WITH A HEAVY HEART

WITH A HEAVY HEART

Confessions Of An Unwilling Spy

SAM TAGGART

iUniverse, Inc.
Bloomington

With a Heavy Heart
Confessions of an Unwilling Spy

iUniverse books may be ordered through booksellers or by contacting:

iUniverse
1663 Liberty Drive
Bloomington, IN 47403
www.iuniverse.com
1-800-Authors (1-800-288-4677)

ISBN: 978-1-4502-8835-4 (sc)
ISBN: 978-1-4502-8836-1 (dj)
ISBN: 978-1-4502-8837-8 (ebk)

Library of Congress Control Number: 2011901682

Printed in the United States of America

iUniverse rev. date: 3/10/2011

This story is dedicated to the people of Bauxite, Arkansas, and especially to those who worked the mines and production facilities during WWII.

CHAPTER 1

"Morning, Jen," Maggie Harris said as she breezed through the front door of the Bauxite Antique Barn.

Jenny looked up from her book. "Morning, Maggie," she said. "Want a cup of coffee? It's fresh."

"Sure, that would be nice," Maggie said. She walked over to the checkout counter and sat down on one of the tall, wooden stools.

Jenny set a cup of coffee down on the counter and pushed it toward Maggie. "If you got time, I need for you to do me a favor."

"I got all kinds of time. What do you need?" Maggie asked.

"In the back of the consignment area, there are a couple of pieces of pottery that are still in boxes and might be worth looking at. They just came in yesterday. One of the Baxley women died; the kids cleaned out her house, took what they wanted, and decided to sell the rest. They asked me to do the pricing. Take a look, and see what you think," Jenny said.

The consignment area was a large open space fronted by south facing windows. The shelves in front of the windows were filled with bright blue and green glassware, which gave a bluish tint to the room. Guarding the entrance to the area was a large, old, floor model radio that had long ceased to function but would make a great furniture piece in the right home.

As Maggie approached the new pottery, the first thing that caught her eye was a small, wooden, shipping crate. Written across the top, between the supports, were the words OLD VASE.

For Maggie, this was like Christmas. At estate sales, she bought odd boxes that were taped shut and labeled "miscellaneous." She would take these boxes home, unopened, and save them for a rainy day. With a bottle of wine, she could spend an entire evening going through old recipes for Mexican cornbread, clippings from the *Ladies Home Journal*, dark, single socks, or pictures of someone's husband holding a large trout; there was always the excitement of what she might find.

She opened her pocketknife and gently pried the wooden lid away from the case. Someone had removed the lid in the recent past, because the nails let go easily. The box was filled with loose wood shavings cut to resemble straw. Pulling back the first layer of straw, she revealed the prize. It was a beautiful, fourteen-inch, swirl vase with the sharp cream, red, and blue layers of color that were used in the late thirties. When she lifted it from its bed, her suspicions were confirmed. On the bottom was the black ink stamp of FITTS that Larry Fitts had used between 1937 and 1943. When this piece was made, it had sold for ten dollars, but now a good piece would go for nine hundred dollars at a minimum.

She slid her hand into the narrow mouth of the vase and ran her index finger around the rim. As her finger explored the border, she felt a roughened area and then a sharp pain in her finger, as if something had bitten her. By reflex, she jerked her hand out of the vase, almost dropping it.

She regained her composure, laid the vase back in its straw, and then looked at her finger. What she thought was a bite turned out to be a cut, a nice, clean, knife-like cut. She reached into her purse and pulled out a tissue to stop the bleeding. She covered the wound with a small dressing and went back to the vase. From her purse, she pulled a small penlight and shined it down into the vase. The culprit was not some ferocious insect or a sharp edge from a clumsy repair attempt; instead, it was an envelope—an old, yellowed envelope. The envelope adhered to the side of the clay vessel, and her knife was not long enough to break it free.

She looked around for something to loosen the paper from the lacquered surface. On a desk next to the pottery she found an old, wooden spatula and slowly guided the dull utensil under the edge of the aged paper. Reluctant at first, the old envelope and its contents finally released their hold and fell free from the wall of the vase. She reached in, grasped it between her index and long fingers, and slowly withdrew it from the vase. *What a find*, she thought as she pulled it from its hiding place.

It was a letter that had been sequestered in the vase many years before and forgotten.

The letter was addressed to:

> Andy Valencia
> Imperial Imports
> Mexico City Mexico

She gingerly opened the letter and removed the contents. In the left, upper corner of the page was the date—July 18 1942. The letter read:

Dear Senor Valencia or whoever reads this

It is with a heavy heart that I write this letter This will be my last communication with you Not to be too melodramatic but I may not survive the next few days I am writing this to set the record straight I am not a Nazi and never was What I did I did for my mother and sister For years I have deluded myself into thinking that my part of this intrigue was meaningless but it isnt The heinous act your friends have planned would involve the death of many of my new friends, and I simply cant do that

The decision to write this letter is the hardest that I have ever had to make and I pray to God that I am doing the right thing It would be a much easier task if it were only me that had to be considered but my mother may still be in the line of fire

The long ton production figures are provided in the usual form

J L Stein

Maggie finished the letter and then read it again.

This must be a joke, she thought. *This just can't be. J. L. Stein couldn't be a spy.*

When Maggie was a teenager in Bauxite, J. L. had been her softball coach. He had been the announcer for the Miner basketball and football games. When the aluminum company dismantled the town in the sixties, he had been a leader in sitting up the community hall as a museum. Even though he had lived in Benton, his kids had gone to school in Bauxite. When a Bauxite kid had needed help, he knew where to turn—J. L. Stein.

Larry Fitts and J. L. Stein knew more about art pottery and fine custom furniture than anyone in the region. Either one could take a pottery shard or a picture of an old piece of furniture and date and authenticate it in no time. Maggie had learned most of what she knew about Mission Art Pottery from those two.

The old men from Bauxite had always talked about a rumored spy at the Bauxite mines during the Second World War. If this letter was true, there was a spy, and he was still there.

This just couldn't be, she thought. *J. L. Stein couldn't have been a spy for the Nazis. I've got to ask him about this, but how?*

CHAPTER 2

Fitts and Stein's old building was built in the style of the turn of the century—a long, narrow, brick building with a low, sandstone facade on the front. Looking in the window, Maggie was struck by the simple beauty of their work. In the right front window sat one of Larry's grandson's latest creations. It was a tall, four-foot pot of New Buffalo swirl that had been inspired by the multicolored rock cliffs along the Buffalo River. In the left front window sat a wooden, padded rocker with an adjustable platform, its arms and back created in the Stickly style.

Hooked above the front door, a bell rang each time the door opened. Entering the building, Maggie saw J. L., dressed in a dark suit, white shirt, and tie, at his computer screen, scrolling through eBay looking for bargains. Larry, dressed in tan-colored, work shirt, and pants, was at the drawing table over by the south wall, working on the design for a pottery display case for his grandson.

J. L. was the first to notice her. "Well, Maggie," he said. "Isn't this a wonderful surprise?"

At the mention of her name, Larry looked up from his drawings and smiled.

"Hello, Maggie," he said. "What do you know?"

"Not much. I got a couple of things I want you guys to look at," Maggie said.

Larry eyed the distinctive wooden box she held under her arm.

"Is that what I think it is?" Larry asked.

"Yeah, I think it is, and wait till you see what's inside," she said.

Maggie was always surprised at how well these two old men moved. They were both in their late eighties, but they carried themselves like men of fifty.

When asked how they managed to stay so fit, Larry's stock response was, "Chasing women and running from jealous husbands."

She carefully set the box on the work counter.

Larry looked the box over and pointed to a mark. On one of the end supports of the box was burned, in small, black letters, FITTS-1942.

"Not bragging," he said, "but do you realize that the box alone is worth about a hundred bucks?"

"Wait till you see what's inside," she said as she pulled out her penknife and slowly opened the box.

"Be careful," J. L. said as the three crowded around the box.

She lifted the lid and the top layer of wooden straw.

Larry smiled.

"How wonderful," he said. "That's a fourteen-inch swirl from the early forties. Looks like I just laid it in there." He paused for a second, "But, how did it get in the box? I only used those to ship out west or up east."

Now came the part that Maggie wasn't completely sure how to approach. How was she to accuse her friend of being a German spy?

"I think it was originally meant to be shipped to Mexico, but I'm not sure," she said, looking at the two men.

J. L. asked, "Why do you say that?"

"Because of the other thing that I found inside," she said.

"What?" he asked.

She reached into her purse and pulled out the old yellowed letter and handed it to J. L.

A look of recognition dawned on his face, and tears began to well up in his eyes. He stumbled as if he'd been hit with a bat. Shaken, he looked around for a chair to sit down in.

Maggie had the feeling that she had done something terribly wrong.

"What is it?" Larry asked. He picked up the letter from where J. L. had dropped it on the countertop and read it out loud.

"Is this what it looks like it is?" Maggie asked.

"Yeah, it is," Larry said as he laid the contents of the letter back on the table. He walked over to the chair where J. L. was sitting. "Are you okay, old friend? Do you need your nitroglycerin?"

J. L. shook his head. "No, I'm okay. This is the happiest day of my life," he said.

"I bet it is," Larry said, patting him on the shoulder.

Somehow this was not the response that Maggie had expected. To say the least, she was confused.

"Why would he be happy?" she whispered to Larry.

"It's a long story. A very long story," Larry said.

CHAPTER 3

The year was 1909. It was a fresh spring evening in central Vienna, and the music of Mozart was being played by a street quartet. Students of The Institute of Civil Engineering had just completed their final exams, and there were several tables of graduating students on a mission to get drunk in Gruber's Beer Garden.

At table number eight were four young men who seldom ventured forth from their labs but this was a special day. Among this group was Wilhelm Stein from Linz. Willie was the son of a master carpenter, who had scrimped and saved to send his youngest son to the institute in Vienna. He was a shy young man who loved to tinker and find out how things worked. No one in the group could remember him dating; there had just never been time. He had begun drinking the sour white wine made locally, and by mid-evening, he was intoxicated.

A pretty young waitress was serving the three tables nearest the street and, in the process, walked back and forth in front of the table of young drinkers. The owner had taken the task of watching after the drunken students; it seemed safer that way.

On one trip as the waitress came walking by with a large tray of wine mugs, Willie said in his newly learned English language, "I wonder what is the name of the cute waitress black-headed with the pretty breasts?" His friends, who had just completed the same English course, roared at his joke.

A few minutes later, the waitress walked by the table and handed him a note that read, "My name is Helena Edit, and I speak four other languages. By the way, your English sentence structure isn't very good."

Willie was awestruck and embarrassed—this pretty little angel who spoke five languages had understood what he had said. When she came back by the table, he stood to apologize for his remarks. In his attempt to stand, he stumbled and fell into her, causing her to spill her tray onto the next table. Realizing the problem he had caused, Willie sat on the floor and cried.

Willie would tell his children years later that he was lucky to have met their mother after his testing was completed, because had he met her earlier, he would have surely failed and ended up a derelict on the street with only his unrequited love for her to sustain him. Coming from someone else, that might have seemed to be a dramatic overstatement, but from Willie, it was taken as it was meant—the absolute truth.

Helena Edit was a woman of many passions. She was born in April of 1889. Her mother died in the process of childbirth, and she was raised by her father.

Franz Edit was the rabbi and schoolteacher for the village of Aigen, near the border between Austria and the Czech Republic. He had a fascination with language, and young Helena's life was immersed in French, English, Spanish, and German. Franz loved to say, "A people's history is written into their language, into the way they write and speak, into the structure of their sentences, into their euphemisms and phrases. It can be said that, after a while, language takes on a life of its own and directs those who speak it. Look beyond the words and how they are put together; they are but a shadow of reality." For Helena, each day was a word puzzle in one of the five languages.

Helena took to the spoken and written word in the same way that her father had. By the time she was ten, she was assisting him in teaching his classes. The rabbi took great pains to expose his young daughter to all of the ideas that had taken root in the nineteenth century: the ideas of universal suffrage for men and women, the philosophy of feminism, the concept of liberalism, and the role of government as an instrument of good for all of the people and not just for a privileged few. The Edit home was full of newspapers and books from Munich, Prague, Paris, Vienna, and on occasion, America. He dreamed that, one day, she would move across the sea and establish a new life for herself in America.

In the fall of 1908, Rabbi Edit became ill; it was a consuming illness that came on fast and with great force. As Franz lay dying on his bed, he said to his daughter, "Sweetheart, I have very little, but what I have is yours. There are no debts to settle; there is no property to sell. You know where I keep the reserve. It isn't very much, but it's yours. If you stay here and marry, you will become the overweight wife of a dirt farmer and have a house full of dirt farmer children. Don't get me wrong; there is nothing wrong with dirt farmers and their children, but you are meant for something more. You are the best student I have ever had, and I'm not saying that because you are my daughter. There is enough money for you to leave this town, go to Munich or

Vienna or Salzburg and find a way to continue your education. Promise me you will do that. Will you promise me that?"

"Of course, I will, Father," she said.

A few short weeks later, Helena was living in a women's hostel in Vienna and waiting tables at Gruber's.

It took days for Willie to build up the courage to return to the scene of the crime and ask Helena out for a date. Helena was waiting for him to ask; she was lonesome with no plans for her future and no family to fall back on in hard times.

On Friday evening just before the evening crowd began to descend on the garden, Helena caught sight of Willie standing across the street, watching her as she went about busing tables. Each time she came from the kitchen, he had worked himself closer to the front entrance. She gave no hint of noticing his presence. Finally, as she came out to wipe down the front tables for the third time, he stepped forward.

"Miss Edit, my name is Willie, Willie Stein," he said. "I got drunk and caused you to spill your tray last Friday. I would like to sincerely apologize for my behavior. I hope that my clumsy drunkenness didn't get you in any trouble."

"No, there was no trouble, just a few broken mugs. Nothing big. Do you drink that much very often?" she asked.

"No, no; I never get drunk. Well, not very often. We were celebrating. I passed my exams. I'm a certified civil engineer."

"What does a civil engineer do?"

"We build bridges mainly—roads and bridges. Jack of all trades, I guess you would say," he said.

"I hope you're better at building bridges than you are at holding your liquor," she said, smiling.

"Me, too." Willie hesitated and put his hands in his pockets. After a long pause, he continued, "Would you like to see my favorite of all man-made things?"

"Why, Mr. Stein, are you asking me for a date?"

"Well, yes, I guess so. I guess I am. Is that okay?" he asked.

"Of course, it's okay," she said.

"When do you have a day off?"

"Sunday. After the lunch hour, about two. I don't have to be back for work 'till six," she said.

"Should I pick you up here or at your place?"

"Here would be best," she said.

"Fine, here it is. Sunday at two."

As Willie walked from the garden, there was a spring in his step. Unlike the stylish men in their fine linen suits, his khaki work pants hung loose from his hips, the frayed cuffs of his pants dragged behind his heels. His coarse cotton shirt was a size too big for comfort and hung over his belted waist. His sandy colored hair was just a little too long in the back—not to make a statement but because of neglect.

Helena knew that her attraction for Willie was for real; she didn't know why, but she did know.

When Helena told her housemates at the hostel of the Sunday afternoon date with an engineer, they insisted on dressing her up. For two days, they planned and schemed. She only had two work dresses, neither of which was adequate for this first date. One evening was spent altering an old dress that belonged to the proprietor of the hostel. As for makeup and perfume, Helena could honestly say that she had never used either. The girl from Prague who lived upstairs took on Helena's makeover as a project.

"I don't want to look like I'm going out whoring," Helena said as the girl proposed an especially bright red lipstick. "Is there anything more subtle?" she asked.

In the end, they had taken a plain, country girl and changed her into a beauty.

Helena wore her regular dress to work for the lunch crowd, and then she changed as the cafe patrons began to thin out. Willie was there promptly at two. His shirt was ironed, his hair was trimmed, and he had on a brightly colored tie. In his right hand, he was carrying a small bouquet of cut flowers. Helena was cleaning one of the front tables when he came into the garden. He walked right by her and asked Gruber if he knew where Helena was.

Gruber smiled, grabbed the boy by the shoulders, and pointed him toward Helena.

Willie was speechless.

Helena walked over and pointed at the flowers. "Are those for me?" she asked.

He nodded his head.

"Are you going to say anything?" she asked.

"Wow," he said.

"You like it. It's not too much is it?" she asked.

"No, you're beautiful," he said, smiling.

"Where are we going?" Helena asked as they walked toward the canal.

"To the park across the river. Have you been there," he asked.

"No, not really. I've been meaning to go, but it has been cold all winter, and I work a lot."

"Well, I've got something I want to show you," Willie said. "Are you hungry? We could stop and get something to eat if you want."

"No, I'm okay. What is it you want to show me?"

"I want you to see the Ferris wheel," he said.

"What's a Ferris wheel?"

Willie had assumed everyone knew about the giant ride in the park. "Do you really not know?" he asked.

Helena shook her head.

"This fellow, Ferris, invented it for the World's Fair in ninety-four. It's just amazing. The most wonderful thing is how big it is."

While they were speaking they walked around a corner.

"Look over there beyond those trees, and you can see it," Willie said.

As he extolled the virtues of the engineering marvel, Helena stared at the height of the giant contraption. He finally got around to asking, "Would you like to take a ride?" In his excitement, Willie didn't wait for her to answer and left to go buy a pair of tickets.

When she was a child, Helena's father had taught her a trick to overcome fear. He would have her stand on a narrow stool facing into a corner as a way of improving her concentration and will. While Willie went to buy the tickets, she began to focus on the stool in the corner, attempting to steel herself against the fear of falling from the giant wheel. It didn't work, and she was tempted to tell Willie that she simply could not ascend to those heights. The other problem was that, like her mother before her, she had a weak bladder and was fearful that, even if she didn't fall to her death during the ride, she would surely pee on herself.

As it happened, neither occurred, even when the cabin they were in came to a stop at the very top of the circle. When the ride was complete and she stepped out of the bucket that had imprisoned her, Helena sighed in relief and swore never to set foot on a Ferris wheel again, even if she did have to admit to being a weak sister; pride was just not worth it.

When Willie took her back to the Garden, he asked, "Now, we have been where I wanted to go, where would you like to go?"

Helena smiled and pointed into the Beer Garden. "Here," she said.

"Here?"

"Yes, here," she said.

"But you come here every day. Why here?"

"Because I want sit at these tables and join into the conversation. I long to sit at the table and discuss the ideas in my head. My father taught me to think and not to accept, to reason and not to follow blindly. He taught me to search for the right path and then take it. I want to be drunk on ideas. You don't know how lucky you are as a man to have the opportunity to go to school, to have the doors open and be able to go in and choose what you want. Not just to survive or accumulate money and things—that's unimportant to me—but to have the power to make decisions that affect my life."

Willie stood with his mouth agape; he was enthralled with this boyish little girl. He was a level-headed, clear thinker, an engineer at home with numbers and formulas, a man who found solace in order and form, and here he was falling in love with a political whirlwind.

For Helena, Willie was a touchstone of reality, a solid place to light on. From that day on, they were inseparable.

The first crisis in their relationship occurred in the following winter. Willie was working at one of the local factories, and he hated every minute of his job. On a visit back to his school to check the job board, he ran into one of his favorite professors.

"Willie," the man said, "there is an American company that's looking for young engineers to go to the Far East. The representative will be here on Thursday, and I would be happy to give you a recommendation."

Two days later, Willie had an interview and, within two hours, a new job in a place called the Philippines. Prior to the interview he had never heard of the Philippines much less known where they were. The personnel man from McAlexander and Associates, a firm out of Atlanta, Georgia, in the United States, offered him a job building roads, bridges, and schools at three times the money he was making in Austria.

When Willie sat down at his usual table, Helena sensed quickly that something was amiss. "What's the matter?" she asked.

"I—we—have a problem we need to talk about," he said.

"What's wrong? Did I do something?"

"No, no. It's nothing like that. This factory work is not what I went to school to do," he said. "My father has spent his life building furniture and homes. The things he built will be here centuries from now. They have his mark. At the foundry, I'm nothing but a cog in a wheel. I won't spend my life as a passive conduit. A funeral—no matter how sophisticated—is still a funeral, and I don't want to get to my end and see that I really haven't added anything. I want to leave a mark. You know, I have been looking for another job, anything but what I've been doing."

"So what's the problem, quit your job, move in with me till you find another one," she said.

"I've already found a new job."

"That's great. So what is the problem?" she asked.

"It's in the Philippines."

"What are the Philippines?"

"They're islands in the Pacific, off the coast of China," he said.

"Oh, I see," she said.

"And I have to leave in two weeks."

"Oh, yes, I see."

For a minute, Helena thought and didn't say anything. She picked up his beer and took a drink. She set the beer down, looked at Willie, and asked, "Can I go?"

"What do you mean?" he asked.

"I mean, can I go with you?"

"You mean you would go with me?"

"Are you kidding? I would give my eyeteeth to get a chance to travel," she said.

"Helena Edit, are you proposing marriage to me?" Willie asked, somewhat incredulous.

She smiled. "I guess I am. Will you?"

"Yes," he said as he started to cry. The Stein men cried when they were happy.

The McAlexander firm provided Willie and Helena with wonderful quarters on the outskirts of Manila, leased from the US government. They lived in a beautiful five-room home with a garden and a maid and a houseboy who were at their beck and call. Helena was delighted by being treated as a princess, but at the same time, she was bored.

She applied to teach at the military base school, but she was informed that, since she had no teaching certificate, there was no way that they could allow her to teach on the base. She was referred to the Methodist Mission compound that was just off of the base. It was the stated mission of this group to provide health care and education to the people of the Philippines. They were always in need of teachers and nursing personnel. Even without papers, Helena was welcomed as an additional set of hands.

The compound where Helena worked primarily served the upper class Philippine nationals who were being groomed as the eventual leaders of the future. It was at that compound that she realized that central European Jews weren't the only people looked down on because of color, nationality, or race.

Helena was assigned to assist a young teacher from Ely, Minnesota. The teacher was ten years older than Helena but naive to the point of being painful. The two became fast friends, Helena taught language to the children and the teacher from Minnesota focused on religion.

Despite the advice of the US authorities and the church, the two women traveled widely in the region around Manila and discovered that the rosy picture of a satisfied population of indigenous peoples ruled over by a benevolent military government was, at best, inaccurate. In the eyes of the general population, people from the United States were no different than the Spanish. They were there to rule the people and to take advantage of them. Except for a few of the powerful politicians at the top, no one believed that the Filipinos would have an opportunity to rule themselves.

Soon, Helena became pregnant with her first child. It was a proud day in the family when she delivered an eight-pound, six-ounce boy. She named him Franz after her father. Two years later, on the sixth day of August, her second son, Jean Louis Stein, was born. She told her work partner that, as a true cosmopolitan woman, she wanted to have four children. Franz would be her German child, Jean Louis her French child, and the last two should be her Spanish and English children.

With the birth of Jean Louis, Helena began a habit that lasted until the children were grown. On Mondays, they spoke only French in the house; on Wednesdays, they spoke only English; on Fridays, they spoke only Spanish, and the rest of the days, they spoke German. In that way, the children grew up fluent in all of the languages.

In early 1914, Helena became pregnant with her third child. At that time, they received word that Willie's father had suffered a heart attack, and they were needed back in Austria. The young family packed up and prepared for what they thought would be a short visit to Austria. When they arrived in Linz, it was obvious that Willie's father would survive but be unable to return to work.

Helena delivered her third child, Anna, and within weeks, war broke out, consuming their lives. Willie was drafted into the Austrian army and sent off to rebuild and repair roads and bridges destroyed by the war. Helena and the children began the war living with the Steins in Linz. There were several points of conflict between the two Stein women that had festered for years. The fact that Helena was Jewish was first on Mrs. Stein's list. The family had a long solid unbroken history of Catholicism and having a Jewish daughter-in-law who had no intention of converting was galling to the elder Stein. To make matters worse, Helena made the decision to keep her own last name with a hyphen—Helena Edit-Stein.

Now that there were children in the picture Mrs. Stein's focus changed. The conversation with Mother Stein was repeated many times, but the essence was the same.

"If these children are going to live in my house, they are going to a real school" (by which she meant Catholic school) "and to the Church."

Mrs. Stein was adamant about the education of the children.

"Mother Stein, I respect you and your feelings, but these are my children," Helena said.

"And my grandchildren."

"Yes, and your grandchildren, but they are my children, Willie's and mine. We have agreed that we want them to go to a nonreligious school," Helena said.

"Well, if you want my opinion—"

"And I don't."

"You are ruining these children. They will grow up with no moral compass," the elder Stein said. "They run around like little natives, half dressed, as it is. I just can't believe that Willie would abide by this."

That evening as Helena sat in her room, she wrote a letter to Willie.

> Sweetheart,
>
> All is well with your father. It seems that this will allow him into slip quietly in a form of retirement. As we both know, he will never quit, but at least now, he won't push himself as hard.
>
> The children and I will be moving to Vienna soon. Your parents have said nothing, but it is obvious that we are a big load for them. I am going to leave the two boys here in Linz for a few days. Little Anna and I will go to the city and find a place to live. We will be safe. I will see if Mr. Gruber will give me my old job back.
>
> Please keep yourself out of harm's way. You can be so absentminded; I don't want you to get hurt. I do not know what I would do if anything ever happened to you. You and the children are my world. I love you so.
>
> Love,
> H.

Within days of arriving back in Vienna, Helena was back at work at the beer garden. Nothing had changed except for the faces; there were the same arguments and the same intensity. However, unlike the shy seventeen-year-old girl of 1908, Helena was no longer satisfied with café conversation; she quickly became involved in the Oldenberg movement.

Louisa May Oldenberg was a Serb-born woman who, like Helena, had come to Vienna to seek her fortune. In 1895, she met and married Fredrick Oldenberg, who promptly died. Louisa said that the only occupations open to women were those of a whore or a wife, and she hated cleaning windows and washing clothes. "In life, you find a way to get along. If you are lucky, you make it; if not, then you don't. Trust me, I was lucky. I never got a disease, and nobody killed me. There was nothing glamorous about my life until the old man came along. He didn't have anybody to answer to, so we got married. I cared for him till he died, and then I got the property."

With the money left to her by the old man, Louisa determined that she would help many of the women who had been less fortunate than she. Over the years, her large, three-story home became a meeting place.

Each day she took her mid-afternoon coffee at Gruber's. By World War I, Louisa was involved in the women's suffrage movement. Helena migrated to this group of women who surrounded the Oldenberg house.

Eventually, Helena and the children moved into the home along with all of the others.

The war years were spent in that large, rambling house full of every description of causes—women's rights, suffrage, communism, feminism, labor unions, socialism, state-sponsored day care, birth control rights, anti-war movements.

By the end of the war, Helena quit her job at the Beer Garden and was teaching classes for women at the home and writing for their newspaper. The group found in Helena an effective speechwriter and thinker.

It was in this mélange of ideas, thoughts, and philosophy that Franz, Jean Louis, and Anna spent their young years. The three would ultimately go their own separate ways, but the foundation for their differences was present in the life created in that house. From the first, Franz had an aggressive streak. The idea of fighting the French filled his head; Helena contended that he had been turned by Mother Stein, a devoted nationalist. During the war years, the boy spent most of his summers with his grandmother, and each time he returned, Helena declared never again. Like her mother, Anna spent her life at a high level of intensity. Unlike her mother, Anna did not have a critical eye and would often cling to hopeless and lost causes. She never learned the skill of picking her battles. Jean Louis, the middle child, the peacemaker, was a happy child who loved a good time. He found joy in the smallest things.

When the armistice was declared, Helena, like most of the other war widows, held her breath. There was no way of knowing if Willie was alive or if he would return. After the first week, word began to circulate that some of the men were making their way home, but there was still no word from her husband. Early one morning as Helena was preparing breakfast for the children, there was a knock at the back door of the house.

"Franz, see who's at the door. I have my hands full," Helena said to her oldest son.

Franz put down his schoolbook and walked to the door. In the absence of his father, he had become the man of the house. Before he opened the door, he looked through the window beside the door. "It's a beggar," he said. "Looks real dirty. Want me to tell him to move on?" he asked his mother.

"Tell him to wait on the porch, and I'll bring him some food in a few minutes," Helena instructed her son.

Franz undid the main lock on the door but left the chain latch in place. "You wait on the porch," he said "Mama will bring you something to eat in a little while."

The man standing on the porch had on a ragged army uniform, he had a gaunt look about him, he hadn't shaven in weeks and even through the crack in the door Franz could smell him.

As Franz was about to close and relock the door, the man said, in a quiet voice, "Franz, I'm your father. Go tell your mother." Behind the rough beard, the man smiled at Franz.

Franz was flabbergasted; he simply stood and stared at the strange man.

After a few awkward seconds, the man said again, "Go tell her."

Franz left the door and, shortly, Helena screamed.

She ran to the door and tried to unlatch the door. In her excitement, she fumbled with the locks and chains. Franz walked up behind her, moved her out of the way, and methodically undid the locks.

"Willie, is that you?" Helena asked as Franz unlatched the door.

"Yes, it's me," Willie said, smiling.

When Franz opened the door, Helena rushed out and threw her arms around him. The force of her embrace caused him to stumble.

"Are you okay?" she asked.

""Yeah, I'm okay, but I'm very tired, and I need to sit down before I fall down," he said.

Helena turned toward the two younger children, who were sitting at the table. "Kids, get up and give your father a seat," she said.

Both children did as their mother said and got up from the table. Franz pulled one of the chairs out from the table for his father. "Can I get you anything?" Franz asked.

"I would love a good strong cup of coffee and as many of those biscuits and honey as I can get in my mouth. I haven't eaten in days," Willie said.

Both of the younger children moved around behind their mother. When Helena noticed their fear and uncertainty, she turned to them. "Children, this is your father. He has come home from the war. Say hello," she said.

Anna's response was to hide behind her mother. Jean Louis stood looking at the strange man. Helena reached down and gave Jean Louis a nudge, but the boy didn't move.

"Give them time," Willie said. "They don't know me. But one thing is for sure: I'll never ever leave again. It was the thought of all of you that kept me going, and I don't ever want to be away from home or separated from you again."

Willie returned from the war a changed man. Any wanderlust that he had had was banished by the war. Along with wanting to be with his family, Willie wanted to live out his life in Austria doing a job that he loved. Within days of returning home, he had a job in the Prader working on the giant Ferris wheel, and the family had found a small apartment in Florisdorf.

Willie's determination to live out his life in Vienna solved a problem for Helena. Working at the Oldenberg, she had become involved in the suffrage movement and, in the process, had been appointed the chief of staff for Adelheid Popp-Dworak. Helena and Mrs. Popp edited the weekly paper, *Freedom,* a socialist, feminist newspaper.

Helena invested herself in the process of creating a clear vision of what the movement was all about. In the immediate post-WWI era, it seemed that the sky was the limit. Overnight, the right to vote was granted, and there were women in the parliaments helping to write new constitutions. In the United States, the American president, Mr. Wilson, proposed a League of Nations, which, if accepted, would go a long way toward breaking down the barriers that helped to sustain nationalism and impede human rights. These were heady times for the women of Oldenberg and their socialist newspaper.

AND NOW WHAT

It is all well and good to shout from the rooftops—DESTROY, DOWN WITH CAPITALISM. But what do you replace it with? If we are to do better at this job than those who we replaced, then we must have an idea where we want to go. We must have a *realistic* plan of action, and that requires that we understand who we are and what we stand for.

Today, I would like to put before you several issues that are paramount in our discussions:

We are not just citizens of Austria, we are citizens of the world, and it is a world that is getting smaller every day. The women of the Philippines long no less for basic freedom than we do; they want no less for their children than we do. When we say that we are Austrian, do we mean the Austria of the Holy Roman Empire or Austro-Hungary or the little country that is now Austria? Which is it? For all of history, boundaries have reshaped and reformed like all of the unholy alliances of the 19th century.

Let us view ourselves as guardians of a new future; one where national barriers are broken down, where the rights of one nation are not predicated on the submission of another, where the laws that apply to one apply to all.

Rights can no longer be predicated on one's sexual organs or the color of one's skin or one's religious beliefs. It would be foolish to suggest that I as a European woman am no different from my husband or a pygmy headhunter in Borneo or a hooded North African or the Pope; but the law should see no difference.

Through most of recorded history, men have ruled, and the abiding principle guiding their relations has been force. Like children on a playground, the one who is biggest or strongest is the winner. We must redefine a new way of doing things. As women we bring to the table a new and different way of looking at things. Conflict must be settled by law and not by force. Under that law, all men and women must be equal.

Rights without the wherewithal to act are empty words. The privilege to vote when your stomach is empty rings hollow. Call it what you will, but along with equality under the law, each and every one of us should be compensated fairly for our work. Capitalism flourishes on low paid labor, and at the bottom of the heap are women and children. This cannot be allowed to continue.

Our children are our future. If they are not fed, if they are not clothed, if they are forced to work in factories when they should be in school, we will never advance as a people. We are the ones who can and must represent their interests.

Now is the time for all to bring our interests to bear on the system and reshape the world we live in.

Helena

With this and other articles that she wrote in the late teens and early twenties, Helena came to the fore as one of the clear thinkers of the women's movement. In most instances, she could be counted on to find a middle ground among diverse opinions. She would sit for hours in meetings where a feminist would be followed by a Catholic nun who, in turn, would be followed by a communist. After all was said and done, she would clearly summarize it all and begin to look for areas where compromise was possible. There was never any attempt to coerce change; if no compromise was possible, it was left at that, but each of the participants would leave knowing that her point had been aired.

The Oldenberg became a meeting place for all interests. As the crowds grew, the need for a meeting place grew. Louisa knocked out a wall between two of the larger downstairs rooms to create a meeting room. The forum created a constant flow of ideas and people that floated through the house like a stream.

When the social democrats took control of the city government of Vienna, one of the first tasks was to build housing for the workers. The Edit-Stein family was one of the first to move into the Schlingerhof, one of the largest of the new complexes. The Schlingerhof was a large project. Built in a square, it took up four blocks. It was three stories high and had its own school and market. In the center of the project was a large park that became the center of life for the community.

On the morning of Helena's thirty-fifth birthday as they were sitting down for breakfast, Anna noticed a large object covered by a tarp in the courtyard outside their apartment. Standing near the tarp-covered object was a pony, eating on a mound of hay.

At first, Helena only noticed the pony.

"Oh my, someone's donkey is loose. I wonder where it came from."

"I don't think it's a donkey," Willie said in a playful way. "Looks like a pony to me."

"Well, what in the world is a pony doing in the courtyard?" As she finished the statement she stopped. "Okay, I get it. It's my birthday and you've got me a surprise. What is it? I know you didn't get me a pony for my birthday."

"Why don't we go see?" Jean Louis said, giggling.

Except for Franz who was still in his room, the Stein family traipsed into the courtyard. With great ceremony, Willie and Jean Louis climbed two small ladders on either side of the tarp and threw the tarp skyward and back, uncovering a ten-feet-tall, four-bucket Ferris wheel. The machine was designed to be operated by hand or, if they had the luxury, by a pony walking around and around in a circle.

With great ceremony, Willie bowed to his wife. "For my wife, you can now have a Ferris wheel ride and not feel like you will pee in your pants." He motioned to Helena who stood a few feet away. "Madame, would you care for a ride?"

She smiled, "I certainly would." She offered her outstretched hand to Willie, and he opened the guard to the first seat. "Take care with the first step."

Willie turned to his coconspirator and asked that he strike up the music. Jean Louis cranked the record player and gently placed the needle in the track. Out came the sounds of a Mozart concerto. When Helena was well seated, Willie joined her. On a cue from their father, Jean Louis and Anna hooked the pony up to the mechanics of the wheel, and off they went.

It was a picture book painting of a happy family, except for one thing. As the wheel made its third revolution, Helena glanced toward the bedroom window of her oldest son. Looking out the closed window, Franz had the sad, pained expression of an outsider on his face. The instant he became aware of her attention, he turned and walked away from the window.

Helena loved all three of her children, but Franz was different. He had been different since he was very small. He found something negative to say about any situation. He was seven when the war began, and when his father left, he assumed the role of male protector for his little brother and sister. During the summers, he spent extended periods living with his grandparents in Linz. Franz became a favorite of Mother Stein, and he adopted many of her attitudes: the war had been a good, noble war, and the only reason it was lost was because of the betrayal of the socialists and communists; anything that was good for Germany was good—period; Austria was really only southern Germany, and if they couldn't have the Hapsburgs, their future lay with Germany. No amount of talking by Helena or Willie altered his view of the war or the German-Austrian future.

Fourteen-year-old Jean Louis had trouble understanding all of the turmoil that bubbled around in Franz's head. Like many middle children, Jean Louis was easygoing, and politics was the last thing on his mind. In fact, the first, middle, and last things on Jean Louis's mind were girls. He played football, read regularly, and enjoyed spending time helping his father build things, but pretty faces, breasts, butts, and legs floated through his mind in all but the deepest of sleep. This fascination with females had begun during the war when the family had lived at the Oldenberg house. The women and girls who came and went from the mansion had doted over the dark-haired little boy with long eyelashes. He moved from room to room as if each was his own. The content of the political speech that was ever-present was beyond him, but the atmosphere of warmth and love infused his life.

Jean Louis spent a great deal of his spare time with his father working at the park, and Willie was proud of his middle son. He seemed to have such a level head on his shoulders.

One morning as they were replacing a worn gear ring on the giant Ferris wheel, Willie turned to Jean Louis. "What are you going to do with your life, son?" he asked.

"Well, I've thought about it a bit. I like working here with you; I like to build things like you do, but I'm interested in what things are made of. I think I want to be a chemist."

"You mean you want to mix drugs and compound stuff?"

"No, I'm really interested in how things are put together and how to use them."

"You mean like a chemical engineer?" Willie asked.

"Yeah, I guess so."

"It's a great field. It would have been my second choice."

As his father finished the word second, Jean Louis got a whiff of a girl's perfume as she walked by.

"Did you smell that?" he asked.

"Yeah," his father said.

"Nice, wasn't it?"

"Sure was."

"That was a chemical, wasn't it?" Jean Louis asked, smiling.

"Yeah, sure," his father said.

"Well, I definitely want to study that."

"Plenty of time for that. We got work to do," his father said.

Willie, Helena, and the kids settled into a life they had hoped for but not expected. With the exception of Franz and his problems, life was going well.

In was a summer afternoon in 1925, Willie was working on his beloved Ferris wheel when the first pains began. At first he thought it was indigestion. He had had an extra serving of sausage at lunch, and it had not sat well in his stomach. Next came an overwhelming weakness, along with a feeling of pressure in his chest. When he broke out in a cold sweat, Willie knew it was more than heartburn. Before he could lay down his wrench, he fell off of the apparatus and to the pavement below. Like his father before him, Willie Stein had his first heart attack at age forty-five. Unlike his father, he did not survive to enjoy his retirement.

Most summer days, Jean Louis went to work with his father, but on that day he had stayed home to help his sister clean up their part of the courtyard. As they were finishing the cleanup, Helena came through the walkway. It was most unusual for their mother to be at home during the day; both kids knew that something was wrong.

Helena was crying. "It's your father," she said. "He died. They don't know what happened. He fell from the Ferris wheel."

Jean Louis would remember that instant as one of numbness with a violent urge to run as hard as he could from the news as if that would make it not true. For Jean Louis and Anna, their parents were their world. Instead of running, he simply slumped to the ground from weakness. Anna began to cry. She ran over to her mother and hugged her as tightly as she could.

For a few minutes, they said nothing. All three sat and looked at the Ferris wheel their father had built. It was a black day for the Stein family.

The results of the autopsy revealed a coronary thrombosis, and as a result, the city made the decision that Willie's death was not related to his work; there would be no pension. Soon Helena and the children moved from their apartment back to Oldenberg. In the process, Anna gave up all of her animals, but Helena refused to give up the Ferris wheel. At first, it went into storage, and then it was placed in the park across the street from Oldenberg. On the base of the wheel, she put a plaque that read:

In memory of Willie Stein, the Ferris wheel man.
Before you stands the smallest working Ferris wheel in the world.
Each part was handmade and tooled by Willie Stein.

In the years that followed, Helena would be faced with many difficult situations and decisions; most of those decisions would be made on Willie's Ferris wheel.

CHAPTER 4

By the mid-twenties, Franz had begun to roam the streets with a group of young men who called themselves the Vienna Front Fighters.

One summer day, Helena was working in her garden in the back of the house when her friend Hubert Gruber came looking for her.

"Morning, Helena," he said.

"Morning, Hubert," Helena said. "What are you doing in this neck of the woods? You're a little out of your territory, aren't you?"

"Yeah, I guess a little bit, but we have a problem," Gruber said.

"What is it?"

"It's your son, Franz."

"What is it? Is he okay?" Helena asked. "We haven't seen him in a week."

"Oh, he's okay for the time being, but he is going to get hurt. That bunch of thugs he runs around with, the ones who call themselves the VFF, they attacked a group of Jewish kids over at the Technical Institute. Franz and his friends used steel pipes and chains on them as they were coming out of class, because they were Jewish. It seems that Walter Riehl, the national socialist firebrand, got them all stirred up at a meeting over in Branden Hall. Then these kids went looking for trouble. They put a couple of kids in the hospital. The police just stood by while they attacked.

"I've listened to the kids at the Garden. They say the police don't ever do anything; that's why the Jewish kids travel in groups. They don't go anywhere by themselves anymore. Probably nothing would have come of this, except one of the kids was from America—New York City. His daddy's a lawyer. They called the American embassy, which called the mayor's office, which in turn called the chief of police and chewed his ass out. Next thing the VFF knows, the same cops who stood by smiling as they beat the crap out of the students came to arrest them.

"Most of this gang of kids … their parents agree with their attitudes, and they've got money. So they pick up the phone and call dear old mom and dad to come bail them out. The only problem is your son is in a dilemma. He's told his friends that his last name is Gruber. They all know who you are, and being the son of that Jewish, feminist, socialist Helena Edit-Stein wouldn't help his credentials as an anti-Semite."

"So you went down and bailed him out?" she asked.

"Yeah, sort of. It was a formality more than anything else. I didn't have to put any money down. This was all done to satisfy the Americans. Nothing will ever come of it. I told them that I was his uncle."

"Hubert," Helena said, "I am so sorry that you had to get involved in something like this. Do you have any idea where he is right now?"

"Well, sort of. I really couldn't get him to talk to me when we came out of the jail. His friends were all hanging out across the street when we left. They took off without so much as a how-do-you-do. I've heard talk that they have an apartment on Heldienstrasse in the Ottaring, but I don't know where, for sure."

"Hubert, I'll tell you again how much I appreciate what you've done. You are a real friend. The difficulty is I'm not real sure what to do about this. Franz has been a problem for years."

"And I'm not sure what to tell you," Hubert said. "I'll keep my eye out and let you know if anything else happens. I've got to go. Got to get the Garden open. I'll keep my eyes open for any news. If I can do anything, let me know."

Late one evening, soon after the conversation with Hubert, Helena was reading in the front study and waiting for Anna to come home when she heard someone moving around in the kitchen. She put her book down and walked down the hall. Much to her surprise, Franz was sitting at the table, eating a sandwich of leftovers.

"Well, well, look what the cat dragged up," Helena said as she looked at her son from across the room and forced a smile.

"Hello, mother," he said. "I was hungry."

"We eat here at least three times a day, and you're more than welcome to join us for any or all of those meals," she said. "You also have a nice, soft bed upstairs to sleep in anytime you wish."

"Don't start preaching to me, Mom," Franz said, an edge creeping into his voice.

"I'm not preaching to you, son, I'm just—"

Franz interrupted his mother, "Don't you realize I'm not your little boy anymore? You don't control me." He picked up the sandwich from the plate and stormed out the back door.

It was then that Helena knew that the answer to their problem would not be found through reason.

That evening, Helena sat down and composed a letter to her brother-in-law Karl Stein. Karl had left for the United States long before Helena and Willie had met. Her only contact with him had been through letters, but he had always seemed eager to help his younger brother. When Willie had died, this loyalty had transferred to Helena and the children.

> Dear Karl,
> Since Willie passed away, Franz has begun to run with a really rough crowd, and if we don't intervene, he may get into some real trouble. I believe that he needs a change in scenery. If I can find a way to convince him to go to the United States, could you assist him in making a new start?
> Love,
> Helena

Karl's response was quick and unequivocal.

> Dearest Helena,
> I would consider it an honor to assist you in your time of need. Nineteen-twenty seven has been a great year and 1928 looks like it will be even better. As the assistant personnel director here in Pittsburgh for Republic Mining, I spend most of my days looking for qualified workers. We are even paying to educate some of the better workers to fill all of the spots we have. As for a place to stay, the boy can live with me. All you have to do is tell me when to meet the boat in New York.
> Love,
> Karl

Helena's plan was drastic, and she understood that, but she could see no other way of breaking Franz free from the morass he was immersed in. When all of the letter writing was finished and travel papers were assembled, Helena created a poster with her son's picture and a very clear message. On the assigned day, she had a group of her associates tack the poster all over the neighborhoods where the young Nazis hung out.

At one o'clock in the afternoon, she stepped off of the streetcar on Heldienstrasse. It was different from the ordered world that she lived in. The buildings were run-down, garbage littered the street, people slept on the sidewalks, and beggars accosted her every few yards. Every available surface was covered with posters tacked on top of posters:

KILL THE KIKES   POLES SUCK
THE ONLY GOOD CZECH IS A DEAD CZECH
ARYANS REIGN   GERMANY-AUSTRIA UNITE
SLAY THE NOVEMBER CRIMINALS
SEND THE JEWS BACK WHERE THEY CAME FROM: HELL
THIS COUNTRY BELONGS TO US; FOREIGNERS GO HOME

In the two blocks that she walked, Helena saw descriptions of every vile act depicted in graphic fashion and every group reviled.

She was looking for 643 Heldienstrasse. When she arrived, it was easy to pick out. Across the front door of the building was a large red flag with the Nazi swastika in black outline on white. On the stoop of the building were a number of young men in their teens and early twenties, sitting, laughing, and drinking beer.

As she neared the steps, one of the men noticed her. Helena was hard not to notice. Even though she was no longer twenty and the stress of life had taken its toll, she still had a dramatic presence. Her dark hair and sharp facial features demanded attention.

"What do you want, lady?" one of the young men demanded to know.

"I'm looking for my son."

"Don't I know you?"

"Probably not. I doubt if you and I run in the same circles," she said.

"Well, la-te-da, aren't we on our high horse?"

"Look, son, I didn't come here to spar with you. I am looking for Franz Gruber, my son. He was one of the kids arrested over at the Technical Institute."

"Those kids stay up in apartment ten on the third floor," one of the other men said.

"Thank you," she said.

Helena had always lived with the hate that was concentrated in this building and neighborhood. It hadn't really changed. When the economy was bad, the anger, hate, and violence spilled over into the real world. When life improved, the vehemence subsided, but it never really went away.

The door to apartment ten had no latch and was standing half open. She gently tapped on the door. When there was no answer, she knocked soundly.

From deep inside the apartment she heard, "Who in the hell is it? Go away. We're trying to sleep in here."

"I'm looking for Franz Gruber, my son," Helena said.

"Somebody wake Gruber up."

A different voice farther back in the cave shouted, "Gruber, get your butt out here. Your *mommy* wants to see you."

For what seemed like an eternity, Helena stood in the doorway. Just as she was about to push the door open and begin to explore, Franz came out to meet her.

"What are you doing here?" he asked.

"I came to see my son."

In a whisper, he said, "If these people knew who you were, you would be in real danger."

"I know that, but you are my son, and I am worried about you," she said.

"I'm doing all right," he said.

"You ended up in jail. I wouldn't call that doing all right."

"That wasn't anything. They just picked us up because of the American. I guess Mr. Gruber told you about it. How did you find me?"

"You and your people leave a pretty clear path."

"What do you want, Mother?" he demanded.

"I—we—want you to come home."

"I am home, Mother. This is where I live now."

"Why do you hate me so?" she asked.

"I don't hate you."

"You hate Jews, and I am a Jew."

"But you're different," he said.

"Why? Because I'm your mother?"

"I don't hate you."

"I am scared for you. I am worried that you will get killed. These people breed violence."

"We never strike first. We only react to what those people do."

"You can't possibly believe that," she said.

"Look, Mother, we are the victims, not them. They started the war and then betrayed our country. They ended it when they couldn't make any more money off of it. You, your newspaper, and the politicians sit up there and justify everything that they do and vilify us at every step."

"Have you forgotten, son, that you are Jewish?" she said.

"No, Mother, I am not," he said. "True, I have some Jewish blood in my veins, but long ago, my eyes were opened to the true nature of Jewish villainy."

"Son, before we go any further, I want you to know that I love you dearly and what I must do pains me greatly. In my view, you have set out on a course that can only bring you to ruin. I have arranged for you to go to the United States to live with your Uncle Karl."

"I won't go," he said.

"Well, you might not have much choice."

"What do you mean?"

She handed him the poster that she had held, rolled up, under her arm. He unrolled it and slowly read the text. Across the top of the paper in sixty-point type were the words: JEW SPY. Below that was a photo of Franz and his mother, taken two years before at a family gathering, blown up with a circle drawn around his face. The text of the poster read:

> Jew spy, Franz Edit-Stein, assumed the name Franz Gruber a year ago and has infiltrated the Austrian Nationalist Socialist Party. In the last year, he has betrayed the party on a number of occasions by revealing secret party plans to the elders of the Jewish cabal in Vienna. He has disappeared with important party documents and plans to sabotage the party's operations. He must be stopped. If anyone knows of the whereabouts of this Jew spy, please contact the office of Dr. Walter Riehl. Twenty mark reward for information.

"This isn't true," he said.

"Those guys back on the stoop don't know that," she said.

"But it isn't true," he said angrily.

"Tell that to them when they come at you with their pipes and chains. I knew that you would not come with me, so these posters are being distributed in all of the neighborhoods right now."

"This is a death warrant."

"You're probably right … if you don't come with me right now," she said.

The young man dropped his head in his hands and sat silently for a minute. When he looked up, there were no tears; there was no emotion except hate.

"Mother, you were wrong," he said. "Before today, I didn't hate you. I didn't like your politics or what you stood for. I felt like you were misguided, but I didn't hate you. But for this, I hate you. You are no different than you say they are. By doing this, it is as if you have stuck a gun to my head and said, 'Do as I say, or I will kill you.'"

"Franz, it may be hard to understand, but the only reason that I have done this is because I love you. I feel that, somewhere along the way, I have failed you, and this is the only way I know to give you a chance of getting back on the right track. I am going home now. I will warn you that the posters are already up in this neighborhood, so I wouldn't waste any time if I were you. I brought you a hooded jacket to wear to keep people from recognizing you. Your train ticket for the port is for the day after tomorrow. Will you come with me?"

"No."

"Very well," she said.

As Helena got up and walked away, she had no idea if she had done the right thing or what the end result would be.

Franz wandered the streets for the next twenty-four hours, seeing the signs with his picture. Twice, he was noticed by members of the party, and each time, they gave chase.

The next morning, Franz boarded a train at the central station with his immigration papers in hand, headed for the port. It was the last time that Franz would see Vienna.

CHAPTER 5

Soon after Franz left for the United States, Jean Louis started his schooling at the Technical Institute. As with everything else, he did well at school. It was a foregone conclusion that he would be accepted into the engineering tract of study, and he was. As the son of a veteran, he was allowed to attend school at no cost, so the only problem was how he and his family would live. For that reason, Jean Louis considered not accepting a position at the school and going to work to support his mother and sister. When Helena heard of this idea, she threw a fit. She was adamant that he not delay his plans to attend school. Again, Mr. Gruber came to the rescue of the Stein family. He gave young Jean Louis a job busing tables. It didn't pay much, but it was enough so Jean Louis would not be a drain on the family, and it helped him pay for his books.

His time at the school was among the happiest times of his life. He had inherited his father's fascination for how things work, and he was working toward a life goal that would let him do that for the rest of his life.

Then the depression struck. Again, Jean Louis considered quitting school, but Helena was insistent.

Rudy Holtoff waited tables along with Jean Louis at Gruber's. Like Jean Louis, Rudy liked girls, but the difference between them was that Rudy had no future; despite his good looks, Rudy was not very smart.

"Did you see the tits on that one out at table ten?" Rudy asked as he brought a wash pan full of dishes back to the kitchen.

"Yeah, that's just too much for me."

"Not me, the bigger the better. By the way, you want to head for the country this weekend—have a few a beers, meet some girls? Maybe get lucky?"

"I'd love to, but I got to study. Tests are coming up soon."

"Hell, where is all of this studying going to get you? You're wasting the best years of your life with your nose stuck in a book when it needs to be between a set of tits."

"Look, Rudy, I have no intention of busing tables the rest of my life."

"Me neither, just as soon as the Depression lets up—and it will soon—I'm getting a Union job at the brass foundry south of town. I got a cousin who works there, and he says he can get me on."

"My mother would kill me if she thought for a minute that I wasn't going to finish school. Anyway, I haven't got a cousin in the Union," Jean Louis said.

"If you ever change your mind, I'll talk to my cousin."

"Thanks."

From the other end of the kitchen they heard Gruber's deep voice: "All right you two lazy clowns, get back to work. I don't pay you to stand around."

Rudy laughed.

"Hell, old man, you don't hardly pay us at all."

"Well, I'll tell you what, wiseass, if you don't like it, then quit. I got twenty men a day come by here looking for a job, most of them with families." This was a conversation that the two men had every day in one way or another. Rudy was Gruber's sister's youngest boy; Gruber wasn't going to fire him, and Rudy knew it.

Gruber turned back to the serving window.

"Olga, order up."

Olga walked by the two young men, and they both followed her with their eyes. Rudy nudged Jean Louis with his elbow and smiled.

"Wouldn't that be nice?" he said. "I mean a weekend on the river with Olga. All the beer you could drink."

"She's not interested in you, Rudy. She's got the hots for that painter from the Art Institute."

"I know but it never hurts to dream. Maybe someday."

Jean Louis never talked politics, but by the age of sixteen, Anna had shifted her affection from stray cats to stray causes. She took her mother a step further and, by the summer of her sixteenth year, declared herself first an anarchist, then a communist, then a feminist communist, and then a Zionist. Unlike Jean Louis, who did as his mother suggested, Anna did not finish her schooling. She refused to go and chose instead to stay at the Oldenberg and help her mother. Like Ruddy, Anna was a woman of action. Why stand around and wait for something to happen? Why plan for days, weeks, and months? If a thought occurred and it seemed like a good idea after an hour of reflection and two cups of coffee, then it was time to act.

When jobs did not materialize, Rudy began to chatter about how wonderful the Nazis were and how great things were going to be when they finally came to power in Austria. Anna embraced communism and raged against the inequities of capitalism. Jean Louis studied and absorbed. In a quieter more stable time, he most likely would have completed an advanced degree and gone on to teach. In the recesses of his mind, that was his dream.

By1933, Jean Louis had completed his studies at the Engineering Institute, but there were no jobs to be had. Life in Vienna was in chaos—the Nazis had taken over just north of the border; the rail workers were threatening to strike; and the economy was in shambles. To make ends meet, Jean Louis continued working the evening shift at Gruber's.

One evening in early January, Jean Louis came home late from work. He stopped at the front door of the Oldenberg and brushed the snow from his boots; four inches of new snow had fallen during the evening. Once inside the door, he removed his hat and coat, hung them on the rack, and walked up the stairs. At the top of the stairs, he noticed that the door to his mother's study was open and the light was on. He stuck his head in through the doorway.

"Burning the midnight oil, are we?" he asked.

Helena, his mother, looked up from her work and smiled.

"Sure, I guess. Sorry, I didn't hear you come in," she said.

"Must be serious," he said, pointing at the paper in her typewriter.

"Oh, it's just an article for the paper. I promised this piece last week, but you know me and deadlines. Come in, and sit down," she said.

"I didn't mean to interrupt you," he said.

"No, no, you're not interrupting. I needed to talk to you anyway."

"What are you writing about?" he asked as he sat down on the sofa near the window.

"Same song, third verse. On the one side, you got your sister and her friends in the rail workers union, and on the other is that idiot Dollfuss and his government. If the union strikes and either one of them does something stupid, then Hitler and the Nazis will jump in with both feet. You know as well as I do that, outside of our small group of people here in Vienna, most people in this country would welcome that Hitler with open arms, including your friend, Rudy."

"Mom," Jean Louis interrupted her, "it's not Hitler they want. It's jobs and money they want. It's a nice place to live and a future. People like Rudy aren't looking for a hero; they're looking for a savior. If the devil came along and said, here's what you need to survive, they'd be right in line behind him."

"Yeah, I know, and that's what scares me," Helena said. "In the process, they're going to bite off more than they can chew. If they ever let this silly clown loose on the world, then the rest of us will have hell to pay."

Helena picked up a letter from her desk, got up from her seat behind the desk, and walked over to the sofa where her son had taken a seat.

"Enough about the Nazis," she said. "We've got something more pressing to talk about. I got this letter from your Uncle Karl in Pittsburgh a few days ago. He finally admitted that he hasn't heard from or seen your brother, Franz, for the last couple of years. I'm really scared that something dreadful has happened to him, and the worst of it is that it's entirely my fault. If your father had survived, this wouldn't have happened. He would have been able to handle Franz, but the boy never would listen to me."

Helena began to cry. Jean Louis moved over to her side of the sofa, pulled out his handkerchief, and gave it to her. While she wiped her eyes, he put his arm around her shoulder.

"I haven't slept any in the last two days, worrying about this," she continued. "I hate to ask you this, because I know it will be a big sacrifice on your part, but you're the only one he will listen to. Would you go to the United States and see if you can find your brother? Will you go find your brother and be his family? Will you do this for me?"

Jean Louis had seen this coming, and he knew that he would go. He knew that it would scare him to death, but he would go. He would because his mother asked him to go.

"Yes, of course I will," he said

In an exchange of letters, Karl assured them that Jean Louis, with his degree in chemical engineering, would have a job and a place to live waiting for him in Pittsburgh. One morning as the date approached for his departure, Jean Louis and his mother were having breakfast. He was reading an article his mother had written. He began laughing, took a sip of his coffee, and looked across the breakfast table at his mother.

"Mom," he said, "that is really strong stuff. You aren't going to make any friends in high places with writing like that. I especially like the swipe you take at the Nazis." He picked up the paper and looked again. "'Bully children,' that's good."

Helena had a worried look on her face. "I'd like to be stronger than that," she said, "but the word is that the government is going to start closing down some of the independent presses as a way of putting pressure on the big boys. I think we're at the top of the list." She took a sip of her tea and changed the subject. "Now, let's talk about your trip. I've been thinking about making a family holiday out of your trip to the coast. It's been a while since the three of us did anything together. What do you say?"

"I think that's a great idea," he said.

"Won't cost much. We can catch a sleeper through the mountains to France and then on to Amsterdam. I have some friends who will put us up for a few days. I haven't talked to Anna yet, but maybe we can pull her away from her meetings long enough to go with us."

Anna Edit-Stein had grown into beautiful woman with a quick wit, dark red hair, blue eyes, and a mischievous grin. There was no mistaking that she was her mother's daughter. The red hair came from father Stein, but otherwise she was an Edit. From the time she was born, Anna was always immersed in a cause. Jean Louis always said that his sister collected causes like other people collected stray cats.

"What's the latest thing?" Jean Louis asked. "Anarchy or communism?"

"It depends on who the latest boyfriend is," Helena said, smiling. "I haven't figured out yet whether she falls in love with the man or the movement first. Either way, it lasts about the same length of time."

Helena found her daughter in the Ottaring among the Schutzbund, the military wing of the social democrats, planning the coming confrontation with the Dollfuss government.

"Go with us to Amsterdam," her mother begged.

"I can't, Helena." Anna said. She had taken to calling her mother by her first name. She had explained to her mother that the bonds of family must be broken, that the first devotion must be to the party. She continued, "You, of all people, should understand that we are at a point of crisis. We've got to fight the fascists and the Nazis. If we don't, they will take control. I leave on a mission tomorrow."

What she didn't tell her mother was that, the next day, she was to cross the frontier and go to Prague where she and Andre, her cell leader, were to pick up a shipment of guns for delivery to Linz.

"Can you at least have supper with us tonight?" Helena asked.

"Can I bring Andre?" Anna asked.

"Of course you can," Helena said.

"Where do you want to eat?"

"Gruber's?"

Anna thought for a minute. "Yeah, that's safe enough," she said as she leaned over and gave her mother a hug and a kiss on the cheek.

Helena said, "Anna, sweetie, one thing."

"What's that?"

"Take a bath, sweetheart. You smell bad. There isn't anything noble about smelling bad."

Hubert Gruber and his Beer Garden hadn't changed. Hubert's hair was grey, and his potbelly had grown, but he was still the same good-natured man who had hired Helena and her children when they needed jobs.

When he saw Helena and Jean Louis, his face lit up.

"And what can I bring two of my favorite people in the whole world?" Gruber asked.

Helena stood and hugged her friend. Jean Louis extended his hand, but Gruber brushed it away and gave him a bear hug.

"How are you my son?" he asked.

"Good, I leave for the United States in a few days," Jean Louis said.

"So this is a farewell dinner. I'll tell you what: the meal is on me. You order anything you want. If I don't have it, I'll go out and get it."

"Before you get too generous," Helena said, "I warn you we have two others joining us—Anna and her new boyfriend."

"And what do we know about *this* young man?" Gruber asked with mock seriousness.

"Nothing," Helena said, "but, knowing my daughter, I suspect that his politics are somewhere to the left of Trotsky."

As they were talking, Anna and her new beau walked into the garden. Anna heard "left of Trotsky."

"That wouldn't be hard. Trotsky's downfall was because he was conservative and reactionary," Anna said. She poked Gruber in the side with her finger. "Hello, Tubby."

"Ah, it's Paprika," Gruber said. "My favorite spice and my favorite color, all in one." He hugged the petite redhead.

Anna turned to her brother and hugged him. "Big brother, Helena told me you are going to America."

Jean Louis nodded and smiled.

Then she remembered that Andre was standing behind her. "Jean Louis, Helena, and Hubert, this is Andre."

Andre was a tall, dark, brooding, young man who was painfully thin. He wore a black suit that was two sizes too large, and he didn't appear to have shaved in a week. When Hubert and Jean Louis extended their hands to greet him, Andre nodded and then sat down in a chair that was pulled away from the table.

There was an awkward silence, and then Gruber asked, "So what would everyone like to drink and eat? Remember, it's on the house."

Helena and Jean Louis ordered a beer and goulash with sides of dumplings.

"And what will my little Paprika and her friend have this evening?" Gruber asked.

Anna looked at Andre, and he simply waved his hand. "Bring us two cups of fig coffee and some dry bread," she said.

Jean Louis made a face. "Fig coffee and dry bread," he said. "What's that all about? It sounds perfectly horrible."

"It's what the workers eat every day," Anna said, "and we're no better than they are."

"That may be true," Jean Louis said, "but fig coffee?"

Helena just smiled. "What kind of work do you do, Andre?"

"I work with my hands," he mumbled.

Gruber returned with the beers. "The fig coffee will take a few minutes—we don't get many requests," he said.

Anna was anxious to turn the conversation away from Andre. "Tell me, big brother, when do you leave for America?" she asked.

"The boat leaves from Amsterdam in ten days. We, Mom and I, are going to take the train a few days early and take a holiday. I sure do wish you would go."

Anna smiled. "Yeah, me too, but you know, duty calls. We've got work to do."

Andre made a grunting sound and then stood up.

"I'm leaving," he said. "I can't take any more of this." He looked at Helena. "I read what you published in your paper today. I hope you understand how stupid that is, especially the crap about not using force. That is a recipe to make sure the fascists win this war. Mark my words—if they even think about attacking us, we will hit them with so much force they won't know what happened." He turned and looked at Anna. "Come on, we've got work to do."

Anna reached out and put her hand on Andre's arm. "But, honey, we just got here," she said.

"You either come with me now or don't bother showing up anymore," Andre said. With that, he stormed out.

Jean Louis looked at his little sister. "He's a keeper, Sis, what rock did you find that clown under?"

Anna was crying. "I'm sorry. I love you both, but I have to go with him. I love him and what he stands for. Good luck in your grand adventure, big brother." She turned to Helena. "I love you, Mom. I'll see you soon. You understand, don't you?"

Helena nodded. "Yeah, I understand. You go on with him. Please be careful."

Anna leaned over and hugged her. When she did, Helena stuck a few bills in her hand. "Keep this for yourself. Just in case." There was the smell of fresh soap on her daughter's neck.

As Anna was leaving, Gruber walked to the table with the two orders of fig coffee.

"So what am I going to do with these two fig coffees?" he asked.

"Set them down here. We'll drink them," Helena said.

"Better not offer too fast," Hubert said.

Jean Louis took a sip of the hot, black liquid and then made a face. "No wonder Andre is so mad."

The three of them began to laugh.

CHAPTER 6

Karl Stein arrived in New York a day before Jean Louis's ship was slated to dock. He checked into his hotel near Battery Park and made his way to the headquarters of the German-American Bund on East Eighty-Sixth Street. He was met at the door to the Bund by a pair of young men dressed in grey shirts and black pants with daggers on their right hips. Each of the men saluted him with their arms extended and their palms facing the ground.

"What is your business, Herr Stein?" the first young man asked.

"I have a meeting with Chief of Staff Krause," Karl said.

The two young men turned and saluted Karl, completing the salute with the words, "Frei Amerika." They separated and allowed Karl to enter the building.

The building was an old bank that had gone belly up early in the Depression; the Bund had rented it for next to nothing. In what had been the atrium of the bank sat the commander of the guards, John Michael Krause, the son of the chief of staff. The younger Krause stood, stepped out from behind his desk, and saluted Karl. Karl returned the salute.

"Good morning, Herr Stein, it is so nice to see you. I hope you had an uneventful trip from Pittsburgh," Krause said.

"Yes, it was nice. The countryside is beginning to green up, and the weather was pretty," Karl said.

"My father is expecting you. Please step into his office," John Michael said, pointing toward the back of the building.

Karl had always enjoyed the company of Dr. Adolph Krause. The two men had been friends, dating back well before the Great War. He couldn't say the same about this young man. By appearance, he could just as easily have been a freshman college student from Princeton, but if half the stories Karl had heard were true, this young man was bad news. The very public show of uniforms, saluting, and daggers attracted far too much attention to the work they were trying to accomplish.

"My old friend," Adolph said as Karl entered the room. The elder Krause came around from behind a desk and hugged Karl. "It is so good to see you. I know we talk on the phone all of the time, and I think I have at least one position paper you sent me that isn't even opened yet, but it seems like I never see you in person. Please have a seat. How are things going in Pittsburgh?"

"Things are going well. I have been working day and night just trying to keep up," Karl said. "How is your health? I hear you were in the hospital last month."

"Well, you know how it is. Life eventually catches up with us. I'm now paying for the indiscretions of my youth. My angina gives me fits if I get too worked up, but the nitroglycerin pretty well takes care of that. The big problem over the last month was the yellow jaundice. My doctors have pretty well convinced me that it's alcohol. For the most part, I've completely quit drinking." He looked toward the desk where his son was working. "I still sneak a toddy from time to time," he said, whispering and winking at his friend.

Karl reached out and put his hand on his friends arm. "I worry about you, Adolph. Sometime, soon, you should take some time off. You and I could take a week off and go out to Camp Stuttgart, do some fishing, forget about politics for a few days. Winnie, the resident cook, can fix anything you want."

Adolph smiled. "You know, that is a nice thought. First off, let's get a little business out of the way. Did you get a chance to review those papers I sent you? The ones that Bill Parkus from Sunnyville, Mississippi, wrote?"

"I did. There's some pretty good stuff in what he writes, but it's really rough around the edges. It's too anti-Catholic for my taste and far too many ain'ts and us'ns. The man needs a good editor."

"You're right there, but I've known this fellow since the war, and his heart is in the right place. If you have time, I would appreciate it if you would clean it up a little, because I would like to use some of it, and you're the best speechwriter we have."

"I can make it sound like it came right out of your mouth," Karl said.

Krause poured Karl a cup of tea. "I understand that your nephew is coming in from Austria tomorrow."

"Yes, that's right," Karl said. He hesitated and then added, "But, how did you know?"

Adolph looked at his friend. "Didn't you tell me when you called last week? Yeah, you must have told me then. I really don't remember where I heard it."

"Maybe so," Karl said, smiling weakly. Karl would be the first to admit that his memory was not as good as it once had been, but he had mentioned the arrival of Jean Louis to no one. He had always been a man who kept his own council about personal matters, and the arrival of his sister-in-law's son, the son of a Jew, the son of a socialist—a woman who was opposed to everything he and the Bund held near and dear—was not something that he was inclined to share with the party. Karl knew, without a doubt, that the source of information was John Michael, but the question was "How did he know?"

"I'll tell you what," Krause turned to John Michael, "clear my appointments for tomorrow. I am going to spend the day with my friend, if he wants me too."

Karl nodded and smiled.

John Michael started to protest. "But father …"

"No buts; Karl is right. A day off would do me good."

Karl and Adolph were waiting on Pier 43 in the area just outside of immigration when Karl spotted Jean Louis working his way through the various lines, turnstiles, and clerks.

"There he is," Karl said to his friend. He handed the picture Helena had sent to him to Adolph.

"That's him all right," Adolph said.

The boy was unmistakably his nephew. He had the Stein nose, eyes, chin, and slope of the forehead. The only problem was that the boy appeared to be drunk. Each time he was asked for his paperwork, he seemed confused, and on several occasions, he stumbled, dropping his bags. His clothes were in disarray, and he did not appear to have shaved in a week.

When the last official stamped his papers, Jean Louis walked out into the atrium, where the two men stood. The elder Stein walked up to his nephew.

"Are you Jean Louis?" he asked.

The younger man nodded and leaned over to put his bag down. In the process, he lost his balance, falling into his uncle.

"Son, are you drunk?" Karl asked. "If so, this is not a good start for us."

Jean Louis regained his balance and put his hand on his uncle's shoulder.

"No, sir. I'm not drunk. In fact, I haven't had anything by mouth except water and juice for the last two weeks. I've had the worst case of seasickness in the world. I've been dizzy and throwing up since we left Amsterdam," Jean Louis said. "I really do need to go somewhere and lay down in a bed that is rooted to solid ground."

"Of course. By the way, Jean Louis, this is one of my oldest and dearest friends, Adolph Krause."

Jean Louis nodded to the older man. "Nice to meet you, sir."

"Your uncle has told me all about you." Adolph said. It was a nice lie; the truth was that they had barely mentioned Jean Louis in the last twenty-four hours. Adolph and his son knew far more about Jean Louis than they let on, and Karl knew that they knew. Nothing else needed to be said.

Karl took Jean Louis to the hotel, and while Jean Louis bathed, Karl emptied the boy's suitcase and took his clothes to the laundry downstairs. He brought a bowl of soup and some crackers back upstairs just as Jean Louis was preparing to go to sleep.

"You think you could eat this?" Karl asked.

"I'll try. It smells wonderful."

Karl pulled the end table around to the edge of the bed and set up the meal. Jean Louis began to slowly eat the soup.

"I will never," he said emphatically, "ever, under any circumstances, get on a boat again where I can't see the other side. I started to get sick when we first lost sight of land. That was two weeks ago, and I have been sick ever since. When I was up on the open deck of the ship, I felt better, but the rolling of the ship was much worse. When I was in my room down in the hole of the ship, I would get claustrophobic, and the vertigo would get worse. There was nowhere I could hide to get relief. I tried everything the staff and the ship's doctor suggested, but nothing helped." He stopped talking and took several more bites of his soup.

Karl sat, smiling at his nephew.

"You know Jean Louis you speak very good English for someone who has never been here."

"Mother insisted that we work on it every day. It really helped when I was at the Academy; several of my teachers were American."

"The other thing is that you really do look and sound like your father," he said. "You're beginning to get a little color back in your cheeks. Do you need anything else?"

Jean Louis shook his head. "No, what I really need to do is get some sleep, if that's okay."

"If you feel like it," Karl said, "we can go down to Mulberry Street for supper tonight."

Supper on Mulberry Street didn't happen; Jean Louis didn't awaken until the next morning.

"Good morning," Karl said as Jean Louis sat up in bed and put his feet on the floor. "How are you feeling?"

"I'm starving," Jean Louis said.

"That's a good sign. There's a great little restaurant downstairs, off of the lobby. Get dressed, and we'll go get some food."

In a few minutes, they were sitting down to a full breakfast that Jean Louis quickly devoured. While they ate, Karl noticed that one of John Michael's men was sitting in the third booth down from them. It wasn't hard to pick out the young man. He appeared to have just stepped out of a fashion magazine.

"We've got a ticket out on the seven PM train," Karl said. "It's not an express, so it will take most of the night to get home. We've got a couple of hours. Is there anything you'd like to see?"

"Where is the Statue of Liberty from here?"

The sun was shining and there was a gentle breeze coming in off of the harbor. Karl and Jean Louis walked over to an observation point in the park. Jean Louis dropped a nickel into the binocular glasses and aimed the glasses at the statue.

"That's really something," he said. "You may not remember it, but when I was a little kid you sent us a small bronze copy of Miss Liberty. Miss Liberty—that's what it had written across the base. That plus the Lazarus poem about golden doors. Anyway, it sat on the mantel of our fireplace all the time I was a kid. She lost it when we moved back into the Oldenberg. It was one of her favorite things."

"You ought to buy her another one," Karl said.

"That's a good idea. Think I will."

Karl took a sip from the cup of coffee he was holding.

"You know, Jean Louis. You don't seem to be much like your brother."

Jean Louis looked up from the binoculars and smiled. "I think that's a fair statement—that is, unless my brother has changed. How is he doing?"

"Son, I haven't seen your brother in several years. He only stayed with me for a very short time. He lived with me at first, and I got him a couple of jobs. He wouldn't show up for work, and he would stay out all night. I live a pretty ordered existence and keep a very neat house. I like for all of my stuff to be left alone. Let's just say that Franz didn't respect that, and we had a parting of ways. The boy was always mad about something, and he didn't take baths. I heard about him from people in the community for a while, but then he just sort of faded away."

"I promised my mother that I would make every effort to try and find him. I may need some help in getting started on my search when we get to Pittsburgh," Jean Louis said.

"I'll do what I can," the older man said.

CHAPTER 7

It was early spring of 1934 when the fighting began. No one was sure who fired the first shot, but in the end, it made very little difference. The rail workers in Vienna went on strike, and the Dollfuss government responded by opening fire on the strikers, their homes, and their families. In the early days of the revolt, as the government labeled it, large government artillery pieces were hauled into the city and proceeded to bombard the communities where the workers lived. After several days of bombing, they sent in the troops and the Heimwehr—nothing more than street thugs—who rounded up anyone who had any sympathy for the strikers. The families of the strikers were thrown into the streets, their homes were looted, and the houses were given to those sympathetic to the government. There were a small number of more hardcore workers, socialists, and communists, who decided to fight to the finish.

On the first day of the bombing, Helena was at her desk, working on a letter to the editor, begging each side in the conflict to step back, take a deep breath, and find a way out of the impasse. She had just finished the second paragraph of the letter when she heard what sounded like thunder. She gazed out of her second-story window and searched the sky for dark clouds. What she saw was a large puff of smoke rising from the Karl Marx Hof just blocks away.

Just as she turned from the window, Judith Keller, her assistant, came to the door. "Helena, there are government men at the front door. They insist on talking to you."

Helena was quick to size up the situation. "Judith, listen to me, and do as I say, quickly," she said. "While I go and talk to these men, you leave by the secret passage into the building next-door. Go and warn everyone else you can find, but try not to attract attention to yourself."

"But what about you?" Judith asked.

"I'll be okay. I have done nothing wrong," Helena said. "By the way, if you see Anna, tell her I am okay and not to worry."

"But—" Judith began to object.

"No buts, just do it now, or it may be too late. Now go," Helena demanded.

From the top of the stairs, Helena could see that the officers had let themselves into the house and were beginning to spread out through the front rooms. She glanced over her shoulder to make sure that Judith had done as she was told. There was no sign of the young woman.

Standing in the entryway were two army officers and a young man in the rough uniform of the Heimwehr. She quickly recognized the young man as Rudy Holtoff, Jean Louis's friend.

"Good morning, Rudy, and to what do I owe the pleasure of seeing you this morning?" she asked.

Rudy averted his eyes from Helena. The officer in charge quickly intervened.

"This is not a social call, Mrs. Stein," he said.

"It's Edit-Stein. Helena Edit-Stein."

The man nodded. "Yes, Edit-Stein. Anyway, you need to come with us to the station. We need to talk to you," he said.

"And what might the charges be?" she asked.

"There are no charges at this time."

"What am I to be questioned about?"

"You will be told that at the station," the officer said.

"I see. So you are taking me to the station on a fishing expedition. Is that right?"

"That's enough talking," the other officer said. "You're coming with us one way or the other. You can make it difficult or easy. It's up to you."

"Of course, I will come with you, but I happen to know the law on this issue, and it says that if I am under suspicion for something I must be told what for."

The first officer intervened again, "We are now in a state of rebellion, and you can be held without cause. Now come along with us."

"We need to speak to two other women. Your daughter, Hannah …" the second officer said.

Rudy tapped him on the shoulder and said, "Anna; the daughter's name is Anna."

"Right, Anna. And a woman named Judith Keller."

"As for Anna, I haven't seen her in weeks. I have seen Judith this morning, but I have no idea where she is right now."

As she finished her last statement, a thunderous explosion rocked the house and shattered the windows in the front hall.

They all went to the floor.

"Damn," the first officer said. "I wish those artillery were more accurate. We had better get out of here, or the next one will be right on top of us."

The four of them got up and dusted themselves off. The two officers and Rudy escorted Helena to a waiting black police van.

Instead of being taking to the local station, Helena was taken to the central station, booked on suspicion of subversive activities, and put into a cell.

Hours turned into days and days into a week. The only sign of another human being was the matron who brought her food and fresh linens. Any attempt at questioning the guard resulted in only a cold stare.

While in jail, she was plagued by self-doubt. It wasn't her situation as much as it was her children that bothered her. Her oldest son had reacted so violently, and now her daughter had gone off to join the communists. *What if—?* she thought many times, sitting in her cell. *What if I had been less of a politician and more of a mother? What if Willie had lived? What if this is all my fault?*

After eight days, an officer of the prison came to her cell and opened the door.

"You may go," he said, and then he turned to walk off.

"What do you mean I may go?" Helena demanded. "I want an explanation of why I was brought here. Why was I held without charges for over a week? This is a civilized country. You can't do this to innocent people."

"I wouldn't know about any of that," the officer said. "All I know is that I was told to come to this cell and tell the prisoner that they were free to go."

"I demand answers," Helena said.

"You'll have to go above my pay grade to find answers, lady. I just do what I'm told. Now you need to leave," the officer repeated.

Walking out of the jail, she had to shield her eyes from the bright morning sun. The day she was taken to jail, it had been raining lightly, and there had been patches of dirty snow along the road. Now the snow was gone, and it was a warm morning as she crossed the bridge over the Danube, heading for home. And there were a number of other differences: there were no guns firing or sounds of bombs going off; there were police and soldiers everywhere on the street; and no one was smiling. A warm winter day that held the promise of spring always brought forth smiles from people on the streets of the city but not this day.

When Helena walked out of the jail and onto the streets of central Vienna, she was torn between walking back into the central station and demanding an explanation and setting off on a search for Anna. When she rounded the corner onto the boulevard where she lived, Helena was overwhelmed. Many of the large trees that filled the park across from the Oldenberg were lying on their sides. When she walked up to the front steps of her house, the stair-minder asked her where she was going.

"This is my house. I have been away, and now I have come home." She purposely didn't tell him that she had been in jail.

"This house is now the property of the city. It is occupied by the soldiers who were protecting the street."

"But what about my typewriter, my bed, and furniture?" she asked.

"Anything that wasn't destroyed was taken to a central warehouse over on the other side of the river. I don't know where exactly," the man said.

"Well, can I at least go in and look for some of my things?"

"You will have to get permission from one of the people who live here now, and no one is at home. You could come back and try again," the man said.

Helena realized that she wouldn't be able to get anywhere with this man, so she left and went across town to Gruber's. The gate to the garden was closed, so she went around back and knocked on the door.

When no one answered, she knocked on the door again. "Hubert," she said, "it's Helena. Are you in there?"

She could hear shuffling behind the door, and then the door cracked open.

"Helena, thank God. We thought you were dead." He opened the door and pulled her in. "Come in, quick, before they see you. We thought you were dead. Where have you been?"

"I'm all right. I wasn't hurt or anything." She looked down at his bandaged leg. "What happened to you?"

"I got a little close to one of the explosions. It's nothing really, just a little burn. Where have you been?"

"I've been in jail," she said.

"Were you beaten?" he asked.

"No, there was nothing. They didn't question me. They just put me in a cell and kept me isolated for the last week."

"Many people have been beaten. Many have lost their homes."

"Do you have news of Anna or Judith?" she asked.

"I know nothing about Anna, but Judith has been in and out since you left."

"How can I get word to her?"

"From what I know of the situation, you probably don't need to go looking. Someone from the police most likely followed you when they let you out of the jail," Hubert said. "You should stay here and let me find out what I can. I have to go to the wholesaler to pick up some supplies, and while I'm out, I'll make some connections."

Waiting at Gruber's was almost as hard as sitting in jail. It took several hours for Hubert to make his rounds and return with a truckload of supplies.

"Did you have any luck?" Helena asked as he walked into the kitchen.

"See for yourself," he said. Since his hands were full, he motioned toward the back door and the two men with caps pulled down over their faces who were bringing in small boxes of cabbage and potatoes. The first man put his box of cabbage on the cutting table and looked up. It was then that Helena realized that the young man was Judith.

Helena ran across the room and hugged her friend.

"I'm so glad you're okay," she said. "Tell me what happened."

"It's been just horrible," she said. "When the bombing was over, they went house to house and kicked out everyone they even suspected of being allied with the workers. There are whole families wandering the streets with nowhere to go."

"What about Anna? Is she okay? Where is she?"

"She's okay, now. She was hurt on the first day of the bombing, but she's patched up now and in a safe place."

"Where is she?" Helena asked.

"She's at a small vineyard across the river from Durnstein on the Danube."

"You said she was hurt. How bad is it?"

Judith hesitated.

"Tell me how bad it is, Judith," Helena insisted.

"She lost part of her left hand and a portion of her left ear. But like I said, she is doing well, and the medical people say she will recover."

"When can we go to her?" Helena said.

"Tonight. You and I should be able to get to one of the safe houses, where they can help us catch a boat upriver. I don't think we can risk the train right now." Judith turned and motioned to the other person standing in the shadows. "Before we go, there is someone here you need to talk to. She may be very important to us. She is from England and can get the story out about what really happened here." Judith turned and addressed the other woman.

"Naomi Mitchison, this is Helena Edit-Stein."

Naomi Mitchison stepped forward, out of the shadows, and removed her gloves. "Ms. Edit-Stein, it is a great privilege to meet you," she said. "I have followed your work at the Oldenberg since you worked for Adelheid Popp after the war. I am sorry we have to meet under such circumstances."

Helena smiled, stuck her hand out, and shook hands with Ms. Mitchison.

Judith began again. "Helena, the official government line is that the strike was a communist revolt. They have taken the opportunity to do away with as many of their enemies as they can, and so far, they have been able to keep any word of the truth from the press. Ms. Mitchison came from London with funds for the strikers and to attempt to find out what is really going on."

"Ms. Edit-Stein, anything that you want to get published in England, I will do my best to help," Naomi said.

"It may take a couple of days for me to get something for you, but it will be done," Helena said. "Right now, I need to find my daughter."

"I understand," the English woman said.

That night under cover of darkness, the three women began their trip up the Danube and, by dawn, had arrived at the ferry dock due north of Durnstein. They walked through the small village to a small home in the middle of a vineyard on the hillside overlooking the valley below. They knocked on the door. An elderly woman came to the door and asked them what they wanted at that time of day.

"We are here to see the girl," Judith said.

"And who are you?" the woman asked.

"I'm the girl's mother," Helena said.

The woman nodded her head and let the three women pass. They walked through a narrow passage way and up half a flight of stairs. At the end of a narrow hall was a doorway that led to the attic.

The woman knocked twice on the door and then opened it. In a small room that had once housed the children of the household, Anna was sleeping on a small metal cot. She was on her right side, facing the door. It took a minute for Helena's sight to adjust to the dim light of the room.

"Anna, sweetheart, are you awake?" Helena asked.

Anna stirred from her sleep. "Who is it?"

"It's your mother," Helena whispered.

"Who?" she asked.

The old woman leaned over to Helena. "You will have to speak up," she said. "The explosion affected her hearing. She was almost killed by an artillery shell during the bombing, but she is doing better."

Helena leaned over to avoid hitting her head on the rafters and moved toward her daughter. When she was at her daughter's bedside, she took her hand and leaned close to her ear.

"Sweetheart, it's your mother. I've come to help."

"Mama, I'm scared. My ears are ringing. It's so deafening. I've been so scared. I'm so glad you are here," Anna said, crying.

Helena reached out and caressed her daughter. "Everything's fine, sweetheart. I'm here, and I will be here. You don't have to worry."

Over the next several days, Helena was able to construct a picture of what had happened to her daughter. She and Andre had made several trips across the frontier into the Czech Republic, bringing back guns for the strikers. On the night before the bombing, they had collapsed from exhaustion in an upper-story flat in the Florisdorf.

The first artillery shell had come through the roof of the building and exploded as it hit the floor beside the bed where they were sleeping. Andre had been lying with his face toward the window and was killed instantly. The concussion of the explosion had thrown them against the wall. Andre's body had been mangled, and the last three fingers of Anna's left hand were gone.

For twenty-four hours, she had lain unconscious in the rubble before anyone got to them. At first, they thought that both were dead, but when they pulled Andre's cold body off of Anna, they realized she was warm and still breathing.

Carefully, they had transported Anna to a more secure area, and after a few days, they had moved her up the river to the house where she was now staying.

The farmhouse faced to the south and east, so the early morning sun flooded the attic room that was now Anna and Helena's temporary home.

"Here, I have some soup for you to eat," Helena said.

"I'm really not hungry," Anna said.

"Eat anyway. You have got to build up your strength," Helena demanded. "You can never tell when we might have to leave this place."

Anna acquiesced to her mother's commands. She was turning into a good soldier.

In between spoonfuls of the hot soup, Anna questioned her mother. "Have you figured out why they put you in jail?" she asked.

Helena nodded her head.

"People with guns are easy for these fascists to fight. All they have to do is pick up a gun and shoot back. The pen is harder to fight. Their only recourse is to shut down the papers and put us in jail. Unlike the Nazis in Germany, we have a semblance of civil society and rule of law left, so they are restrained. I think that is why they let me go. But this isn't the end. The minute I start to write, they'll be back."

Helena reached over and touched her daughter's hand. "How does your arm feel?"

"It's okay. It's the ringing in my ears that bothers me. It may be a bit better than it was, but it's still there."

"We are going to have to start thinking about what we're going to do when you get better," Helena said.

"When I'm strong enough, I'm going back to the fight," Anna said.

"Honey, I don't think you understand. The fight is over. The fascists won," Helena said.

"No, Mom, it's you who doesn't understand. In the same way that you have to go back to writing, I have to return and join my friends. That is my life now. Andre gave his life, and I will give mine, if it's necessary."

There was something in her daughter's voice that made it clear to Helena that this was an issue that was not up for discussion.

One night several weeks later, a small group of men and women came by to check on Anna. After several hours of talking, Anna got up, packed a small bag, and left for the frontier.

The next morning, Helena returned to Vienna. She was fully expecting a major confrontation, but on the day of her return, there was an attempted Nazi coup, and Dollfuss was killed. A new government was quickly formed, and the coup was suppressed, but for the time being, the government had more important things to deal with than a few socialist writers.

CHAPTER 8

Dear Jean Louis,

I suppose you are somewhat surprised at getting a letter from London. It seems awfully cloak and dagger to correspond like this, but since the revolt, the mail is very irregular, and we are convinced that most of our correspondence is read. Naomi—that's the lady who is getting our mail out—tells me that the people outside of central Europe don't get an honest picture of what's going on. If you haven't heard, I am now officially an outlaw. The government has declared all of us social democrats outlaws. Isn't that a hoot? After the revolt, the Nazis killed Dollfuss and tried to take over. Your friend, Rudy, was involved somehow. Anyway, it didn't work, and we now have his fellow, Schuschnigg. If he could, this guy would bring back the Hapsburgs, but he's got a real problem—he has Hitler and his boys putting the pressure on one side, and on the other, your sister's communist friends are taking shots at them. The only friend he has is Mussolini across the Alps in Italy.

Your sister was hurt in the revolt, but she has completely recovered, and the last I heard, she was heading for Palestine with a bunch of her friends from Poland. It seems like they have given up on us Europeans and decided to go start anew in the desert.

Despite being an outlaw, I am getting a few things published. I don't use my own byline anymore, so if you see anything by the Dissenter, that's me.

I hope you are doing well and staying out of trouble. Have you met any nice girls? I guess that's a stupid question; you always meet nice girls. I hope you are enjoying your work and getting on well with your uncle.

Naomi said in her last letter that she may be coming to the US in the next few months. She is going to somewhere in the Mississippi delta to work with tenant farmers.

Anyway, I love you and hope you are doing well.

Love,

Mom

CHAPTER 9

Karl Stein lived in a modest but immaculate Craftsman home in a quiet Catholic neighborhood. At precisely five thirty each morning, his alarm rang. At five forty, the sounds of a Mozart concerto or Beethoven sonata filled the house and spilled over into the small yard that separated him from his neighbor of thirty years. By six, he had bathed and shaved and was sitting at his dining table, eating a simple breakfast of meat, cheese, and bread. He left home promptly at six thirty-five every morning for work—that is, every day but Sunday. On Sunday, he went to ten o'clock mass at St. Joseph's followed by lunch at Emmy's Schnitzel House, and then he went to work. On his rare day off, Karl spent his time buying and selling antiques. Karl's comment, "I live an ordered existence," was repeated often enough to make the point clear.

Jean Louis's room was at the top of the stairs and to the rear of the house. When he ascended the stairs, there were several oak planks that made a distinctive sound; it was impossible for him to come in late without waking his uncle. Meals were served precisely at six AM and six PM, and the evenings were spent reading and working on Bund papers. The few times that Jean Louis missed a meal, he heard for several days about wasting food.

One evening over supper, Jean Louis broached the subject.

"Uncle Karl," he said, "I've been thinking about getting a room on my own."

Karl raised his hand to object. "Nonsense. That would be wasting money."

"It really wouldn't be, and besides, I feel like I am getting in your hair," Jean Louis said.

"Rubbish—that's the silliest thing I ever heard," Karl said. Despite his objections, Karl was tickled to death. He cared for his nephew and found him to be good company, but living alone for thirty years had created habits that were hard to break.

"Anyway," Jean Louis continued, "I found a place close to the office that's really cheap, and I'll probably be moving out after the next paycheck."

"Well, whatever you say. But I want you to know that you're always welcome here."

"I really do appreciate it, and I might have to take you up on the offer again somewhere down the road."

While Jean Louis had lived with his uncle, Karl had discouraged him from attempting to find his brother, partly out of fear that the older brother might decide to move back in.

As soon as Jean Louis settled into his new apartment, Karl put him in contact with some of the leaders of the German immigrant community. Jean Louis showed a picture of his brother around. No one had seen him.

One night as he having supper at the Europa, a small rathskeller near his apartment, Jean Louis showed the picture of his brother to the waiter.

"Have you ever seen this guy?" he asked.

"I don't know. What's his name?" the waiter asked.

"It's my brother. His name is Franz Stein, but this picture is at least ten years old."

"There used to be this guy who came in here, but he hasn't been in here in a while. The last time I saw him, he didn't look too good. He tended to drink too much and get rowdy. One time, the manager had to ask him to leave. If I were you, I'd check the dives over around the river near the rescue mission."

The neighborhood around the mission had the look of Heldienstrasse, where Franz had hung out in Vienna. The first bar along the strip was the Hindenburg. Jean Louis walked into the darkened room and up to the bar. Without an order, the bartender brought him a beer. The bartender turned to walk away, and Jean Louis stopped him.

"Need to ask you a question. Have you ever seen this guy?" He handed him the picture. "He may go by the name of Frank."

"Who wants to know?" The bartender sounded suspicious.

"His brother. I'm his brother. I just moved here from Vienna. I haven't seen him in a few years."

"What did you say his name was?"

"Last I heard, he called himself Frank, but his real given name is Franz."

"No, I mean his last name," the bartender said.

"I don't know what name he's using, but my name is Stein."

"Don't know of anybody named Frank, but there was a fellow used to come in about two years ago looked like this fellow." As he was talking, a thought occurred to him. "Wait a minute." He shouted over his shoulder, "Hank, come out here." The bartender looked back at Jean Louis. "Hank's my dishwasher. He and the guy I'm thinking about went out drinking a few times."

Hank came out of the kitchen drying his hands. "What do you want, boss?"

"You remember this guy? What was his name?" He showed the picture to the dishwasher.

"Oh, yeah, Stephen Holder. He hung out over at the Bund. I haven't seen him in a while. Real mad, always looking for a fight. If he is anywhere around this part of town, Jerry, the evening supervisor over at the mission, will know about it."

Jean Louis was showing the picture to the meal supervisor at the mission when he heard his brother's voice. Franz was having an argument with one of the cooks.

"I demand that you give me more potatoes," Franz shouted. "I know what you're doing. You're saving them for your kike friends. Well, I know my rights."

The supervisor excused himself from Jean Louis. After a couple of quick hand signals, a large, black man and a dark-skinned Italian surrounded Franz, getting between him and the server, a small, bucktoothed man.

"Look, Bud, nobody's getting shorted here," the supervisor said. "If you don't like the way we run things, you'd better just leave."

"What a bunch of crap," Franz shouted.

"Look, friend, we are here to help. If you feel like that, why don't you just set that tray down on the table over here, and we will help you out the door. And, if you had any idea about throwing that tray on the floor, I assure you that you will clean it up if you do. Do I make myself clear?" the man said, without raising his voice.

Franz said nothing, but his body language spoke volumes. Everyone within a twenty-foot radius, except for the four combatants, took a step back.

In German, Jean Louis said, "Franz, don't." He knew what his brother was preparing to do.

Perhaps it was the sound of Jean Louis's warm, soft voice, the memories of laughter as they chased each other through the Oldenberg and rode the Ferris wheel at the Prater, the taste of hot sausage, kraut, and strong Austrian beer. Franz paused.

"It's me, Franz, your brother."

The two men made eye contact. Jean Louis continued, "Come with me. I'll get you something to eat."

The meal supervisor reached out and took the tray from Franz. "Did you have a coat, friend?"

Franz shook his head.

"Would you like one?"

Franz nodded.

The black man went around the corner and, in a second, returned with a ragged cloth coat. "This isn't much, but it'll keep you from freezing to death."

As they walked onto the street, Jean Louis and Franz moved along in silence. It was a cold winter night, and the wind made it feel even colder.

"Do you want something to eat?" Jean Louis asked.

"I'd rather have a drink."

"How about both?"

"Sure," Franz said. "There's a little place just up the street. Got good beer and passable food."

"Lead the way," Jean Louis said.

By himself, Jean Louis would have been afraid to go into Mac's bar, but with his brother leading, they walked in and took seats at one of the tables near the bar.

A waitress came up to the table.

"We'll have two beers," Franz said.

"You got money?" she asked. "I am not getting stiffed by you no more."

"He's paying," he said pointing at this brother.

"Let's see the money."

Jean Louis reached in his back pocket, pulled out his wallet, and demonstrated that he had more than enough to pay for the food and drinks.

"Okay, what do you want?" she asked.

Jean Louis asked, "Do you have veal?"

She smiled.

"Are you kidding? This isn't the Waldorf."

"How about steak?" he asked. "Bring this man a big steak and a plate full of potatoes."

Jean Louis smiled at the waitress, and she smiled back.

"How did you find me?" Franz asked.

"Persistence and a little help from Uncle Karl."

"You don't go telling that old fag where I am. He's one of them," Franz said.

"Why do you call him an old fag? And who is them?" Jean Louis asked.

"Come on, Jean, you can't be that dense. Karl's never been married, and he collects artsy pots and lamps. He may be smart and good at his job, but he's as goofy as a three-eyed flea. And then there's those friends of his."

"What do you mean 'those friends of his'?"

"Haven't you met the boys in his club? The ones who dress up in their silly, little army costumes?"

"I don't know what you're talking about," Jean Louis said.

"The old clown might have cleaned up his act in the last couple of years. But he and the boys used to meet in the back room at Emmy's on Sunday morning."

"He still goes to Emmy's, but as for friends and Army outfits, I never saw any of that. Anyway, enough about Karl, how are you doing, and why did you change your name?"

"Because they're still after me," Karl said.

"Who's after you?"

"They've got a lot of names. You know them as Nazis, but they got all kinds of covers. They still think that I'm a spy."

"Come on, Franz, that was a long time ago and halfway across the world. Nobody cares about that anymore."

"Open your eyes and look around. These people are everywhere. You just don't know. No matter what name I use, no matter where I go. Any time I settle in one place for a few days, they let me know, and most of the time, they aren't very subtle about it. Those people tonight … they knew. That's why they kicked me out of the shelter. Sometimes, the people in the bars make threats at me. They know. They're just waiting for a chance to take me out. You don't know what it is like to be afraid all of the time." The longer he talked, the more agitated he became. The waitress returned with the beers. "A bunch of idiots, that's what they are."

"Who are you calling an idiot?" she asked in a defiant manner.

"Shut up and get out of here. Leave us alone. Can't we have a little privacy?"

Jean looked at the waitress. "He's just a little upset. We'll keep it down."

She turned and walked back to the kitchen.

Jean turned back to his brother, "Franz—"

"And don't call me Franz. Every time you call me Franz, you make it easier for them to find me."

"What do you want me to call you?" he asked.

"Don't call me anything. I don't want a name. A name gives them a place to start and something for me to run from."

"Will you come home with me?"

"How stupid do you think I am?" Franz demanded, getting loud again.

"What do you mean?"

"I mean, you and I both know that they've been tailing you ever since you left Austria. If you weren't careful, they are probably waiting outside the door right now."

"Oh, please," Jean Louis said. "That is the craziest thing that I've ever heard."

"Are you calling me crazy?"

"No, of course not."

"Who sent you? Was it Karl?" Franz said.

"Your—our—mother sent me."

"Do you mean that Jew bitch who raised us, the one who started all of this?"

"Don't talk about my mother like that," Jean Louis said.

"Look, stupid, she's the mastermind behind this whole thing. You can't be stupid enough not to see that."

"Quit talking about our mother like that." Jean Louis's anger was building.

About that time, the waitress arrived with the food.

Franz took one look at it and said, "I'm not eating this slop."

He downed his beer, got up, and headed for the door. He threw open the door and looked into the street. At the top of his lungs, he shouted, "I'm not a spy. Leave me alone. I am not a spy." With that, he ran into the street and into the darkness. Jean Louis stood and watched as his paranoid brother disappeared into the night.

Jean Louis paid for the beer and food and walked out into the street. He had hoped that he could find his brother, help him, and be the peacemaker for the family. For the first time in his life, things hadn't gone like he had planned, but it wouldn't be the last time.

CHAPTER 10

Dear Mother,

You're right. We get a very distorted view of what is going on in that part of the world. The thought of you as an outlaw is comical, but please be careful. The United States is a wonderful country. It isn't perfect, but the freedom of thought and expression here is amazing. You would absolutely love this place, and I think you should hog-tie my sister (if you can find her), get on a ship, come here, and continue your writing.

The news about Franz is good and bad. I did find him, but he really isn't doing well. He drinks too much and moves from place to place. I will try to keep contact with him, and if the opportunity arises, see if I can help him dry out. But, then again, I'm not sure that would do much good. He is just as angry and pained as he always was. He takes a lot of his meals at the rescue mission, and I'm keeping in contact with the supervisor down there.

Love,
Jean Louis

CHAPTER 11

The Americanization of Jean Louis Edit-Stein began soon after his arrival in Pittsburgh. The name Jean Louis was the first problem. Instead of pronouncing it like it was spelled, most of his fellow workers tried to call him Gene or Lewis, both of which he hated. Soon, he shortened it to J. L., and the only time he marched out his complete first name was when he was trying to pick up girls. Most women seemed to like the way he dragged out the syllables in Jean Louis. When Karl introduced him around the office, he did so as J. L. Stein, dropping the Edit, and so, to most of the people in his new home, he was J. L. Stein.

As for language, J. L. was a quick read. It didn't take long for his classroom English to convert into an easy, flowing, conversational tone. Like his father before him, he had a warm smile, a quiet voice, and a soft touch. Soon, he was one of the favorites in the office.

His first job was that of special assistant to his uncle, and a major part of their job was the recruitment and placement of personnel to match the needs of the company as the economy began to expand. The Roosevelt recovery was in the full swing, and people were going back to work. Plans for new plants that had been on the shelf for the last six years were being taken down, dusted off, and reevaluated. J. L. was right in the thick of things.

If there was a point of contention between J. L. and his uncle, it was politics. When the conflict in Vienna was reported in the news, Karl tended to dismiss it as the ranting of the liberal European press.

"The communists and the socialists have taken over the newspapers and the universities. Anytime something upsets their little apple cart, you would think that the world was coming to an end. Dollfuss and his people didn't have any choice. Now don't get me wrong, Dollfuss was a fool. What we need is strong a leader. All of this garbage about voting for everything guaranties that the people who ascend to the top are fools," Karl said.

"You mean we need somebody like Hitler?" J. L. asked.

"No, no. He's just a crackpot. What we need is the return of the Hapsburgs."

J. L. was amazed. As a child, he had heard this same stuff from his grandmother when he had gone to Linz in the summers, but hearing it come out of his uncle seemed somehow different "You mean you want to bring back the king?" he asked.

"Yes," Karl said, "that would be a good start. What we need is order. And respect for the church and God. All this democracy crap does is create disorder. At least with the Hapsburgs, the brighter people floated to the top."

J. L. had never been one to discuss politics, but it wasn't because there hadn't been chances. Between his mother, his brother, his younger sister, and now his uncle, there had always been endless opportunities to argue. As a child, J. L. had watched and learned the ability to question and glide through these conversations without angering the one across the table. There was one difficulty with this approach: if the person sitting across the table did not have a good social monitor, he would leave thinking that J. L. agreed with him. On more than one occasion, this did happen with Karl.

It was a Thursday afternoon in the fall. Karl walked by J. L.'s office door. "I am going to a German Day Festival for the weekend. It's at a camp run by some of my friends in the southern part of the state. Would you like to go? It should be a lot of fun," Karl said.

"Will there be any women?" J. L. asked.

"Yes, there will be a lot of women," Karl said. "There might even be a few under the age of fifty."

"Sounds like fun. When do we leave?"

"Pack a bag and bring it to work tomorrow," Karl said. "We'll leave straight from work."

"Will do," J. L. said.

It was almost dark when Karl pulled off the highway onto a tree-lined dirt road. Since the last small town, about ten miles before, they had taken several turns onto smaller and smaller roads, going further into the country.

"Wouldn't be hard to get lost in this country, would it?" J. L. said.

"First few times I came out here, I stayed lost most of the time," Karl said.

"If I was trying to raise a crowd, I think I would at least put up a few signs."

"The size of the gathering isn't important. Anyway, the people who need to be here already know where this place is. This gathering is not for everyone."

J. L. saw no need to reply to the last statement. He would find out soon enough.

Several hundred yards down the road was a closed metal gate. Off to the right of the gate was a group of young men standing around a small campfire. Each wore black pants, a white short-sleeve shirt, and a black tie. When the lights of the car flashed on the gate, one of the young men got up from the fire, walked out to a position in front of the gate, and came to a smart parade rest.

Karl stopped the car and the young man came around to the driver's side. The young man shined a light in Karl's face and asked for identification in German. Karl handed him a packet of papers with a picture ID. The man examined the papers closely.

"Very good," he said, this time in English. "And who is this?"

"This is my nephew," Karl said. "He is with us. I will vouch for him."

"You may pass," the guard said. "Drive straight to the lodge. There are security patrols out with dogs. The dogs can't tell friend from foe."

The young man then went to the gate, undid the chain that held it in place, and walked the gate around to the open position. As Karl drove the car through the gate, the young man raised his extended arm shoulder high, with his palm facing the ground.

As they passed, he shouted, "Frei Amerika!"

J. L. sat staring out the window of the car. The road led down a long hill with multiple switchbacks. From the middle of the turns, he could see a large camp set on the banks of a small mountain stream. The stream made a U-shaped turn, and in the middle of the turn was a finger of land that held a number of rough, wooden cabins. Just to the west of the stream, outside of the turn of the stream, was a large, wooden structure that was obviously the lodge that the young man had mentioned. Just south of the lodge was a large, well-lit, open area with bleachers on either side. On the west end of the field was a stage decked out with hundreds of flags.

At the bottom of the hill, they passed under a large arched sign that read:

Welcome to Camp Stuttgart

hearty welcome

The sign was festooned with red, white, and blue bunting, and on each side of the sign were paired, crossed United States flags.

"Somebody is going all out," J. L. said.

"This is really a pretty important weekend. There will be a lot more than beer drinking and partying here this weekend."

Karl pulled through the gate and drove toward the lodge. Across the stream on a small peninsula of land, lantern lights were beginning to come on in the cabins.

"I need to go in and get us a cabin. We're staying on the point this weekend," Karl said with a certain amount of pride. "That's where all of the action will be." There was excitement in his voice; he was like a small child at Christmas.

The lodge was a large, pine, log structure with vaulted ceilings. On the right as they walked in was the check-in desk with a bulletin board detailing all of the weekend activities. At the other end of the atrium was a large fireplace with a blazing fire, and in front of the fireplace were nests of river birch furniture covered with overstuffed cushions. On the slick, smooth, hardwood floors, children were playing shuffleboard. The parents of the children were lounging on the sofas and laughing as the children played. In the back of the room were wide double doors that led into a cafeteria.

"The coffee bar is just inside the cafeteria," Karl said, pointing toward the double doors. "Get me a sandwich while you're at it, will you? Ham and cheese, if they have it."

"Sure," J. L. said as he headed for the open doors.

When J. L. returned with the sandwiches, he and Karl got back into the car and drove across a low-water bridge. At the other end of the bridge, another young guard asked to see their IDs and then directed them to one of the cabins near the end of the point.

As they unloaded the bags, Karl said, "I have some business I have to attend to, but I should be back in an hour or so. I believe there is a dance scheduled at the main lodge at about eight."

J. L. nodded. "What's so important about this weekend?"

In the distance, a hand bell rang.

"I don't have time to get into it right now, but here's some literature to look at," Karl said. He reached into this suitcase and pulled out a stack of newspapers, newsletters, and brochures. "Take a look at these. This meeting may go on for a while, but if you're still up when I come back, we can talk." Karl picked up the leather satchel that he carried back and forth to work every day and was out the door.

J. L. sat down on the metal cot that was to be his bed for the weekend. There was a strong smell of cedar and mothballs permeating the air. He picked up the papers that his uncle had dropped. In the stack were copies of the *Steuban News* and *Social Justice*.

The *Steuban News* appealed to German-Americans to get involved in politics. The editor described Hitler as "an idealist and a man of tremendous energy who endeavors to unite the German people and fill the nation with hope for a new future." A second article that caught J. L.'s eye was an article about an attack by the Nazi youth of Vienna on Cardinal Innitzer. The article detailed the confrontation and then went on to say that the attack was only an attempt to compel the priesthood to keep out of the affairs of state.

Social Justice was more blatantly anti-Semitic and anti-Roosevelt. An editorial by the Catholic priest Father Francis Coughlin read, "For ten years, this country has suffered under a depression, and it was no accident. It was deliberately created by the Jews."

J. L. had seen most of these things before, but that was back in Austria. Before Franz had moved out, he would bring this stuff home and leave it lying around their room. It was obvious that Karl was mixed up in something, but most of it seemed a little radical for his uncle's taste.

After he tired of looking through the magazines, J. L. wandered outside for a cigarette. It was a pretty, fall night, and the air was crisp. At the end of the point, the river made a sharp bend, and on the opposite side was a high bluff. In the middle of the water was a wooden floating platform that was used for swimmers in the summer. A series of ladders had been built into the rock bluff with diving boards extending out at various heights. He finished his cigarette and walked across the swinging footbridge that led back to the lodge.

In the two hours since they had checked into the camp, a swing band had set up in the corner of the room where the children had been playing shuffleboard. The band was playing one of Glen Miller's tunes when he came in. He went to the deli and purchased a beer.

When he emerged from the deli with his beer, he immediately began to search for young, attractive, unattached women. Since it was early in the evening, there were only a few people on the floor. Most were groups of couples sitting around tables, absorbed in conversation, but at the front of the room was a table with one young lady who seemed to be alone. She was reading a magazine and sipping on a cola through a straw. Her legs were crossed, revealing a pretty calf.

"Would you care to dance?" J. L. asked.

She looked up from her magazine and smiled. It was a warm smile that filled her face. "I would love to," she answered, "but first may I know who is asking? I don't recognize you."

"Excuse me, that was rude on my part," J. L. said. "My name is Jean Louis Stein." As he said it, he dragged out his first and middle names.

"What a lovely name," she said. "It almost sounds French."

"Well, in a way, I guess it is, even though I am not French. I am Austrian, and my mother loved the sound of the name."

"I think it is a perfectly delightful name. All of the men around here have adopted the disgusting habit of calling each other by their initials," she said.

"And whom do I have the pleasure of addressing?" J. L. asked.

"Hannah Nabholz," she said.

"Sounds like the name of a queen," he said.

"It's funny you should say that. I have had several people tell me that in the last year."

"Maybe it's because you have a noble way of saying the name. There's something to that, you know. My sister's name is Anna, and even though she is a pretty girl, there is nothing regal about her. She's a bit of a bohemian."

As they were talking, the band began a slow easy tune. J. L. extended his hand and assisted her to her feet.

"Madam," he said, "the dance floor is calling."

J. L.'s mother had loved to dance and, even when they were at early ages, would put a record on the machine and force her children to dance with her. Anna and Franz had both detested the exercise, but J. L. had always found it very natural. He was able to pick up any new step in just a few short moves and was light on his feet.

As they eased across the floor, J. L. caught a smell of Hannah's perfume. The soft warmth of her hand and the sweet smell of the fragrance she wore entranced him, but there was one thing that puzzled him. "Why is it that you were sitting by yourself and no one had asked you to dance?"

"It may be because of my boyfriend," she said.

J. L. had been in that situation before, and in fact, in Austria that same scenario had resulted in him being trounced by an angry boyfriend. So when Hannah said "boyfriend," J. L. slightly loosened the grip he had on her hand and backed up just a fraction of an inch.

"Don't worry; he won't hurt you. It's not like that."

"But there must be some reason, if all of those guys over by the wall shy away from you."

"Well, part of it is that, for most of them, he is their boss. Michael is head of the Young Guard. They are the security arm of the Friends of New Germany. His last name is Krause. John Michael Krause." She looked into J. L.'s face and then added, "That doesn't mean anything to you does it?"

J. L. shook his head. "I haven't been in this country but a couple of years, and most of time I've spent working."

"His father is Adolph Krause, a retired physician from New York. He's kind of a powerbroker behind all of these various groups that come together from time to time. Anyway, John Michael is head of the security group. You remember those guys at the front gate? Those were his men."

"Now that you mention it, I think I did meet his father my very first day in the country, but I was so seasick when I got off the ship, I wouldn't remember him. This John Michael sounds like an interesting guy," J. L. said.

"He's nice to me. And don't worry; as far as I know, he doesn't have a jealous bone in his body. If he walked through and caught us making out on one of those sofas over there by the fireplace, he'd just ask us to keep down the noise so he could work."

J. L. made up his mind—no matter how pretty this little girl was, no matter how much he enjoyed her company—just as soon as this song was over, he would find an excuse to work his way to the door and back to his cabin. He had no intention of becoming closely acquainted with the head of security—nice guy or not.

He was plotting his exit strategy when Hannah stopped dancing, grabbed him by the hand, and headed for the door.

"Speaking of the devil," she said. "Come with me. I want you meet him."

J. L. had expected a large, burley man with a square jaw, close-cropped hair, and a brusque German accent. Instead, John Michael had fine, almost girlish features and dark hair. He had on a dark cardigan sweater and tie. When he saw Hannah and J. L., his face lit up, and he began walking toward them.

"John Michael, I want you to meet my new friend, Jean Louis Stein," she said.

"You must be Karl's nephew. I just left a meeting with your uncle. Fine man. He's a little conservative for my tastes but still a fine man. Over the years, your uncle has done a great service for the Bund."

"He has certainly helped me since I arrived in this country."

As he spoke, J. L. realized that he was still holding Hannah's hand and quickly released it.

The band began to play another song, and John Michael motioned to his girlfriend. "May I have the pleasure of this dance?" He then turned to J. L. "You will excuse us," he said.

John Michael and Hannah turned and danced across the floor. As they did, J. L. noticed that most of the eyes in the room were on the young couple.

When he walked out into the night air, he was taken by the smell and feel of the fresh air as contrasted by the smoke that seemed so pervasive in Pittsburgh.

Back in the cabin, Karl was laying out a uniform for the next morning.

"J. L., my son, I'm glad you are back. How was the dance?" Karl asked.

"It was nice enough."

"Were there any young women that suited your fancy?"

"Yeah, I danced with a really pretty girl," J. L. said.

"What was her name? I know most of the families," Karl asked.

"Hannah Nabholz."

Karl frowned. "Yes, fine family. But I believe she's engaged to the Krause boy. Adolph's son."

"Yes, I got that impression."

"A word to the wise: Be a little cautious when you deal with that boy. Looks can be deceiving. He didn't get to be head of the security forces by being a boy scout."

J. L. decided that it was time to talk about what this was all about. "Tell me, Uncle, why does a group of people like this need a security force? You folks just look like a bunch of people getting together for a weekend of fun."

"It's not quite as simple as that. The meeting we just completed was an attempt to put the final touches on a plan that will help to create some real power for us. Dr. Krause, John Michael's father, has done a masterful job of bringing these people together. You will see tomorrow when we have the big celebration on the parade ground. There are all sorts of people here who share the same goals: to create some order in the world, to protect our family values, and to fight the communists. Some of the groups have German roots, but most are just patriotic Christian groups who love this country. This isn't about Hitler or Mussolini, even though there are some people here who think they are the answer to our problems."

"So what's your role in all of this?" J. L. asked.

"I'm more like a glorified secretary. I take notes, create speeches, and write things down so we can keep them straight."

"You mentioned how you felt about the Hapsburgs. Do you really think they will ever be brought back?"

"I was more confident of that several years ago, but now it looks less likely. Even without them, we need a strong leader, someone who can set us on the right path. Right now, one of our big pushes is to keep this country out of any conflict that happens overseas. That is why we have worked so strongly for the Neutrality Act. I am particularly proud of my own role in helping to have that passed. The United States has no business sticking its nose in the affairs of Europe."

"What about Roosevelt?" J. L. asked.

"He started out okay, but now he is being led around by the nose by a bunch of socialists who have mush for brains."

J. L. had heard about all he needed to hear. Karl had made a point of seldom talking about J. L.'s mother, but it wasn't hard to figure out where Karl stood on Helena.

"I'm going out for a cigarette," J. L. said.

The next morning began early. When the sun rose over the camp, the security troops were out doing their early morning run. In the camp ground just west of the lodge, the food, arts and craft booths, and games were being set up for the day. J. L. emerged from his cabin to a beautiful fall day. The oaks, elms, and maples were beginning to change colors. The early morning sun was just beginning to rise.

Karl came out of the cabin dressed in his uniform. It was well cut and tailored, befitting an officer in the old Austrian army.

"Don't you look spiffy," J. L. said.

Karl smiled. He was proud of his youthful physique.

"I've worn the same size for the last twenty-five years."

"Is this for your big parade?" J. L. asked.

"Yeah, this should really be a show."

"When does it start?" J. L. asked.

"The rally is set for ten thirty."

The two men began to work their way toward the lodge for breakfast, and as they did, J. L. noticed that Karl was not the only one in costume. There were all variety of gowns, robes, and uniforms. The most startling were the white hooded figures of the Klan.

After breakfast, they worked their way to the parade ground where the official band of the campground was tuning up. Karl turned to J. L.

"You are more than welcome to join me on the podium if you want."

J. L. shook his head.

"I'll just stay in the background if you don't mind," he said.

Camp Stuttgart had been transformed from a vacation spot to an armed encampment of fanatics. Men, women, and children were dressed in the costumes of one hate group or another. John Michael's security troops were out in full force. The dress shirt and tie had been replaced with grey shirts, black pants, and a dagger on the hip. Every few minutes, J. L. was accosted by someone in the crowd selling a different brand of anger.

J. L. found himself a seat in the bleachers on the south side of the parade ground. No sooner was he seated than a chorus of trumpets announced the beginning of the march. At the lead was a flag team, at the center left were the American stars and stripes, and just to its right was a slightly smaller version of the Nazi cross. Flanking these two were a variety of smaller flags representing the Christian Patriots, the Brotherhood of the Chosen, the Ku

Klux Klan, the Free Germans, and last but not least, a much smaller version of the Austrian Hapsburg flag.

Behind them were the Silver Shirts, a company of John Michael's finest, all spit and polished. At the halfway point on the field, the security company began peeling off and forming a perimeter around the western end of the field. When they were in place and the flags were stationed on the platform, the real procession began. A succession of small groups of men, preceded by the flag of their organization, marched down the field and then seated themselves in a prearranged area of folding chairs. Once the groups were seated, a fanfare sounded, and everyone stood to watch the last line of marchers.

Leading this group were Fritz Kuhn, the newly elected president of the German-American Bund; Dr. Adolph Krause, his chief of staff; Karl Stein, executive secretary of the organization; and John Michael Krause the chief of security.

When they had assembled on the podium, Kuhn stood and surveyed the crowd. He then extended his right arm and shouted at the top of his lungs, "Frei Amerika!"

The crowd responded with raised right arms, "Heil, Amerika!"

When the crowd had quieted, he continued, "Today we have established, here in this place, a little piece of German soil, a Sudetenland in Amerika. It is our duty as good Germans to carry forth the good fight. We must impel American politics with a pure German feeling. We must demand that candidates for office always use their office to keep the United States out of any European conflicts. Our task is to consolidate all of the German groups and use that influence as power in American politics. And second, American Germandom must become dynamic and turn against its adversaries. Our battlefield is right here, and here is where we must fight it out."

By that time, most of the crowd was on its feet. J. L. was sitting at the end of the bleachers near the lodge, watching the crowd with a certain degree of detachment, when he felt someone sit down beside him. In the brief moment that it took for him to turn and look at the person to his left, he knew before he looked; it was the aroma that was a mix of her and the perfume that she wore.

"Good morning, Mr. Stein," Hannah said.

The night before, J. L. had gone to sleep thinking of her beautiful smile and the soft feel of her hand.

"Hannah, what a delightful surprise. I thought you would probably be up there on the stand among the important folks," he said.

"I don't much go in for politics. Anyway, I would have just been in John's way." She handed him a piece of paper.

"What's this?" he asked.

"It's my address and my own telephone number. I still live with my mother and father, but I have my own number. I would like to see you again."

"What about young Mister Krause?"

"What John Michael doesn't know won't hurt him."

"But what he does know might hurt me," J. L. said.

"No guts, no glory," she said smiling. "See you around."

J. L. sat in the bleachers and watched as she walked away. The way her hair fell down over her shoulder, the way her hips moved in the summer dress she was wearing, her warm smile and the aroma of her perfume—all flooded his mind. And here she was giving him her telephone number and inviting him to call. On the other hand, there was John Michael and Uncle Karl's warning. It was an interesting dilemma.

By mid-afternoon the two men were driving back toward Pittsburgh.

"Uncle, I've got a couple of questions," J. L. said.

"Shoot," Karl said.

"I notice that the Klan people were part of your group."

Karl nodded.

"Well, I know that you are a devout Catholic. From what I know about the Klan, I thought they were anti-Catholic. How does that work?"

"That is the southern Klan. These are members of the northern Klan. They are only anti-Jewish."

"Oh." J. L. wasn't sure how to respond to that. "You seem different from a lot of those people. There were some really hateful speakers on that stage today."

"That's politics, my son. You're absolutely correct; there were a number of those folks that I would not take home to meet my family, but in politics, sometimes, you have to make compromises." He laughed and then added, "You know the old line: there are two things you don't want to see made—sausage and politics."

When J. L. got home that night, he emptied his pockets on the dresser. There among the change and keys was the slip with Hannah's number. He picked up the slip, lay back on his bed, and stared at the numbers. The last thing he had expected was to meet a beautiful dream on his weekend in the country with Uncle Karl. He had agreed to go only because he was bored. There had been something about the vision of Hannah as she had walked away from him on the parade field earlier in the day—he knew that sooner or later he would see her again.

Each night when he returned home from work, the slip still lay on the dresser, and one evening before he knew what he was doing, he picked up the phone and began to maneuver through the series of operators to get to the

Scranton exchange. On the third ring, the phone was picked up, and Hannah was on the other end.

"Hello," the soft, quiet voice said.

J. L. was overwhelmed by the sound of her voice.

When he didn't speak, she said again, "Hello, who is this please?"

"It's your new friend from Camp Stuttgart. Jean Louis."

"I thought you would never call. I thought maybe you had lost my number or something."

"No, I didn't lose it. In fact, I have looked at it every day since I saw you." Jean Louis said.

"Where did you go?" she asked. "I looked for you on Saturday night and Sunday morning."

"Uncle Karl had to get back to town."

"Do you ever come to Scranton?" she asked.

"No, I don't think I've had the pleasure. We may have come through on the train coming from New York."

"It's a nice enough place, but it's boring. How about Chicago?" she asked.

"Been there a couple of times with friends," J. L. said.

"I'll be there over Thanksgiving. There's a car show there that my father goes to every year."

"Could we see each other?" J. L. asked.

"The Friday after Thanksgiving. Dad is always at the show. Mama will have one of her sick headaches—she hates Chicago, and she always drinks too much on Thanksgiving. I go shopping by myself. Anyway, I'll meet you outside of the museum down by the lake. Do you know where that's at?"

"Yeah, I went there the last time I was in town," he said.

"One o'clock?" she asked.

"One o'clock it is."

"By the way," she added, "you didn't give me your number."

"Yeah, sure."

He gave her his number and address.

The train trip into Chicago was filled with anticipation for J. L. In his young life, he had had a number of relationships, none of which had lasted very long. Since coming to the United States, he had dated a few of the girls in the office, but nothing was serious. Secretly, he feared that she wouldn't be there and he would be left standing alone on the steps of the museum. He got out of the cab and made his way across the crowded street and through the small park that led to the museum.

To his relief, there she was standing on the front steps, dressed in a long, dark coat with a large, black hat holding her hair in place. She was looking across the lake and didn't hear him as came toward her.

"Hannah," he said when he got close.

She turned at the sound of his voice and a broad smile spread across her face. "I thought you might not come," she said. She removed her hat and kissed him. Despite the setting and the beautiful woman, it was a kiss full of desperation.

"Let's go for a walk," she said.

For the next several hours, J. L. and Hannah walked by the lakefront and through the downtown of Chicago. She told him her family history—how her father had come to the States without a penny to his name and, in fifteen years, owned his own car dealership; how her mother longed to return to Germany so she could be close to her family; and how Hannah was caught in between. J. L. talked about his family and about being raised in the Oldenberg, about his mother's politics, and how it was her idea for him to come to the United States.

"I'm going to have to go soon," Hannah said. "My family will be worried."

"Would you like something to eat before you go?" J. L. asked. They had stopped in front of a small café near the Drake Hotel.

"Heavens, no," she said. "After yesterday, I don't think I'll eat for a month, but a cup of coffee would be nice.

J. L. escorted her into the restaurant, and they found a table in the back that was quiet.

"I've enjoyed the day," J. L. said.

Hannah reached out and put her hand on his. "So have I," she said.

"When can we meet again?" he asked.

"Can you come to Scranton?"

"Yeah, sure. But what about John Michael?" J. L. asked.

With the mention of John Michael's name, Hannah began to sob.

"I don't want to marry him," she said. "He puts on this show of being nice and all, but he's mean. He's hit me a couple of times when he got mad—nothing serious, but it scares me. I'm trying to figure out a way of breaking up with him right now, but my father is against it. He likes John Michael." She stopped for a minute and thought. "That's not completely accurate. He likes the business he gets from Dr. Krause and his people. My father isn't much into standing up and shouting his politics, but he puts a lot of money in affairs like that weekend at Camp Stuttgart. Anyway, he really likes the fact that I'm dating a Krause."

J. L. moved his chair closer to hers and put his arm around her shoulder. When he did, she began to cry more. Her tears moved him to tears.

"Is there anything that I can do?" J. L. asked.

"No, just be there for me."

"I will," he said.

The waitress brought the coffee to the table, and they sat quietly for a few minutes, not wanting the evening to end.

"I really do have to go," she said.

"I'll call you Monday night after work. Okay?" J. L. said.

"I should be home, unless something happens."

The train trip back to Pittsburgh was a blur. In fact, the next three days were a blur. On Monday, J. L.'s body showed up at work, but his mind was still preoccupied by the Nabholz girl—her smile, the way she had looked with the wind blowing in her hair, the taste of her kiss, and the soft touch of her hand. The day at work dragged by; he spent most of the afternoon watching the large clock in the hall outside of his office. The instant the clock struck five; he was out the door and headed home.

Most evenings, J. L. lingered at the Europa cafe three blocks from his home. On occasion, he would go to a local bar for a couple of beers, but that night, he went to the deli and bought a sandwich to go. A block from the house was an especially busy intersection where the city had recently installed a stoplight. J. L. was standing on the corner, waiting for the light to change, when he looked to his right, and there stood John Michael Krause.

"Why Mr. Krause, what a pleasant surprise," J. L. said.

Krause stared straight ahead, his face a mask of anger. "Stein," he said. "You couldn't be that stupid. First off, if my being here is a surprise to you, then you must think I am a total idiot. You catch a train to Chicago, take my fiancé out on a date, and you don't think I'm going to know about it. And second, there's going to be nothing pleasant for you about this visit."

"I didn't ..." J. L. started.

Krause held his hand up and stopped J. L. mid-sentence. "Don't even try to explain. I know you. I know your kind. If you're interested in staying alive, pay close attention to what I tell you. First and most important, stay away from my girlfriend. If I even suspect you have been trying to cuckold me, I'll kill you, and if you got any ideas of being brave and sacrificing yourself for her, I'll kill her too."

"Wait a minute," J. L. started.

"Shut up, Jew spy," Krause said.

"What are you talking about? I'm no spy," J. L. said.

"Look, Stein, we've known about you since you got off the boat in New York. I must admit I was a little surprised that you had the gall to show up at Stuttgart."

"Look, John Michael, I'm a chemical engineer. I work for an aluminum company. I'm not a spy. I don't care about your politics."

"Right, so what's with all of these letters you've been sending to this Mitchison woman in England? How stupid do you think we are, Stein?"

"How do you know that I have even been writing letters, much less to whom?" J. L. demanded.

"Look, stupid, I know everything there is to know about you, down to your underwear size," Krause said.

The red light turned, and J. L. stepped from the curb. A black, Hudson sedan came speeding by within three inches of him. J. L. jumped backward and, in the process, tripped over the curb.

"Watch out for these city drivers. They can be really dangerous. That's probably what happened to your brother," Krause said.

J. L. looked up as he brushed himself off. "What are you talking about my brother?"

"I'm talking about the other Stein Jew spy, the drunk idiot. I heard tell they got him in the morgue. Hit and run was what I was told."

"You rotten son-of-a-bitch," J. L. said.

John Michael smiled. "That's the first true thing you've said. And another thing you can count on: I'll do what I say. If you mess with me, you will pay dearly. Don't even think about going to the police, because I've got sources everywhere. Now go cry over that piece of shit brother of yours."

John Michael turned and walked away.

It was Franz in the morgue, and it had been a hit and run. Eyewitnesses said that J. L.'s brother had stumbled out into traffic and had been run over by a new, black Hudson sedan. No one got a look at the license plates or the face of the driver. The man lying on the metal table was undoubtedly Franz, but J. L.'s boyhood friend and Helena's little son had long since disappeared. The only ones at the graveside were the gravediggers, the chaplain, J. L., and Karl. The chaplain who worked for the funeral home said a few words and then turned and walked away.

As the men with the shovels began to cover the casket, Karl asked, "Have you written your mother yet?"

"Not yet. I haven't quite figured out what to say."

"I'm sure you will be gentle. You're good about those things, I can tell." Karl paused for a moment. "I'm sorry about your brother. Somehow I feel like this is at least partially my fault."

"What do you mean, Uncle Karl?"

"I mean, J. L., you've made some enemies, some enemies you wouldn't have made if I hadn't taken you to Stuttgart," Karl said.

"Don't worry about it. I'm a big boy. You warned me about Krause," J. L. said.

"The problem is that it's not over," his uncle continued. "I know these folks, and they're vindictive. I think it would be best if we found you a job somewhere else so you would be out of their line of fire."

"Like where?" J. L. asked.

"You know those projects we've been putting together for East St. Louis?

"Yeah," J. L. said.

"Well, there are a couple of chemical engineer slots that we could fit you into. What do you say?"

J. L. nodded. "Okay," he said, "let's do it.

J. L.'s last act before he left for East St. Louis was to write a letter to Hannah.

> Dear Hannah,
>
> It grieves me to write this letter, but I fear that we should cease having contact. I have not been completely honest with you. The truth is that I am married and have a son. They are still back in Austria, and one day, I will bring them to this country.
>
> At first, I thought that I could somehow separate my life into two halves and live with that fiction; but I can't do that to you. You are a beautiful, warm person, and you deserve much better than me. I hope you have a wonderful life.
>
> Your dear friend,
> Jean Louis Stein

CHAPTER 12

Dear Mom,

I hope all is going well with you. I have news of my brother, but I'm sad to say it's not good. Franz was killed in an accident. He stepped out in traffic and was killed by a car. It seems that he had a problem with alcohol for a while but had dried out and was working in a mission. He left Uncle Karl's address with a man at the mission, just in case anything ever happened to him. The neighborhood he lived in was really rough. When he died, they called, and I went and identified him. It was a nice funeral with a number of his friends there. I have enclosed the little cross that Grandma gave him, the one he wore around his neck. I thought you might want it.

I will be leaving Pittsburgh soon. I am moving to a city in the center of the United States called East St. Louis, right on the banks of the Mississippi river. Our company has a big plant there, and I will finally get to be a chemical engineer instead of a pencil pusher.

What is the latest word about Anna? The last time you mentioned her, she had left for Palestine. I hope they are ready for her.

As for you, please stay out of the way of the Nazis and the fascists; they sound like a dreadful bunch of people.

Love, your son,
Jean Louis

CHAPTER 13

Dear Jean Louis,

It was wonderful to hear from you. It broke my heart to hear the news about Franz, but I had my suspicions that something bad would happen to him. It seemed like he always lived under a dark cloud. Thanks for sending the pendant.

As for your sister, she is living on a farm outside of Hyfa in Palestine. Surprise, surprise, she is taking care of animals. For her, it sounds safer than being here. Our fascist government is really cracking down on anybody they even think might be a communist.

As for Judith and I, we are doing okay for the time being. I think I told you before, but we never got back into the Oldenberg. We rent a place across the river in Florisdorf. We can't get any of our writing printed in the big papers, but we are still putting out *Freedom*. Naomi has been a great deal of help getting some of the work published in the labor papers in England, but they are very nervous about upsetting either the Nazis or our homegrown fascists. There is another crisis brewing here.

Love,
Mom

CHAPTER 14

As a young solider during WWI, Bill Parkus had been assigned the job of assisting Dr. Adolph Krause in examining the eyes of the incoming hoards of immigrants to Ellis Island.

Dr. Krause was a German immigrant who had fallen prey to the demon, rum. Each day, he made the boat ride across the harbor from his enclave of proper Germans in Manhattan. He inspected the men and women who came through his station as if they were cattle.

"The good people would never be in third-class steerage," Krause said to Bill. "Those people are processed in a different place. The people you see before you are the scourge of Europe and the future of America.

"The people who come through these golden doors," he said, voice dripping with sarcasm, "these people are the reason we have this war now. This war was forced on the Germans. My country is not the enemy of the United States. These Slavs are nothing but scum. They fight over little scraps of land that aren't worth having. For centuries, they've married their cousins, and everybody gets stupid. They've fought the same war over and over again for the last five hundred years.

"If you want to get a true picture of what my people are like, we have a group called the German-American Bund. You people call it a club. You don't have to be German to come. You might enjoy seeing what the real Europeans are like."

Bill attended these meetings and found it hard to disagree with what those folks were saying; these were right-thinking people who understood the way things should be. Long after returning to Sunnyville, Mississippi, he maintained his ties with that group of scholars and wise men.

Over the years, Bill had refined his own message and honed it to a sharp edge. He knew the names of all of the Jewish peddlers who plied their trades up and down the delta. He knew the names of all of the absentee owners with foreign sounds, all of the companies that were based in Chicago, New York, or Pittsburgh.

The events of the 30s made Bill's message seem prophetic. The economic collapse of '29 with the corrections instituted by the Roosevelt administration in 1933 confirmed everything that he preached and believed.

"The Jews caused the Depression. For years, they've pushed us to the left, and now they have nominated and elected Roosevelt. The worst part is that he's a Jew, and his wife is a communist. I've got proof."

By '33, the bottom had dropped out of the cotton prices, and one of the first acts of the Roosevelt administration was the passage of the Agricultural Adjustment Act. This act required that one third of the cotton planted in the year of 1933 be plowed under.

Bill's response was immediate and sharp. His next newsletter read:

MULES GOT MORE SENSE THAN ROOSEVELT

Last month, Roosevelt forced the Congress to pass a law that says we have to plow up one out of every three rows of planted cotton. Now, I don't pretend to be no genius, but when you tell a man whose kids are going hungry to plow up his crop, that don't make no sense.

I got an old mule by the name of Jake. He's been taught since he was born that a row of cotton is sacred. He knows that if he tramples on the cotton, he's gonna get a whipping. If I tried to get him to plow down a row of cotton, he'd balk and bray loud enough that you could hear him clear to Memphis. Now ask yourself: Who come up with this fool idea? Are they just stupid? Are they just a bunch of mush-brained socialists who ain't never been outside of Washington? Or, is there more to it than that?

If you think they're stupid, you ain't been listening to me for the last ten years.

This is the kind of approach they would take in communist Russia, comrade. When we don't have enough good clothes for our children, this approach don't make any sense.

Before you think they have singled you out, listen to this: in Iowa, they are plowing up corn; in Illinois, they are killing little pigs; and in Kansas, they are burning wheat.

This is a country where our children are going to bed hungry every night, and YOUR FEDERAL GOVERNMENT is destroying our crops and livestock.

WHY?

It's money and power, my friends. They have most of it, and they want it all.

What can you do? I'll tell you what you can do. When the agent of this foreign government comes and tells you to destroy your crop, show him the door.

Here they come, my friends!

Stand up for yourself!

Seventeen-year-old Junior Parkus was rebuilding the carburetor on the family's Ford pickup. Bill was leaning on the front bumper, smoking a cigarette.

"How long is it going to take you to get that truck running?" Bill asked.

"About an hour," Junior said.

"Good. We got to go to a meeting over on the Arkansas side."

"What's up?" Junior asked.

"According to the boys in Sandy Banks, the Jews done brought in that white-haired communist, Norman Thomas, and a communist woman named Mitchison or something like that from England."

"England, Arkansas?" Junior asked

"No, no, no, England across the sea."

"What are they doing in the delta?"

"I can see the handprint of Mitchell and East from Tyronza in this little party," Bill said.

Bill's form of radicalism was not the only movement to rise up in the delta during the '30s. While Bill and the Brethren of the Chosen were preaching their brand of paranoid racism, another group on the other end of the political spectrum had emerged. As Bill had suggested in 1933, the Agricultural Adjustment Act backfired. Within a year, many of the sharecroppers and tenant farmers across the south were bankrupt, dispossessed, and on the move.

In July of 1934, H. L. Mitchell and Clay East from Tyronza, Arkansas, formed the Southern Tenant Farmers Union. These men embodied everything that Bill and his clan hated. They were confirmed socialists, and worse than that, they were devoted to an integrated union. Their goal was to overthrow the plantation system that they viewed as legalized peonage. Of the eight million farmers who were affected by the government plow order, five million were white and three million were black. Mitchell's vision was to pull these poor, working farmers—black and white—into a strong union, capable of striking and bringing the plantation system to its knees.

The new union developed strong ties with the Arbeiter Ring Hall, a fraternal Jewish organization in Memphis. The Hall itself was closely aligned with the national socialist party in Chicago and New York. Norman Thomas, the patriarch of socialism in the United States was making the first of several trips to the delta in support of the fledgling union.

"You sure you made the right turn back there, boy?" Bill asked his son as he looked out the passenger side window.

Junior nodded but said nothing. When he was old enough to see over the steering wheel, he had become his father's driver. It gave Bill time to collect his thoughts and prepare for his next talk.

"We get lost in these Little P bottoms, we wouldn't ever find our way out," Bill added.

"We're going the right way, trust me," Junior said.

"Son, tonight, you're gonna to be my eyes and ears. I know most of these people, and they know me. It wouldn't be safe for me or you if I went into that church tonight."

"What do you want me to do?" Junior asked.

"Mitchell's been going all over the country, stirring up the coloreds, talking about taking over the big farms."

Junior looked across the truck at his father. "You want me to kill his ass? I can do it, and nobody will ever know."

"Wouldn't solve anything. They aren't the only ones," Bill said.

"If we killed enough of 'um, it would."

"We don't have the men to fight a war right now," Bill said. "What I want you to do is just go into that church tonight and find out what they're up to. There's a pecan orchard just north of Sandy Banks. It's only about two miles from the colored church where they're having the meeting. I want you to leave me and the truck at the orchard and walk to the church. If there's any trouble, I want you to get the hell out of there. Jigger Morton, the sheriff, is a mean son-of-a-bitch—the kind that shoots first and then asks questions—and he won't know that you ain't one of them."

"I can handle myself," Junior said.

Bill knew that his son was right. The boy wasn't very big, but he was tough as nails. As a child when Bill would whip him for some infraction, Junior had never let out a whimper. When they hunted together, Junior had the ability to blend into the woods in a way that you would never see him unless he wanted you to.

"There's the turn for the pecan grove," Bill said, pointing off to the right. "Pull in there."

Junior turned off the road onto a rutted trail and parked far enough off of the road so that Bill could build a fire and not be seen from the road.

Bill pulled out his pocket watch and looked intently at the face.

"You better get a move on, boy. That meeting starts in about an hour. To get in, you got to know the password and have something red in your hand." He reached into his pocket and pulled out a red bandana. "When they ask where you're from, you say New York City. If they ask you where you farm, tell them you just got kicked off a farm over in Mississippi."

"That's stupid," Junior said.

"I know, but that's how these people are."

Mount Bethel Church sat on the south bank of the Green River, high on a bluff. The sun was beginning to set when Junior turned off the main road and headed for the church. Up and down the church road was every description of old truck, car, and mule wagon. Off to the left near the river were several large groups of white men and women. On the right side of the road, near the edge of the woods, was a group of black men.

Junior looked for familiar faces in the white crowd, but he didn't see any. As he neared the church, a large black man walked out onto the narrow road.

"Where you from?" the man asked Junior.

"New York City." Junior held up the red bandana.

"Don't know you. I knows most everybody around here. This here meeting is for sharecroppers only; where you farm?" The man pulled back his jacket to reveal a sidearm.

"I just got kicked off a farm over in north Mississippi."

"You look awful young to have done much farming. You wait right here," the black man said. "I'll be right back."

The man was gone for a few minutes. When he returned, he was accompanied by two large, white farmers.

"What's your name, boy?" one of the men asked.

"Ain't your boy," Junior said.

"I don't care whose boy you is. I ask you what your name was," the man said.

"John David Paul. My daddy, a'fore he was killed by a colored man, was Bill Paul. We lived outside of Clarksdale."

"How did you know about this meeting?" the other white man asked.

"Folks at Birdsong told me what was up."

The three men walked a few paces away, had a brief discussion, and then returned to where Junior was standing.

"Okay," the black man said, "you can come in, but if you got a gun, you need to be giving it to me. You can tag it, and I'll give it back after the meeting."

The black man motioned for him to lean up against the tree while he patted Junior down. Just as the man finished, the sound of a bell rang out from the church steeple.

"Ya'll come on up here so we can get started," announced an elderly black man dressed in a white suit. "We was going to have this here meeting indoors, but we got way too many people here to fit in the church. So we set up this stage out here so everybody can hear."

Junior was pleased that he didn't have to go into the church. It was easier for him to stand in the shadows among the pecan trees. The white sharecroppers lined up around the front of the stage, and even though it was their church, the black farmers grouped themselves on the right side of the stage, more to the back, out of habit.

"Ya'll folks be quiet now so we can get started," the black minister dressed in white said. "Brother Mitchell done brought us some special guests tonight. I'll let him introduce these new friends. Brother Mitchell."

H. L. Mitchell walked to the foot of the stage along with a tall, white-haired man and a small white woman. The trio took the stage with the minister. She seemed to be a proper English lady with refined manners, more at home serving tea and crumpets to her bridge club. As she had walked up the steps toward the stage, Ms. Mitchison had placed her arms around the black minister and kissed him on the cheek. There was an audible gasp from the audience.

Mitchell directed Ms. Mitchison and the white-haired gentleman to their seats on the stage and then turned to the audience.

"My friends, what's at stake are our lives. There are people with money and power who are against us, and they will use everything they have to keep us from being successful. What we have is the law. Tonight, I brought with me some people who are here to tell you that we aren't alone. On my left is Ms. Naomi Mitchison. She's a member of the British socialist party and author of the *Vienna Diary*. I asked her to share with you what she found in Austria last year. On my right sits the next president of the United States and a true man of the people, Mr. Norman Thomas." He turned and motioned to the lady. "Ms. Mitchison."

Ms. Mitchison walked up to the podium.

"Men and women of the delta, have no fear. You are not alone. You are at the front of a battle that is being waged the world over, and the whole world is watching you. Most of the world is rooting for you. There is a small group of people that controls the purse strings, who juggle the markets, make money from war, keep you poor while they get richer, and pass all of that on to their fat, lazy children. Those people are not on your side, but the rest of us are. The rest of us know that you are out there fighting for decent wages and a better life for all of us, and we will do what we can to support you.

"A couple of years ago, I was in Vienna, Austria, during a labor revolt not unlike yours. Those men and women, like you, were striking for better wages and better living conditions. The fascist government called out the troops and attacked those good people. The government expected those men and women to just roll over and give up, but they didn't. They fought for their rights. What I saw in those people is what I see in you. You are in the right, and you know it. You have the moral high ground. Because of that, in the long run, you will win, and they will lose."

The crowd was on its feet, clapping and shouting loudly. When they began to quiet, she continued, "In Vienna, there was one particular group that stood out—the women of the Oldenberg house. This group was led by a writer, Helena Edit-Stein, who has a clearer understanding of what the world is about than anyone I've ever met. She's a mother, a wife, and a defender of right. I spent time with her, talking to her, and watching her work. When the bombs started falling, she moved from place to place as if she had no fear. When the fighting stopped, she took her pen and denounced the treachery of her government. She did both with a clear determination that her children would not have to live with this in the future.

"I see that same look in you and your leaders. Men can only be driven so far. There is a point where each of us has to stand up and be counted. My people and I are behind you one hundred percent, and that is not an empty pledge. Today, I gave Mr. Mitchell an envelope with one hundred dollars from our party funds to help establish a strike fund when you go out on your next strike. Thank you, and keep up the fight." Ms. Mitchison raised a clinched fist. "Workers of the world, unite."

The applause brought down the house. Naomi went back to her chair and took a seat. Mitchell eventually turned to the crowd and held up his hand.

"My friends, that's a hard act to follow, but the man to my right is up to the task. He has spent his life in public service to the common man, and I believe he will be the next president of the United States. I present to you, Mr. Norman Thomas.

The stately looking gentlemen rose from his chair and walked up to the podium.

In a deep voice he began, "Ladies and gentlemen—"

From the back of the crowd came an equally loud but angry voice: "There ain't no ladies in this here crowd tonight, and there sure as hell ain't no gentlemen on the platform tonight. And you, you white-headed, Yankee son-of-a-bitch, can go back up north where you came from." As the man spoke, he moved slowly toward the front of the crowd. When he entered the light of the kerosene lamps that lit the stage, Junior recognized Sheriff Jigger Morton.

Thomas was not to be put off that easily. "Sir, the Constitution of the United States and the state of Arkansas guarantees me the right of free speech."

Morton looked around at the farmers standing around the stage and lingered for several seconds on the black farmers at the edge of the crowd. Then he looked back at Mr. Thomas.

"I don't give a damn about the Constitution. This here is the best county in the whole United States, and we can take care of our own farmers. We ain't gonna have no white-haired, Yankee telling us what to do. Now I declare this meeting over." He waved to the farmers. "All you boys go on home, and I don't want to hear nothing about no strike, 'cause if I do, there will be some head knocking." He turned and looked at the blacks on the edge of the crowd. "If I as much as hear a peep out of you jig-a-boos, I'll ride you out of town on a rail." He turned his attention to the stage. "Now as for you clowns on the stage, you got two choices. You can go to jail right now—"

"On what charge?" Thomas spoke up.

"I'll think up something," the sheriff said. "Your other choice is to get in that car of yours, and one of my men will escort you to the county line. It don't make me much difference which you decide."

Mitchell walked up to Mr. Thomas and Ms. Mitchison and indicated that it would be best if they did as the sheriff had dictated.

Junior was at the back of the crowd, watching the show. He had heard very little of what was said. After the English woman had kissed the black preacher, the rest of the words that had come from the stage had meant nothing. If not for the promise to his father, he would have stayed around on the edge of the crowd, stalked the man and the woman, and killed them both. His father had been right; these people were evil.

Back at the truck, his father was anxious to get on the road back to Sunnyville and hear all of the details of the meeting. They were heading east, and Junior was filling in as much as he could remember when they noticed headlights on the road up ahead.

Junior came to a stop thirty yards from the headlights.

From the other car, Junior heard the now familiar voice of sheriff shout, "Parkus, you and the boy get out of the truck and stand in front of the headlights where I can see you. If you got guns, leave 'um in the truck."

Bill and Junior walked around in front of the headlights, and the sheriff came out to where they were standing.

"Now, boys, I want to make myself clear. There are a few things where we see eye-to-eye, but let's get one thing straight. We don't need no stupid Mississippi rednecks over on this side of the river, stirring up trouble. This ain't Elaine, and we don't need you. I got about as much patience with your kind as I do those communists at the meeting tonight. This is going to be the last time that I'm going to tell you this. Stay the hell out of my county. This is the only warning you will get; next time, it will come out of the end of a gun. Do you understand?"

Bill nodded but didn't speak. Junior just stood there.

"One other thing: you might wonder how I knew you was here. Old buddy, I got eyes in the back of my head and spies behind every tree. Now, get your skinny little asses back to Mississippi."

CHAPTER 15

INDEPENDENT VOICE

I am sorry to say that this will be the last regular issue of this paper. The Austria that we all know and love will soon cease to exist. Hitler and his German Reich, with the aid of a homegrown, rabble-rousing element, have succeeded in bringing our dear country to its knees. Our fair-weather friends at the academy have informed us that, after today, we will no longer be able to use their presses. The Nazi party has never been accused of being stupid. They clearly understand the power of the press and the free exchange of ideas. For those of you who welcome this beast, mark my words: he will bring us all to ruin.

Helena Edit-Stein

For two years, Helena and Judith had seen the handwriting on the wall. First, their sources of financial aid began drying up. Many of the more influential writers who made up the backbone of the movement opted for emigration. Their support in the academic community slowly eroded. During the winter, gangs of Nazi youth harassed anyone who came and went from the university. The young men spent their time lounging in the park across the street from the hostel where the women lived. Each morning, the women writers were met with a chorus of catcalls from across the park.

"When you lesbos want some real sex, I got what you need here in my shorts."

"What a waste of white meat."

"We're coming after you pretty soon. Don't walk down any dark alleys."

Helena and Judith understood that, when the Nazis took over, they would be some of the early targets. They were committed to a nonviolent course of action and discussed at length what their response would be if they were arrested. If an attempt was made to arrest them, they would simply sit down on the pavement, wherever they were.

When it became apparent that the Nazis would be taking over the next day, both women took most of their meager belongings and exited the hostel where they lived under cloak of darkness. A friend of the movement provided them with an apartment in a quiet working neighborhood across the river.

The first month after the Anschluss went smoothly as the Germans busied themselves with the more public, political figures. The women acquired a mimeograph machine that produced a passable print copy. They tacked copies of their paper to billboards and other public places. As they watched the abuse that was heaped on non-Aryan members of the community and especially the Jews, the ladies made it their mission to accurately document the events that took place and make sure it got to the outside world. That was where Naomi came in.

It was a Saturday morning in late May. Helena got out of bed and discovered that they were out of coffee and milk. She shouted at Judith through the bathroom door, "I'm going to the market; be back in a minute. Do you need anything?"

"Nope," Judith said.

The nearest grocery was two blocks away—no more than a ten-minute walk. She purchased her supplies and began the walk back home. As she turned the corner at the end of the block, Helena realized that something was dreadfully wrong. There were three Nazi cars surrounding the entrance to her apartment. A crowd had gathered to see what all of the commotion was about. Helena stood at the edge of the crowd and watched as Judith was walked out of the building. She was handcuffed and very solemn.

All Helena could think was, *Cooperate with these people. Please cooperate with these people. Forget the nonviolent stuff. Just go along with them.*

As if on cue, Judith went to her knees. This was how they had rehearsed it.

Please get up. These clowns will not put up with this. They'll pistol-whip you, Helena cried to herself.

The young officer who seemed to be in charge walked up to Judith and said something. She shook her head. He reached to his belt, undid the clasp on his holster, pulled out his gun, put it to her forehead, and pulled the trigger. As the shot rang out, the crowd, in unison, took one step back and gasped.

The gallant woman who had been Judith Keller was now a corpse lying on the pavement with a pool of blood outlining its form.

Helena stood paralyzed in fear and horror. Her person was consumed with a silent scream that would be with her until the day she died. She looked at the face of the man holding the gun. He was smiling. It was Rudy Holtoff, J. L.'s friend, the good-natured kid from Gruber's.

Rudy turned to the crowd. "Do you people see what we will do if you don't do as we say? We are in charge now, and if you don't do as we say, you will die. So that you will clearly understand, we will leave this freak of nature here on the sidewalk for the rest of the day. If you know where her queer friend is, you need to tell us right away. The quicker we rid ourselves of these perverts, the better we will all be."

Helena was standing just outside of a small clothing store. She heard the lady who ran the store. "Pssst, Pssst—sweetie, come here," the lady said. "Get out of the street. There are people on this street who will give you up in a second. You can go out the back. You best not come back here." She reached into one of the bins and pulled out a hat. Here, put this on your head so they won't see you."

"But what about Judith?" Helena asked.

"We'll take care of the body."

Helena took a small piece of paper and scribbled the name and address of Judith's parents on the paper.

"This is her family," she said.

That night, in a small inn on the outskirts of Vienna, she penned a letter to J. L.

> Dear Son,
> I saw them shoot her today. They shot her in the face. My friend, my soul mate, was killed for kneeling in the street when she was told to stand. She was one of the smartest, brightest repositories of human knowledge, one of those people who understood the "why" behind the "way" things work. In one instant, a stupid bull calf of a man who barely shaves, who believes what he is told to believe, shot her dead. I stood paralyzed with fear and horror at this dreadful act of man's inhumanity.
> From this day until this horrendous storm passes, I have gone underground. That sounds overly dramatic; the truth is I am in hiding.

Your mother,
Helena

This copy was found tacked to the large posting board on the campus of
the Academy.)

Independent Voice
Hitler and his henchmen will be judged quick and early
as the incarnation of evil. The people of Germany and
Austria who stand by and watch this abomination take
place, doing nothing to stop it, will live with this for
generations. You may pretend that you do not know,
but you do. You will write the history and say that
you did this to save the country. The sad truth is that
Hitler is no aberration. He is a product of our culture,
taken to the extremes of perfection, purity, violence,
and intolerance. In the end, the only real weapon we
have is the sure and certain knowledge that each of us
possesses, deep in our soul: none of us is perfect. We
all have our own deep, dark secrets that, if exposed,
would find us judged inadequate. It is this knowledge of
inadequacy that creates understanding and acceptance
for our fellow humans. We can only hope that this
knowledge will keep us from falling off into the abyss
of self-righteousness.
God, if you exist, please have mercy. Please have mercy
on our souls.
Helena Edit-Stein

When Helena was captured, it was almost by accident. She stepped out of
a bookstore and was headed to an apartment that she shared with four other
women. All for one reason or another were fearful that they too would be
picked up. A uniformed solider walked out of the shadows and asked to see
her ID. He had mistaken her for one of her roommates. When she handed
him her papers, he shook his head, slapped her, and arrested her for carrying
forged papers. He was still convinced that she was the other woman. It wasn't
until they arrived at the substation that the sergeant in charge realized whom
they had in their hands. A quick call to headquarters, and she was whisked
away to a more secure building.

SS Officer Rudy Holtoff had several reasons to get his hands on Helena Edit-Stein.

First, she was a socialist newspaper writer and, as such, was one of the opposition's most important voices. She had to be silenced. Among the political "unreliables," she was now near the top of the list.

Second, she was Jewish. Even if she made no claims to a Jewish heritage, her father and mother most certainly were Jewish. That by itself made her a risk.

Third, she could be used for other purposes.

Rudy had a plan for this woman. It did not require her cooperation, but that would make it easier.

"Good morning, Fraulein. It is nice to see you again," Rudy said as Helena was led in by the guard.

"You will understand if I don't share that emotion," Helena said.

"I hear that Jean Louis is doing well in America."

"How do you know anything of my son?"

"I have sources," Rudy said.

"What do you want from me, Rudy?"

"Fraulein, it is Lieutenant Holtoff. We are no longer at Gruber's, and I am not a child."

"Whatever. What do you want from me?" she demanded.

"You are here for your protection."

"Oh, is that all? And who are you protecting me from? Some stupid fool with a uniform who shoots unarmed women point-blank in the face? Let me have a paper and a pen, and I will sign away all of my rights to protection, and then you can let me go," she said.

"I am afraid it's not that simple."

"I didn't think it would be. Now, I ask you again, what is it that you want from me?" she said.

"To begin with, we need to know the whereabouts of the five other women—make that four women—who were living in the apartment with you." He picked up a sheet of paper and read out loud: "Louisa Wright, Olga Tariff, Claire Fortner, and last but not least, your daughter, Anna."

"Of the other women, I know nothing. I believe that my daughter has gone to Palestine. We are not close."

"Bullshit. You're like two peas in a pod. You know good and well that your daughter is working for the communist underground."

"As I told you, the last I knew of my daughter, she was heading for Palestine," Helena said.

"The captain told me to expect nothing from you, but I told him that you would help us, because you were a reasonable woman." While he talked, Holtoff walked around the room.

"You were wrong. A reasonable conversation requires two people who have good sense," Helena said.

Rudy walked up behind Helena and, with the broad side of his hand, hit her in the head, knocking her from her chair.

"Bitch, I have no patience with the likes of you. I will turn you over to the people who really know how to interrogate Jews."

With that, he stormed out of the room. That was the last that Helena Edit-Stein ever saw of Rudy Holtoff.

The next day, she was shipped off to a newly organized work camp just south of Linz on the Danube—Mauthausen.

CHAPTER 16

Dear Bill,

As you know, the Bund has recently been embroiled in a financial crisis. Several of our upper-level people got greedy.

To my point of writing, I will be in Memphis on a fundraising drive the first of August, and I would like to meet with you if that is at all possible. My country and I have a big favor to ask of you.

Yours truly,

Adolph Krause

Bill sat down that day and penned a letter back to his old friend.

Dear Doctor,

I was overjoyed to hear from you. I will be of whatever assistance that I can be in your cause. I am rather uncomfortable in the city of Memphis, because of the number of Jews and coloreds.

Just south of Memphis at Horn Lake, we have a safe house that is run by one of my associates. The place is called Betty's Eats. The food is good. I'll be in the back room.

I will be there on the second of August, and I would love to have a chance to see you.

Bill

Bill and Junior arrived in the early morning and talked for several hours with John and Betty as they prepared the noon meal. At one PM, an old Dodge pulled up in front of the cafe. There was no question about who the visitor was. Betty escorted him to the back room, where Bill and Junior were sitting. When Krause and his son entered the room, Bill rose to greet him.

"Doctor, it is so good to see you," Bill said.

"Likewise, my friend."

"Would you like a drink?" Bill asked.

"No, I think not. That is one pleasure that I had to give up," the doctor said.

"I don't drink much anymore, either. I just don't think clearly when I drink too much. By the way, this is my son, Junior." He turned to his son. "Junior, this is the great man himself, one of my early teachers."

The two men shook hands. Krause turned to John Michael and motioned him forward.

"You probably remember my son, John Michael. He's the head of security for our organization, and I must say, he is making quite a name for himself," Krause said.

John Michael smiled at Bill. "It's nice to see you again, Mr. Parkus. You may not remember, but we met at Camp Stuttgart a couple of years ago. I hope you had a safe trip home from Stuttgart."

"I did, thank you," Bill said.

"Bill, I will get to the point, because time is of the essence," Krause said.

"As you know, your country has already taken sides in the war in Europe. I have read your newsletters for years, so I know how you feel about Roosevelt. I can tell you that the forces that were at work twenty-five years ago have not changed. They are pushing the Jew to join this war on the side of England again.

"Hitler is the man we've been waiting for. He understands the true nature of Politics with a capital P. He understands the racial issue better than any leader in the last two centuries. We need your help.

"This war will be won and lost with airplanes. About two hundred miles across the delta is the largest source of bauxite—the raw material for aluminum—in the continental US. We have no one there to serve as our eyes and ears. We were wondering if you had anyone who we could trust who could go to the mines, work, and provide us with information."

"I don't think I would be of any value to you," Bill said. "My face is too well known in this part of the country. Most of my good men are married and needed for our mission. There are a few in our group who would go, but I really don't know if I can trust them."

Junior, who had sat quietly listening to the two men talk, spoke up.

"Dad," he said.

"What?" Bill answered.

"I'll go. I'll go to the mines and work. I'm old enough, and if I stay around here, they'll draft me. You've always said how you don't want me going into the army."

In his wildest dreams, Bill had never thought of asking his son to do anything that smacked of real danger. He knew that, at some point, his son would have to grow up and do something with his life … but be a spy?

"Junior, do you know what you are saying?" Bill asked. "This could be dangerous."

"Yeah, I understand," the boy said proudly. "I may be scared, but that won't never stop me."

The boy had just recited back to Bill one of his own mantras. That moment was a confirmation of Bill Parkus's whole life. He had preached and lived the truth for twenty years, and now the truth was to bear fruit. Bill turned back to the doctor.

"What do you think Doc?"

"I would consider it an honor to have your son work for us."

"What are the mechanics?" Bill asked.

"It's really very simple. We know that the mines at Bauxite are hiring right now. If he shows up at the gate, he will get a job. We have a contact in Hot Springs, Arkansas, at the Spa City Cigar Store on Central Avenue. Once a month, Junior will take the train to Hot Springs like any normal tourist, drop off the information that we need, and pick up the an envelope of money and instructions."

Bill interrupted the doctor. "Make sure that there is only enough money to cover the expenses that he incurs—train trips, meals, etc. We're not in this for money."

"I understand. How long can the boy stay?" the doctor asked.

"He can stay as long as is required," Bill said.

"We may go for long times when no help is required."

"That's fine. One lesson we learned from the socialists was patience."

"What about acts of violence and sabotage?" John Michael asked.

"Violence is not something we seek out, but it has its place, and we are willing to do our part," Bill said.

Junior nodded in agreement.

"Fine. No—wonderful," the elder Krause said. "When can he leave?"

"He should go home and see his mother, but he could be on the road in the morning."

"Excellent, but we don't need him that fast," Krause said. "He'll need to change his name. With your notoriety, the name William Parkus Jr. would draw unnecessary attention. I have connections that can get him a set of papers in a week."

"Mail them to Sunnyville, general delivery."

"Done."

Krause got up from his chair, joined his son at the door, and saluted Bill and Junior with an upraised arm salute.

"Frei Amerika."

Three weeks after the meeting at the café, Junior had a new identity and was on his way to Bauxite. When he walked out of the house to get into truck, he had a small bag in one hand and his shotgun in the other.

"You ought to be leaving that gun here," Bill said.

"How come? They ain't got no game in Arkansas?" the boy asked.

"No, that's not it. You got a job to do. With that temper of yours, the gun is liable to get you in some trouble. You get in trouble, that means you are of no value to us. Now put the gun on the porch, and let's get out of here," Bill said, pointing back toward the house. "And, by the way, I'm driving today. I got to learn all over again. With you gone, I've got to learn to be my own driver and mechanic. You've spoiled me."

The two men drove across the delta through Little Rock and south on Highway 67.

By two in the afternoon, they were nearing the county line of Pulaski and Saline counties. On the left was a small tavern called the Red Gate.

"Would you like to have a beer?" Bill asked his son. Bill seldom drank. He rarely consumed alcohol in public, and he had never offered his son a drink.

Junior turned and looked at this father. He had a faint smile on his face.

"This is kind of a special occasion," Bill replied to the unstated question.

The Red Gate was quiet at that time of afternoon. The two men found a table, and Bill ordered a couple of beers and sandwiches.

"I can't tell you how happy I am that you're doing this. The fact that you spoke up and said you wanted to do this made me as proud as a man can be. We don't really know what you are getting into here, and I want you to understand that, if you ever get tired of working over here, you can always come home. The one thing I'm most worried about is your temper. You're going to have to figure out a way not to be going off on people," Bill said. "By the way, how do you like your beer?"

Junior made a face and shook his head. "Don't. Tastes bitter."

"Probably for the best. Finish your sandwich, and let's get out of here."

On the way out the door, Bill asked the bartender, "Where are the bauxite mines from here?"

The man pointed west. "Go three miles out on the highway, and you'll see a sign for Bryant. Take a left and go through Bryant. The plant is about three miles south of town.

Like Mississippi, Arkansas was a quiet place where life moved slowly, but not so in Bauxite. If there was any place in the country where it was obvious that the United States was preparing for war, it was in this small, rural community. Bill's old truck was dwarfed by the large, earthmoving equipment and trucks that roamed the gravel roads to and from the mines, leaving great plumes of dust in their wake.

Bill pulled up in front of the train depot and came to a stop.

"I think I probably ought to drop you off here," he said. "I need to get back to the river bottoms before dark overtakes me. If you need anything, you know how to get hold of me. Any extra money you make, you send it home. We need it for the cause. Keep your nose clean, and don't screw up. Remember, you got a job to do; hold your temper, and do as you're told."

Bill gunned the old truck and started a U-turn back onto the road. Just as he did, a large truck loaded with ore came around the corner just missing the back of the truck. Bill sheepishly smiled at his son, completed the turn, and headed back east.

Two old men were sitting on the edge of the train station platform. Both had what appeared to be cotton sacks over their shoulders and cut-off broom handles with sharpened nails on the ends.

One of the men said, "Looking for work?"

Junior nodded.

"Well, son, we are the official greeters and trash picker-uppers for Republic Mining. This is the company's idea of retirement. When your back gives out and you can't get a hard on, they put you out to pasture."

The other man pointed in the general direction of Bill's truck. "Your friend damn near got killed, pulling out in traffic like that. Where you from, boy?"

"South Mississippi," Junior said.

"I would have guessed that. In my experience, most people from Mississippi ain't got much sense," the first man said.

His friend agreed and then looked back at Junior. "Well, boy, if you're looking for work, you ain't gonna find it standing out here in the middle of the road. Personnel office is just up there on the left."

"You read and write?" the lady behind the counter asked Junior.

"Passable," Junior said.

"Good, that'll save me some time," she said as she handed him the application form. "Take this form over to the table and fill it out. You ever been in trouble with the law?"

He shook his head.

"By the way, you got any special skills?"

"Mechanic," Junior said.

"Honey, everybody out here is a mechanic. I mean like welding, driving heavy equipment, explosives."

Junior shook his head.

"Just as well. Everybody starts out doing grunt work in the mines. You got family here or somebody you know that already works at the mines?" she asked.

He shook his head.

"Then I guess you'll need a place to stay?"

He nodded.

"While you're working on the forms, I'll see what I can do."

Thirty minutes later, Junior had a job and a place to live.

Early the next morning, Junior Parkus, alias Sandy Scroggins, reported to the mine area, where he, along with thirty other men, boarded a small dingy train that carried them to Nielion, one of the last of the old underground mines. Before descending into the mine, each man was issued a hard hat with a carbide lamp and either a pick or a shovel. The men then boarded another small train that served double duty—once they were at the mine face, the cars were used to haul the raw ore to the surface.

The train cars were small, forcing the men into close proximity. In the dark, the others fell into the loose conversation of familiarity while Junior sat, waiting to see what would happen next.

Someone in the lead car shouted back, "We got two new men in car three, did anybody tell 'um about the mine snakes?"

"No, boss, we didn't," Charley Morgan shouted back.

"Better let 'um know a'fore we get down there. Wouldn't want any of these new guys getting hurt," the lead man said in all seriousness.

Charley turned to his new work mates, "Either of you men ever worked in mines a'fore?"

Junior and the other new man both shook their heads.

"I didn't hear you," the man said.

Both realized their mistake.

Junior spoke up, "I ain't never worked in no mine. Ain't never heard nothing about no mine snakes either."

"I ain't neither," said the other new miner.

"Well, you boys better be careful. These mine snakes is tricky little critters. They're about the size of a green snake, as black as coal, but they got more poison than a copperhead or a cottonmouth. They like to hide in cracks and dark, warm places like lunch boxes and stuff. Don't be picking up no loose rocks before you kick 'um."

"Everybody light up," the man in the lead car shouted, referring to the carbide lamps on their hard hats.

Despite the fact that Junior was convinced that the snake story was a ruse to shake up the new guys, he and the other new men spent the day gently turning over rocks, fearful that they might pick up one of the infamous mine snakes.

At the lunch break, the other new miner reached into his lunch sack. Charley had placed a night crawler in the sack. The man fainted dead away.

One of the other miners leaned over to Junior. "Charley does that to ever one of the new miners. It was funny the first dozen times, but it's kinda getting old."

Junior decided that day that he didn't like Charley Morgan.

The men in the mines had learned to live in that world of darkness, and for most of them, it had become a way of life. The work was hard, but Junior was young and had a strong back.

The one drawback to the digging was that he was required to work in close proximity with some very black men, and he was often required to use picks or shovels that had been used by a black man on the shift before him. For that reason, he began to wear gloves at all times. It wasn't the dirt and grime or the wear and tear on his hands; it was his repulsion against touching things that had been touched and used by the blacks. This repulsion was magnified by his fear. In the recesses of his soul, Junior knew that, in the darkness of the mines, they could read his thoughts. No matter how he held his tongue, they could read his mind.

Once he was settled into his new job, Junior went to Hot Springs. It was a short bus ride to downtown Benton, where he caught the train to Hot Springs. When he disembarked from the train, he knew that it was not his kind of town. Well-dressed blacks and whites walked the streets, and whores propositioned him before he could get off of the train.

At the Spa City Cigar Store, he was confounded by an angry, old man behind the counter. Tommy, his contact, was a slick-looking Italian man who met him on the back stairs of the store. The man gave him a manila envelope that he was instructed to destroy once he had read its contents.

Riding the train back to Bauxite, he decided that going to Hot Springs would never do. The next day, he mailed a letter to his father in Sunnyville.

From that time on, all of Junior's communications passed between him and his father at the Red Gate Tavern in Alexander.

CHAPTER 17

For Helena, it seemed like centuries since she had come downstream on the Danube to forge her life in Vienna, and now, she was heading back upstream to a far different life. This time, she was riding in an open cattle car, shackled to seventy other people whose offenses ranged from vagrancy, robbery, murder, and rape to the heinous crime of being Jewish.

Passing through the village of Durnstein, she glanced across the river to the house where her daughter, Anna, had hidden after the revolt of 1934. She couldn't help but think about the mistakes she had made in her life. What if she had gone to Pittsburgh when Willie had died? What if she had been more of a mother? What if she had raised her children in the church, any church? Would her son, her father's namesake, be alive? Would her daughter have married and given her grandchildren instead of fighting a war against all odds? Would her gentle son be by her side smiling?

There was no way to sit down in the cattle car; they were packed as tightly as the guards could force them.

That morning when Helena had been awakened from her sleep, the only instruction had been, "Get out of bed, and leave everything but what you have on." Despite the instructions, she had stuffed her notes and pencils inside the lining of her jacket. Once she was outside the cell, she had been chained into a line of prisoners and marched out of the jail to the central train station.

Any questioning—"Where are we going?"; "What are you going to do with us?"—was met with dead silence. Since the Nazi occupation of Austria, the disappearance of prisoners had become an accepted phenomenon.

The train crossed the river at Krems and proceeded north and west until it stopped at a small village.

"Where are we?" a man behind Helena asked.

"This is Mauthausen," she said quietly. "They appear to be taking us to the work camp at the Wienergraben, the old rock quarry on the top of that mountain over in front of us."

"Good," the disembodied voice said. "They aren't taking us to Germany. At least the people here are civilized."

Helena thought but did not say, *You misunderstand, my friend; this was Austria, and now, it's Germany.*

After disembarking from the train, the shackled prisoners were marched up the mountain through a gauntlet of suspicious stares. At the edge of the village, a group of rowdy children shouted insults and threw small rocks at the ragtag chain of humans.

At first, the Germans had imported prisoners from Auschwitz to construct the fortress on the hill that surrounded the old stone quarry. Most of the streets of Vienna had been paved with stones from this hillside. It was common knowledge that the camp at Mauthausen was worked with the most elemental tools and often with bare hands. In the new Germany, there was an endless stream of prisoners who could be brought to bear on any task.

When a prisoner could no longer stand up to the job, she was discarded. Many were dispatched with carbon dioxide in the gas chamber below the sick bay. At first, the SS dealt with prison deaths using a local crematorium, but when the numbers rose, ovens were constructed on-site to deal with the unwanted bodies. It was this process that created the sweet sick odor that permeated the air around Mauthausen.

At the top of the hill, the column of prisoners was called to a halt before the oversize, wooden doors of the prison. The solider in charge of the detail presented his list of orders to the sergeant of the guard. The sergeant compared his list to the expected shipment, made a series of check marks on both sets of papers, and then authorized the door guard to open the doors.

Inside was a large roll-call yard the size of a football field, and occupying this yard were several hundred other humans who had been brought to this place and were waiting to be processed. Like the group from Vienna, the prisoners were shackled, and on either end, the chains were locked to rings that were embedded in the grey, granite walls of the courtyard.

Soon after Helena and her group arrived, there was a commotion on the walkway well above the yard. An entourage of soldiers with flags walked smartly out onto the upper walkway, followed by Commandant Franz Ziereis. For the first time, the prisoners were directly addressed.

"Listen to me," the commandant began. "You are here for a purpose. You are here to work. Your life has no other purpose. It is as simple as that. The rules here are just as simple: you will not talk unless told to, and you will do as you are told. If you break the rules, you will be punished quickly and severely.

You now know the rules. They will not be repeated." The commandant then turned and left the walkway.

Within a few minutes, a squad of soldiers and several men in long white coats, who appeared to be physicians, made their way into the roll-call yard and began to sort the inmates. On the first pass-through, they picked those who appeared to be on their last legs.

"Take this one to sick bay; he won't last a day in the quarry."

"Take this one to Harthiem; she is of no use to us."

"This one needs to be deloused and sent to Melk."

"This one needs the fresh air of the farm at Gusen."

All of those identified on the first pass-through were detached from their respective chains and herded through a small, round door that led down a narrow staircase into a white, porcelain room. Once in the room, the doors were sealed; the room was flooded with carbon dioxide. Thirty minutes later, they were all dead and being fed into a pair of small crematoria just down the hall. The smoke stack for the ovens discharged just above the roll-call yard where the next group was being sorted.

The older of the physicians wandered through the group of new arrivals, looking for those with interesting tattoos, well-formed heads, and perfect sets of teeth. This was a smaller group. These individuals were separated from the others, and they, in turn, were led through a second rounded door and down a series of stairs and herded into a large cell. Over the next few days, the doctor who had picked them out would dissect each of the inmates, taking their tattooed skin for use in the making of lampshades and luggage. The well-formed heads and teeth would be cleaned and used as paperweights.

The rest of the charges left in the yard awaiting their fates were slowly but meticulously processed. While one soldier sitting behind a small, wooden desk asked them a series of questions, a second sat and heated an inked branding iron with a seven-digit number and letter brand. With the brand on their arm, these men and women were reduced to numbers.

As the sun began to set, a cloudbank rolled in from upriver, and it began to rain. The soldiers and medical personnel packed up their equipment and moved into a small storeroom just off the yard. The lines of leg-chained prisoners were still secured to large, round hooks on the granite walls of the yard, and the soldiers disappeared for the night.

During the night, several of those on Helena's chain passed away from hypothermia, and early the next morning, they were removed by the rested soldiers.

When it came time for Helena's evaluation, the soldier's first question was, "What was your name?"

"Helena Edit-Stein," she said.

The soldier looked up from his paperwork.

"That name rings a bell. I was supposed to be on the lookout for a name like that." He fumbled through a sheaf of papers and came to a list of names. "Ahh, yes, here it is. We were supposed to be on the lookout for a couple of women by the name Edit-Stein. Did you say Anna or Helena?"

"Helena," she said.

"Good. The commandant has something special in mind for you."

"And what would that be?" she asked.

He looked up at her and said, "Shut up. I did not ask you for a response."

He made several marks on her paper and handed it to a young soldier standing beside him.

"Take J476159 to the bunker and give the permanent copy to the commandant's secretary. He will be interested in this one."

If Mauthausen was the end of the road for most of the inmates, then the bunker was where the road disappeared. Buried deep below the prison walls were a series of cells where high-profile political figures were kept in complete anonymity. After the war, there would be no record that these people had ever existed.

CHAPTER 18

The aluminum refinery in East St. Louis, Illinois, was a large, spread out affair located on a tract of land once owned by John Jacob Astor. It extended from Forty-Second Street to the bluffs along both sides of Missouri Ave. Although officially outside of the city, it was hard to tell where the country ended and the city began.

The company provided J. L. with an apartment duplex near his work, where almost everything was provided.

For the first time, he had an office of his own and was in the position of supervising a lab. It was a promotion from personnel, and he was pleased. Here, he would actually get to do something and not just think about it.

It was a Monday morning in late September. He arrived early, grabbed a cup of coffee, and sat down to read his mail. On the top of the stack was an unstamped letter addressed to him. In the return address spot was the name Rudy Holtoff.

> Dear Jean Louis,
> Long time no see, old buddy. Thought I would write and bring you up on the latest goings on here in old V-town. Life has changed a lot. You remember the girl Olga who worked at Gruber's. Well, she and I tied the knot a couple of years ago, and now we have a couple of little yard apes running around. Imagine me with kids. It really isn't so bad. I still get a little strange on the side.
> Never got that union job, but I did even better. I got hooked up with some folks here a couple of years ago who had connections in Berlin. We buy and sell stuff on the black market. I've made a killing.

Well, I have always been lucky. Anyway, this fellow came through recruiting for the SS. Now, this is a deal. Good job; don't have to work much. It's mostly using my connections. Our job is to make sure that the union of Germany and Austria goes off smoothly. You and I know that there are a lot of troublemakers out there, and our job is to make sure that they understand what's at stake—if you know what I mean.

Let me tell you, your mother has put herself in a really bad situation. She kept printing lies about us, and the hot shots in the party don't like it one bit. It was hard to find her, but a few days ago, we found her living in a ratty, little, old basement, cranking out that vile crap she preaches. She's in protective custody now. I am working hard to make sure that she has everything she needs, but she is not being in the least bit cooperative. You know what your mother is like.

Anyway, it looks like you plan on sitting out the effort while the rest of us try to put our people back on top where we belong. As a true, red-blooded Austrian patriot, I know you will want to do your part. From time to time, we will need information about the United States' ability to produce aluminum. These fellows tell me that aluminum and airplanes are really going to be important in this war. We expect you to provide information when we ask for it.

For my part, I will try to make sure that your mother gets treated well. It will be much easier for me to help if you help me. If you don't help, she will probably go to one of the labor camps in northern Germany, and then it would be completely out of my hands. So, I guess, old buddy, it is up to you.

If you have any idea about telling anyone about this letter, forget it. We've got people in places you wouldn't imagine. We pretty well know where you've been and what you have been doing for the last few years.

Heil Hitler,

Your friend, Rudy

J. L. laid down the letter and began to cry.

Dad and Franz are dead, Mom's in jail, and heaven knows where Anna is, he thought. *And now these people want me to spy. Hell, I'm not a spy; I'm an engineer. I don't have access to any secrets. In fact, I don't even know if there are any secrets.*

Jean Louis did not have a political bone in his body. He was one of those people who could live with any system of government and most conditions of life. Give him a structure, a set of rules, and he would figure out how to play the game. He would survive. His happiness wasn't based on having a new car or a big house or a prestigious title. He loved good food, dark beer, and pretty women. He loved his mother and respected her positions. He had looked through the anger and madness of his brother and seen a flawed human who wasn't whole. He loved his sister and her intensity for life. He and his father had been kindred spirits. Underneath the engineer who studied and measured the world was a little boy, sitting under a honeysuckle bush and sucking on the sweet end of the flower in awe of the world around him.

For Jean Louis, the child, his family was life. Now his father and brother were dead, his sister was in Palestine, and his mother was in a prison camp. The first three he could do nothing about, but he could help his mother. J. L. didn't want to spy for the Germans, but it was the world constructed for him.

After a while, J. L. wiped his eyes and strengthened his resolve. As a child, he had dreamed of spying and intrigue. The great adventure of being a spy who saved his country—the whole idea seemed so exciting. And here he was being forced to spy for a cause he didn't believe in to save the only person in life he truly cared for.

The only thing he knew for certain was that he would do anything to help his mother.

For weeks and months, he expected some person in a long trench coat to come to his door at night and demand the blueprints to the refinery or production figures or the secret sex life of the plant manager—none of which he knew anything about.

When the request came, J. L. was amazed at the simplicity with which it was delivered. Every day, there was a stream of couriers who walked up and down the halls of Building 28. He stepped down the hall for a cup of coffee, and when he returned, he noticed a young man leaving his office.

"May I help you?" he asked.

"Memo from Planning," the young man said, walking away from J. L.

"Who in Planning?"

"Got me. Just says Planning," the young man said as he disappeared around the corner.

When J. L. looked at the envelope, he realized it was designed to look like company stationary, but there was something different about the typeface. In addition, it was sealed. Memos in the plant were never sealed. Sealing wasn't efficient; it took time to open, and the envelope couldn't be used again. Another company rule was that everything must have a clear return address, and this one said nothing.

It began:

> Good day, Stein,
>
> One of the new engineers in your section is working on the preliminary plans for a new ore reduction process involving extracting alumna from low-grade ore. His name is Donald Wilson. He works in Section 10 office 4 in your building. We need copies of all of his notes. We don't much care how you get it, but do it. When you have obtained the information, go to Taylor's Import and Export on Collinsville. Buy a piece of pottery, and ship it to Andy Valencia, #3 Camino Reale, Mexico City, Mexico. When we are notified that you have accomplished the task, you should receive word of your mother.
>
> Rudy

It turned out that the process of obtaining the information was much easier that he had expected. Most of the time, Building 28 was empty from Saturday night until early Monday morning. The duty engineers stayed in the plant and never got close to their offices. There was a master schedule where the duty roster was posted, so it was easy to know when Wilson had been on duty and when he would be on next.

To get into the plant at night required only his standard ID pass and a statement of purpose.

It was interesting that the building that seemed so alive with life during the day had the feel of an abandoned school at night. The slightest noise echoed through the halls and glass-encased cubicles.

J. L. took every opportunity to look over Wilson's office space. Like most of the engineers, Wilson seemed rather obsessive, with everything organized just so. The metal desk where he kept the keys to his file drawers had a simple lock, nothing fancy.

One Saturday morning, J. L. stopped the janitor and asked to use the master key, indicating he had left his own key at home. While he had the master, he made a wax impression and, from that, a key that allowed him access to all of the offices in the building.

On the evening of his first spy venture, J. L. checked in and went to his own office. He put on a pot of coffee, turned on the radio, pulled out one of his own projects, and began working. All was quiet in the halls. He timed the rounds of security.

Confident that he was alone, J. L. walked the two corridors over and opened the door to Wilson's office. He carefully opened the drawer in the desk and took the key to the filing cabinet. He opened the cabinet and removed the file marked Refine-R experiment.

Back in his office, J. L. spent the rest of the evening carefully copying every detail. The drawings were somewhat rough, but the numbers were exact.

By the time the evening was over, J. L. was convinced that Wilson was a very bright man and would go far in the company.

At five AM, he waited for the guard to make his rounds and then took the file and replaced it in its prescribed site. When he returned to his desk, he began to look again at the data that he had transcribed.

The next thing he knew, the guard was gently rapping on his door.

"Mr. Stein, are you okay?" the guard asked.

J. L. held his head up, looked around, and realized that his stolen treasure was lying out on the table before him, and no one knew the difference.

"Yeah, Fred, I'm fine. Just dozed off."

"See you tomorrow. I'm going off in a few minutes."

"Yeah, I'll see you later," J. L. said.

J. L. gathered up the data he had obtained, slid it into his briefcase, and walked out of the plant. Despite his misgivings about the job he had been assigned, it had turned out to be easy.

Taylor's Antiques was a dark place, full of inexpensive pottery, lamps, and plates.

The little man behind the counter appeared to melt into the walls as if he was one of the pots sitting in the display case.

"May I help you?" he asked.

"I'm looking for a nice pot to send to a friend in Mexico City."

"Would that be Mr. Valencia?"

"Yes," J. L. said.

"Oh, then you would like some of the things we have in the back. Follow me," the man said as he walked out from behind the counter.

In the back, through a heavy curtain, were a variety of larger pots and flatware. The man turned back to J. L. "Would you mind me leaving while you pick out your piece and pack it in one of those cases? I have other customers to see to, if you don't mind."

J. L. was left in this bazaar of shapes and sizes. It seemed a shame to purchase an expensive pot. Why waste money on something of value. On the other hand, he did not know the fate of the pottery, it would be sad to know that the nice pot he bought was destroyed. In the end, he picked out an ornate piece with a wide neck.

J. L. looked around to make sure that no one was watching, and then he withdrew the papers from his waist and folded them into the pottery. As soon as he finished laying the pot in the bed of straw, the old man immediately came back into the room.

"It seems you have made a fine selection."

"Thank you. How much will that be?" he asked.

"We will put it on the bill. It will get paid."

"I have Mr. Valencia's address here."

"Oh, I don't need it. I send things to him all of the time. You keep it; you may need it sometime."

Within days, J. L. received a letter at his duplex from his mother. It was postmarked Vienna.

> Dear Jean Louis,
>
> I was recently moved to Mauthausen, the old rock quarry. We have it very nice here, but of course, we are still in custody. The security forces assure me that, as soon as things are stable, they will allow us more freedom.
>
> Louisa was killed when a mob attacked the Schlingerhof. Renee and Greta have gone into hiding and hopefully are safe.
>
> Your Uncle Karl wrote and told me that you were doing well. I love you dearly and hope to see you soon.
>
> Love,
> Mother

In unguarded moments, J. L. would admit to himself that there was a perverse pleasure in being a good spy. Even though he was forced to side with the guys in black hats, J. L. took pride in doing a good job; sloppiness and inaccuracy would only endanger his mother.

From the start of the war in Europe until early 1940, he provided regular information about shipments of ore from the Caribbean and South America, about the quality of the ore, about the shifts in production to materials used for sheet metal. Right along, he was asked to give updates on the work of Donald Wilson. Very little of the information seemed of major importance to J. L. and most of it could be obtained from other sources in a less clandestine fashion.

As it became painfully clear that the United States would eventually enter the war on the side of the Allies, his passing of information made him subject to execution if he was caught. Guard towers were erected, and floodlights illuminated the plant day and night. The government took over security for the plant.

In the time since his first letter from Rudy, J. L. received a series of letters from his mother. All were short and to the point. This was something that his mother had seldom been. Whereas most of her professional writing was clear and concise, her personal letters were rambling and stream of conscious. Not so the letters that were postmarked Vienna.

After the first two or three letters suggesting that she would soon be freed from the camp, she changed her focus to life in the camp. Most of the talk was of picnics and her days of study in the camp library. After the first year, no further mention was made of his sister.

In the dark times when J. L. became convinced that this would go on forever, he couldn't allow himself to think that maybe, just maybe, these letters might be forgeries, that his mother was dead or lost in a system of prison camps and would never be heard from again. In those times, the marvelous facility of denial came to his rescue and forced his concerns into the subconscious, protecting him from his worst fears. For days on end, he read and reread the letters, looking for clues and hints as to the real circumstances of her life.

CHAPTER 19

Stein,

There are plans to build a large production facility in a little, out-of-the-way place called Bauxite, Arkansas. Soon, you will receive notification of your transfer to that facility. Forty miles away by train is the spa resort of Hot Springs. Your new contact will be at the Spa City Cigar Store on Central Avenue. Ask for Tommy; he and his people are couriers and do not know the nature of your work.

Rudy

Roosevelt's Lend-Lease program was a thinly veiled way of assisting the Western allies and, at the same time, maintaining American neutrality. As the production of planes, ships, and weapons increased, the need for aluminum skyrocketed. Several years earlier, the company had begun to upgrade the facilities in Bauxite, Arkansas, where most of the reserves were. With the development of Wilson's new process, it made it feasible to reopen many of the mines that had been closed during the Depression. Republic Mining had already put large amounts of money into improvement of the existing mining facilities. Now the company and the US government had joined forces to build the largest aluminum production facility in the world in Bauxite, Arkansas.

Dear Jean Louis,

I have heard good reports of your work there in East St. Louis. I am sure you have heard the rumors about the facility that is to be built in Arkansas. Well, those are no longer rumors. The company and the government are going to throw a lot of resources into this project. You will be reassigned after the first of the year to the mines in Bauxite.

By the way, Saline County is the home of a friend of mine. His name is Bullet Hyten of Niloak Pottery, and he lives in Benton, just a few miles down the road. We've become acquainted at shows in Chicago and New York over the years; you probably remember me speaking of him. He was an odd, little man, but he makes beautiful pottery. His most famous pieces are made of something he calls "swirl." I have one of his bigger pieces; it sits at the foot of the stairs in my house. It's the one you tried to use as an umbrella stand until I told you what it was. Anyway, when you get to town, look him up and tell him I said hello.

Some friends of mine have told me that your mother is in protective custody at Mauthausen on the Danube. From what I hear, it's probably better that she's there than on the street. With your mother's tendency to speak her mind, it could be very dangerous for her right now.

No one seems to know where your sister is; I heard she had gone to Palestine and then disappeared. If you hear from her, tell her to write me, and I will do my best to help her get into this country.

I realize that it is a long way from Pittsburgh to Arkansas, but I would really like to see you. Maybe we can arrange to meet somewhere in between for a holiday.

Love,

Uncle Karl

Was it all a coincidence that Uncle Karl knew so much about his mother and his sister? Who were the friends who had told him about her whereabouts? Were John Michael and his father involved in this? How did Rudy know about his transfer? All of these people and their pottery seemed to keep popping up; did they have anything to do with the Germans? What would they do to a Nazi spy if they caught him in Arkansas? Probably string him up in a tree and use him for target practice.

Being a spy kept getting more complicated all the time.

CHAPTER 20

Helena's cell was dark most of the time. The only illumination was the dim light from the hallway that entered through a slot at bottom of the door. The watery gruel and dry bread that constituted her one meal a day was slid through that same slot. The floor of the room sloped to the center, where a drain hole had been placed, providing her a place to relieve herself. Every other day, the door was opened, and a guard would hose down Helena and the floor.

Several days passed after she had been marched into the cell and the door had been closed. Helena had no idea if she was being treated differently from anyone else in the prison.

The guard came to her cell, opened the door, hosed her down, and then, instead of closing the door, threw her a towel.

"Dry yourself off," he said. "And make it quick."

Helena did as she was instructed.

"Now, come with me," he said.

They ascended a series of switchback stairs and emerged onto the walkway above the roll-call yard. The sun was bright and hurt her eyes.

When she attempted to shield her face, the guard shouted, "Put your hands down, walk with your hands at your side."

At the west end of the walkway was the administration tower where the commandant's office was. Helena and the soldier entered a small, outer office, and the soldier approached the secretary.

"The commandant requested prisoner J476159 be brought here."

"I will tell him," she said, without looking up. She rose from her desk, walked over to the office door, and knocked.

A muffled voice said, "Come."

She opened the door, entered, and said, "The prisoner you requested has arrived."

"Bring her in," the voice said.

The secretary motioned to the soldier to bring the prisoner forward.

"Remove her shackles," the commandant instructed the guard. "And then you may leave. We have some talking to do."

The guard did as he was instructed.

Ziereis looked Helena over and then smiled.

"You're not at what I expected. I thought you would be some giant, hulking woman with arms the size of lampposts. But you're nothing but a skinny little Jewish woman, just like the rest of them. I guess that's true of most of us though, isn't it? Take away the outer layers, and we are nothing but puny little humans." He motioned to the teapot on his desk. "I saw you look at the tea. Would you like a cup of hot tea?"

Helena nodded her head.

Ziereis poured her a cup of tea.

"Have a seat," he said, handing her the teacup. "Let me tell you why you were brought here. You have a gift. It is a perverted one, but it is a gift nonetheless. Many of the people in this camp grew up reading the drivel you have written over the years, and when you write something, they believe it. The purpose of this camp is work, and we will get more work out of these people if they believe that you and people like you are behind us. So what I want you to do is write notes and letters that we will allow to be circulated around the camp. I want you to start rumors that the conflict will end soon, that everyone will get to go home, that hardworking prisoners get sent to better camps. That woman in England—your friend Mitchison—has become a real pain in the ass. I want you to write her and tell her how good things are for you here."

"I won't do that," she said, shaking her head.

"You don't understand. I control everything about your life," he said. "You live and die based on my whim. I took away your identity. I can have the guard come into this room, gather you up, take you into the bowels of this prison, kill and incinerate you, and in an hour, you will be history. There would be no record that you ever existed."

"That may be true, but you don't control my soul," she said.

"Oh, but I may," he said smiling.

"What do you mean?" she asked.

"I mean you have two children: a son and a daughter. Jean Louis, I think is the boy's name—the engineer in America. We always know where he is and what he is doing. If you do not cooperate with us, he could easily be struck by a runaway car, just like his older brother. If you do cooperate, we will forward some of your letters to him."

"What about my daughter?" Helena asked.

"Your daughter is another matter altogether. She's not in custody, but she and her friends will be caught, because they're stupid. It's just a matter of time. If you don't help us, she will die in the process of being captured. If you do help, we will go easy on her. So, you see ..." he hesitated, picked up a piece of paper in front of him, "J476159, I do control your soul."

Helena did not answer the commandant, because she did not need to.

"You're dismissed," he said.

The guard returned to the office and put her back in handcuffs but did not put the shackles back on her legs. Helena and the guard retraced their steps back to the cell, but when they arrived, several things were different. The empty cell she had left earlier now had a small cot with a mattress and blanket, a commode with a lid, an electric lightbulb in the ceiling receptacle, and in the far corner, a table with pens and paper.

CHAPTER 21

Charley Morgan, a big, meaty man, was the lead man on Junior's line, and part of his job was to show the new men the ropes. The joke about the mine snakes hadn't sat well with Junior, and it had set the tone of their relationship.

One afternoon as they emerged from the mines, Charley said, "Yeah, there ain't nothing in Mississippi but colored half-breeds and river rat idiots 'cause they all screw their sisters and mamas."

"You don't know what the hell you're talking about, you stupid hillbilly," Junior said.

"Well, at least I know who my daddy is," Charley said.

Before Charley knew it, Junior was all over him. Charley outweighed Junior by fifty pounds and had a six-inch arm length over the smaller man. Junior had no experience boxing, but he was quick. In an instant, Junior landed two punches to the face and chest of the big man. Charley grabbed his attacker and held him close so Junior couldn't land any more punches. When Charley's head had cleared, he shoved the smaller man away and squared his feet.

"Come on back, you little river rat, and I'll feed you my fist for supper," he said.

All of the other men formed a tight circle around the two combatants and began egging them on. Charley was a decent boxer, but he was slow. Of the three solid licks that he landed, two to them sent Junior staggering.

Junior was preparing to respond to the last blow when one of the men on the edge of the spectators said, in a loud voice, "Evening, Mr. Mac."

All of the spectators and Charley came to a halt. Junior, focused on Charley, landed a blow to his chin. The bigger man was dazed again and went down.

Mr. McDermott was a small, wiry man who was legendary at the mines. He had been raised in South Africa and fought in the Boer Wars. After the war, he had worked in the diamond mines near his home and then moved to the United States. For years, he worked in the silver mines of New Mexico and eventually moved to Bauxite, where he had worked his way up to be chief mining engineer for Republic Mines. He was a very precise man who dressed in jodhpurs and high leather boots and carried a riding crop. In his earlier years, he had had a career as a lightweight boxer. When he first came to the mines, he established a boxing club that soon became known throughout the region.

Mr. Mac looked at the men, smiled, and said, "You men go on and finish up what you started."

Charley seemed mad now. No one had ever beaten him in a scrap in the mines. He sized up his opponent again and launched a right-handed haymaker. Junior ducked and landed a solid punch to the nose; this time, Charley went down for good. With Charley down, Junior jumped on top of him and began to pound him around the head and neck.

Mr. Mac fired a round into the air from the pistol he carried on his hip.

"That's enough. It looks like old Charley is down for the count. Pull the kid off of him."

Several of the men pulled Junior off of the unconscious Charley.

"Come here, boy," Mr. Mac said.

Junior was covered with blood and dirt. His anger was only slowly beginning to subside.

"You're a fair fighter. Where did you learn to box?" Mr. Mac asked.

"Didn't."

"Well, for somebody who never learned to fight, you take pretty good care of yourself."

Junior nodded.

"You just whipped the third best heavyweight fighter in Bauxite. I was grooming old Charley to take over the top slot in three or four years. How would you like to come fight for me?" Mr. Mac asked.

Junior shrugged his shoulders.

"Is that a yes or a no?" the older man asked.

"What's in it for me?"

"First off, if you want out of the mines, I can get you a job as a Uke driver. And I feed my fighters real good—lots of steak and potatoes. By the way, we'll put about fifteen pounds on you and fight you as a heavyweight. You're fast enough and you can take a punch. Charley landed a couple of punches that would have put most people down. What do you say?"

"I'll think about it," Junior said.

"You better not take too much time. Charley isn't going to take kindly to being showed up in a fight. If you go back down in the mines, keep your eyes open."

The next morning, Junior showed up at Mr. Mac's office, saying he would take the offer. Being one of Mr. Mac's boys had a number of privileges. As a truck driver, he spent most of his time alone, and being above ground, he was not forced to be in contact with the black men in the mines. Being one of Mr. Mac's boys meant he was on the day shift, because his evenings were spent training.

The work at the gym was at least as hard as the mines. The first night he reported to the gym, Junior expected to be thrown into the ring with the other fighters. Instead, Mr. Mac looked at him and said, "Run to the railroad tracks in Bryant and back. I'll give you an hour and ten minutes."

An hour and eleven minutes later, Junior dragged his body back into the gym.

Mr. Mac's only response was "You're late; hit the bags."

By the time the evening was complete, Mr. Mac had run him through the bags, the rope climb, the heavy bag, and another sprint to the train depot and back. For the next few weeks, that was the extent of Junior's boxing career, and then one night, he came prepared to make the run to Bryant, and Mr. Mac told him to stay in the gym and stand behind him. For the rest of the night, there was no physical work; his job was to stand and listen to what the coach told the other fighters.

At the end of the evening, the coach turned to Junior.

"Did you learn anything tonight?"

Junior said nothing but nodded.

"Show me," the coach demanded. Mr. Mac crawled under the ropes and began to put on a pair of gloves. "Come on up here, boy. I haven't got all night."

Junior climbed into the ring and put on a pair of gloves.

"Now hit me," the coach said.

Junior positioned his hands and then took a jab at Mr. Mac.

The coach shielded the blow and landed a solid right to the boy's chin.

"I hope you can do better than that," the coach shouted.

Frustrated, Junior tried again, and this time, the coach landed one to his chest and another to his chin. The combination put Junior on the tarp.

The coach took off his gloves.

"Looks like you didn't listen very well," he said. "Get your gloves off and sprint to the depot and back. I'll give you eight minutes."

With that, he hit his stopwatch.

The training was hard, but Mr. Mac expected no more from anyone else than he did from himself. Occasionally, Mr. Mac would take the whole team out for roadwork. On those evenings, he ran backward in front of the men, making fun of each of them in one way or another. He had a nickname for each of them, and Junior—Sandy as Mr. Mac knew him—was called Sandman.

It was a month into Junior's training when Mr. Mac first let him into the ring with one of the other fighters. The other fighter was "Soapy" Hand, a veteran of the Bauxite boxing team. In the middle of the first round, Junior decked the veteran twice with solid punches to the mid section followed by a straight right jab.

After that evening Sandy "Sandman" Scroggins became a mainstay on the Bauxite Miners Boxing Team.

It was the first time that anyone had really ever expected anything from Junior Parkus, and he liked it.

CHAPTER 22

J. L. didn't know what to expect as he stepped down from the train onto the concrete platform. It was a cold winter day. A layer of sleet and snow covered the station and all of the surroundings.

A small, white sign hung over the doorway to the small depot, and it read BAUXITE, ARKANSAS. The loading dock was empty except for J. L. and the conductor. A young man in uniform with a patch on his arm that read WAR PRODUCTION BOARD stepped out through the glass door of the warm depot. As war had become more of a threat, these young men had replaced company security.

The young solider walked over to J. L.

"What's your business here in Bauxite?" he asked. "Do you have a job? Because if you don't, you need to get right back on the train."

J. L. pulled out his papers with his company ID card and held them out to his questioner. "I'm a chemical engineer. I'm here to work at the mines."

"That's an odd accent you have," the young man asked with a skeptical look on his face.

"I'm originally from Pittsburgh." J. L. realized that, as he traveled further south, his accented English became more apparent. First in Pittsburgh and then in East St. Louis, he sounded more or less the same as everyone else, but in the rural south, his classroom English set him apart.

"How about them Pirates?" the young man said.

"Oh, they'll do better next year," J. L. said.

"I'm a Cubs fan myself."

The solider handed him back his papers.

"Everything seems to be in order. The plant is behind the depot and straight down the road," he said, pointing south. "You'll come to a T in the road; that's Benton Town Road. The entrance to the plant is on your left.

The main office is just up the hill on the right. This snow pretty well brought everything to a standstill around here—at least for the day. These people around here don't do so well with snow and ice. If you see a car coming from any direction, give it a wide berth. The company decided it was cheaper just to declare an unofficial holiday. There aren't many people up there, but Maxine—she's the operator—will get you started. I'll call up and tell her you're coming. You need help with your bags?"

"No. All I've got are these two suitcases," J. L. said. "Thanks, anyway."

The young solider disappeared back into the warmth of the depot. The thought occurred to J. L. that he might never go home again. His mission in Bauxite had its dangers. All of the cloak-and-dagger stuff had turned out to be pretty routine in East St. Louis. There, he would secret a document out of the plant and ship it to Mexico. Here, it was different; this was more like the old west. If they caught a spy here, they would just string him up to the nearest tree, and no one would ever know.

Traveling on the trains from Pittsburgh and then St. Louis, J. L. had been amazed at the great expanses of open country in Ohio and Illinois. Parts of the country seemed to be almost unoccupied when compared to Austria. This might be his new home, this strange land with strange people and strange customs.

Before he had left Pittsburgh, his uncle had warned him not to make an issue of being part Jewish and to keep his mouth shut about race. Despite the differences, many things were the same, take for instance the relationship between Germany and Austria. The Germans considered themselves more civilized and intelligent than their neighbors to the south, much like the peoples of the north and east of the United States.

The ice and snow formed a thin, white blanket over everything in sight, and all was quiet except for the sound of the train whistle nearing the town of Benton, four miles down the road. Giant floodlights lit up the plant like an ice palace.

J. L. walked down the middle of a wide boulevard with the town on his right and the plant on his left. At the three-way stop stood a sign post with three large arrows: to the south was SHERIDAN, 20 MILES; to the west was BENTON, 4 MILES; and to the north, toward the train station, was PINE BLUFF, 40 MILES. On the Pine Bluff sign, someone had painted NEW YORK, 1000 MILES.

Sitting at the switchboard, Maxine turned her head and acknowledged J. L.'s presence.

"Yes, my name is Stein, J. L. Stein. I was told to report here. I'm the new chemical engineer from East St. Louis."

"Well, you're out of luck for the day. Everyone's gone home early except for some of the shift people, and they wouldn't know what to do with you." She reached into a file folder on her desk and removed a sheet of paper, made several marks on the paper, and then signed it.

"You take this over to Mr. Alred at the guesthouse just up the hill. He'll give you a room for the night." She handed him the voucher, good for one night's lodging and two meals. "He'll feed you and get you bedded down for the night. Be nice to that old man; he can make your life hell if he wants to.

"You will probably be in the guesthouse for a while. We don't have enough housing, and they haven't started building any new stuff yet. There is a rumor that they are going to build something over across the tracks, but so far, it is just rumor.

"By the way, this plant turns out almost as many rumors as it does tons of bauxite. Don't believe anything until you see it with your own eyes.

"If you need anything, my family and I live at 220 Center Street just across the road and up the hill.

"You need to be here tomorrow at eight thirty. The people in personnel will get your paperwork started. Better be ready for a busy day. Since those War Production Board people got here, we've all been on pins and needles. They look at everything. They'll have to get your fingerprints and take a picture. They put the picture on a badge, and I guarantee you won't get in that gate without your badge. My father-in-law, Jeff Davis, sees to that."

"Your father-in-law?" J. L. asked.

"Yeah, he's the constable, and during the day, he works the front gate," she said. "If he doesn't know you, you won't get in."

"Sounds like you folks have a pretty good security system."

"Yeah, I'd say we do. I'm not sure why. We been through the two depressions, a war, and the Wobbles, and nothing's happened yet."

"Well, this is a different world we live in these days," he said.

"Yeah, I guess you're right."

A bald old man was in the kitchen cooking supper. J. L. rang the bell on the front counter, and the old man looked up from his stove.

"The lady over at the main office sent me over here. Said I should talk to Mr. Alred," J. L. said.

"That would be me. What do you need?" the bald-headed man asked.

J. L. handed him the voucher.

"I need a room for the night."

"Damn-it-to-hell, these people must think I'm Houdini," Alred said. "I can't make rooms appear out of thin air. You and half the people in eastern Saline County need a room. Worse, they send you over here on a day when it's snowing and none of my colored help showed up. I'm half a mind to quit this job, buy a tin cup, sit on the street, and beg. You'd think, if they can organize the digging and shipping of all that ore, the least they would be able to do is provide housing for their people."

"You mean you don't have a room?" J. L. asked.

"Well, yes and no. Lucy Dodge—I mean Storer, her name was Dodge, but she married Jim Storer, one of the assistant managers over at the plant. She moved out yesterday, and I haven't had a chance to clean her room yet. She moved over to Silk Stocking Row on the other side of the community hall. She is schoolteacher. Good-looker, too. That's how she got Storer. She timed her walk every day. Really, I don't know whether it was her doing the timing or him, but every day, they passed right down there on Benton Road. His wife died a couple of years back, about the time Lucy came to town. One of the other girls told me that she set her sights on Storer the minute she got here.

"The other thing is that I got a waiting list for that room. What do you do at the plant?" he asked.

"I'm a chemical engineer," J. L. said.

"You got a degree?" Alred asked.

"Yes sir, I do."

"Well, that pulls you up the list. You'll find that there is a pecking order around here. If there is another engineer on the list with more time in the company, he gets the room, but I don't think there is.

"Anyway, if you will help me clean the room, we will have a room at least for the night. It's free for the first night, then it is one dollar a night—that includes a room, breakfast, supper, and a late-night sandwich for those who work the three-to-eleven shift. The rules are no alcohol in the guesthouse, and I would encourage you not to be seen drinking around town. Jeff Davis, the constable, will haul you up, try you, convict you, and fine you in about fifteen minutes."

"Speaking of having a drink, where can a man get a drink in town?" J. L. asked.

"Well, we don't have any bars in town, but from what I'm told, liquor is easy to come by. There is a fellow over at Paron, who makes deliveries. Kind of like a milkman. If you end up in a house that has a sleeping porch, you just leave your empties on the steps, and he drops off the full ones. Late at night, you can hear his clinking bottles all over town. The people who use his services have accounts, and he collects at the end of the month.

"Now you understand, that's what I've been told. Never used his service myself." This last he said with a twinkle in his eye. "You can buy beer and wine over in Benton. There are a couple of bars downtown. One is in the pool hall, and there's the Spot out on Military. If you're heading into Little Rock, there is a little place that a lot of the boys like called the Red Gate."

"What about Hot Springs?" J. L. asked.

"That's a long way to go for a beer."

"A friend from East St. Louis told me about it. Said it was a fun place to go—horse racing, gambling, women—you know?"

"Unless you got a car, the easiest way to get there is to take the bus to Benton and take the train over to Hot Springs. Better be careful; there are some rough folks over there. You get on some of those people's bad sides, and you'll end up at the bottom of Lake Hamilton."

J. L. already knew what to expect in Hot Springs. Before leaving Illinois, he had been instructed to go to Hot Springs and find the Spa City Cigar Store on Central Avenue. He was supposed to ask for Tommy.

"I know you been traveling all day," Alred said, "but if you feel like it, the fights start at seven over at the community hall.

Five miles down the road in downtown Benton, Larry Fitts was admiring his new truck. It was sitting out in front of his store and covered with a layer of fresh snow. Larry decided that when the weather dried up, he would build a shed for his newly acquired truck.

The truck wasn't really new, even to him—he had driven it for twelve years. Mr. Sims, the coroner and undertaker had decided that the 1925 Dodge was no longer appropriate for funerals and had purchased a brand new Ford truck that had been converted to an ambulance and hearse. Larry had worked as the ambulance driver for Sims for the last twelve years. He convinced Sims to let him have the old truck and work it out in services. As time had gone on, Larry had found it inconvenient and costly to depend on Bullet Hyten of Niloak Pottery or Sims to deliver his products. The day that he took possession of the truck, Larry took it down to Thomas Auto and had them paint, in large white letters, FITTS CUSTOM POTTERY AND FURNITURE.

In the early thirties, Larry had befriended Jack Eggy, the old man who lived on the corner of Market and River streets. The old man had suffered a stroke and couldn't care for himself. Dr. Gann, who lived just two doors down on South Market, had suggested to Eggy that he ask Larry to move in with him and help take care of him. Eggy had no other family, and when he died, Larry inherited the land and house. He sold the house to one of the local builders with the stipulation that it be moved, and with the money from the house, he had built his building.

He had worked part-time for Sims at the funeral home, driving the ambulance and building caskets and furniture. Part-time, he had also helped Bullet Hyten at the Niloak kiln. In exchange for his work, Bullet had allowed him to fire his pieces of pottery at the same time. He had discovered that there was a lot more to making a living as a potter or furniture builder than making his product and setting it on the shelf for sale. He had never been in danger of going hungry, but at the same time, he wasn't making anything.

He was standing in front of his truck when Dr. Gann Sr. came walking up the street.

"See you bought you a truck," he said. "Looks like Sims's old ambulance."

"It is. He's got a new one. I figured now was as good a time as any to buy me a truck. I know this old truck backwards and forwards. He gave me a good deal. I don't need anything new like he does. This one isn't like those new ones. I can fix anything that breaks on this thing with baling wire and glue. Those new ones got all that complicated equipment; you spend more money keeping them running than you pay for them."

"How's your business doing?" the doctor asked.

"Oh, it's okay," Larry said. "I don't make much, but then again, I don't spend much."

"Well, any time you get tired of being your own boss, there are any number of people in this town who will take this building off your hands."

"Doc, this is the first time in my life that I ever had or thought I'd have anything that was my own. Things would have to get awful bad for me to close up shop and go back to working full-time for somebody else. The folks in this town have been good to me, but one of the things that Eggy told me before he died stuck with me. I was moaning and bitching about how hard life was and how unfair everything was. He just laughed at me and told me to quit feeling sorry for myself and get off my butt and do something about it. 'If you don't take no risks, you ain't gonna get nowhere,' he said, and he was right. I may go through some bad times, but I am going to make a go of my art and this business. If I don't, at least I'll go down trying."

"I wish my son had a dose of your gumption," the doctor said, shaking his head. "By the way, how are you boys going to do at the fights over in Bauxite tonight?"

"Don't know, Doc. They got this boy fighting in the heavyweight division that I'm told is fast as greased lighting."

"You talking about that the guy they call Sandman?"

"Yeah. How do you know about him?" Larry asked.

"I've seen the product of his work. He worked over an old boy from Sheridan a couple of weeks ago. That kid didn't walk straight for a week. Who are you going to throw in the ring with that kid?" the doctor asked.

"Don't know for sure. Tubby Burks is our best boxer, but he can't take a punch. There is this country boy from up at Kentucky Church that I'm taking with me. His name is Sam Duvall. He's not scared of anything, and he weighs in right around three hundred pounds. I might just throw him in at the last minute. It makes Mr. Mac mad that I won't send him a lineup in advance."

"Well, I hope you guys don't need my services tonight."

"Me, too," Larry said as he crossed his fingers.

Down the hill from the guesthouse was the community hall. Bauxite was a company town with its fair share of churches, a school, a movie theater, a post office, a small golf course, and a hospital. Surrounding the central core of the town were a number of semi permanent neighborhoods with names like Sand Hill, Pine Haven, Swamp Poodle, Crumby, Dirt Dauber, the Woodlands, Mexico, and Alabama Camp.

After eating a bite and getting settled into his room, J. L. walked down the street, turning onto Silk Stocking Row, where all of the managers lived. On the left was the community hall. It was a big, white, two-story affair with large antebellum columns. Out on the front lawn, someone had started a fire in an old barrel. There was a small group of black men standing around the fire, warming their hands and smoking.

J. L. walked through the large double doors that led into the entry hall. On the left was a small table where a pretty young lady was selling admission to the night's fights. In front of J. L. were two old men, who complained about the fact that they had to pay.

"In the old days, they never charged us to get into our own hall. Damn place is going to hell in a hand basket if you ask me," the first old man said.

"Well, stupid, I guess they didn't feel like they had to ask you, did they? Now pay your money, and let's get in there, so we can get a seat before it fills up," the second old man said.

The two men paid their money, and the young lady behind the table stamped their hands with a small, red ink stamp.

The noise was beginning to build inside the hall. J. L. worked his way through a second set of double doors. In the center of the hall, a makeshift ring was surrounded on all sides by bleachers ten rows high. There were small, high balconies with three rows each on two sides of the hall. The hall was packed, with every seat filled. There was a small contingent of Benton supporters, but most of the hall was filled with miners. On the far wall of the hall in the most distant corner of the balcony was a small area roped off for blacks.

J. L. worked his way around the ring until he found a place he could stand and get an unobstructed view of the ring. He was standing next to a tall, bald-headed miner. The man acknowledged J. L. and offered him a cigarette.

"You new around here? Ain't seen you before," the man said.

"Name is Stein. I'm a new engineer with the company."

The man stuck out his hand.

"I'm L. T. Barnes. I work for the B & N Railroad. When did you get here?"

"Just today."

"Well, you ought to enjoy this. Mr. Mac is one of the best fight managers in the south, and he's always got a good team. Coach "Gimpy" Fitts from Benton never has a good fighting team. Now don't get me wrong; they're always good at baseball, but they can't fight their way out of a paper bag. The fun part about this Benton team is to see what screwball thing Fitts comes up with next." The man pointed toward Larry. "See the riding pants and the safari hat that Gimpy is wearing? Nobody in the county wears those things except Mr. Mac. Gimpy just does it as a joke just to see if he can get Mr. Mac's goat. The other thing he does is change the lineup at the last minute, and that pisses Mr. Mac off. One night, he tried to throw a woman in the ring against one of Mr. Mac's fighters."

While the two men talked, Mr. Mac and Gimpy handed the referee a sheet of fighters. McNeil, the referee, looked at both men and asked if they were both okay with the changes. Gimpy grinned, and Mr. Mac nodded.

"Ladies and gentlemen, we have had change on the program for the night. Instead of Tubby Burks fighting in the heavyweight division against Sandy 'Sandman' Scroggins, Sam 'the Mountain' Duvall will be substituted.

"We will begin with the lightweight fight in ten minutes."

The arena was heavy with smoke, and the noise was deafening. The first three fights were easily won by the Bauxite team. The first fight was a total knockout or TKO after two rounds. The second went to a four-round decision, and the middleweight fight was won with three punches in the first round.

Sandy "Sandman" Scroggins had become a crowd favorite. He was small for a heavyweight, but he was fast and could take a punch. Rumors had begun to circulate that Mr. Mac was going to take him professional, like he had with Lloyd Montgomery a few years before.

Sam Duvall weighed in at 350 pounds. His fight career consisted of three fights—all of which had taken place in the town of Sandy Banks on the banks of the Green River. The last fight was why Duvall had moved to the Kentucky Church Community. Sam was on the giving end of a punch that resulted in the death of one Paul Hodge. Paul's family was one of mussel shell divers on the Green River, and they had vowed revenge for his death. Sam was shipped off to the hill country to help prevent a war between the two families.

McNeil called the two men to the center of the ring. The contrast between the two fighters could not have been greater. Sam was a giant of a man with coarse features, a big head, a prominent brow, and a thick neck. His long arms hung almost to his mid-thigh.

In comparison, Sandy appeared to have been chiseled out of stone. Standing beside the big fighter, he looked like a child. Mr. Mac had trained him day and night; there wasn't an ounce of fat on him, and every muscle he had was finely tuned.

"No hitting below the belt," McNeil said, "and when I say break, I mean break. Now have a good fight. Fighters, go to your corners."

Back in the corner, Mr. Mac advised his fighter.

"Stay out of this guy's reach. His arms hang down halfway to his knees. Get in a few licks and then back out. Go for the head. You could pound him with body blows all day long and never make a dent."

Sandy nodded as he put in his mouthpiece.

The bell rang. Sandy was on his feet and in the middle of the ring as Sam rose from his stool. Before Sam could get his hands into a defensive position, Sandy threw two quick punches to his face and took three steps back. The second blow was a sharp right that caught Sam just above the left eye and opened a small bleeder. The partisan crowd went wild.

The rest of the first round, the two men sparred, each landing a few blows, but no one was hurt.

"Score one for us. You're doing good," Mr. Mac said as Sandy sat down on the stool and spit out his mouthpiece. "But watch out for that right hand."

When the bell for the second round sounded, Sam was on his feet and heading for Sandy's corner. For the first half of the round, Sandy couldn't get out of his way. The big man came in close and began to pound on Sandy's middle. Any punches that Sandy landed had no strength. This quieted the crowd, and by everyone's count, the second round went to the big man.

In round three, the two men stood in the center of the ring and matched blow for blow—Sam pounding on Sandy's middle, and Sandy going to the face with jabs and hooks.

Back in the corner after the round was over, Mr. Mac summed it up. "It's pretty well even, unless we get a break. Keep after his face."

When the fourth and final round began, both men squared up and began to exchange punches. The question was: Would one of them come up with a lucky punch? As the time ran down in the round, it looked like there would be a draw. Just before the bell, Sam pushed Sandy against the ropes, and just after the bell sounded, he hit him with a solid right to the jaw. For years, the Bauxite loyal would contend that it was a late blow. Whether it was a late shot or not, Sandy crumpled to the mat and was out.

Mr. Mac quickly made it into the ring and began to administer smelling salts to his fighter. Sandy began to come around, and soon, they moved him to his corner.

At a Bauxite-Benton match, there was no such thing as a neutral observer, but most of the crowd had the two fighters at a dead heat until the last blow.

When Sandy recuperated enough to be brought to the middle of the ring, McNeil grabbed both men by the hand. Sam was on his left, and Sandy was on his right. The announcer came to the center of the ring and held his hand up to quiet the crowd.

"The judges awarded thirty-six points to Sam Duvall, a two-point penalty for a late hit for a total of thirty-four, and thirty-five points to Sandman. The winner is Sandy 'Sandman' Scroggins."

There was a roar from the crowd that shook the rafters. The instant Sam realized that the decision had gone against him, he used the referee as a fulcrum and came around with a left-handed haymaker, landing a glancing blow to Sandy's jaw. The smaller man went stumbling back against the ropes.

The miner standing beside J. L. grinned and said, "Here we go. Now the real fight begins."

"What do you mean?" J. L. asked.

"I mean, this one will be finished up out front. Around here, fights never end on a dirty blow."

As they were talking, all of the spectators began to file out of the arena, heading for the frozen front lawn.

In Sandy's corner, Mr. Mac was talking to his fighter.

"I'm not going to stand in your way, but you won the fight, and you don't have to go out there and fight again."

Sandy did not reply. He completed removing his gloves, stood up, and looked over at the other corner.

"Hey, you, lard ass, I'll see you out front."

Sandy stepped through the ropes and walked toward the front door. As he did, the crowd parted and gave him a path.

There were no rules to a grudge match. Constable Jeff Davis was the only thing that resembled a referee, and his most important job was to make sure that no one got killed. The fight started when the first man threw a punch and ended when one man was left standing.

The two men squared off and began to exchange blows. Soon, the snow and mud that covered the front lawn was mixed with blood, most of which was coming from Duvall's right eye. With the blood and swelling around the eye, his vision was limited.

When it was obvious that Sandy, with his blows to the face, was getting the upper hand, Duvall rushed him, pushing the smaller man backward, overturning the fire barrel that had been used earlier as a hand warmer. Coals and large pieces of charred and burning wood were then mixed with the mud, snow, and blood. Duvall, seeing an opportunity, fell on the recumbent Sandy and began to beat him around the head. Sandy picked up a piece of the burning kindling and hit the larger man upside the head. The bigger man was stunned, giving Sandy the chance to push him off. While Duvall was holding the side of his head, Sandy began to kick him in the face. When Duvall moved to protect his face, Sandy began to pound on his chest wall. Soon it became apparent that Duvall was not going to get up, but Sandy continued to pound.

When Larry Fitts realized that Sandy wasn't going to quit, he moved in and began to shout at him to stop, but Sandy continued to pound on the unconscious Duvall. It was at that point that Constable Davis moved in to stop the fight. In the end, it took five men to pull Sandy off of the unconscious Duvall.

Larry and his other fighters loaded Duvall into the converted ambulance and took off for Benton.

Soon, the only people left on the front lawn were Sandy and his coach.

"You're a good fighter, boy. But you are going to have to learn some control," the coach said. "Let's take you in and get you cleaned up."

He helped the fighter to his feet and walked him back into the community hall.

CHAPTER 23

It was a slow day at Sims Furniture and Undertaking. Mr. Jim Sims and John Hampton, the black man who kept the store clean and assisted Sims with the bodies, had just finished the embalming of an elderly woman. Larry Fitts was watching the store and working on a mantelpiece that Dr. Gann had asked him to carve.

Sims emerged from the back of the store, adjusting his tie. As usual, he was immaculate. He was dressed in a black suit, black tie, and freshly starched, white shirt, and he had a spit shine on his shoes.

"Larry, if you expect to be successful in business," he said as he took a cloth to the toes of his shoes, "you'll need to dress the part. It's not that you aren't neat and clean, mind you, but everything you wear looks like a workman's uniform. If you'd go over to Gingles, Henry Brown would have you fixed up in no time."

Larry looked up from his carving and smiled. This was speech number twenty-five; he heard it once a month.

"How about I buy you some lunch?" Sims asked. "I need to talk to you."

"Yes, sir, have I done something wrong?" Larry asked.

"No, son, you haven't done anything wrong. I need you to do something for me."

Sims walked over to the telephone behind the cash register and picked it up.

"Minnie," he said into the phone, "give me the house. I need to talk to my wife." He stood waiting for a few seconds and then continued, "Won't be home for lunch. You and the girls go on and eat. I got some work to take care of." He paused. "No, my leg is okay," he said. "Yeah, I'll talk to Dr. Gann about it today. Love you, and I'll see you tonight. Bye." Sims put down the phone and then walked toward the back door. There was a noticeable limp when he walked. "John," he shouted, "Larry and I will be over at the Lone Star. Come get me if you need anything."

Sims was known for three things. First, he was a very thorough man who never left anything undone. Second, he was always serious, and recently, he seemed to be more so. Third, he was tight as a preacher's hatband. For Jim Sims to offer to pay for lunch was a big deal and suggested that something big must be up.

The Lone Star Café was two doors down from the funeral home. The two men walked down to the café and found a seat in the back. Jo Ragan, the waitress, brought a couple of menus, a pair of roll-ups, and two glasses of iced tea.

"What can I do for you two gentleman this fine day?" she asked.

Larry looked at the handwritten list of specials attached to the top of the bound menu. "I'll have roast, mashed potatoes with gravy, and green beans."

Jim put his menu down. "Make that two, except hold the gravy."

Jim took a drink of his tea and then said, "You know, Larry, my job as the Coroner means that I'm the FBI identification officer, and that has put me in an interesting situation. That file cabinet that sits over in the corner of my office has the fingerprints of every person who has died in Saline County in the last ten years. The other day, two fellows from the Federal Bureau came down from Little Rock. When they called and said they wanted to come down, they wouldn't say what it was about. I was worried that they were getting ready to indict one of our local politicians, and I really didn't want to get involved. Anyway, what they wanted had nothing to do with our politicians; it had to do with this fellow, Hitler, over in Germany. They asked me to keep a file on any unusual people who might show up here in Benton."

"What in the world would anybody be interested in Benton, Arkansas, for?" Larry said, laughing.

"That's what I asked. Why Benton? They pointed out that any war in the future will be won with air power, and airplanes are made from aluminum. Bauxite is the only place in the continental US with any real reserve of bauxite ore. Most of the bauxite that we use right now comes from high-grade sources in Surinam and Jamaica. If we ever go to war with someone who has a big navy—Germany for instance—they could shut down our ability to produce aluminum.

"They want me to watch out for anybody who looks suspicious. At one time or another, I've been in just about every house in the county. The problem for me is there is a whole group of people that I never have any contact with. Now, I don't say this in an accusing fashion, but you run with a different crowd. I need your help. When people drink, their tongues get loose. If any of that rough crowd you run with starts talking about things that would help, I need you to tell me."

"You mean you need me to spy on my friends," Larry said, shaking his head. "I don't know if I can do that."

"Listen, son, if they're spies, then they aren't your friends. Do you know what I mean?" the older man said.

"Yeah, I guess you're right, but I still don't feel comfortable with it."

"Well, you think about it, and if something comes up—anything—please let me know."

"I'll think about it."

The idea of spying on his friends didn't sit right with Larry. When people drank, they often said stuff that was outrageous and, at times, just an outright lie. There were more than a few people who didn't like Mr. Roosevelt. Back in '35, one of the old men at the courthouse had crowed about the fact that, if the train with the president stopped at the station, he could save the country a lot of pain just by shooting that Jew from the East Coast.

On a different level, Larry had no interest in politics. For the first time, he truly enjoyed his life. With his pottery building complete, he had moved into the back and spent all of his free time and money on his pots and custom furniture. Furniture-making was becoming a major industry in the little country town. McCoy-Couch was dominant in the upholstered goods, and Owosso had converted from the pallet business to wooden furniture. From time to time, someone needed a special piece, and that was where he came in. Larry's reputation had grown quickly, and soon, his one-of-a-kind pieces with intricate carvings were in demand.

Working for Sims was a source of steady income, and Sims was desperate to have him continue working, because he was reliable, but there were several points of conflict between the two men. Larry's lack of desire to have anything to do with the preparation of the bodies would eventually lead to his replacement, but it was Larry's choice of friends and his drinking that Sims complained about more than anything. Sims received regular reports of Larry's adventures at the Red Gate Tavern at the county line. When old man Payor was picked up for bootlegging, there was a question for a while as to whether Larry might get charged as well.

On his weekends off, Larry caught the train to Hot Springs, fishing on Lake Hamilton and enjoying the pleasures of Central Avenue.

It was Larry's contacts in Hot Springs that Sims what to take advantage of. The city of Hot Springs was a haven for the crime elements from up north. The bosses of the various gangs declared it a neutral ground, where they could all go for a time out. That didn't mean that their business was curtailed, only the killing. The Southern Club, the Vapors, the big hotels with their baths, and the racetrack were all places that the criminal element tended to congregate. Sims's thinking was that, if spying were to take place, it almost certainly would begin there.

CHAPTER 24

A poem written by an anonymous source on a piece of toilet paper found in
Mauthausen:

> Deal another hand,
> please.
> if you don't mind.
>
> We could
> you know,
> just start over again
>
> all of us,
> everybody

Junior was sitting at the back table against the east wall, where there
was very little light, when Bill came into the Red Gate Tavern. Until his
eyes adjusted to the light, Bill didn't see his son. When he did spot him, Bill
worked his way over to the table.

"What happened to you?" Bill said as he looked at his son's black and
blue face.

"I won the fight. The other guy looked worse than me," Junior said.

"What in the hell are you doing fighting?" Bill asked.

"It wasn't a fight. It was a boxing match." Junior hadn't bothered to tell
his father about his boxing career. Bill had always frowned on sports as a
waste of time.

"What are you doing boxing?" Bill replied.

"Coach Mac says I'm the best heavyweight fighter he's ever had."

"Wait a minute. Start from the first. What's this all about?" Bill demanded.

Junior explained to his father how he had ended up on the boxing team.

"Okay, now think about this, son," Bill said, interrupting him. "Your job is to spy for us. Your job is not to be noticed. Now you tell me how you plan on not being noticed when you're the "best heavyweight fighter" in Bauxite."

"Listen, Dad, since I've been on the boxing team, I'm no longer doing grunt work in the mines. I'm up above ground, driving a truck all over the place. The minute something new happens, I can see it and report it. My coach is the chief engineer of the mines. I'm in and out of his office at least twice a day."

Bill wasn't convinced, but he was seeing a side of his son he had never seen before.

"I really don't think I like this idea of you drawing attention to yourself. Remember, boy, this isn't about you. This is about our mission. The minute this boxing starts getting in the way of the mission, I want you to drop it like a hot potato."

"Sure, of course I will," Junior said. He didn't bother to tell his father that the coach was talking about taking him professional.

Larry Fitts spotted the two men sitting over against the wall. He ordered a couple of extra beers and took them over to the table where Bill and Junior sat.

"What do you want?" Bill said as he looked up at Larry.

"I just wanted to buy the Sandman a drink so he'd know there weren't any hard feelings about the other night," Larry said.

"Go to hell. We don't want your damn beers. Now get out of here; we're having a private conversation," Bill said.

"Pardon the hell out of me," Larry said as he turned back toward the bar. He set the two extra beers down on the bar and turned to the bartender. "Do you know that guy with the Sandman?" Larry asked.

The bartender looked over toward the men at the darkened table.

"Can't see him real clear, but I don't think it's anybody I know," he said.

"Well, whoever he is, he is a real jerk."

CHAPTER 25

When he was a child, Helena had regaled J. L. with stories about America, about New York City and the Statue of Liberty, about Washington DC, the capital of freedom. He had seen newsreels of the American South with its plantations and cypress swamps with large alligators, of New Orleans with its French-Spanish sensibility and pleasures. He had seen movies of the American West with cowboys and Indians, great herds of longhorn cattle, and buffalo roaming the grand prairies.

Bauxite, Arkansas, was none of these; it was a no-nonsense place where the reason for existence was bauxite ore. The town had not been there forty years before, and when the ore played out, it would be gone. There was no sense of history, because there was no history, except for what the town and its people could contribute today. Though the United States was not at war, everyone who worked and lived in the small community knew, without a shadow of a doubt, that he was contributing to a war effort.

Benton, on the other hand, only five miles down the road, had been a place for over a century—not much of a place but a place nonetheless. Sitting on the banks of the Saline River, Benton had begun as a river crossing, but it had quickly moved up the hill away from the river to get away from floods, mosquitoes, and malaria. When the railroad came through in the late nineteenth century, Benton had been at the center of a flourishing timber and furniture industry. The other principle reason for its existence was the presence of a blue clay called kaolin. By the beginning of the twentieth century, there were six active commercial potteries in the hills around Benton. Bullet Hyten, Karl Stein's friend, was among that group of people.

Mr. Alred had been correct in stating that housing was at a premium in Bauxite, and new housing wasn't high on the priority list. It took a short time for J. L. to realize that living at the guesthouse was worse than living with his uncle in Pittsburgh. Alred was determined that everything would be done just so, and all the rules would be obeyed. J. L. could have tolerated that for a while, but it became increasingly clear that Alred was in and out of the rooms each day, checking on the conditions.

In the old days, that wouldn't have bothered J. L.; after all, he had been raised in the Oldenberg with more than twenty women—there was no such thing as personal space or privacy. Now, however, he had a new role in life that demanded privacy and secrecy. In East St. Louis, he had devoted a small closet in the back of his apartment to all of his transcriptions and letters. After the first two days at the guesthouse, he purchased several small locks and put them on his bags.

On his first day off, J. L. took the morning bus into Benton to look for a place to live. Most of the men on the bus were returning home from a night at the mines; they got priority in seating. J. L. was the last one on the bus, and when he boarded, there was only one seat left. A tall, thin man with narrow, sloping shoulders was sitting near the back. He was covered with a grey-pink dust that gave him a ghostly appearance. With his hard hat removed, the top of his bald head was the only clean spot on his body.

"One back here," he shouted from the back of the bus when he saw J. L. looking to see if there was a seat.

J. L. acknowledged him with a wave of his hand.

"Have a seat," the man motioned to J. L.

"Thanks," J. L. said.

"Don't sit too close, or you'll look like me by the time we get to Benton. Name is Manuel Tyson," he said.

"J. L. Stein," he said. "Nice to meet you."

"You one of those new engineers they bringing in to work the mines?" Manuel asked.

J. L. was a little surprised that he was so easy to spot.

"Yeah, I've been in East St Louis for the last few years, working in research."

"Knowing this company, they're liable to put you in the typing pool. Me, I was a diesel mechanic with Rock Island back in the twenties. I thought maybe these folks would have put me to working on the B & N, their little railroad; but no, they put me to work doing grunt labor in the mines. Go figure."

J. L. grinned at the man.

"Well, for the time being, they got me working in administration. It reminds me of working in personnel in Pittsburgh, but we'll see what happens. I really would like to get out and get my hands dirty doing some real work."

"Don't worry, it's hard not to get your hands dirty in this place," Manuel said. "What with the rain we've had recently, there hasn't hardly been any dust. When it dries out in the summer, this place is just one big cloud of dust."

"What do you know about places to live in Benton?" J. L. asked.

"They are few and far between, and from what I hear, you pay top dollar for next to nothing," Manuel said.

"I guess I'll get a copy of the paper and see if there's anything available," J. L. said.

Manuel shook his head.

"By the time it gets in the paper, it either ain't fit to live in or the folks are awful proud of what they got. If I was looking, I'd look on the bulletin board in the Lone Star Café or go talk to Jim Sims at Sims's funeral home."

"Why the funeral home?" J. L. asked, a bit surprised.

"Mr. Sims is the coroner, undertaker, furniture maker, and business man. He knows every time somebody is born, dies, moves in, or moves out in this town. Now, if Sims can't help you, my nephew, Larry Fitts, probably can."

"Why does that name ring a bell?" J. L. asked.

"Were you here for the big fight a few weeks ago?" Manuel asked.

"Yeah."

"His name is Larry Fitts, but they call him Coach Gimpy," Manuel said.

"Oh, yeah, the guy in the safari getup," J. L. said, smiling. "If you don't mind me asking, how did he get the name Coach Gimpy?"

"Boy was born with a clubfoot, and when he was about sixteen, he damn near lost his good leg falling off a cotton wagon over in the river bottoms. Anyway, to make a long story short, he ended up living with my wife and me over at the mines for a while. That didn't last long, and he come over here to Benton and went to work for Sims at the funeral home.

"One day, he was down at the baseball field, and one of the teams was short a player, so he filled in. Turned out he wasn't a very good player, 'cause he runs like a wounded deer, but he was one hell of a coach. Somebody starting calling him the Gimp, and that became Coach Gimpy.

"I'm real proud of that boy. Nobody from that side of my family ever amounted to anything, except for that kid. He can do anything he puts his mind to. He carves, makes furniture, and is a great potter. He's got him a nice little shop over on Market Street catty-corner from the Baptist church. Even works part-time for Bullet down at Niloak."

"You talking about ... wait a minute," J. L. reached into his pocket and pulled out a slip of paper. "Are you talking about Bullet Hyten?"

"Yeah, that's the guy."

"My uncle, who lives in Pittsburgh, told me to look that fellow up, said he was a really good potter," J. L. said.

"Now, you got to understand I ain't never met the man, but I hear tell he's a good fellow. Larry speaks real high of him. The problem I got is why would anyone want to spend that much money for something you pour water out of—no matter how pretty it is?"

J. L. just smiled.

"By the way, friend," Manuel continued, "if you need a place to stay till you find a room, we can always fit in one more. Me and the wife got about six or seven kids; I can't ever keep track, but one more wouldn't be noticed."

"I really do appreciate that, but I got a room at the guesthouse for the time being," J. L. said.

"Finding it a little hard to get along with Alred?" Manuel asked, smiling. "That's okay, so does everybody else."

As they were talking, the bus came to a stop at the station at the northeast corner of Main and Sevier streets. All of the tired miners got up out of their seats. It was hard to tell how old the men were because of the layer of dust and grim on their work clothes, but most moved with a slow, stiff gait.

Manuel and J. L. were the last to file out of the bus. Manuel pointed south on Main.

"The Lone Star is in the next block on the other side of the jail, and the funeral home is just beyond it."

"Thanks, Mr. Tyson, you've been a great help," J. L. said, offering his hand.

Manuel accepted the offered handshake. "You don't have to call me Mr. Tyson; it's Manuel. And remember, the offer of a room still stands if you don't find something."

"Thanks again," J. L. said.

When he had been a child in Florisdorf across the river from the old part of Vienna, people had looked out for each other. No one had anything extra, but they never thought about being poor. There was always enough to eat, a warm place to sleep, and friends. New York, Pittsburgh, and East St. Louis were different; you were on your own, sink or swim, live or die. Now, here, in the country in rural Arkansas, a total stranger had just offered him a room in his house. *I like this place,* J. L. thought to himself.

Across Sevier and a few doors down was the Lone Star Café. J. L. had left Bauxite early and missed breakfast, so he was hungry. He went in to the café, found a table near the front so he could look out onto the street in front, and sat down. The waitress came up to the table and automatically put down a glass of water and a cup of coffee.

"You want cream with your coffee, sweetie?" she asked.

"No, thank you," J. L. said.

"What do you want to eat?" she asked.

"Got anything special?" he asked.

"Yeah, we do. Got a fresh ham just yesterday," she said.

"How about a piece of that ham, a couple of fried eggs—over easy—and biscuits and gravy?"

"Sounds like a winner," she said. "Have it for you in a couple of minutes."

"I hear you folks have a bulletin board with places to rent?" J. L. asked.

"Yeah, it's back on the wall by the restroom," she said, pointing toward the back of the café. "But I don't think there's anything new."

"Thanks."

Most of the items on the bulletin board were beginning to look a little frayed around the edges. There were a few business cards from drummers who made the café part of their circuits, two or three old cars for sale, and one item that caught his attention. It read: ROOM FOR RENT, REASONABLE RATE, VERY QUIET. 860 BAUXITE HIGHWAY.

J. L. took the note down from the board and took it back to his table. He sat back down at the table just as the waitress brought his plate of food. She smiled at the note on the table.

"I'd be real cautious about even going out to talk to them folks. He's as crazy as a three-eyed flea. That crap about quiet is true only if you are deaf. The old man's deaf, and he's beginning to lose his mind. He hollers at that poor wife of his day and night."

"Thanks for the head's up," J. L. said.

J. L. ate his breakfast, paid for his meal, and walked back out onto the street. There was a constant stream of traffic in front of the café.

Two doors south of the café was Sims's Furniture and Undertaking. The store was quiet. Back in the middle of the store was a desk, and behind the desk, a man sat, whittling on a piece of hickory. He had a burlap sack spread out on the floor to catch the shavings. The wood was a piece of a hickory limb that had grown in a twisted fashion. He had carved away enough of the wood to reveal the face of a lovely young girl with long, flowing hair that draped off her left shoulder. She was looking backward over her shoulder and smiling. He was totally immersed in his work as J. L. walked up.

"Good morning," J. L. said.

"Sorry, good morning. I didn't hear you come through the door," the man said.

"Don't let me interrupt you," J. L. said. He walked over and took a closer look at the carving.

"You're not interrupting anything. I'm just piddling around."

"That is really nice work," J. L. said, pointing at the carving. "This may seem really stupid to you, but how do you know where to start. I mean, I have trouble sharpening a pencil," J. L. said.

"Really, it's simple. You just cut away the part that's not supposed to be there," he said. He pointed at the figure he was holding. "This is Marty, the best short-stop, male or female, in Saline county and, in addition, one of the prettiest and smartest girls to set foot in Saline county in the last half century. She works for Bullet Hyten at Niloak and has the prettiest red hair. I see her face in everything I pick up. I think I may use this as a model for a piece of pottery. The idea would be to have her with her arms surrounding the top and her hair sweeping down around the vase. It would be a little hard to do, but I think I can make it work."

"My name is Stein, J. L. Stein," J. L. said, extending his hand.

"Larry Fitts."

"You're the coach, right?" J. L. asked.

"Yeah," he said.

"I just met your uncle Manuel on the way in from the mines," J. L. said. "He really bragged about you."

"He and his wife are two of the dearest people in the whole world. If it hadn't been for them, I would have ended up on the street begging after I hurt my good leg. The rest of our family ain't worth shooting." Larry put the wood carving down on the desk and began to clean up his mess. "But my guess is you didn't come in here to talk about my pedigree. May I help you with a piece of furniture or some bedding?"

"I may need some stuff later, but right now, I'm looking for a place to stay. I was told that Mr. Sims or you might be able to help me."

"You looking for a house or a room?" Larry asked.

"Well, I would rather have something like an apartment. My experience with rooms in someone's home hasn't worked out really well," J. L. said.

"The man you really need to talk to is Mr. Sims. If there is anything out there, he'll know about it. He and John L. are finishing up on a body. He should be out here in a few minutes."

As if on cue, Jim Sims came walking out of a door near the back of the store. He was immaculately dressed in a navy blue suit. He stopped at a small mirror and gave his hair one last stroke with his wooden comb. Out of the corner of his eye, he noticed Larry and J. L. on the opposite side of the store. He turned and began walking toward them.

"Good morning, sir, how are you?" Sims said, addressing J. L. "Are you being served?"

"Mr. Stein is looking for a place to stay," Larry said. "I told him I didn't know of anything."

"Stein, is it? You're not from around here, are you?" Sims said.

"J. L. Stein. No, sir, I'm not. In fact, I'm brand new to this area. I'm a chemical engineer out at the mines.

"What is it you are needing, Mr. Stein?"

"I'm looking for an apartment where I can have some privacy. Right now, I'm living at the guesthouse in Bauxite," J. L. said.

"Enough said. Alred is a good man, but he doesn't make things easy," Sims said. "Off the top of my head, I don't know of anything, but I'm speaking to the rotary at lunch, and I'll ask around. If you can drop back by about one o'clock, I should know something by then. On second thought, would you two like to go to the meeting with me as my guests?"

"Thanks anyway," Larry said, "but I got work to do."

"How about you, Mr. Stein? It wouldn't hurt to meet some of our folks and get acquainted," Sims said.

"Sure, why not," J. L. said.

"Before I begin my prepared remarks," Sims addressed the assembled group, "I would like to introduce my guest, Mr. J. L. Stein, a chemical engineer with the mines in Bauxite, who has just come to us from East St Louis and before that Pittsburgh. Please welcome him to our meeting."

The group of men looked toward J. L. and clapped. He smiled, stood, did a slight bow, and then sat back down again. In Pittsburgh, he had gone through this routine with his uncle Karl, and in East St. Louis, his supervisor had taken him on similar rounds. The names of the organizations were different, but the impulse was always the same.

Sims then turned back to the podium and his sheaf of papers.

"My friends," he said, "we must prepare ourselves for the turbulent times ahead. There are enemies—seen and unseen—around every corner. We all did our part in the Great War, and now it appears that, someday soon, we may be called on again. There are forces out there in this world that would have us involved in the European war today.

"Representative Dice and his Committee on Un-American activities have done a wonderful job in exposing the enemies, the wolves who come in sheep's clothing. It's now our duty to stand guard against those who would bring down this great nation.

"The director of the FBI, Mr. Hoover, made it clear that he is depending on us to act as his eyes and ears. If you see someone who is suspicious, report him or her to me. As the FBI identification officer, I have a direct line to the regional office and can make your information count. Do not act alone, because you might inadvertently interfere with an ongoing investigation. That piece of information you have about the little fish might help the agency catch the big fish, so don't tip him off.

"It is apparent that the mines at Bauxite will play a big role in any effort in the future, and because of that, our vigilance will be all the more important."

Sims had given this speech repeatedly over the years; only the culprit was different. First, it was Chicago gangsters who flooded Hot Springs; then, it was the communists and socialists; and now it was the Nazis.

Sims's speeches always went on just beyond the comfort level, and several of the men were looking at their watches.

"Remember, friends, keep your eyes and ears open. Thank you."

His friends smiled. Sims saw a spy behind every bush.

Sims and J. L. left the rotary and went back to the funeral home. Sims handed J. L. a slip of paper. On the slip was an address: 537 Sevier Street.

"These folks are in need of a little extra money, and they have just remodeled the storeroom over their garage. I've not seen it, but John Roberts is a wonderful carpenter, and he never does anything halfway. Sevier Street runs west just south of the court house. It's only a couple of blocks from downtown. Tell them I sent you," he said.

The furnished garage apartment on Sevier Street sat under a canopy of maples, oaks, and pecan trees that were beginning to green up. Mr. Roberts had divided the space over the garage into four small rooms. He had built a set of stairs on the east end of the garage, so the tenant wouldn't have to enter the garage to get to his rooms. At the top of the stairs was a small landing that served as a porch. The door to the apartment opened into a small living room. Near the middle of the room, a small door opened into the kitchen and the bathroom. On the west end of the living room, a door opened into a room that ran from back to front and served as a bedroom. J. L. loved the small apartment. It was quiet and, most importantly, private.

Once the deal was done, J. L. went back to the funeral home and thanked Sims for his help.

"Mr. Tyson mentioned that Larry Fitts had a pottery shop somewhere here downtown. How do I find it?" J. L. asked.

Sims pointed south.

"Just follow Main south. At the end of this block, it angles off to the southwest and becomes River Street. The first street it crosses is Market. Larry's building is on the left just across from the church.

Larry was loading his truck when J. L. came walking up. He had a number of thrown pieces that he was taking down to the kiln to be fired that night.

"Looks like you have been a busy man," J. L. said to Larry as he carried a particularly large piece out to the truck.

"Hello, friend. How did your house hunt go?" Larry asked.

"Good. Mr. Sims put me on to a place over on Sevier Street. The name is Roberts," J. L. said.

"Good folks," Larry said.

"Forgive me for asking, but you're an awful young guy to be owning your own building, having your own business," J. L. said.

"Yeah, I know. The truth is that most of it was luck and old man Jack Eggy. That's his name up there on the front of the building," Larry said as he pointed up to a large, white, stone plaque high up on the front of the building. It read: JACK EGGY BUILDING 1937. "Egg—that's what everybody called him—was a great, old man. Anyway, Egg lived in a house on the north corner of this property. When he died, he gave me the house and the property to the corner. One of the local builders bought the house and moved it, and I used the money to build the building. A lot of the materials were seconds from McCoy-Couch Furniture and Acme Brick. I designed the building and did most of the work myself. If you got time, I'll give you the grand tour."

"Sure," J. L. said.

The grand tour was composed mainly of Larry pointing in the general direction of a wall and saying things like, "When I get some money, I'm going to put a big showcase right there."

"You can get standard furniture anywhere, so I'm trying to make a name for myself making one-of-a-kind pottery and furniture. Take that chair over against the wall," he said, pointing at a small, oddly shaped chair frame. "That's for a little woman who couldn't be more than four and a half feet tall, and her back is the shape of a dog's hind leg. Her husband asked me to build her a chair she could be comfortable in and wouldn't have to struggle to get out of it. So far, we have been through about three versions, but we're getting close. When she passes away, they'll probably have to throw it away, 'cause it won't fit anybody else.

"I don't make any money doing this kind of thing, but at least I'm having a good time."

"There are worse ways to spend your life," J. L. said. "One of the reasons I wanted to come by is because of my hobby. Besides being an engineer, I buy and sell art pottery. My uncle in Pittsburgh got me involved, and now I've really gotten interested in it. I have a family connection in Mexico City who will buy just anything I send him. You think you might be interested in selling some of your stuff? Don't have to worry about the one-of-a-kind stuff, 'cause these folks won't know the difference."

"Are you kidding? Of course I would," Larry said. "Bullet Hyten sells pots by the train car load out in Manitou, Colorado. You see those mugs over along the wall? Those are part of a contract that Bullet has with the navy. When he gets more work than he can handle, he subs a little out to me. You figure out what you want, I'll come up with some samples, and we'll get this train rolling. Boy, am I glad you came in today. In fact, this is worth a celebration. How would you like a beer?"

"Sounds great to me," J. L. said.

"Let me finish loading the truck, and I'll be ready to go," Larry added.

J. L. helped him to load the last of the pots destined for the kiln. Larry put a sign on the front door that said BE GONE FOR A WHILE. IF YOU NEED SOMETHING, LEAVE A NOTE.

Heading south on Market Street, Larry pointed out the various points of interest—the Baptist church, Dr. Gann's home and office, the football field and high school, the icehouse. Just before he crossed the train tracks, Larry turned right onto Hazel Street and then left into the lot of the kiln.

The Niloak kiln was a weather-beaten old building that appeared to be falling in on itself. Inside it was a beehive of activity: potter's wheels, workers smoothing out the rough edges of the raw product, molding casts, and seconds strewn about. In the back of the building was the kiln itself—a circular brick affair with a small, curved door that they had to lean over to carry the pots through. Larry and J. L. unloaded the pots that were to be fired that night and put them on a table near the opening to the kiln.

"I need to make another stop at Bullet's retail shop, but it's on the way," Larry said.

"I'm with you. I'd like to meet Mr. Hyten if he's there," J. L. said.

From the kiln, they headed back up Market Street, passed downtown and out onto the Little Rock highway.

Niloak Pottery sat on a tall, clay hill just north of town. The building had a stucco facade with the feel of an old Mexican hacienda. The showroom floor was composed of Niloak clay tiles with large swaths of red, blue, and cream. The room was best seen in the late evening, when the red glow of the sun flooded the room and highlighted the swirl pottery that Bullet Hyten had perfected.

Larry pulled his truck into the parking lot of the retail shop and told J. L. to wait in the showroom while he saw if Mr. Hyten was in the back.

J. L. walked up to the open door of the shop and noticed a young woman working in the showroom. She was sweeping near the front window, raising a shower of dust particles that created an image of a Christmas ornament that snows when shaken.

Quietly, she went about her work as he watched from the doorway. She had cream-colored skin and auburn hair that hung down around her shoulders; prominent cheeks bones highlighted her blue eyes. She moved in unison with the broom as if she was dancing.

When she turned in his direction, J. L. diverted his gaze to a large pot near his left hand.

"May I help you?" she asked. "Are you interested in that piece?"

Before he had time to answer, Larry walked in from the storeroom. "Marty, have you seen Mr. Hyten?" Larry asked the girl.

"No, Coach, I haven't. He left early this afternoon to deliver a shipment of pots to Camden. Don't expect him back until late."

"I'd like you to meet someone," Larry said. He pointed at J. L. "This is J. L. Stein. He's an engineer at the mines, is going to be living in the Roberts's house on Sevier. He wanted to meet Mr. Hyten." He turned back to J. L. "J. L., this is the Marty Elrod, the girl I told you about. You know, the beautiful girl who won't give me the time of day," he said, smiling.

J. L. smiled and extended his hand.

"Nice to meet you," J. L. said. As he spoke, he allowed his accent thicken and his speech to slow.

"Me, too." Marty said, smiling broadly. She accepted his hand and then stood there.

"So, Larry tells me that you're a really good baseball player?" J. L. asked.

Marty smiled.

"Yeah, well, he exaggerates. We have a women's league, but sometimes when Coach is short a player on the men's team, he'll throw me in just to get the other side riled up. I'm not the only one. One time, he played a guy with a cast on his leg. Another time, he had Kim Lee, the Korean grocer with one eye, playing center field. The best one is when the boys from Jenkins Ferry come to town; he's always got a Negro kid on the bench—really does make those rednecks mad. Only one time did he ever play one of them, and that was my friend Dirt Hampton. Dirt is real good, and he hit a home run to win the game."

"I'm a bit of a baseball fan myself," J. L. said. "And I would love to watch you play sometime."

"I'm not playing as much as I used to be. Between my two jobs and helping Dad, I don't have much free time," she said.

"Marty, we're going to the Red Gate to have a couple of beers," Larry said. "You want to go along?"

"Can't. I've got to close up here and then cook supper for Daddy. He's not doing well. Dr. Gann can't figure out what's wrong with him. He's talking about sending him to St. Vincent for some tests. Truth is I think he's still depressed because of Mama dying last year."

"Can we do anything?" Larry asked.

Marty shook her head.

"I don't think so, but thanks for asking."

Larry claimed his usual table in the Red Gate. The bartender brought two beers and sat them down in front of Larry and J. L.

"Hope you wanted a beer," Larry said.

"Yeah, that's fine," J. L. took a drink. "Boy, you weren't kidding about Marty being a real knockout. And I bet she has a big ugly boyfriend who likes to pound on guys when they talk to her."

Larry shook his head.

"She's never shown any interest in the guys here in Saline County. She and her family moved here in the early thirties. Her father is the chief potter at the kiln. She's only been out of high school a couple of years. They're Catholic, and her mom insisted that she go to St. Mary's in Little Rock, so she has never been part of the young crowd that runs around town. When her mom died, they both took it hard, and other than working and taking care of her dad; she has been scarce in the last year. On top of that, she's really serious, says she wants to be a newspaper writer and maybe a novelist. In addition to working for Mr. Hyten, she is a stringer for the *Courier*; that's the local paper."

"You think she would go out with me?" J. L. asked.

"I only know one way to find out, and it isn't asking me," Larry said.

"Everybody around here seems to think you are a pretty good baseball coach. Some of the guys over at the fights were laughing about you trying to get Mr. Mac's goat by dressing like him. Marty said something about a colored player you played one time, just to make some guys mad."

Larry smiled.

"Yeah, that was Dirt. Dirt Hampton, the son of John L. Hampton, the old black man that works at the funeral home. He was a really good player; if he had been white, he probably would have played in the majors. He was a legend in the colored league up on the hill, south of the tracks. The folks from Jenkins Ferry made it clear a long time ago that they don't want no black folks in their part of the country. They came up to play us, and I asked Dirt to just come sit on our bench. It made Eric, the other coach, so mad they almost stormed off the field. I told him, if he did, that was a forfeit—a win in our column and a loss in theirs. The truth is I didn't have any intention of playing Dirt, but they made such a stink about it that I put him in for the last inning. The first pitch they threw to him was high and inside, but the second was right over the plate. He hit the ball so hard it was still rising when it crossed Richards Street."

"What ever happened to him?" J. L. asked.

"He played on one of the colored All-Star leagues for a while, but he got to drinking, and they finally cut him loose. Last I heard, he was working as one of the gardeners for the principal of the schools in Bauxite. Dirt never did like working very much."

CHAPTER 26

Junior stood in the back of the Southern True Gospel Church. It wasn't much of a church; in fact, it wasn't a church at all but the back bedroom in the home of Virgil "Tee" Clark.

A makeshift podium made of sawhorses and planks was set up in the front of the room. On the right was a small American flag and on the left the KKK flag. On the back wall of the room was a large Confederate flag.

Tee was holding forth on the evils of modern society.

"If us Southerners don't stand for our own rights, ain't nobody gonna do it for us. Look around you; these people are bringing in all of the scum of the earth—Jews, niggers, Mexicans, and Catholics. At some point, we're gonna have to stand up and say 'enough is enough.' I don't know about you men, but—"

Before he could finish his sentence, the door to the room flew open, and in walked Major John Dormer and four of his men. The major was familiar to all of the men. He was the commander of the War Production Board troops that provided security for the bauxite mines.

"Good evening, gentlemen," Dommer said. "It is good to see that we have all of the usual suspects here; that way, I won't have to say this but once." He stopped and looked around the room. "I want to get something straight right here and now. The Reverend Clark has got that sign-in book up there on the desk. Any of you who signs the book or lends your name to one of his schemes is out of a job. The work of this plant is to mine ore and produce alumina, and anything that you men do that interferes with that work is against the law. And understand, boys, I am the law."

Tee pulled himself up and interrupted the Major, "Now wait a minute, we got First Amendment rights, and you can't do anything about that."

"To hell with your First Amendment rights. As long as you are on company property and working for this plant, your ass is mine," Dommer said as he walked toward the front of the room. "Now I understand how you boys feel. Fact is, most of the people at the plant agree with you, but that's beside the point. Right or wrong, we can't have anything that disrupts the work of this plant. Now, you boys get on home, and we'll just forget that this little meeting ever happened." He turned to Tee. "As for you, Mr. Clark, I think you have outlived your usefulness at this plant. You go on and pack up your flags and get your sorry ass out of here. I got your final check here in my pocket." He handed a small envelope to Tee. "We'll expect you out of here by the morning."

Junior stood in the shadows and said nothing. He and all of the other young men filed out of the house and disappeared into the dark. He wasn't terribly disappointed in the events of the evening. Like his father before him, Junior had never been impressed with the Klan. They made a lot of noise and drew a lot of attention, but when it came down to doing something, they were just paper tigers. By disrupting this little group, Dormer would get a false sense of security and, in the long run, make Junior's job easier. Junior had more important chores on his plate.

The town of Bauxite was divided into a series of small communities. Each had its own special identity—Alabama camp, Little Italy, Crumby Town. The blacks lived in Africa, Mexico, and Dirt Dauber. In the 1910s, a large population of Mexicans had been moved in to do the work that the whites wouldn't do. When the Depression hit, most of those folks were rounded up, taken back to the border in Laredo, Texas, and instructed to go home. During the Depression, as blacks and whites began to flee the cotton farms of the south, the mines were a convenient first stop.

The managers who ran the plant lived in large homes on Silk Stocking Row, just west of the community hall. Each morning, a group of black house-and-garden workers gathered on the road that led into town from Mexico Camp. They walked in double file and were all dressed in white. Near the end of the file of domestic workers was Dirt Hampton. After parting company with the Mid-South All-Stars, Dirt had drifted back to Saline County, worked for Bullet Hyten for a while, and then signed on as the yardman for the principal of the school at Bauxite.

Each morning as these workers headed for Silk Stocking Row in their white, cleaned, and starched uniforms, they were met by the nightshift making its way home from the mines. The miners were covered with dirt and grime, tired, and ready for bed. Unlike most of the others who walked silently, looking straight ahead and never making eye contact, Dirt always greeted the mine workers—"Morning, y'all get you some rest." Most of the men returned his greetings with a smile and an occasional bit of banter—"Yeah, we ain't got a cushy job like working somebody's vegetable garden and sitting under a shade tree with ice water all day." The truth was they all worked hard for very little money; there weren't any easy jobs at the Bauxite mines. The mines tended to chew people up and spit them out when they couldn't work anymore.

To Junior, Dirt's smile was a mock—"Look at me: I got me an easy job. I don't have to get my hands dirty like you white trash, so to hell with you."

For the first time in his life, Junior "Sandy Scroggins" Parkus was in love. Her name was Martha Jordan. The problem was Martha was in love with a lot of men, and not all of them were white.

Between Alabama and Mexico camps was a strip of woods that created a fiction of separation of the two races. Early on, Junior found a large pin oak tree where he could sit, perched, and watch the activities of life as they unfolded on both sides. It was in this tree that he fell in love with Martha Jordan.

It was common knowledge that Martha and her husband, Lloyd, were married in name only. With time, she developed a complex system of signals to notify her suitors of Lloyd's absence. The most common signal was a bright blue quilt strung out on the clothesline like a flag at sea, signaling clear weather. When the great blue sail was on the line, some freshly shaven miner with hat in hand would soon be at her back door.

Junior's ambition was to be the next in line at Martha's back door.

It was a warm evening. The sun was setting over the pine ridges to the west. The red sun cast its long rays over the town of Bauxite. Junior was sitting high in the pin oak tree. Martha walked out of her house with the blue quilt in hand, but instead of stopping at the clothesline, she walked around the outhouse and kept on going toward the woods. At first, Junior thought she was going to walk straight up to the base of the tree and invite him down. For an instant, he puzzled as to what he would do. When she entered the woods, she turned and walked almost to the other side, stopping at a honeysuckle jungle growing on the edge of the forest.

Martha took her blanket and spread it out in a secure, little spot protected from all four sides but not from the top. Junior had a clear picture from his position. Out of the corner of his eye, he saw a movement that, at first, he thought was a deer, but then he realized it was Dirt Hampton. The young, black man had been hiding in the tall grass on the Mexico Camp side and was now walking toward the woods with a bottle of wine and a big grin on his face. It seemed that Martha had decided to expand her territory.

Junior felt a hot flush of jealousy and moral outrage as he watched the black and white couple engage in the universal act of procreation. Every principle he had been taught since he had been small was being violated. Here was a white woman, who could have her pick of white men, and she chose instead to lay in the honeysuckle with this black man. Hampton was simply following his instincts. This was a transgression of God's law, a violation of every common rule that governed man's life. That boy needed to be taught a lesson. So did the woman, but that would wait until later.

After the couple consummated the act, they propped themselves up against a tree and began drinking from the wine bottle. The sun disappeared over the last ridge, and darkness began to descend. A large, full moon appeared in the eastern sky, filling the woods with its own light. Martha, over the protests of Dirt, redressed and headed back to her house. The blue quilt was left in place; it would be there the next evening and the next, until Martha tired of her black lover.

Quietly, Junior climbed down out of his tree and slowly advanced on the reclining black man. Dirt was basking in the afterglow of sex, the warmth of the evening, and the sweet peach wine.

"Hold it, boy," Junior commanded.

"What? Who is that? What do mean 'hold it'? I ain't doing nothing." As he spoke, Dirt strained to see the form of the disembodied voice.

Junior stepped from beyond the tree and, in one motion, shot Dirt in the right thigh with the .22 pistol that he carried strapped to his leg inside of his boot. He had actually aimed at the belly.

"I said, hold it," Junior said.

"What the hell are you talking about?" Dirt said as he grabbed at his leg. "You silly shit, you just shot me."

"And I'll do it again if you don't stay where you are."

"I'm bleeding. You shot me," Dirt said.

"I'll shoot you again, if you don't shut up," Junior said.

"Mister, I didn't do nothing to you. Why did you—"

Junior fired again. This time he aimed for Dirt's chest and hit him in the left arm. The pistol was a discard Junior had found in the rent house where he lived in Crumby Town.

"Now if you are through talking, take off your belt. Don't talk; just take off your belt." When Dirt had the belt in hand, Junior added, "Now put the belt around your knees and snug it down real tight. I don't want you going nowhere."

As Dirt worked with the belt, blood began to pool on the quilt.

"You got to understand. You and your people can't go mocking us white folks like this. Most of your people know their place, but it is obvious that you don't. Every time you have sex with a white woman, you thumb your nose at us. We just can't let you do that."

"Who in the hell do you think you are?" Dirt asked.

"Well, tonight, boy, I'm your judge, jury, and executioner." He walked over to Dirt, put the gun up his left temple, and fired. The young man slumped over dead. The interchange had taken less than a minute.

To the dead body, Junior said, "I told you to shut up."

This was Junior's first time killing a human. It was easier than he had expected. It wasn't a lot different from killing a deer.

Junior leaned against a tree opposite the black man to calculate his next move. His heart pounded in his chest, the hairs on the back of his arms stood erect. He was exhilarated. It wouldn't do to have this opportunity go to waste. In his death, this black boy needed to be an example to any other colored man who had ideas about white women. Once the adrenaline rush subsided, Junior began to make plans as to how to best use the body, and in a short time, he had a plan. He removed the belt from the Dirt's legs and looped it around his chest under his arms. With the belt secure, he dragged the body through the woods, north to where the woods opened onto Church Street.

He left the body lying in the woods, went over to the waterworks, and found a piece of painted white, pine board. Using a pencil that he carried in his shirt pocket, he wrote the words:

STAY AWAY

FROM

WHITE WOMEN

He propped the body up against a pecan tree that faced the road, folded the man's hands in front, and put the sign across Dirt's still chest.

Junior was now a true warrior in the battle to save his country. By dispatching this black man to the other world, he had finally struck a blow for his race.

The next morning, the domestic workers in Mexico Camp gathered in the dark at the appointed site and began their quiet walk, double file, to Silk Stocking Row. Leading the file was William Cummings, the head deacon of the AME church and the yardman for the plant superintendent. He had spent many evenings in prayer over the children of the church and especially over young Hampton.

At first, he thought the young man was sleeping off a drunk, but as he approached the body, he realized it was far more serious than that. He stopped and held his hand up to those behind him.

"Y'all hold up. There is something wrong here. Johnson, take the women over to the other side of the road." He redirected his attention to the boy by the tree. "Dirt, boy, you all right? Wake up boy."

Closing in on the dead man, he saw the blood covering his leg and arm. The bullet that had entered his head had left only the slightest of holes and wouldn't be discovered until the coroner examined the body. When Mr. Cummings leaned over to nudge the young man, he realized that Dirt was cold and stiff.

Cummings turned to the others, now standing across the street, and motioned for his daughter to come to him. He met her in the middle of the street and, in a low voice, said, "Go on down to the office and tell them we need some help. Tell them Dirt is dead, and it looks like he has been killed."

As she ran off toward the office, William returned to the body, took off his work coat, and laid it over the boy's face.

"What a waste," he said to himself. "What a waste."

The daily administrative meeting started promptly at seven AM. The superintendent presided over the gathering most of the time, but he and his family had boarded a train for Georgia the evening before. That left Jim Storer, his assistant, in charge of the mines for two weeks. The men were standing around the coffee pot waiting for the 7:00 plant whistle when Maxine came in.

"Mr. Storer, we have a problem," Maxine said. "There has been a killing."

"You mean someone has died. You should say there has been a death," Storer corrected her.

"No, sir. It looks like there has been a killing. Dirt, the colored man who works for the principal has been shot. Willie Cummings and his people found the boy when they were on the way to work."

Storer wasn't prepared for this. He had expected a train derailment or a major equipment failure but not a killing. He looked around at the men standing around the coffee pot. They'd all stopped talking and were listening to the conversation.

"Who has the duty for the day?" Storer asked.

"I do, sir," J. L. said, stepping forward.

"Stein, good. Get someone to take over your load for the day. Get with Maxine here; I know the superintendent has a procedure for this."

Before he could finish the sentence, Maxine extended her hand with the appropriate protocol turned to the correct page. There was a checklist of things to do.

Storer continued, "You stay with this as long as it takes, and keep me posted about what's going on. Use my car if you need it."

"Yes, sir."

J. L. put his coffee cup down and followed Maxine.

"You can mark off number two and three. I called Jeff Davis, the constable, and Jim Sims, the coroner," Maxine said as they walked out the front door. Despite what the superintendent thought, the plant could get along well in his absence, but that would not have been true of Maxine.

Number one on the checklist was to secure the scene of the death. At that point, it made no difference whether it was a killing or an accident; J. L.'s most important job was to keep anything from being moved or changed so the coroner could accurately assess the scene.

By the time he had made the walk back up to the body, Jeff Davis had arrived and was in control of the scene. This left J. L. free to simply observe and be the eyes and ears for Mr. Storer. At the instruction of Mr. Davis, he and Mr. Cummings made a circle ten yards out from the body, using baling twine and sawhorses.

Jim Sims was shaving when Maxine called the house. His wife answered the phone on the second ring.

"It's for you," she said. "It's Maxine from the plant."

"Tell her I'll call her right back," he shouted from the bathroom. Sims hated shouting from room to room.

Mrs. Sims relayed the information and then came into the bathroom.

"She said she needs to talk to you now. There's been a murder; it's Dirt Hampton."

"Oh my," was all he said. He quickly wiped the shaving cream from his face, walked into the hall, and picked up the phone.

"Morning, Max. Are you sure it's Dirt?" There was a slight delay. "Has anyone told his father?" Again, there was a delay. "Has Jeff secured the site?" He nodded his head. "Good, I'll run by the Hampton house on the hill and make sure everything is okay with John." He then hung up phone and went back to finish his shaving.

His wife came and stood in the doorway.

"Are they sure it's Dirt?" she asked.

"Yeah, looks like it," he said. "You know, the sad thing is we've all seen this coming. Just last week, John L. was talking about how the boy was drinking too much. Folks at the plant came by to check up on him after he didn't show up for work for a few days."

Sims slapped a little Old Spice aftershave on his face and went back to the hall. He picked up the phone and tapped the cradle twice.

"Morning, Minnie. Has anyone called the grocery store up on the hill?" He waited for a second. "Good," he said. "We can assume that John L. knows about his son. If you get any calls for me, I'll be out at the plant. It may take a while. Now, ring Larry over at the store. Thanks."

After three rings he heard, "Good morning. This is Fitts Pottery and Custom Furniture. Larry speaking."

"Larry, it's Jim Sims. I need your help. There's been a killing at the plant over in Bauxite. It's Dirt.

"Oh, no, what happened? Was it an accident?" Larry asked.

"Don't know much at this point. They found him leaned up against a tree. I think John L. already knows. Minnie said there had been a couple of calls from the plant to Jackson's Grocery on the hill. That would be John's people. I'm going to need an extra set of hands. Could you drive for me?"

"Yes, sir, I'm at your service. Have you had your coffee?"

"No, I haven't," Sims said.

"Good. When you come by, I'll pour you a cup in one of my new navy mugs I'm making on subcontract for Niloak."

"I'll be there in about twenty minutes. I've got to go by the office and pick up my bag."

"I'll be ready," Larry said.

Sims drove to the funeral home and picked up his bag, his camera, and his fingerprinting kit and then put a sign on the front door, indicating that he should be back by noon.

It was a short distance to Larry's place. Larry was waiting out front, sitting in an Adirondack-style chair. Sims slid over to the passenger side, and Larry jumped in behind the wheel.

"Let's run by John L.'s house before we go to the plant. Won't take a minute. Constable Davis should have everything under control," Sims said.

"You're the boss," Larry said as he pulled out from the curb.

Down the hill at the end of Market Street, the road crossed first the Hot Springs track heading west and then the main line heading south. Just beyond the track, the paved road stopped and became a dirt path. It made a left and then, a block later, a right leading up the hill. At the top of the hill was Jackson's grocery and, just beyond that, the home of John L. Hampton.

To most of the white community, John L. Hampton was just another old, black man who worked as the hired hand for the Sims, but in the black community, John L. was the man who got things done.

When Larry pulled up in front of the Hampton home, it was clear that the word had arrived. There were people filling the front yard and the small porch. Everyone turned and watched as the hearse came to a stop in front of the house. Larry and Sims were like family to most of these people; these two white men had often come up to the hill to retrieve the body of an old person, a baby that had died from diarrhea, or a man in his prime who had dropped over from a heart attack.

Sims got out of the car and made his way through the crowd. The group silently parted as he made his way into the house. No one wanted to touch the undertaker.

John L. and his wife were sitting around the kitchen table. Mrs. Hampton was crying, and John L. sat with a blank look on his face.

Sims walked around behind the older man and put his hand on his shoulder.

John L. looked up at him and asked, "You been out to the plant yet?"

"No, John, I haven't, but the constable should have everything under control. I just wanted to come by and check on you, make sure you're okay. Can I do anything for you or your wife?"

"No, sir, we is doing tolerable well. Well as can be expected. You think they'll find out who done this to my boy?" John asked.

"I hope so, John, I really do hope so."

"You do what you can?"

"I will," Jim said.

Back on the road, Sims was quiet. Larry broke the silence.

"It sure is nice that they've paved this road." Larry said as they left Edison Avenue and headed out of town.

"Yeah, don't eat near as much dust," Sims said. "How's business?"

"I'm doing fine. I don't need much. Don't have any bills. I sell a little furniture right along. I do some work for Bullet. Unlike some of these kids here in Benton, all my wants and needs were met by the time I was twenty-two."

"You ever thought about getting married?" Sims asked.

"Man, I can't afford to get married," Larry said.

"I hear you been spending some time up at the Red Gate and over at Hot Springs."

Larry smiled.

"You got ears everywhere, don't you?" he said.

"That's part of my job. Mr. Hoover says we always have to be on the alert. You haven't heard anything that sounded suspicious, have you?"

"Well, Jim, I can't say that I've listened real close. But to answer your question, no, I haven't heard anything you would be interested in. Most of the guys I run around with brag about women and how much money they're going to have." Larry wasn't comfortable with idea of spying on his friends, even if he was doing for the man who was more like a father than anyone he had known.

"The scuttlebutt is that we will be at war within the year," Sims said, "and if that happens, those mines will get real important, real quick. You know they're building a processing and reduction plant out here starting this fall?"

"Yeah, I heard about that."

"They say that there will be several thousand new jobs. Can you imagine that?"

"Thousands?" Larry said.

"Yeah, thousands. They don't have any housing either. A lot of those folks are going to be looking for a place to stay in Benton. In fact, the security people from the plant and the FBI office in Little Rock came by the funeral home a couple of months ago. They asked me to let this man and his wife live with us. He's going to be the structural engineer for the new plant. He's bringing the blueprints with him when he comes. Name is Sebastian. He had something to do with developing the process where they extract the alumina from the low-grade ore out here. Anyway, he's going to be living with us. He and his wife are supposed to show up in about three weeks. We walled off our front room and turned it into a small apartment. I had a carpenter build me a second bathroom. If we hadn't, I would have had to share a bathroom with five women. That would never have worked."

Larry smiled.

"Yeah, I know what you mean. You know anything about who killed Dirt?"

"No, I don't," Sims said.

"Who found him?"

"Some of his family, I think. I just hope they didn't mess with the scene too much. That's the problem most of the time. These folks feel like they got to make the body comfortable. If Jeff got there pretty quick, he will have everything set up for us."

Just past the community hall, they took a right up past the office and waterworks to where Center Street veered to the left. Well before they got to the scene, it was clear where they were heading. There were two groups of people standing on the north side of the road, one black and one white. Across the road were Jeff Davis, his horse, and J. L. Stein with his clipboard.

J. L. was relieved when he saw Sims's truck round the corner and head up the hill. Once they had roped off the site, there wasn't a great deal to do except stand around and wait. The War Production Board men came through soon after J. L. arrived, made sure the truck traffic could get through the crowd, and then had gone about their business. Their job was to keep the plant moving.

"Morning, constable," Sims said as he got out of the truck.

Larry got out and circled the truck.

"Morning, constable. Morning, Stein."

The two men shook hands, and then J. L. explained that he was there to represent the plant. Sims nodded his head.

"I understand," he said, "and I'll keep you informed of everything we do, especially as it pertains to the plant."

Sims then turned his attention to Jeff Davis. "Anyone mess with the scene?"

"No, Willie Cummings laid a coat over the body, but that was all," Jeff said.

Jim Sims had been the coroner for a long time, and over the years, he had become methodical in his approach to crime scenes. He had learned early not to depend on his memory. In his bag, he carried a large, box camera. His first chore was to photograph the scene and the body. In addition, he took several pictures of the crowd that surrounded the scene.

Once Sims had the feel for the scene, he moved on to the body. Carefully, he photographed Dirt from all angles. The pant leg over the right thigh was covered with blood, but there did not appear to be any blood on the ground. The shirtsleeve on the left arm was bloody, but again, there was no blood on the ground around the body. The body was stiff so, if it had been moved, the moving had taken place immediately after the death.

While Sims began to examine the body, Larry put up a series of screens around it. Sims carefully removed the sign from the dead man's chest and packed it away in a special case he had made to keep from obscuring latent prints. While he was leaning over the body, he noticed the small entry wound in the young man's thick matted hair. It wasn't the leg or arm wound that had killed the boy; it was that bullet bouncing around in his head.

In the meantime, Larry and J. L. searched in a slowly expanding circle, looking for clues as to how the body had gotten there. They quickly found a trail of blood and broken brush that led into the woods. Whoever had placed the body next to the tree had not tried to cover his tracks. It led right back to the blue quilt and the half-empty bottle of wine.

Larry stayed at the site and sent J. L. back to get Sims and his camera. Jeff returned with Sims, and when he saw the quilt, he immediately looked toward the Jordan house.

"I think I can tell you a little about that quilt." Jeff proceeded to tell the men about Mrs. Jordan and her various paramours.

"Constable, I need to talk to that woman," Sims said.

"Sure."

Sims and Larry secured the site and began to collect the evidence. Davis and Stein made their way across the woods and to the back door of Martha Jordan's house.

Davis knocked on the screen door and then, in a loud voice, said, "Martha, you need to come on out here. We got a problem, and we need to talk to you about it."

Martha came to the door, drying her hands on an old ragged towel.

"Morning, Mr. Davis. What can I do for you? Ain't nothing wrong, I hope. Has Lloyd been hurt?"

"No, Martha, there has been a murder. His name was Dirt Hampton."

When he said the name, Martha looked visibly shaken, but she quickly steadied herself. "Don't think I know him. All them colored boys look the same to me."

"Martha, I didn't say he was colored," Jeff said.

"Well, I mean, I don't know any white men named Hampton, so I just assumed he was colored."

"You better come with us."

The two men and Martha retraced the steps she had taken the night before. When they arrived at the honeysuckle jungle, Martha realized that she had left her blue quilt. She began to cry.

"I didn't hurt nobody. I ain't done nothing wrong."

"We aren't accusing you of anything. When did you last see Dirt alive?"

"After we finished, I hightailed it back to the house. I had to get Lloyd's supper ready. He don't care about me screwing around, but he wants his supper ready when he gets home from work. Truth is, the colored boy wasn't very good at screwing, and I wasn't in any mood for small talk. He wanted to sit here, get drunk, and go at it again. All twenty-year-olds—whites, coloreds, and Mexicans—are the same, slam-bam, thank you ma'am. It don't take them more than a minute to get through."

"What would Lloyd have said if he knew you was over here in the bushes with a colored man?" Sims asked.

"He wouldn't like it none, but if you think Lloyd would kill somebody over me—colored or no—then you don't know Lloyd very well."

Jeff knew Lloyd, and Martha was right.

After questioning Martha and gathering up the rest of the evidence, Sims indicated to J. L. that he had accomplished all he could at the site and that they would be taking the body back to Dr. Gann's for the autopsy. While Sims and Larry wrapped up the scene and loaded the body, J. L. returned to the office and reported to Storer—it was a murder; the man had been shot three times; and just before he died, he was having sex with a white woman by the name of Jordan. Storer gave J. L. the use of his car for the rest of the day, so he could get to and from Benton without having to wait for the bus.

In the company car, J. L. followed the hearse back into Benton. Sims pulled his hearse up behind Dr. Gann's office. J. L. and Larry helped him move the body onto a small surgical table in the back. While Sims prepared the body for autopsy, Larry and J. L. stood out back and smoked.

When Sims was finished with his preparation, he came back out and joined them.

"When will we find out something about the autopsy?" J. L. asked.

"Dr. Gann will get around to it sometime this afternoon. He is pretty prompt with his report, and we should have something in the next couple of days," Sims said. "Would you two like some lunch?"

"Sure," Larry said quickly.

"Yes, sir, that would be nice, but I wouldn't want to be a bother," J. L. said.

"It wouldn't be a bother. My wife makes enough for an army."

Sims drove the hearse back to the funeral home. J. L. and Larry picked him up and they headed north on Main Street, and J. L. turned to Sims.

"Where do we go from here with the investigation?"

"Well, this pretty well completes my part. I'll turn this over to the sheriff and Constable Jeff Davis. They will question anyone who knows the boy, and all of the men folk that have availed themselves of Mrs. Jordan's pleasures. From what Jeff Davis told me, that could amount to a lot of men."

"What do you think will happen?" J. L. asked.

"Nothing," Sims said in an offhand fashion.

"What do you mean 'nothing'?"

"I mean we got a colored boy screwing a white girl. He gets killed. Whoever did it was wrong, but there is not a jury in the history of this county that would convict that person. Now if it was a colored boy killing a white, he or somebody else would already be in jail. That may not be right, but it is the way that it is." Sims pointed off to the right. "Here we are. This is my house. Pull around back."

J. L. pulled the black Chevrolet sedan up to the Sims's house.

"Let me show you what we have done to the living room."

He gave the two young men a tour of the apartment with its bathroom facilities, which they had created out of a sitting room.

"And the good thing is, the company paid for the whole remodeling."

"Who did you say this was for?" Larry asked.

"Fellow named Sebastian."

"I'm going to be working for him after he gets here," J. L. said.

"Really?"

"Yeah, they say he doesn't drive, and someone is going to have to drive him to and from work every day."

"Well, it looks like we will be seeing quite a bit of each other. Do you know anything else about this guy?"

"No, I've been told that he is real smart but doesn't have a lot of common sense. The rumor is that his wife is some kind of actress and she is really upset about having to come to Arkansas," J. L. said.

From the back of the house, Mrs. Sims shouted, "Soup's on. Everybody get cleaned up."

Chapter 27

Any situation that offers a group of people, like the Nazis, the opportunity of behaving badly is one to be avoided at all costs. When cowardice, venality, and betrayal become not only useful but also esteemed and revered, these people come into their own. The same people who, under normal circumstances, would never show this side of themselves are triggered into action.
Helena's writing on a piece of scrap paper

J. L. received a brief letter postmarked Pittsburgh that said, "We have a message from your mother. Inquire at the Spa City Cigar Store in Hot Springs."

On Saturday, he got up early, went over to the Lone Star for breakfast, and began flirting with Jo.

"How about going to a movie with me tonight? There's a new comedy playing over at the IMP."

"My boyfriend wouldn't like that very much," she said.

"He doesn't have to know," he said.

"You haven't lived here very long, but you're bound to have noticed that there is no such thing as a secret in this little town. He's heading this way from New Mexico right now. Just bought a new motorcycle and wants to take me on a road trip. How long do you think us going to the movie would stay a secret? Thanks anyway."

"Can't blame a man for trying," J. L. said as he took his wallet out and paid the bill. "I'm going to Hot Springs for the day, you got any tips?'

"Yeah, don't catch nothing," Jo said, smiling.

Market Street was a bit out of the way, but J. L. needed to check on Larry. He opened the front door to the shop and shouted, "Anybody in here alive?"

Larry emerged from the bathroom in the back of the shop, holding his head. "Yeah, but I think I'm coming down with something. I've got a dreadful headache."

"I wonder if it has anything to do with how much beer you had last night," J. L. said, laughing.

"Well, that's the pot calling the kettle black."

"At least I could find my way home. By the way, I left your truck keys on the counter over by the wall."

"Thanks," Larry said. "You want a cup of coffee?"

"No, don't think so. I had breakfast over at the Lone Star, and I'm on my way to Hot Springs. Uncle Karl wrote and asked me to look at some antiques in an auction house on Central Avenue. You know much about those folks?"

"They're awful proud of their stuff, but other than that, not much. Won't be hard to find though. There are auction houses all up and down Central Avenue," Larry said. "Are you going to be back tonight?"

"Don't know. Depends whether I get lucky or not," J. L. said.

"Don't catch nothing," Larry said.

J. L. purchased his ticket and boarded the Missouri-Pacific short train to Hot Springs. Just west of town, the train picked up speed and crossed the narrow bridge over the Saline River. In the bottomlands west of the river, cornfields, cotton fields, and cow pastures surrounded the tracks. Beyond the bottomlands, the train began its ascent into the Ouachita Mountains. The train track followed a gradual incline, generally following the high ground along the banks of Ten Mile Creek. From the top of the mountain, a view of the Ouachita Valley opened up.

It was easy to see why Hot Springs had stayed isolated for so long; there was no easy way to get to the springs. The original European explorers had followed the Ouachita River up from the delta. The animal traces they had followed were steep, rocky, and for significant parts of the year, impassable paths. To the south, west, and north, the springs were guarded by imposing mountains that made anything but foot traffic impossible. The original train tracks were narrow gauge and required constant maintenance. In the end with the lure and mystery of the healing springs, human persistence had prevailed, and several lines of rail traffic had been established.

The isolation of Hot Springs had allowed it to develop in its own way. Unlike most small towns across the South, Hot Springs had developed as a mecca of sorts. Indian legend has it that the early tribes had gone there to repair their wounds and recover from the battles. The fiercest of enemies would put down there knives and bows while they were at the springs. The other tradition that developed along with this peaceful pact was the idea that it was rude to notice; what you did was your business and nobody else's. It was this idea that allowed the advent and prosperity of gambling, horse racing, and whoring with little interference from the powers that be.

The train ride down the slope of Ten Mile hill and into the city of Hot Springs, with a number of small streams paralleling the track, reminded J. L. of his home in Austria.

The Missouri-Pacific station sat at the south end of Central Avenue. Just to the north of the station, Hot Springs Mountain on the east and West Mountain on the west formed a hollow where the town was nestled. The creek that emptied the waters of the springs had long since been covered, and in its place was a broad avenue of shops, hotels, and bathhouses. At the south end of the main stretch was the Spa City Cigar Store.

J. L. stood and watched from across the street for a few minutes as a steady stream of men in dark suits walked in and out of the store. When there was a break in traffic, he walked across the street and entered the store. He seldom smoked, but the strong, rich aroma of the tobacco was intoxicating. Behind the counter was a bald-headed, old man sitting on a stool with an unlit cigar in his mouth. While he waited for the last customer to walk out, J. L. picked up *Stag* magazine and mindlessly thumbed through it.

The old man behind the counter spoke, "You looking or buying?"

"How much does it cost?" J. L. asked.

"To buy, fifteen cents."

"How much to look?"

"Twenty cents," the old man said.

J. L. smiled at the man and then put the magazine back on the rack. The old man never looked up.

When the last of the other customers walked out, J. L. walked up to the old man and said, "Do you have message from my mother?"

"What in the hell are you talking about?" the man asked as he looked up above his reading glasses from his racing form.

"I want to know if you have a message from my mother," J. L. asked again.

"Look, fella, all I got is newspapers, beer, and cigars. You want messages, go to Western Union. What do I look like the post office?"

"Are you Tommy?"

"Hell, no, I ain't Tommy. That's my nephew. What do you want with him?"

"He is supposed to have a message for me."

"He's upstairs. What's your name?" the old man said. "I got to tell him who's looking for him. He's an important man, and he ain't got time to be talking to every Tom, Dick, and Harry that comes walking in off the street."

"My name is J. L. Stein."

"What kind of accent is that? I know you ain't from around here."

"I'm from Pittsburgh," J. L. said.

"Oh."

The old man picked up a small, black phone and tapped the receiver a couple of times. "There's a fellow down here named Stein asking about a letter from his mother. Yeah, okay, I'll tell him." He hung up the phone. "Tommy will be down in a minute."

"Thanks."

The old man grunted and went back to his form.

On the floor in front of the counter were papers from Chicago, Detroit, Gary, and Minneapolis. In the rack were girlie magazines, and toward the door was a stack of the *Daily Racing Form*. J. L. had just reached down to pick up one of the *Forms* when a thin, young man with a dark complexion came walking down the back stairs. J. L. had never had anything to do with gangsters, but for years, he'd been fascinated with the newsreels of the great shoot-outs between the mob and the FBI. He didn't know what he had expected Tommy to look like, but it was certainly not like this. This young man could easily have been the poster child for the chamber of commerce. Every hair was in place. His shirt was starched and neatly pressed. His black shoes were clean and shined. There was not a hint of anything unsavory about the young man.

"May I help you?" The young man asked.

Again J. L. posed the question, "Do you have a message from my mother?"

"What is your name?"

"Stein, J. L. Stein."

"Yes, I do. Follow me."

Tommy led J. L. to the back of the store, where they climbed a series of narrow switchback stairs leading to the third floor of the small, brick building.

At the top of the last flight of stairs, the top floor was one large room. The north wall of the room was a tote board with two men working fast with different shades of red, blue, and green chalk as the odds changed from second to second. In the middle of the room were a series of desks, each filled with multiple, ringing telephones. The men at the desks scribbled cryptic notes on small pieces of paper and then placed them on the front of the desks. A young boy, no older than twelve, picked up the papers and handed them to the men at the tote board. The rest of the walls were lined with large windows and sheer curtains that shifted in the warm, spring breeze.

Along the far wall sat a young pregnant woman with a small child in her arms. Several other children ran around the large room in an active game of tag.

"Almedia, keep the kids back away from the tote board," Tommy said. "Those men got work to do. They don't have time to be a hiding post for these kids' games."

"It's all right, Boss. They ain't in our way," one of the men said as two of the children circled his leg.

Tommy shook his head.

"My papa would never have let me get away with half the stuff these kids do."

At the back corner of the room was a glassed office.

"Mr. Stein, come with me. I have most of your stuff in my office."

When they were seated in the office, Tommy opened a small floor safe, pulled out two manila envelopes, and handed them to J. L.

On the front of the first envelope was written "Helena." J. L. quickly began to open it.

"Please don't open these here in the store. It's part of the rules. If you don't open it, then I can honestly say that I don't know what it contains. I'm just a courier, and I don't want to know what's inside," Tommy said.

"This isn't all I have for you. There is another package for you at our place out on the lake. We, the family, run a small travel court and fish camp out on Lake Hampton. It's called Lorio's. If you have time, we'll feed you supper and give you a room for the night. I can get you back into town for one of the trains tomorrow. That is, if you aren't in a big hurry."

"I'm in no big hurry," J. L. said. "I really don't have to be back to work until Monday."

"Good. You be back here about five when we close the store."

Tommy got up from his chair and walked to the door of the glassed office.

"Almedia, call Mama and tell her to hold cabin number six for the night and, if that's already rented, number eight. Tell her it is for a Mr. Stein." He turned back to J. L. "We start filling up at about three in the afternoon."

He looked at his watch. "Let's see, it's one thirty right now. You need to be back at about four forty-five."

J. L. smiled at Tommy.

"Any place I can get a good cup of coffee?"

"Are you kidding? This town has got some of the best coffee in the world. And if you are so inclined, you can get some of the best Chianti from Florence, some of the best duck from Stuttgart, some of the best chocolate from Vienna. You can get real German Lager."

"All I want is a good cup of coffee," J. L. said.

"Maghee's just up the street. If you are really want a treat, go to the Arlington, get a cup, and go out onto the veranda. That way, you can watch everybody come and go. I understand they are taping a radio show up there this afternoon. Some country stuff. You might get to be in the audience. Now, I got to go back to work. See you at five."

J. L. carried his packages down the stairs and was heading out of the store. The old man behind the counter stopped him. "You spent a long time in my store without buying nothing."

J. L. reached down, picked up the copy of *Stag* magazine, and paid the old man his fifteen cents.

Central Avenue was an open-air circus. There were delights for children of all ages. For the infirm, there were the baths and their healing powers. For the wealthy, there were the big fancy hotels and sumptuous meals. For the family on holiday, there were excursion trips to the top of West Mountain, the Alligator Farm, Sleepy Hollow Photography where they could get their pictures taken with a live bear, a carriage to be pulled down the street by two ostriches, the Jack Tar motel with its swimming pool, exotic-sounding foods like flankin-in-a-pot, sauerbraten, pizza, and fresh oysters. After the families retired, there was gambling at the Southern Club, drinks of every description, and ladies of the evening.

As J. L. walked north onto Bathhouse Row, a large, convertible Hudson slowly moved down the street. Sitting on the back of the seat were three of the most beautiful women J. L. had ever seen. He stood transfixed as the car came to a stop, waiting for traffic.

The young lady sitting closest to him looked and smiled. In a soft voice, she said, "You looking or buying, Mister?"

"Depends on what you're selling."

The girl reached inside her waistband and handed him a card. The card had a large, multicolored peacock in the center, and above it in an arch over the tail feathers was written Madame Peacock's. Below the bird's feet were the words: WE CATER TO YOUR NEEDS. At the very bottom was the name MAYLENE.

"That's my name," she said as the car began to move away.

For J. L., Hot Springs was intoxicating. As a chemical engineer, his life was pretty routine—he did his work, ate his meals, drank beer with Larry and his other new friends, played baseball, and flirted with the girls at work. Here, all of the forbidden pleasures of life jumped off the page and onto his lap. Had it not been for the manila envelope in his left hand, J. L. would have jumped into the car with Maylene, and the bauxite plant might never have seen him again.

I've got more important fish to fry, J. L. thought to himself. He laughed to himself. He was beginning to think like a southerner. Six months before, he'd never heard the phrase "more important fish to fry," and now it had become part of his vocabulary. Living in the South was contagious. Life was slower, and the sensibility was different. If you were the right color and class, many things were possible.

Walking up the street, he made notes of places where he would return: the elegant, old bathhouses; Hammon's Oyster House; Matter's Oriental Palace of Art; Mountain Valley Water Company.

Near the head of Central was the grand Arlington Hotel. Eighteen years earlier, the old Arlington Hotel had burned down and been rebuilt on the corner just opposite the old site. The New Arlington, as it was known by the locals, was a beautiful structure that presided over the affairs of Hot Springs. The rich, famous, and infamous came and went on a regular basis. Joe T. Robinson received official notification of his nomination as vice president with Al Smith in 1920 on the front steps of the hotel. The Vanderbilts, Rockefellers, and Melons had come and gone in the twenties and early thirties. Al Capone and his cronies had used it as a headquarters when they were in town.

It was an eleven-storey, L-shaped building, fronted by two bell towers. Between the two bell towers was a large antenna for the broadcast of radio signals from KTHS. The initials stood for Kum To Hot Springs. The grand entrance was fronted by broad Romanesque steps that led up to a covered veranda. Except for the coldest of weather, there were always small knots of people sitting around on the marbled porch, seeing and being seen. Thin black men in starched white jackets and black bow ties hurriedly moved from table to table with cups of coffee, mint juleps, beer, and food.

J. L. walked up the steps and looked around for an empty table. The head waiter walked over to him.

"May I help you, sir?" he asked.

"I would like a cup of coffee."

"I'm sorry, sir, but a coat and tie are required for service on the veranda and in the lobby in the afternoon. We would be more than glad to serve you in the coffee shop in the shopping arcade on the lower level. Or I might suggest one of the cafés across the street?" The waiter was most polite, but he made it clear to J. L. that he would probably fit in better across the street—that is, unless he was a guest at the hotel.

J. L. walked down the steps and across the street. The Warm Springs Café had seating on the street and didn't require a tie.

After ordering his coffee, he turned to the envelope labeled Helena. There was a nervousness associated with each new missive, the excitement of receiving word with the fear that something bad had happened. With each new letter, he would pore over it for weeks, looking for clues as to the true author of the notes. He looked for a turn of phrase that he could say was something only his mother could have written. He looked for words she used in ways no one else did. Since her capture, most of the letters had sounded the same; all were typed and could easily have been forgeries. If the latter was true and J. L.'s worst fears were true, then all he was doing was meaningless. But that was a black abyss that he could not step off into. His mother and sister were the only family he had. That wonderful, interesting, odd, quirky group of people he had been raised with was gone.

He opened the envelope and took out the one-sheet letter.

> Dear Jean Louis,
>
> I want you to know that I compose a letter every day, but I am told that I can send only one every two or three months. So much happens in between each letter, it is hard to know where to start. It is hard for me to remember where I left off the last time.
>
> Life is hard here at Mauthausen. We carry rocks from one place to the next. We do not get much to eat, and what we do get does not taste good. I would give anything to have a plate of Gruber's sausage and potatoes.
>
> The Nazis tell us that they are winning the war. They say that soon Russia will fall and after that Britain. I only hope that the war is over soon. I am beginning to get weak, and the work is hard. I really don't know how much longer I can last.
>
> They tell me that you are helping them to keep me safe. If that is so, I have very mixed feelings. I would never ask you to do anything against your conscience, but at the same time, I have learned that we must take whatever fate dishes out. If it is your help that is keeping me alive, you must know that no mother could ever ask for a better gift.
>
> When I think about all of my friends and family who have died, it makes my heart sick. The worst is poor Anna

dying. She should never have come back to Austria. I cry every night about her. I wish it had been me instead of her.

The Nazis tell me that you have been sent to the Wild West. Have you seen any cowboys and Indians? We've heard for years about the gangsters in America. I suppose out west there aren't any gangsters. Please try to stay safe and keep your head down; you are all I have left.

Love,

Helena

"Anna is dead," he said quietly. The tears began to flow. He leaned over and put his head in his hands. His dear little sister, the one who had crawled into bed with him when she was scared, the redheaded girl who had been forever adopting crippled animals was gone. Like her mother, she had spent her life at a high level of intensity, but unlike her mother, Anna had not had a critical eye and would often cling to hopeless and lost causes. She had never learned the skill of picking her battles. No doubt she had died fighting the people he was helping, fighting the people who had his mother, the people who ruled their lives.

His first thought was to take whatever money he had and race as fast as he could to revenge his sister's death and rescue his mother. And yet he knew that was an act of futility and would only result in his own death and the death of his mother. His only option was continue to provide the information they asked for. Little as it was, that was his only way of contributing to his mother's safety. For the first time in his life, Jean Louis Edit-Stein felt truly alone, alone in a world of uncertainty with all of the familiar signposts uprooted and cast aside.

J. L. emerged onto the street in back of the cigar shop. Tommy and Almedia were herding the last of the children into a large black sedan.

"Thought maybe you were lost," Tommy said.

"No, just thinking."

"That's one of the things that Hot Springs will get you to doing."

J. L. joined the kids in the back of the car. It was a tight squeeze, but they made it in. About that time, the old man with the cigar came walking out of the back of the store, locked the back door, and then added his bulk to the already overcrowded backseat.

Despite the packed conditions, the ride to Lorio's was not unpleasant. Tommy's family had an easy grace, with everyone, down to the smallest child, filling a comfortable role. Each bump in the road was met with squeals of delight. When they passed Oaklawn Racetrack, the oldest boy, Jerry, shouted to his father, "Daddy, next racing season, I want to go to the races with you."

Amelia frowned at Tommy.

"We'll see," he said.

Two miles south of the track, they turned east onto Amelia Lane, a narrow dirt road.

"Watch out for the deer that lives around this next curve," Rosa, the oldest girl, said as they crested the last hill before the lake.

At the end of the road was a small camp composed of a series of neat, little, white cottages. Near the water's edge was a larger, rough pine lodge where the restaurant and check-in were housed. Beyond the lodge was a boat dock on wooden piers made of railroad crossties. Each slip was occupied by a johnboat with a small, outboard motor. On the west end of the dock was the bait shop and gas pump. Dotted around the platform were chairs and a variety of fishing poles. A middle-age man in grey work pants and shirt with a large, tan, straw hat puttered around the dock, putting things in order.

As opposed to the hurried activity of Hot Springs proper, Lorio's Fish Camp was a study in tranquility. It sat on a quiet, protected bay off of the body of the main lake. Hot Springs Creek emptied into the lake just north of the camp. Before the lake had been impounded, the site where the camp sat was near a small bluff overlooking the creek as it made its way toward the Ouachita River. For centuries, Indians, the Spanish, and finally the northern European settlers had walked and ridden the animal traces that followed the healing waters of the creek. Lorio's was man's latest attempt to settle on or near the creek bed.

Tommy parked the car in front of the lodge, and the children noisily emptied out into the parking lot. J. L. walked toward the dock and stood staring out across the lake.

"Pretty, isn't it?" Tommy said. He pointed at the man on the dock. "That would be Jake. You need to talk to him after supper. Come on inside, and I'll get your room key. I got extra bathing suits if you would like to go swimming. The water is still a bit cool. There is beer in the lodge. Help yourself."

"I will take you up on those swim trunks," J. L. said. "Where's the best place to swim?"

"Right off the end of the dock. Supper is at seven. Don't be late. It makes Mama mad."

After taking a swim, J. L. dried off, changed clothes, and lay down on the bed in his cabin. He opened the large envelope and read the second letter.

Jean Louis,

As you know, our Führer's navy has control of the Caribbean Sea. Many of the American reserves of high-grade bauxite ore are in South America, and if war comes, the ore barges can be blasted out of the water. Because of this, as you know, the Americans have decided to build a production plant in Bauxite, Arkansas, to process the low-grade ore that is readily available.

In the near future, a man by the name of Ben Sebastian will be arriving at the mines. This man will have the blueprints for the new plant. We must have a copy of those prints. Because of the volume of the information, the process of copying will no longer suffice. In a different package, you will be provided the necessary photography equipment to do what we need.

Rudy

Supper was a giant platter of spaghetti and meatballs, fresh bread, and salad and all of the Chianti he could drink. Mama Lorio lorded over the table like a mother hen, pushing a second plate of pasta, and then a third. When it was obvious that everyone was satisfied, they all joined in the process of cleaning up. Tommy motioned to J. L. that he was to follow him.

"Jake takes his meals in his room," Tommy said. "He's a bit of a strange bird, but he is a good dock man. He can always tell you what's biting and what kind of bait to use. He, along with Mama's cooking, are what bring people back to this little place. The politicians keep threatening to clamp down on the bookmaking. If they ever do, I'm going to close up shop and just run this place. The smoke shop pretty well runs itself. We don't make a lot of money out here, but it sure is a great place to live.

"Jake's cabin is down at the end, around the corner." Tommy reached into his pocket and pulled out a couple of cigars. "Jake likes a good cigar. One is for him."

It was beginning to get dark. The sun cast a red glow over the mountains to the east. On his way back into the lodge, Tommy turned on the nightlights for the camp. All of the paths, the dock, and the eves of the cabins were outlined with multicolored Christmas lights.

J. L. knocked on the door of cabin number twelve. From inside the room, he heard a grunt that he assumed was an invitation to enter.

Sitting at a table by the window, Jake was working a crossword puzzle. Without so much as a hi, or a "How do you do?" the man in the grey work shirt asked, "What is a five-letter word for shithead that starts with a *P*?"

"Prick," J. L. said.

"Yeah, that's good."

"Where did you get a crossword puzzle that asks questions like that?" J. L. asked.

"I didn't. I write my own puzzles. More fun than trying to solve those stupid-assed puzzles they sell these days. The exception is the puzzles in the Sunday *Times,* but do you think I can get the *Times* in a place like this? This place is a damn intellectual wasteland. So, I'm reduced to writing dirty puzzles to amuse myself. It's like Shakespeare writing limericks. It's such a waste. What do you want?"

"You're supposed to show me something about a camera," J. L. said.

"Oh, yeah. You're the guy who gets the Zapp's cabinet. Now, the guy who put that thing together was one smart fellow. The only problem with it is that I didn't think of it. You know anything about photography?"

"I've never had a camera in my hands," J. L. said.

"Shit, shit, shit!" In the middle of a string of expletives, he stopped and shrugged. "Well, at least we don't have to overcome any bad habits. The ingenious thing about the cabinet is that you don't have to be genius to make it work. You do have to have good eyes, a steady hand, and know how to count. Can you do that?"

"I hope so, I'm a chemical engineer," J. L. said.

"Well, I won't hold that against you."

Jake handed J. L. a book of instructions.

"Take this book to your cabin and study it overnight. Come back about eight in the morning. I'll have all of my morning fishermen in the water by that time, and I'll give you a run through on the cabinet."

The Germans could be accused of many thing but they were thorough and had an eye for meticulous detail. The book that Jake handed to J. L. left nothing to question. It began with the first photographic accident and walked him step by step to the development of the Zapp's cabinet.

The cabinet was a self-contained photographic studio designed to produce a picture negative of a full page reduced to the size of a period at the end of a sentence. The concept was relatively simple. The cabinet itself was the size of a standard briefcase. When the case was opened, a canvas tent that was impervious to light expanded over the body of the case. A Minox camera four inches long and one inch wide slid into the top of the tent. A small, built-in light provided continuous illumination. The document to be copied was slid under the tent onto a movable tray and photographed.

Once the roll of film was complete, the tent was turned into a small darkroom and a second red light was used to develop the film. This first negative was a half inch by a half inch. Then came the truly ingenious part of the cabinet—the camera slid into a reverse microscope mounted onto the top of the movable tray in the cabinet. When the second roll of film was developed, what appeared was a series of dots on the film. The case contained a hypodermic needle and syringe. Unlike a normal needle that is shaped like a sharp, cutting, knife blade, this needle was rounded and cut a shape like a cookie cutter. Once the developing was complete, the microdots were cut from the film and could be used as punctuation in an otherwise normal letter.

J. L. spent the rest of the evening and early morning absorbing the information contained in the manual. It reminded him of his days at the academy, studying for finals.

Early the next morning, he emerged from his cabin and was greeted by the sun rising over Ten Mile Mountain. The smell of coffee drew him to the lodge. After pouring himself a cup, he stood by the front window and watched as Jake assisted one of his customers in renting a boat and heading out on a fishing adventure.

J. L. walked down to the dock.

"Fish biting?"

"The fish are always biting on Lake Hamilton," Jake replied.

"No, honestly."

"Being as honest as a dock man can be. The secret is knowing what bait to use and where they are."

"You fish much?" J. L. asked.

"Fish, eat, screw, and crosswords. As I see it, ain't much more to life than that."

"When you want to talk about the cabinet?"

A stern look came over Jake's face. "Listen, stupid, if you want me to help, don't ever talk about that kind of stuff outside of my cabin. You'll get me and these folks who run this place in trouble. Just like you and me, no one is quite what they seem. They don't know my business, and they don't need to. What goes on between you and me in the cabin is between us. Like I told you last night, I'll see you about eight. By the way, where is the manual?"

"It's in my room on the table."

"Go up there and get it right now, and don't let it out of your sight," the man demanded.

"Sure, okay."

J. L. hurried back to his room to make sure that the book was where he left it. There it was on the middle of the table with all of the notes he had made during the night. He thought to himself that, if he was going to be a spy, he was going to have to start thinking like one. Otherwise, he might just get himself in big trouble.

After breakfast, he made his way back to cabin number twelve. He and Jake quickly got down to business. They spent the rest of the morning going over his notes and assembling and breaking down the cabinet. Using the *Stag* magazine he had purchased at the cigar store, they took a roll of film and reduced it to dots. When Jake was satisfied that he could handle the equipment, he took all of J. L.'s notes, burned them in the fireplace, dismissed J. L., and went back to his fishing.

As J. L. walked out the door, Jake added, "There is only one thing missing."

"What's that?"

"A four-letter word for idiot."

"What?"

"A four-letter word for idiot. With that, I finish my puzzle. I've been thinking about that all morning," Jake said.

"Got me."

"Shit," he said as he walked off.

On the train ride back into Benton, J. L. mused on the events of the past twenty-four hours, his mother, his poor sister, and the camera in the seat beside him.

CHAPTER 28

"You have been with us for a while," the commandant said to Helena. "My question, Fraulein, is why you have so many special privileges. You have a bed to sleep in, and you eat every day while our soldiers on the Eastern Front are hungry and freezing. Yet, you provide us with nothing; in fact, you complain that we do not provide you with pen and paper.

"We've asked you for the whereabouts of those common criminal friends of yours, and you refuse. You will be happy to know that we will no longer be asking you those questions. Would you like to know why? I'll tell you why. They are all dead. All except for one: your daughter, Anna. And she is now here with us. She was caught trying to blow up an ammunition dump. Would you like to know where she is?"

Ziereis stood and walked over to the window.

"Here, stand with me, and I'll show you." Pointing to the Hartheim Castle, he said, "She's there in the castle in a room next to the crematorium. Now it's she who has information we need, and you are the bait. She knows you are here, and soon, we will let her get a glimpse of you. If she does not talk, we will kill her, but we will tell her that you will die if she doesn't talk just the same as we are telling your son in America. Your son already believes that his sister is dead. You told him so in one of your letters.

"You, on the other hand, have nothing that we need, so as of today, you will join the rest of the Jewish vermin in the rat hole. You are old, and I fully expect that soon you will die. It will be no great loss. Before you leave, let me assure you that your children will not survive either. By the time we are through, there will be no such thing as a Jew. We will destroy you, body and soul."

CHAPTER 29

The sun is never yellow; its cast is red or black. The hazy fog that filters the light and caps our mountain carries an overly sweet, sick smell. It comes day and night from the ovens not made for bread.

Death proceeds, regardless of our level of attention or inattention. Like water behind a dam, we can impede, we can divert, but we can't stop it. That same water flows ultimately to the sea and its primordial soup, where the elements are recombined and the process begins again.

Helena

Ben Sebastian and his wife, Gail, arrived and moved into the front apartment of the Sims's home. J. L. was assigned to be his assistant and driver; it seemed that Mr. Sebastian had lived in New York City all of his life and had never mastered the skill of driving a car.

The two men hit it off quickly. J. L. listened, and Ben talked. Ben had no intention of staying in Bauxite for very long. He had no problem with the living arrangement or the work at the plant; the problem was Gail.

Gail Sebastian was a budding actress whose off-Broadway stage career had been just on the verge of taking off. Her agent had assured her that she would be the next Carol Lombard, only with real talent and not just another pretty face. Because of the move to Benton, she had been forced to turn down an extra's role in a show called *The Girls of Hoboken*. It was a small part, but if you didn't work, you weren't seen. At age twenty-two, she was at her peak. She was a long-legged brunette, full-figured with a narrow waist. Her face was angelic with fine aquiline features. In the last two years, she had lost the awkward vestiges of adolescence while retaining her look of innocence.

Most importantly, she was not happy to be in Benton, Arkansas, and her displeasure was taken out on Ben. Gail refused to take her meals with the Sims and, for the most part, stayed to herself. When Ben returned from a day's work, Gail was ready to be entertained. Most days, he was tired and ready to sit and listen to the radio, but Gail wouldn't hear of it. In an attempt to replace the café society she was used to, she insisted that they go to the Lone Star, the Triangle Café, or the Phoenix and sit for hours over a cup of coffee. Most evenings, she complained about the noise the children made during the day when she was trying to rest. Her second favorite subject was the lack of culture in this out-of-the-way little burg. Ben had better sense than to point out that she was from Newark, New Jersey. Compared to Newark, Benton was mecca.

"I don't know what I'm going to do with that woman," he told J. L. one morning on their way to work. "I love her, but I've got to work, and she just doesn't understand. In New York, structural engineers are a dime a dozen. This job was a great opportunity for me. She listens to that agent. He tells her what she wants to hear. She hasn't had one job in the last two years; not one real acting job, anyway. But to hear her tell it, she would be starring on Broadway if it wasn't for me and this plant."

While Ben talked, J. L. sat and watched the rolled up set of blueprints that sat on the seat beside them each morning as they drove to the plant. As they rode back and forth, he puzzled over how he would ever get an opportunity to copy the documents.

One day when he went by the Sims's home to pick up Ben, Gail came out with the plans and told him that her husband was ill and wouldn't be able to go in to work. She handed him the plans and went back into the house.

When he turned back onto Military and headed down East Street toward Bauxite, J. L. knew that he would never have this easy an opportunity again, the question was timing. He was expected at the plant, the plans were expected at the plant. He stopped his car in front of the cotton gin on East Street and sat there for a few minutes. As he contemplated his next move, Jim Sims pulled up alongside.

"J. L., are you okay?" he asked.

"Yeah, I'm fine. Just thinking about how nice a morning it is. Did you ever think about just keeping on driving? I mean, somebody calls you to come get a body and you get on Highway 67 and just keep on driving?" J. L. asked.

"You're beginning to sound like Fitts," Sims said.

"Oh, I wouldn't do it. I got too much going here, but every once in a while, I think about it."

"Well, I got to get to work. Where's Ben?" Sims asked.

"Wife said he was sick this morning."

"Those two are really strange. You know, they didn't say a word to us."

"Yeah, I know. I think it's the wife," J. L. said.

"I think you're right. By the way, are you and Larry coming to the camp a week from Saturday?"

"Didn't know anything about it."

"I told Larry to tell you," Sims said. "The American Legion is putting on a big get-together for the veterans at Quapaw on the river north of town. We have all of the cabins set aside. Most of us are going to spend the night. We have arrangements for kids, couples, and singles. We're going to have softball and horseshoes and lots of food. We've got boats for those who want to fish. Quapaw is about a mile long, and it has good fishing. For those that want to, they could float down to town and leave the boat there. My whole family is going, and believe it or not, Ben and Gail have said they might go."

"Fitts didn't tell me anything about it, but it sounds like a good idea."

"If you decide to go, let me know by next Thursday. We are trying to get a head count. Got to go; got work to do. See you later."

"Yeah, see you later," J. L. said.

J. L. watched Sims's car pull in behind the funeral home, and it occurred to J. L. that the next Saturday night would be the perfect time to photograph the plans. He and Larry had eaten Sunday dinner with the Sims family a couple of times in the last few months. Sims kept the house key on a nail at the north end of the porch, just under the eve of the house. There was no dog to worry about. The cat, Gracie, wouldn't be any trouble.

The problem was solved.

That evening after he returned the plans to the Sims's house, J. L. stopped by Larry's shop for a beer.

"Evening, Larry, how are you?" J. L. asked.

"Not bad. Look what I finished today." Larry held up a delicate, little vase. It had a bright blue sheen, and impregnated into the fired clay were small pieces of white, blue, and green crystals. It was exquisite. Held up to the light, it cast a series of small rainbows.

"That is absolutely beautiful," J. L. said.

"There is only one problem."

"What?"

Larry took a glass of water and poured it into the vase. The water poured from the small clay vessel like a shower head. "Leaks like a sieve."

"Well, just make it a lamp," J. L. suggested.

"But I want to do a vase. I have just got to find a way to keep the clay from retracting from the crystals," Larry said.

"It's pretty anyway. By the way, are you going to that shindig that the legion is throwing at Quapaw a week from Saturday?"

"Are you kidding?" Larry said, laughing. "Do you want to sit around and listen to a bunch of old guys talk about what they did in the 'Big War'? Besides, there are two things they won't have—beer and women. Back when I worked for Jim full-time, he hooked me into going to that for a couple of years. Talked about the fishing and how we could do a float trip and take out down at the swimming hole at the end of Jackmon Street."

"He told me that too," J. L. said.

"Well, don't fall for that. They just want someone to do the work. In the two years I went, I never got near a fishing boat. Half the time, you end up babysitting the kids. Anyway, I got a date with this pretty little girl from Lonsdale. We're going to go skating that night and drink a little beer. You want to go along? I'm sure that Lenora's got a friend we can fix you up with."

"No, thanks anyway," J. L. said, "I've got a lot of work to get done. By the way, my friend, Valencia, in Mexico City is putting the pressure on for some more pots. You think we could do a shipment next week."

"What kind of things does he want?" Larry asked.

"Let's send him a selection of three or four different kinds."

"That's a good idea. If you get eight pieces, I can give you a discount."

"Don't worry about that. He'll pay what we ask," J. L. said.

"If I give you a discount, you can pocket the rest," Larry suggested.

"No, you just sell them to me at the price you would get if you sold them out of the showroom."

"If you say so," Larry said. "By the way, I lied to you the other day."

"About what?"

"I said, you wouldn't find out from me whether Marty would go out with you or not. Well, she came in this afternoon and asked if I knew if you were dating anybody. When I told her no, she said to let you know that she is working our baseball game for the *Courier* on Saturday afternoon down at the field on Richards street. Sounded like an invite to me. By the way, if I was you, I'd take a bathing suit; most of the time, we end up swimming down at the river after the game."

CHAPTER 30

On Saturday, J. L. caught the bus to the plant. On the days that he didn't have to drive Ben to work, he enjoyed riding with the miners. He had quickly developed a reputation as a miner's friend. Any time there was a task to be done, he could be counted on to jump in and get his hands dirty.

All week, they had been dealing with a sticky problem of speeding up the movement of bauxite from the ore train to one of the big hoppers. By early afternoon, he and a crew of men were fully immersed in the latest of a series of mechanical solutions when he noticed the time. It was three o'clock, Larry's game had started at two and, with that, his date with Marty; he was late.

He explained his dilemma to the crew, quickly made it back to his office, closed up, and ran toward the bus station. Fortunately, he arrived just as the bus was getting ready to leave. With several stops along the way, the bus arrived at the corner of Main and Sevier at about three forty-five. He raced down Sevier to his house and picked up a pair of shorts that could serve as a swimsuit. Just beyond his house, Richards Street took a right and headed directly toward the baseball field.

As he neared the field, he heard a loud roar of approval from the Benton home stands. The second basemen had just hit a solo home run to put the Benton team up by one run in the top of the ninth inning.

J. L. surveyed the stands looking for Marty. She was sitting at the top of the stands by herself with a scorer's book in her lap. Slowly, he made his way through the crowd to the bench where she sat.

"Hey, Marty," he said. "Can I have a seat by you?"

She smiled and patted the bench.

"Of course, I would love for you to. You've been missing a great game. Larry and the boys just got ahead of Lonsdale for the third time in the game. But we've got a problem; Shorty, the third basemen, hurt himself in the last inning and probably won't be able to go back in the game, and Larry doesn't have any other players. He may have to get me to play the last half-inning."

The Lonsdale pitcher struck out the next batter, retiring the side.

Then much to everyone's surprise, Larry took the field playing third base. Most of the time, he made it a rule not to run—even slowly—because when he did, he looked like a wounded antelope.

Slim Davis was the pitcher for Benton, and he was beginning to tire. The first batter hit a pop up into short left field that fell in between the short-stop and the fielder. The next batter hit a line drive to deep right, and the runner on first took off. By the time the fielder had corralled the ball; the runner had rounded second and was headed for third. The fielder lofted the ball with a prayer toward third, but it was too late. While this was transpiring, the runner on first easily made it to second.

Larry called a time out, walked to the mound and had a quick conference with the pitcher. He returned to his position at third. "Get him, Slim," he said. "That clown can't hit the ball. Show him the way back to Garland County."

Slim wound up and threw the ball as fast as he could. It was inside and hit the bat just beyond the knuckles of the batter as he came around. The bat splintered, and the ball sped right down the third base line. Larry was playing just off the bag when the ball was hit; the runner had a two-pace lead toward home; and the man on second had a jump and was running.

Larry had his gloved hand extended to the left when the ball was hit. He hesitated and turned his head to the left, looking toward the outfield. The runners and all of the spectators assumed that Larry had missed the ball. With the runners committed, Larry walked over to third and stepped on the bag. The runner from second was racing toward him, heading for home. Larry opened up his right hand to reveal the scoffed baseball. He'd caught it with his bare right hand. The runner from second stopped dead in his tracks, five feet away from third base. Larry lunged toward him, tagging him with the now very obvious ball.

Marty's headline for the weekly paper would read: COACH GIMPY FITTS WINS GAME WITH UNASSISTED TRIPLE PLAY

For a minute, the whole field went quiet as they considered this improbable occurrence. Then, in unison, the home crowd broke out in uproarious laughter.

Marty turned to J. L. and said, "They may not always win, but they are always entertaining."

Marty and J. L. made their way down to the field as the team celebrated.

"That was one hell of a play," J. L. said to his friend. "I bet your hand is going to hurt in the morning."

"There's no in the morning to it. It hurts like hell right now," Larry said. He exposed the palm of his right hand, and it was already beginning to turn black and blue.

"You need some ice for that," Marty said.

"Sounds like a great idea. We need to get some ice for the beer anyway," Larry said. "Everybody pile into the truck, and we'll head for the river."

The Ice House was at the south end of Market across the street from the Niloak kiln. Old man Gibson was sitting on the loading platform when the Larry pulled up in front. His wood cane chair was cocked up on two legs, leaning against the brick front wall.

"How much ice you boys need?" he asked.

"Thirty pounds ought to be enough," Larry said.

When old man Gibson's chair came down on all fours, he maintained the same bent position. His back was turned like a pretzel from years of hauling heavy blocks of ice. When he walked away, all they could see was the leather shoulder apron that protected him from the ice. He looked like an old buffalo with one hind leg shorter than the other. Every time Larry watched Gibson move away, he thought about how he might end up looking that way one day.

When Gibson returned with the ice, Larry was amazed by how the ice added a balance to the appearance of the old man with the deformed back. With the thirty-pound block of ice suspended from the easy touch of the brass ice tongs over his back, the old man appeared almost like a dancer who was complete only with his partner. He moved down the wooden steps of the platform like he'd done a million times before and gently laid the ice into a metal washtub. From his belt he removed a sharp ice pick and, with a few deft strokes, reduced the ice to a tub of chips.

It was only a block or so over to the parking lot for McCoy-Couch Furniture Factory. John Payor was in his usual spot under the oak tree at the back of the lot. John had built a custom frame over the flatbed on the back of the truck, and painted on the side in big red letters was PAYOR'S DRY GOODS AND PRODUCE. It was a noble attempt at fiction that gave everyone an excuse to turn their heads.

John was a small man and bald except for a small strip of black hair that circled his head just above his ears. In addition to making whiskey and beer, he invented things. Each week, he had a new gadget. An electric curling iron that weighted in at twenty-five pounds, a radio mounted in his truck that took up most of the truck cab, an electronic straight razor that always maintained a sharp edge—John always had an idea, but most of the time, he lost interest by the following week.

"What will it be, boys?" he asked.

Larry jumped from the truck. "Case and a half of orange pop, warm. We got our own ice. We got exchange bottles."

"Coming up," Payor said.

John reached under the canvas that was draped over the back of the truck and slid two wooden cola cases full of Orange Treat bottles. Slim gathered up all of the loose empty bottles from the back of the truck and behind the seat in the cab.

"We're one over on empties."

"Good, I need the bottles. I'll give you credit," Payor said.

Larry and J. L. gently placed the precious orange drink bottles into the ice; Payor was never terribly precise about the way he capped the bottles.

After they paid and were on the way to the river, J. L. asked about the orange pop.

"That way if somebody like a revenuer comes by, Payor will know. The local police don't give him any trouble, but every once in a while, a federal guy will come by and start snooping around. If you ask for whiskey or beer and he doesn't know you, he'll act like he doesn't know what you're talking about. He told me one day that he had a friend in Little Rock who warns him when there's going to be trouble."

The Saline River was a small mountain stream that began in the hills north and west of Benton. A few miles north of town, three small branches came together to form the main river. The town of Benton had begun at a river crossing on the Old Military Road to Texas, one mile south and west of the present town. Malaria and flooding had forced the town fathers to move a safe distance up the hill. A second path, Jackmon Trail, headed due west of town and forded the river at an idyllic site. The rocky shoal that formed the crossing was wide and shallow, providing good footing for men, horses, and wagons. Above and below the crossing were deep holes of blue-green water that were perfect for swimming. The eastern shore had a sand and gravel beach that was good for the little kids. The western side was deep, and the shore was lined with old white and red oak, slippery elm, and cottonwoods with large strong limbs for rope swings.

Johnny Moore from the Mountain View community had built a large gazebo on a mud sled, and each spring after the heavy rains, he harnessed the sled to a big team of mules and pulled it down to the river. The gazebo had change centers and restrooms for those who were shy. For the kids, Mr. Moore sold lemonade, punch, and sandwiches. For the parents, he had wooden-framed canvas chairs and umbrellas for rent.

There were two unwritten rules: no liquor was to be sold and any drinking had to be done at the deep hole on the south side of the crossing, away from the children.

The baseball crew arrived at the river in a cloud of dust. They found a shady place to park the truck, opened a cold beer, and then took turns changing clothes in the cab. Most of the boys made short work of the first beers and started on their seconds. Larry had no bathing suit.

J. L. sat down by him on the bank. "Aren't you going change? I bet someone has an extra pair of shorts."

"No, to be honest with you, I really don't want anybody seeing my legs. They really are gimpy looking." Larry gave J. L. the highlights of all the problems he had had with his legs since he was born.

"Damn, I'm surprised that you can walk, much less play baseball. You mind showing me what they look like?"

Larry shook his head. He reached down, removed his shoes, and pulled up his pant legs. With his pants leg pulled up the extent of his problems were obvious. His left foot was nothing but a stump that slid into his modified shoe. The left leg had multiple scars that ran from knee to ankle and the bony structure that should have been an ankle was a rigid fused plate.

"Man, those do look like they would hurt."

"No, not a lot. I got special stuff in my right shoe."

"You know that makes what you did today that much more special. By the way, what about the triple play?" J. L. asked.

"You want to know the truth?"

"Yeah, sure."

"I don't have the least idea. I looked up, and there the ball was in my right hand. When I was a kid, the colored all-stars would come around the farms and play the home teams. I'd seen those guys do things like that—you know, palming the ball, that kind of thing. But I've never done it myself."

As they were talking, Marty walked out of the gazebo with a towel draped around her neck.

"Get a look at her," Larry said. "What a set of legs."

They both smiled.

"Look a lot better than yours, that is for sure," J. L. said.

"What are you two laughing about?" Marty asked.

"We were just admiring the scenery," Larry said.

"Well, I'm going swimming. Last one to the raft is a rotten egg," Marty said. She was referring to a wooden platform made of one-by-six planks nailed on top of heavy oak logs. It was secured in the deep water by a cable that led to a large bolder in shallow water upstream.

Larry motioned for the two of them to go on. "I don't swim much," he said. "My sister was always protective of me when I was a kid. She didn't want me to drown on her shift. I'll just sit here and drink beer."

Soon, Marty and J. L. were sitting on the raft, dangling their legs in the water.

"Larry was telling me that you haven't lived here very long," J. L. said.

"We've lived here a few years. Before we came here, we lived in Zanesville, Ohio, and Dad worked for Roseville Pottery. In Zanesville, he was just a potter, and Mr. Hyten gave him an opportunity to be the big cheese. It was an opportunity he couldn't pass up. Mom wasn't the least bit happy about moving south, but she knew that Dad couldn't pass up the opportunity, especially during the middle of the Depression. So, we moved.

"I think Larry probably told you, but Mom died last year, and Dad has taken it really hard. He is still blaming himself, I know he is."

"Sounds like a tough situation," J. L. said.

"How about you? How did you end up in glorious Saline County?" she asked.

"Needs of the company. They needed engineers here, and I'm an engineer. It's a pretty good job; for the most part, I'm my own boss, and I get to do a lot of things I wouldn't get to do in East Saint Louis or Pittsburgh."

"What about your family?" she asked.

"Dad died of a heart attack back in the twenties. My dear mother is a newspaper editor and writer in Vienna, but I haven't heard anything from her since the Nazis took over. My little sister is a bit of a radical, and the last I heard of her, she was in Palestine. My older brother came to this country back in the twenties. Mom used him as an excuse to get me to come to the States and look for him. By the time, I found him, he was a hopeless drunk, and a couple of years later, he was run over and killed. I have an uncle in Pittsburgh, but we aren't really close."

"You said your mom was a newspaper editor in Vienna. Did you ever know of Adelheid Popp-Dworak or any of the women of the Oldenberg?" Marty asked.

J. L. was tempted to say no, but before he knew it, the words were coming out of his mouth. "Of course I did. I grew up in the Oldenberg, but how do you know about her?" he asked.

"My junior high French teacher was a feminist and socialist, and she talked about those women all of the time. Who was your mother?"

"Helena Edit-Stein."

"Are you kidding? Your mother has been an inspiration to feminists everywhere. One of the first political essays I ever read was her editorial, "AND NOW WHAT". The pieces of hers that Naomi Mitchison reprinted in England a few years ago were beautifully written. Have you thought about going back to find her?"

"She made me promise that, no matter what, I wouldn't come back until the crisis was over in Europe."

"What do you think has happened?" she asked.

"I have no idea, but I worry about it all the time." With that, J. L. began to cry quietly.

"I didn't mean to upset you," Marty said.

"It's okay. Sometimes it just seems like there is a big black hand over our family. I really do miss them." He wiped his eyes and then attempted to change the subject. "So what are you going to do with your life?"

"I want to own a newspaper," she said. "I want to be the one who decides what is news and what's not. Right now, I'm here because of my father; if he ever gets to feeling better, I will probably leave and go to school somewhere. I'm saving every penny I make to eventually go off to school. He doesn't make enough to send me. He would send me, but it would be a real burden. Right now, I write obits, the police and fire beat, and the occasional sports column for the *Courier*. I'm working on a novel that I started a few years ago, but my heart just isn't in it."

From the bank of the river Larry shouted, "Hey, guys, we're going to town. Are you ready?"

J. L. turned to Marty and asked, "You want to walk back into town?"

Marty smiled. "Sure, that sounds nice."

J. L. shouted to Larry, "You go on. Just leave my clothes on the bank."

By the time Marty and J. L. made it back to the bank, they were the only ones left, and Mr. Moore was getting ready to close up the dressing rooms.

They both dressed and walked back up the hill into town. The sun behind them was just beginning to cast its long red shadow on the town of Benton. The courthouse stood out as a bright reflection.

"You know I have never noticed that light off the courthouse. It is awfully pretty," Marty said. As they talked, she took J. L.'s hand.

"Yes, it is. When I was a child, Dad and I would walk down to the river in Vienna and watch the sun go down. By the way, I didn't ask you where you live."

"I live just around the corner from the baseball field on Gaunt Street." She pointed up the street. "Just there on the left, the little house with the rose trellis. You live on Sevier, don't you?"

J. L. nodded. "Would you like to have a real date some time? I mean like dress up and go to a movie or maybe over to Hot Springs for the day?"

"I would love to," she said.

"How about next weekend? Jim Sims was telling me about this big picnic they are having at Camp Quapaw. I haven't looked at my schedule, but I think I am off all day Saturday."

"I can't next weekend. Dad's family is having a reunion back in Ohio. Dad and I already have our train tickets. I really need to go with him. He looks forward to this every year."

"When will you be back?"

"Wednesday week," she said.

"I'll call you."

"Good, can't wait." She leaned into him and kissed him on the cheek.

J. L. stood and watched her walk through the trellis. As he did, he remembered the story his father had told of his first encounters with his mother. It seemed that J. L. was a great deal like his father; he was most attracted to pretty, smart women.

CHAPTER 31

A group of young resistance fighters were brought into camp. They were forced to climb down the quarry walls instead of using the steps. Several fell and were killed. The rest were required to carry double loads up the steps. Some fell and dropped their loads, killing those below them. The ones who fell were shot on the spot. This morning, the rest were lined up on the top of the quarry and told to climb down the wall again. Instead, they joined hands and jumped to their deaths. The guards laughed, and we went back to work.

Helena

Old-Fashioned Day was set aside to celebrate the past, to relive the time when the early settlers had shared that part of the Saline River Valley with the Quapaw and Caddo Indians. It was to keep alive a memory of times that seemed simpler, times when the most important thing in the life of the family was the changing of the season and how their neighbors fared. For a time, World War I had erased the fiction of isolation. It had brought home the reality and horror of mass wars. The veterans of World War I had returned from Europe, determined to recapture their former lives. They had looked for ways to regain what they had lost. Old-Fashioned Day with its ballgames, horseshoes, and picnics was one of those affairs.

Camp Quapaw was a beautiful hilltop site overlooking the Saline River Valley. Six miles north of town, a small gravel road turned south off of Highway 70. After crossing a small creek, it angled up a sharp grade to a ridge on the north side of the river. On the south side of the ridge, a steep bluff dropped off into a long pool of water, extending up- and downstream. The river made a long wide U with the camp at the base of the U. Across the river were the flat river bottoms, part of which was cleared for cattle grazing. For the most part, it looked like it had when God had first built it.

Old-Fashioned Day had triggered a major tiff between Ben and Gail. After several days of fighting and promises of future favors, Gail had agreed to attend the gathering. She was packed into the Sims's Chevy sedan with the three girls, Mr. and Mrs. Sims, and her husband. Gail had an aversion to touching people, and she said that the idea of being packed in a car with six hot, sweaty people was next to torture.

Except for weekend trips to Hot Springs, visits to the IMP Theater when the movie changed, and their nightly sojourn to the local cafés, Gail stayed in her room.

"What a beautiful place," Ben said as he stepped from the car. A cool breeze blew up from the river. Many of the older women had arrived early in the day, and the smell of fried chicken and homemade bread filled the camp.

"Your cabin is the one over on the other side of the horseshoe pit. Put your bags away, and we'll meet you over by the baseball field in a few minutes. The restrooms are just beyond the lodge," Sims said, pointing toward the west end of the campground.

Gail Sebastian turned heads when she walked into a room. When she emerged from the car, brushing the wrinkles from her skirt, all of the men in the line of sight stopped to look at her. She bordered on being too pretty—that look of beauty and youth that approaches perfection, nothing subtle. Her long, silky, smooth hair fell across her shoulders in a cascade of gold. She wore a simple, blue sundress that strongly hinted at all of the features it concealed. The line of her breasts, her flat belly, and her round bottom touched the fabric in an inviting, suggestive fashion. Her movement beneath the dress was fluid and unrestricted. It would never have done for her to walk through a machine shop where high speed, dangerous equipment required constant attention. One sashay through the plant floor and most of the men would have been injured.

She and Ben walked to the cabin that Sims had pointed out to deposit their bags and change for the softball game. Much to Ben's surprise, she had not objected and, in fact, seemed somewhat excited about the prospects of playing a game of softball. Ben knew next to nothing about her early life, and when he pressed the point, she insisted that it was past history and didn't apply to this life. Another part of the mystery of Gail was the fact that she wouldn't divulge her age or her birthday; after a while, he quit asking.

The yearly game, The Game, was an Old-Fashioned Day tradition—men and boys against women and girls. The loser served the other side the evening meal.

When the game began, it was obvious that this was not the first time that Gail Sebastian had played a game of softball. By the second inning, any pretense of reserve and aloofness disappeared. She was now twelve-year-old Gail, playing stickball on the streets of Newark.

When she came up to bat in the third inning, she hit the ball square on, driving it over the head of the left-fielder, driving in two runs. The next batter drove one into short right field. Gail had a good lead from second and was halfway to third when the ball crossed into the outfield. The right-fielder was Joe Sharp. Other than the pitcher, he was probably the best athlete on the field. When he saw Gail turn the corner at third and head home, he threw a line drive strike right back to the catcher who was waiting, guarding the home plate. No matter how fast Gail Sebastian was, she wasn't going to beat the throw. She was too far from third to turn back, and the outcome seemed certain. The catcher wasn't counting on Gail. As she neared the plate, she went into a crouch and dove directly into him. The collision caused a cloud of dust and when the dust began to settle, the scuffed baseball came rolling out along the first baseline.

"Safe," the umpire shouted.

Gail was joined at home plate by half of the women from Saline County. When celebrating was done, she was the new hero. This was a different Gail—not the beauty queen who had stepped out of the car two hours before. This lady was a down-and-dirty baseball player with her hair pulled back, dirt on her face, sweat under her arms, and a scrape on her right knee from the collision at home plate.

The women went on to win the game fifteen to thirteen and prepared to have their evening meal served to them.

When Gail emerged from the showers, she was again dressed in her sundress, but there was something quite different. She had her hair pulled back in a ponytail. There was no makeup, uncovering a light dusting of freckles on her cheeks. The most distinctive change was her smile. Any illusion of distance and mystery was replaced by an open, warm smile that seemed to go from one ear to the next.

As the sun was sitting, Ben, along with all of the other men, served the meal. The older boys in the group gathered a supply of dried wood, and when the darkness was full, they started a large bonfire. For an hour or two, they sat around the fire while the children played a game of Kick the Can. The old men told stories about what life used to be like in Saline County.

Eventually, Ben and Gail excused themselves and headed for their cabin. Ben carried a kerosene lantern. They walked with their arms around each other's waists, watching for irregular rocks and the potential hapless blind snake that might have accidentally wandered into the campground.

Ben opened the screen door to the cabin. Ben and Gail saw the skunk at the same time the skunk saw them. The kerosene lamp created stage lights for the frightened, cornered skunk as his black and white tail flipped up. The smell was instantaneous. In the close quarters of the cabin the spray of the skunk covered their bags and, mercifully, missed them. In the process of backing out, Ben dropped the lamp that busted, spreading lit kerosene all around the entrance to the cabin.

"Ben, I've got to have my bag," Gail insisted.

"The skunk peed on it, and it's in the middle of a burning building."

"I know, but I have to have it." There were almost no material things in life that had intrinsic value to Gail Sebastian, but in the smelly, wet bag were a small locket with the only picture she had of her mother and a small change purse with two hundred dollars, rolled tightly. It was her nest egg.

About that time, the others, who had heard the noise, came running with old blankets and buckets of water. Before Gail could object, the first pail of water landed on her open bag, soaking it and its contents.

Ben darted back into the building and grabbed the soaked bag, which smelled strongly of skunk.

Without a thank you or an "Are you all right?" Gail said, "Take me home." It was a voice that Ben had heard before; it was not a negotiation voice.

Ben turned to Jim Sims, who was standing beside him, watching the younger men fight the fire. "Would you take us home? I think Gail has had enough of Camp Quapaw."

"Yeah, sure. I understand."

J. L. spent the morning at Larry's, helping with the finishing touches on a daybed he was building for the Caldwell family. It seemed that the old man of the family loved to sleep on the screened porch in the spring and fall. Mr. Caldwell was a rather big man, and standard cots were too narrow and sagged with his weight. Larry had built a heavy, wood frame with a reinforced spring system that was strongest around the middle section of the bed where most of the elderly gentleman's weight would fall. As an added surprise, he had added carvings that depicted scenes of the old man hunting quail.

"This is something they won't get from mail order," Larry said as he smiled at his creation.

"You know, you are quite an artist. Did you ever think about going to New York or Chicago?" J. L. asked.

"No, I got people here. As I see it, there are a lot worse places that I could be right now."

"I can guarantee you that."

J. L. finished the touch-up he was doing on the footboard and sat down in one of Larry's many rocking chairs that sat around the store.

"You might not like the way that chair feels. I built that for Old Highpockets who lives out on Peeler Bend Road. You probably don't know him, but he is shaped kinda funny. He ain't got no middle. His legs come damn near up to his chest. I had to shorten the platform and lower the back. I've been working on that thing for a year. When the old man dies, they'll probably have to throw the chair away 'cause nobody else will be able to sit in it. Sit in that one over there by the wall."

"How did you learn how to do all of this?" J. L. asked.

"I don't know. When you're born like me with a gimpy leg, you learn real quickly: there's always more than one way to solve a problem. I remember the kids at Children's Hospital. Some were born normal and then lost a leg. It was harder for them. I was the way I was from the day I was born, so I started out figuring out ways to walk, make my own shoes, and change the length of my pant legs. When my other leg got bunged up, that was just one more challenge. As for the carving and pottery, that was just to entertain myself.

"That's enough about me. What about you? Don't you have some family or something?"

"No, my family is all gone," J. L. said. "I got an uncle in Pittsburgh, but we aren't real close. We traveled around a lot when I was a kid. My dad was an engineer like me. He died from a heart attack in the mid-20s. He wasn't very old. Real great guy; I loved him a lot. Don't know where my sister is, last I heard of her, she was heading for Palestine. We got a little Jewish blood in us. I'm sure that's why she headed that way. My older brother was a drunk, got run over by a car. Last time I saw him was in a dive in Pittsburgh. Real sad case."

"What about your mother?" Larry asked.

J. L. enjoyed Larry's company. He really wanted to tell his new friend about his mother, his worry for her, and the life that had been forced on him, but he knew that would complicate things in all sorts of ways.

"I don't know exactly where my mother is. She is one of the smartest people that I've ever known. She writes for newspapers. I get letters from her every once in a while. She was all involved in the suffragette movement back in the teens and twenties. After World War I, she was a big proponent of the League of Nations. She really believed that President Wilson was on to something. Anyway, I haven't seen her in a long time."

"Looks like we are in the same boat as far as family," Larry said.

"Yeah, I guess so."

"You want another beer?" Larry asked.

"No, I got to go home. I got some work that I have to get caught up on this weekend. You don't get in any trouble over in Lonsdale."

The talk of family had put J. L. in a sober mood. He had every letter he had received since he had moved to the States. He had read and reread them until they were beginning to tear in the folds.

He fixed a pot of coffee and pulled one of his chairs out onto the landing. The earlier letters painted such a rosy picture of life in Austria and especially Mauthausen. A group of distant relatives that his mother didn't claim lived just outside of Mauthausen. Helena always had a bad taste for that little stretch of country, but then she spoke in glowing terms as to how wonderful things were.

When the sun set, he packed up the camera case and walked the back streets over to Lillian Street, the street that came up behind the Sims's home. Most of the time, nobody in Benton locked his doors. Jim Sims was an exception. The only problem was he left the key on a nail on the north end of the porch. Several times in the last few months, J. L. and Larry had joined the Sims family for Sunday dinner. J. L. had made note of where the key was kept.

None of the neighbors had outside lights that would interfere with J. L.'s progress, so in a short time, he was in the back door and making his way across the combination den, dining area, and kitchen. The door into the Sebastians's room was not locked. Ben kept the plans in a rolltop desk on the north wall of the room. In a short time, J. L. had the plans out and on the floor. He had become adept at setting up the camera and getting what he needed done in a minimum amount of time. The problem with this chore was that the pages were too large for the dark area of the case so he had to photograph the pages in four sections.

He was finishing up the next-to-last page of the plans when a set of car lights flashed through the window and flooded the room with light.

It was Sims's car, and J. L. could hear Ben apologizing for the inconvenience. Just as soon as Ben and his wife were out of the car, Sims backed out of the driveway and headed back toward the river.

J. L. realized that something had gone wrong. They were supposed to be gone all night. The front door was locked. They were coming in the back, and he had no way out. He quickly refolded the maps, getting more desperate with every moment. He was collapsing the camera when he heard Ben open the back door. The bathroom was out of the question; he wouldn't have time to get the window open. The only option was to crawl under the bed and hope that he could sneak out later after they were asleep.

His heart was pounding in his chest, and his breathing seemed as loud as a freight train. As Ben and Gail came in the door to their room, J. L. pulled his second leg under the bed. Ben turned on the light. J. L. was worried that he had left something ajar in the room, but if he had, they didn't notice. They were too busy arguing about what to do with their clothes. Ben sat on the bed to take off his shoes, and Gail immediately barked at him to get off of the bed until he bathed. It was then that J. L. got his first whiff of the skunk. There was still water dripping from Ben's shoes, and the longer they stayed in the room, the more impressive the skunk odor became.

"Look, sweetheart, we can take these clothes to the cleaners," Ben said.

"Ben, you can do with your clothes what you want, but you aren't bringing them back into this house. Now get those wet clothes off, and let's put them out the front door."

Gail moved to the bathroom, disrobed, and handed the smelly clothes out to Ben. By this time, he was in his shorts. He carried both sets of clothes out into the side yard and put them on the line to air out. He was determined to prove to Gail that the odor could be banished.

To add to J. L.'s dilemma, he needed to pee. While first Gail and then Ben showered and used the restroom, J. L.'s problem became increasingly urgent. At one point, he considered just peeing in his pants, but he thought better of it.

Ben and Gail turned out the light and climbed into bed.

"Ben, open the door so the ceiling fan in the hall can draw some air through this room." Ben got out of bed and opened the door into the living room on the Sims's side. Before he got back into bed, he cracked the window in the front of the room.

From their conversation, J. L. had surmised what had happened as to the skunk, the fire, and Ben's dash back into the cabin to get her purse—which she now wanted to throw away.

When Ben got back into bed, he seemed interested in putting the events of the evening behind them and began to talk about the softball game. He rolled over toward Gail and tried to shift the focus to a more amorous subject.

"Not tonight. It's almost that time of the month," she said.

"But it's not that time of them month."

"I know but it's almost that time. I really don't feel like it to night."

Ben had just about had it.

"Well, when in the hell are you going to feel like it? You haven't felt like it for a damn month."

"I'll tell you when in the hell I'm going to feel like: I'm going to feel like it when you get me out of this backwater town."

"Damn," he shouted. Ben got out of bed went around to the closet and pulled out a pair of pants and an old work shirt.

"What are you doing?

"I'm going to get a beer?" he said.

"But, you don't drink," she said.

"I will tonight."

Listening to his friend fight with his wife made J. L. sad, but he was oddly fascinated. The idea of listening to people when they had their guards down had a certain amount of thrill.

The next sound he heard was Ben slamming the back door.

After Ben left, Gail got out of bed and went back to the bathroom. While she was gone to the bathroom, J. L. slid out the other side of the bed, case in hand, and made for the door. Gracie, the Sims's grey tabby, chose that instant to check out all of the noise. As they passed in the dark, J. L. stepped on the cat's tail. The cat screamed, J. L. peed on himself, and Gail came walking out of the bathroom. If the lights had been on, she would have seen him; as it was, all she saw was a motion near the door. She turned on the light and walked to the bedroom door. When she got near the door, Gracie raced back out of the bedroom to the safety of the living room and familiar territory.

Instead of heading for the door, J. L. had turned the corner into the girls' bedroom. For the first time that night, luck was with him. Despite warnings from their father, one of the girls had left the latch off of the window. He slid out of the window and pulled his case after him.

This spy business is getting to be hard work, he thought to himself as he walked away from the Sims's house. He made his way back to the apartment, changed his pants, and headed for the pool hall.

"Fancy meeting you here," J. L. said as he pulled a stool up beside Ben at the bar in the pool hall. "What are you doing down here with all of us losers?" He stopped for minute with a studied look on his face. "Aren't you supposed to be at Quapaw with Sims and his crew?"

"Yeah, we were, but we had a little mishap," Ben said.

"What sort of mishap?"

"Well, the short version is we ran into a mad skunk in a burning cabin."

"Sounds like a movie plot," J. L. said, smiling.

"Yeah, a bad movie. You want to play some pool?"

"Yeah, sure."

"I'm not much good. Haven't played since college."

"Is Gail all right?" J. L. asked.

"Yeah, everybody is all right. We had a little fight."

They both picked out pool cues, and Ben turned to J. L.

"You want to break?" he asked.

"No, why don't you go first?"

Ben lined up the ball and his cue and, with great force, sent the ball sailing past the rack and off of the table.

"Got a little force in that break. Might want to rein it in just a little."

"Don't know how long I'm going to last in this town. Gail is really putting on the pressure to leave," Ben said.

"You mean you might leave before the project is through?"

"Well, if it comes down to the job or my wife, I can always get another job," Ben said.

"I thought you told me they were going to send you to Surinam after this job was complete. If she doesn't like Benton, she really isn't going to like South America."

"Don't say that too loud; no one is supposed to know and especially not Gail."

Before the evening was out, Ben was baring his soul to his friend. It seemed that Gail used sex as a tool. If she didn't like something he did or didn't do, she cut him off for a week or so.

"Tonight, she told me that I could just forget about sex till we left this town. I know she isn't completely serious, because she likes it as much as I do, but it still makes me mad."

By this time, Ben was drunk and speaking in a stage whisper.

"Don't you think you have had enough?" J. L. asked.

"Yeah, maybe you are right. But I think I'll have another anyway."

By the time he had finished the next beer, Ben was barely able to make it to the restroom and back.

"Why don't you let me take you home?"

"Do you think they would let me take another one home with me?" Ben asked.

"They aren't supposed to do that. They could get in trouble."

"All right, all right. Let's go."

By the time they walked back up Main to Military and to the Sims's house, Ben was fully, completely drunk. When they walked into the front yard, he began to shout for Gail.

"Come out here, woman, your husband is home."

The lights came on in the house, and Gail walked to the door, tying her gown.

"Is he drunk?" she asked.

J. L. smiled.

"Yeah, I'm afraid he is."

As he finished, Ben went limp. It was official: he had passed out.

CHAPTER 32

Helena's bed, the one she shared with four other women, was in the back corner of block five—the Jewish barracks. Trun, the kapo or captain of the barracks prisoners, occupied the center of the barracks. An Austrian gypsy and convicted murderer, Trun was mild by kapo standards, beatings were administered on a predictable basis. Like the other kapos, he and his helpers were prisoners who reported the daily prisoner count to the SS overseer, set up work crews, and meted out favors.

In addition to being a barracks, block five served a second purpose. It was the old camp hospital; it was not a hospital in the sense that people went there to get well, but it was a stopping place for those who were too sick to work. More than three days in the hospital meant a prisoner was headed for the crematorium.

It was Helena's job to care for the sick. Commandant Ziereis made it clear when Helena was transferred from the bunker that she was not to be sent to the quarry just yet. He might still have a job for her to do.

"Nurse, help me. I'm freezing," the man in bed five said. He was covered with three blankets and was shaking violently.

"It will pass," she assured him. "You're just having a chill." She had no medicine, and there was little else to do except clean up the mess as she watched the poor man die. It was clear that he had pneumonia or some other overwhelming infection and would not survive long. "You should be better in the morning. You'll see," she said. "I'll be back in a minute."

Helena left her charge and walked down the aisle toward the front of the building. In the center was a potbellied, wood stove; in the winter evenings, most of the prisoners moved as close to the fire as they could without attracting the attention of Trun.

"Sir," she said, addressing the kapo. "The man in bed five will not make the night."

"Are you sure?" he asked.

Helena nodded her head.

"Take him to the infirmary, and bring his clothes back to me."

It was Helena's job to keep Trun apprised of the condition of her charges. When death was imminent, he could ship the dying prisoner off to the crematorium and replace him with someone who could work. There was a constant flow of prisoners into the camp, and Trun was only rewarded for the amount of work that was produced. The principle work of the camp was in the rock quarry, and those who worked the quarry were expected to last no more than six weeks—three months tops. Those, like Helena, who worked a camp detail, could be expected to survive for a year or more.

"We're going to take you to the infirmary. They have medicine there to help treat you," she said to the sick man. He didn't reply; he had already lapsed into a coma. It was no secret what going to the infirmary meant. The end result was death, and it was best that you were unconscious when you arrived. Dr. Kresbsbach and his pharmacist, Waskitsky, had several ways of ending a life—some more painful than others. Besides being gassed and shot, many were injected with a variety of chemicals; magnesium chloride caused the prisoners to die quickly and quietly, but most were injected with benzene or gasoline, which caused a violent, convulsive death.

By the time Helena and one of the other prisoners had moved the man to the infirmary, he was dead. The infirmary assistant signed the physician's name, certifying the death, and the body was moved to the crematorium.

The man in charge of the crematorium helped Helena and her assistant slide the body into the oven.

"Have you had a busy day?" Helena asked.

"Sure have. Kresbsbach thought he had a case of typhus in barracks ten yesterday. They gassed the whole barracks—kapo and all."

Helena shook her head.

Back at her barracks, Helena took out a slip of paper and recorded what she knew about the man who had died. She stuffed the note and her pencil back into the lining of her jacket. What had begun as a ploy on the part of Ziereis had now become a source of hope for the prisoners of Mauthausen. Sometimes her scribbling was found tacked to a post or lying on the roll-call yard. When the notes were found, they were secretly passed from person to person. There was little to smile at in Mauthausen and nothing to cause hope, except for the words of the poet of Mauthausen. There was no agreement as to whether the poet was a man or a woman or even if it was just one person or many, but no newspaper or bulletin was ever read so eagerly as the slips of paper that Helena Edit-Stein penned.

CHAPTER 33

On Wednesday, J. L. was helping Larry put the finishing touches on a shipment of pottery headed for Manitou Springs, Colorado. Each piece was carefully placed on a bed of wood shavings that Larry had salvaged from the pallet shed down by the railroad. "You know, Larry, I been watching when you are working at your potter's wheel. You get completely absorbed in what you are doing." J. L. said.

"I do. I can sit there at that wheel for hours. Between that and carving, I get a lot of satisfaction. What about you?"

"I really never knew this 'till I came here, but I most enjoy planning a project and then managing it to its finish. My work at the plant is the first time I have been in a position of working with and managing a big crew of men."

As they were talking, the bell over the front door rang, and Marty came walking into the shop.

"Welcome back, stranger. How was life up in Yankee land?" Larry asked.

"Actually, it was pretty nice. I haven't seen Dad that happy in a year. All his family was there. We ate and talked and laughed for a couple of days. But I have a problem."

"What's that?" J. L. asked.

"Dad enjoyed it so much he has decided to move back. He is going to tell Mr. Hyten today."

"Does that mean you will be moving as well?" J. L. asked.

"I really don't want to. I had planned to go to Little Rock Junior College this fall. I've got some friends from St. Mary's who are going there and really like it. I could take classes three days a week, ride the Doddle Bug back and forth, and keep my jobs at the paper and with Mr. Hyten."

"Can't you still do that?" Larry asked.

She shook her head. "I just wouldn't have enough money to go to school and pay the rent. It looks like I might have to move back with Dad."

"I can solve that problem right here and now," Larry said. "I got more than enough room back in the back. We can frame you in a private room, and it won't cost you anything. You'd have to share a bathroom with me."

"Are you serious?"

"Of course I am," Larry said.

"That would be great," Marty said. "I don't cook or anything."

"I'm not asking you to marry me."

"It's a deal. I could help tend the shop when you're out and clean up a bit. I've always thought this place needed a woman's touch anyway. But what about the Baptists at the church across the street?"

Larry grinned and shrugged his shoulders. "It'll just give them something good to talk about. Besides, they already think I'm a heathen anyway."

CHAPTER 34

My heart aches
for the warmth of love.
I can learn to live
without a fire to warm my skin,
without a full belly,
without the assurance of tomorrow,
without freedom;
but
I cannot live without love.

Poet of Mauthausen

"J. L.," Ben began, "Yesterday, I got a call from the top brass in East St. Louis. They want me to come up and give them an update on the preparations. I need for you to do a summary of the production numbers for the last three months."

"Already got it. I put it together last week," J. L. interrupted. What he didn't tell Ben was that the summary had been for the Germans, but, after all, it was the same numbers.

"You do remember we had that meeting planned with the mine's people tomorrow," Ben asked.

"Yeah, I can cancel it if you want me to. Mr. Mac won't mind," J. L. said.

"No, I think I'd go on and have it. Tell him that I'm suspicious this is more than just a routine update meeting that I'm going to. They may be getting ready to change the plans. Wilson was real closemouthed when he called. You know Wilson, don't you?"

"Yeah, we worked in the same section in East St. Louis before they sent him to Pittsburgh," J. L. laughed. "Real bright fellow. I wonder if there is any significance to the fact that they sent him east and they sent you and me west?"

"Somebody up there loves us," Ben said smiling. "By the way, I need for you to come by the house a little early in the morning, pick Gail and me up, and take us to the train station."

"Sure."

Early the next morning, J. L. pulled the black company sedan up in front of the Sims's house. Sitting on the front porch of the house were five suitcases, four of which belonged to Gail. Gail was sitting on the largest of the bags, smoking a cigarette.

"Ben," she shouted, "Hurry, J. L. is here."

"Hold your horses," he said, "I've already got the ticket, and the train doesn't come in for at least an hour."

"I just don't want to miss the train," she insisted.

"Okay, okay," Ben said.

The men loaded three of the bags in the small trunk and the other two on the front seat beside J. L. Ben helped Gail into the car, and they were off. It was clear that this was a day that Gail had looked forward to for several months.

At the station, Ben and J. L. unloaded the bags and handed them off to one of the porters working the platform. Ben handed J. L. the plans.

"Protect these and tell Mr. Mac that I may need some men when I come back. Don't know how many."

J. L. nodded to his friend. He looked at Gail. She was smiling and looked like the movie star she wanted to be.

Gail looked back and didn't say anything. She just winked at J. L. as she stepped up onto the train.

When the train pulled out, J. L. watched as it disappeared east on the tracks. He was lost in his thoughts when Larry came walking up beside him.

"Where you running off to?" Larry asked.

"Nowhere. Just put Ben and Gail on the train to East St. Louis for a meeting with the bigwigs. What are you doing here?"

"Well, some of us work for a living. I got this demanding customer who insists that I ship pots to Mexico and gets mad if I don't get his stuff out *yesterday*," Larry said.

"Well, everybody knows that you artist types aren't very dependable. Maybe I ought to help you unload that stuff. Wouldn't want you to get in trouble for not getting the stuff out on time."

"Won't they get mad if you're late to the mines?" Larry asked.

J. L. raised up the blueprints to the new facility.

"You don't understand; I'm *they*."

At the meeting that morning, J. L. relayed the message from Ben to Mr. Mac.

"I'm really pressed for people right now, but give me a few days to think about this. One guy that I can say for sure is being underused is Sandy Scroggins. When I first met him at the mines, I knew he could be a good fighter, but he's turned out to be a bright guy in a rough kind of way. He can do anything I turn him loose on. He's driving a Uke and running errands for me, but he's a jack-of-all-trades. Only problem with him is his temper. So don't get him mad at you," Mr. Mac said, smiling.

J. L. seldom slept during the three days that Ben was gone. He spent the days putting the finishing touches on several subcontracts that were essential to getting the project off the ground. Each evening, he rounded up parts of the data the Germans requested, took it to his apartment, photographed it, and returned it the next morning—that part had become routine. The problem came when he tried to figure out what to do with all of the photographed data. J. L. had more punctuation than he could use. He had more periods, commas, colons, and semicolons; he had more dots than he had *I*s.

He wrote letters to all of his family. To his mother, he wrote about his new home and his new friends. To his sister, Anna, he reminded her of how much fun they had as children, of times when they would stand, washing and drying dishes, harmonizing to popular songs. To Franz, he wrote about the summers they spent in Linz with their grandparents. To his father, he wrote that he was now a successful engineer and was helping to build the largest aluminum production plant in the world.

He took the letters and secreted them away in the pots that he and Larry sent to Mexico City. The one real concern he had was that, if this ever came to light, people might think that Larry had something to do with the espionage.

"Morning, J. L.," Ben said as he opened the door to the car and got in.

"Morning. I thought you were going to call me and let me come pick you guys up at the train station."

"Well, it really wasn't necessary. It was just me and my little bag, and I needed the walk," Ben said.

"What about Gail?" J. L. asked.

"That's another story. It seems that Miss Gail decided this was her chance to get out of town. Night before last when I came home from my meetings, she was packed and dressed. It was quick and sweet. She said she wasn't coming back to Arkansas. She was going back to New York City. Said she would understand if I wanted a divorce, and when I got back to the city, we could try again. Goodbye, and that was it."

"I'm really sorry to hear that," J. L. said.

"Me, too. But I that's not the only surprise I got on this trip," Ben said.

"What do you mean?"

"The big boys want construction started on the plant in two weeks or less, and get this: they want it finished by summer," Ben said.

"You've got to be kidding. It will take at least a year and maybe two to get everything up and running."

"They want to turn the power on by mid-July of next summer."

"Have they told the superintendent?"

"That's what you and I are going to be doing in about …" he looked at his watch, "in about, twenty-five minutes."

"So, Mr. Sebastian," the superintendent began after Ben told him of the change in plans, "where do they think we are going to get the men to start this job three months early? We don't have enough people for the mining as it is."

"I don't know, sir. All I know is that I was told to begin construction in two weeks," Ben said.

"Well, it sure as hell would help if they would communicate some of this information to me. How many men do you need to get started?"

"Well, sir, if we are to finish on schedule by next July, I will need at least two hundred men for the first phase," Ben said.

"Two hundred men! Do you mean to tell me that we have to either hire two hundred new men or take two hundred men out of the mines to meet this new deadline? Damn bureaucrats in Washington. I wish they would come down here and try to run these mines for one week while I sit up there and make the rules. I tell you, if we had a republican in the White House like Dewey, we wouldn't have all of this interference from Washington."

"There are a couple of other options."

"You mean, to having Roosevelt in the White House," the superintendent said.

"No, sir, to the labor problem."

"Oh, and what might that be?" he asked.

"Well, you could increase the hours of each shift or add more shifts at all of the work sites. Some of the sites are only working a day shift," Ben said.

"Right, and the minute I do that, I will have the pissant, little CIO union, breathing down my neck. There's only a few of them, but they can cause a lot of trouble."

"I thought they said they wouldn't strike as long as there was the potential for war," Ben said.

"They don't have to strike to cause trouble. I can see it now. The first thing they would do is file a grievance with the labor relations board in Washington. And then, guess whose fault it would be. Not some clown in Washington or one of the brass in Pittsburgh. No, sir. It will be my butt on the line. When we finish this meeting, Maxine and I will put a letter together, making sure that it is clear whose idea this is so that everyone will get a little share of the blame when it blows up in their faces."

The superintendent was reflecting the opinion of the overall company. If they had their way, the production at the mines would not have been raised, and the new plant would not be built. All of this was the idea of the War Production Board. In other words, it was the idea of Roosevelt, a traitor to his class who was determined to get us into this war with Hitler—one way or the other. These people saw the main enemy as Stalin and not Hitler. If we got into this war, the main reason would be to stop the communists, and for the time being, Hitler seemed to be beating up on the Russians pretty well.

CHAPTER 35

In the past several months, J. L. Stein and Marty Elrod had become a regular feature on the sidewalks of downtown Benton. Marty had enrolled in school, and three days a week, she took the train into Little Rock for her classes. In the evening when she returned, J. L. would meet her at the station and walk her to supper.

On a warm fall evening when the leaves were beginning to turn, there was a small pickup band playing country music on the steps of the courthouse. On the southeast corner of the courthouse grounds a group of old men were sitting and whittling as Marty and J. L. walked up.

"My cousin's daughter works in the typing pool at the plant, and she said that the War Production Board folks are convinced that there is a German spy at the plant. She said it is just a matter of time before they catch him," said one old man.

Another old man chimed in, "Some fellow who owned a furniture store over in Cabot had an airplane drop a little parachute with leaflets for a sale he was having. Somebody started a rumor that it was the Germans preparing for an invasion. They almost had a riot on their hands before they got it all straightened out."

Not to be outdone anther old man added, "My brother lives in Cleveland County, and it seems there was this traveling preacher riding up and down the road on the back of a horse, shouting, 'The war has begun.' Before they figured out that he meant the war with the devil, everybody had gone home to get their guns. Word is they rode that old man out of town on a rail."

Marty and J. L. found a bench away from the old men.

"What do you think?" Marty asked.

"About what?" J. L. asked.

"About war, spies, and the Germans attacking us."

"All you got to do is read the *Gazette* or listen to the radio. I honestly don't see any way that we can stay out of this war. As for Hitler, he is a mean-spirited, devious bully, and the truth isn't in him. When I was a kid and we went to my Grandmother Stein's in Linz, I heard all of the angry, nationalistic talk about how badly Germany had been treated, how superior the German race and its ideals were, how they needed to ascend back to their rightful place in the world. Mom wrote about them for years. She saw it coming."

"You don't really think they have the capacity to actually attack us here on our soil? I mean, we have two giant oceans protecting us."

"I've listened to the American First folks talk about that for the last year or so, and I think they are being naïve. With airplanes, ships, and submarines, those oceans just give them places to hide."

"You know, if you listen to Jim Sims, you would think there was a spy behind every tree. What about at the plant? Do you guys hear much about spies?"

"When I first came to the plant, the lady on the switchboard told me that the plant turns out at least as many rumors as it does tons of ore. And I believe her. Every other day, there is something new."

"Speaking of the plant, I have to put my reporter hat on now. Have you heard anything new about Dirt Hampton and his murder?"

"No, not really. Why?" J. L. asked.

"Dirt and I were close. Despite the fact that he was a drunk, he was a good guy, and everybody liked him. I met him when he worked for Mr. Hyten. He tended the kiln at night when they were firing pots. I'd go down and talk to him about his time in semipro ball. My editor at the paper asked me to do a piece on him that they could use when times are slow. He's even going to give me a byline. It would be my first."

"Did you talk to Jim Sims?"

"Yes, I did, and he gave me a copy of everything he had. I even went out and talked to Martha Jordan. I thought maybe she would tell me something she wouldn't tell one of the men who had been questioning her, but she wasn't any help. She either couldn't or wouldn't remember anything about the men she has been with," she said.

"The thing that Jim and I talked about was the fact that there weren't any fingerprints on the sign. There are only two explanations for that. One is the person is smart enough to know about fingerprints, which I doubt, or he was wearing gloves." J. L. said.

"It just makes me so sad. Dirt was so smart and he had all of that potential. He could have gotten out of the south and made something of himself," Marty said.

"If you don't mind, I have to make an early evening of it," J. L. said. "I've got to get up early in the morning. We have a lot of work to do."

"Sure," she said.

They walked down past the theater. "Would you like to go over to Hot Springs in the next week or two? I can get Ben to cover for me overnight. I've got a friend who runs a little resort out on Lake Hamilton. We can get a couple of rooms, do some swimming. He's got boats, and we could go out on the lake and do some fishing."

"I really don't care about going fishing, but I would love to go to the lake with you for the weekend. Do you want to know a secret?" she asked.

It was a rhetorical question, and he knew it.

"You are the main reason I decided to stay in this town. I know this may sound silly, but I've known from the time I met you that there was a spark there. I saw it your eyes. I felt it as well. Of course I will go to the lake with you."

She put her arms around his neck and kissed him in a way that he had never been kissed before. There was passion and warmth; she could not have shouted at the top of her lungs, "I love you with all my heart" and been clearer about how she felt. It was a kiss he would never forget.

"I'll see you tomorrow," she said. "Get some rest."

J. L. had seen this coming, and he felt the same way.

CHAPTER 36

For those who die,
war is not the answer;
but is war really the answer
for those who kill?

Poet of Mauthausen

One evening after boxing practice, Mr. Mac took the men aside and told them of the plans to build the new plant.

"Until the plant is complete, we will put all of our boxing activity on hold, but as soon as things settle down, we'll stoke up the fires again. Starting in the morning, you men will have new work assignments. It's posted on the board. If I hear of any problems, you'll still be answering to me. You're dismissed." He pointed at Sandy. "Sandman, I need to talk to you."

The other men filed out and Junior came to the front of the room.

"What did I do, Coach?" he asked.

"You didn't do anything, son," the coach said. He motioned to a chair. "I've told you that I think you have potential as a fighter, and I mean it. I've made sure you were assigned to Sebastian and Stein, the engineers in charge. What I am hoping is that will give you some time to get in some training. If you're going to have a career in boxing, you can't afford to take a year's break. When you figure out what your schedule will be, let me know, and I'll meet you at the gym."

"Yes, sir," Junior said.

"I got a new job at the plant," Junior told his father later at the Red Gate. "I'm the driver for the chief engineer. Mr. Mac wanted me to have time off—that way I could do some training—so he got me a job with the head man. The fellow don't drive, and it's my job to make sure he gets around. I spend most of my days delivering him or Stein."

"Who's Stein?" Bill asked.

"He's second-in-charge at the new plant. The other guy, Sebastian, is smart, but Stein is the one who gets things done. Most of the men really like Stein. Those two work around the clock. One or both of them are at the work site all the time; they even got cots in their offices."

"That Stein name rings a bell, but I don't remember from where. Never mind about that, what can you tell me about security?" Bill asked.

"Dommer and his men are a joke. They couldn't find their way out of a tow sack, and they haven't got a clue as to what is going on in that plant. They arrested one of the explosives men the other day because he didn't salute the flag. Really made Sebastian mad."

"Good, that's good. But you really got to be careful," Bill said. "I got a letter from the doctor the other day with fresh instructions. They want you to find ways to slow this plant down, but everything has to look like an accident."

"The best way to slow this plant down would be for one or both of the guys in charge to disappear," Junior said. "I know the woods around the mines like the back of my hands, and there are bauxite pits that ain't got a bottom where these guys could disappear and no one would ever find them. I can do that any time Krause and his people want me to," Junior said.

"That would draw too much attention. Just find ways of slowing down the work," Bill said.

Junior nodded.

It seemed such a waste of time to work around the edges. Why not just kill these guys? It would take several months to get new people in and get them up to speed. If push came to shove, he could disappear into the woods around the mines, and they would never find him. He could sneak back in when he needed to do a job, and security would never know. But Junior was a good soldier, and he would do as he was told.

CHAPTER 37

There was a time in my life when Death was my enemy. I feared him and his friends, Disease and Pain. I worried that I might fall prey to him, that I might die before my time. But here, in this place, Death is my companion; he's always four or five steps behind as I walk up from the quarry, as I lay down to sleep, as I stand for roll call. When I turn to look him in the face, he hides behind a guard, and no amount of coaxing will bring him out, but I know he's there.

Poet of Mauthausen

On a rare day off, J. L. was at Larry's, helping him with a new pottery design when the news came over the radio.

"News bulletin: The Japanese have just attacked Pearl Harbor."

Larry's first response was: "Where's Pearl Harbor?"

"It's in Hawaii," J. L. said. "There are a bunch of ships there in the harbor."

"Damn," Larry said. He sat there at his workbench for a minute and then added, "Jim's been saying something like this was going to happen. Tomorrow, I'm going down to volunteer."

"Fitts, you know they won't take you, not with your bunged-up legs. The doctors will take one look at you and send your butt packing," J. L. said.

"They can't refuse me."

"I bet they can. In fact, I got ten bucks says you don't make it through the first intake station," J. L. insisted. "Hell, they don't even take people with flat feet."

"But that wasn't during war; that was in peacetime. What about you?" Larry asked.

"We talked about this a few months ago at the plant. This is considered a vital defense plant. All of the workers and management will be exempt from the army as long as we work at the mines."

As they talked, J. L. thought to himself, *I could be executed for what I am doing. I work for the country that will be killing men from Saline County. No one would shed a tear for a German spy who has fooled them for years.*

He fully expected the FBI or the army or someone from the War Production Board to swoop down on him, cart him off to jail and throw away the key.

The next morning Ben and J. L. were standing near the first of the foundations being poured for the new plant, when Major Dommer and several of his minions came sliding to a stop in their new, black sedan with green and gold flags painted on the doors. They got out of the car and Dommer pointed in the direction of the two. The armed guards took off at a double time pace.

J. L. watched the men as they neared his position. He had rehearsed this a million times and had wondered how he would respond when the moment came. When the guards approached their position, J. L. felt a sense of relief that he no longer had to lie; a smile of resignation spread across his face. He was preparing to put his hands up in the air and give up.

Instead of stopping, the guards ran past him and surrounded a young man who was pouring concrete. His name was George Hable, one of the best cement men they had. While the guards searched George, Dommer came walking up beside the J. L. and Ben.

"What are you doing, Dommer?" Ben asked.

"Well, I'll tell you what I am doing. I'm catching me a spy, that's what I'm doing. I got good reason to think that Hable here is a German spy," Dommer said.

"Oh, bullshit. George isn't a spy. He's lived in Saline County all of his life. He was talking about it at lunch break Friday. What makes you think he's a spy?"

"I'm not at liberty to divulge that information at this time, but I will say this, he has been engaged in some very suspicious behavior. We've had our eye on him for some time," Dommer said.

"What kind of behavior?" Ben asked.

He motioned to Ben and J. L. to move over to the car, away from the crowd that was gathering to watch the show.

"My superiors are convinced that there is a spy here at the plant that was planted several years ago. They gave me the go-ahead yesterday to pick up anyone who might be a threat to the plant."

"But what makes you think that Hable is a spy?" Ben asked.

"Have you ever noticed that he doesn't salute the flag at ballgames?" Dommer said.

"What? You're going to arrest a man because he doesn't salute the flag?" Ben said.

"Well, that, and other things."

"Look, Dommer, the man's a Jehovah's Witness," Ben said. "It's against his religion to salute the flag. He's no more a spy than J. L. here. God, this is stupid. Look here, Dommer, question him if you must, but I really need him here working, so please make it quick."

As Dommer was preparing to get in his car, he turned back to Ben.

"Be careful with those plans, they would be a hot item if the enemy got hold of them."

Sure enough, George was back on the site the next morning with a warning to keep his nose clean.

CHAPTER 38

"Well, Ms. Poet, I've enjoyed as much of you as I can tolerate," Commandant Ziereis said to Helena. "You were bound to know that these notes you've been writing would fall into my hands, and yet you've kept writing. Why?"

Helena shrugged her shoulders and allowed a half smile.

He picked up a scrap of paper lying on his desk and began to read, "The steps down to the quarry are crumbling; where once there were one hundred and eighty-six, there are now one hundred and eighty-five. The walls that hold us in are shrinking; before they were twenty feet tall, now they are only eighteen. Someday soon, they will disappear."

"I didn't write that," Helena said.

"This has your handprints all over it. Are you denying that you have been writing these notes?"

"No, of course not, but I didn't write that piece. I like it, but I didn't write it."

"So you're suggesting there are more of you out there?" Ziereis asked.

"All I can say is that I did not write that note."

"Why is it that you or whoever is writing this trash does so?"

Helena shrugged her shoulders.

"No, tell me, please. Tell me why," he said.

"Hope," she said.

"What hope? No one leaves here alive. This is your home for the rest of your short life. Where is the hope?"

Helena raised her hand and laid it on her chest.

"What does this hand on your chest mean? Does it mean that the famous nonbeliever has found God and heaven? Did the Jehovah's Witnesses get to you? I actually had to get rid of two guards, because the Witnesses got to them."

"Hope is not something that can be explained; it either exists, or it doesn't," she said.

"Well, Madame Poet, as of today, you will have less time to sit around and contemplate your navel. These notes will stop. You're being moved to barracks fifteen and placed on permanent quarry detail."

CHAPTER 39

Some arguments just aren't worth winning.

Helena

Massive floodlights illuminated the plant site, and the roar of the giant earthmovers and trucks created a constant drone. The men and women of Bauxite attacked the building of the plant as a company of soldiers would an enemy position. They devoted all of their energy to doing their parts. Despite the concern of the superintendent, the men and women set aside their personal concerns and became soldiers in the new army. These men, who were considered unskilled labor, quickly made it clear that they were anything but. When the tools they needed were in short supply, they made their own. They went above and beyond the call of duty to keep things running, and no one complained.

J. L. was down in the middle of them, solving problems, and lending a hand when it was needed. It turned out that he had a knack for supervising personnel. His training in Vienna and his last eight years with the company had been preparation for the job. As his skill level grew, Ben gave him increasing responsibilities. When Ben was called away to East St. Louis, J. L. was placed in charge of the project. He would go for days without thinking about the fact that he was an enemy spy.

The first clue that something was amiss was the derailment of a dummy-line train that ran from the main line to the new plant. Dommer was convinced that it was an act of German sabotage. If he had his way, they would have shut down the construction site for days while he investigated. Luckily, cooler heads prevailed, and by afternoon, the train car had been righted and the track repaired.

"You know, Ben, that was really unusual how the track gave way," J. L. said.

"What do you mean?"

"Do you remember that rain we had two weeks ago?"

"Yeah," Ben said.

"Well, I sent Sandy down there with a crew to check on all of that track to make sure that nothing was washed out."

"And?" Ben asked.

"And they came back and said everything was solid."

"Hold it just a minute, J. L. You're not getting Nazi fever, are you?"

"No, it just seems odd," J. L. said.

"Well, don't tell that clown, Dommer; he would shut us down for a week."

"Don't worry, I won't say anything," J. L. said.

The train derailment had fallen into Junior's lap. It was not something he had thought about or planned. Stein assigned him to the task of managing the crew that checked out the tracks after the rain. That night, he had returned, removed a few spikes and loosened the underpinning at the train trestle.

A number of the large trucks had been put out of commission because of sand and sugar in the gas tanks. Tires were spiked with barbed wire.

Most important on his list of planned targets was the dynamite shed. For several weeks, he worked his shift, went back to the house, had something to eat, and then took off for the woods. He walked cross-country to the plant site, went under the fence, climbed an old gum tree, and watched the explosives men come and go. Junior paid close attention to Leroy Larson, the lead man in charge of the explosive materials. There was general agreement that Leroy was sloppy, and it was just a matter of time before he blew himself up.

The security around the shed was pitiful, and Junior learned quickly that he could come and go with impunity. He jimmied a small window on the back wall and took what he needed from the shed. He assembled a small bomb, using an alarm clock he stole from one of his housemates and materials he had found in the shed. The bomb itself was small but large enough to start a chain reaction. It was set to go off at exactly 8:00 AM.

Ben called the staff meeting to order.

"Men, we have a lot of work to get done this week. First, we need a report from—"

He never finished the sentence. The dynamite shed, a quarter of a mile away on a slight hill overlooking the new plant, exploded in a mass of sound, smoke, and light. The large petitioned window that allowed the engineers a view of the plant construction came showering down on top of the conference table. Instinctively, everyone went to the floor.

"What the hell?" Ben said as the sound subsided.

Everyone slowly got up from their places on the floor, brushing glass from their hair and clothing. A cool breeze was blowing in through where the window had been.

Ben stood and looked around the room.

"Is everyone all right?"

A couple of the men had minor cuts, but for the most part, everyone was intact.

J. L. walked over to the space where the window had been.

"It was the dynamite shed," he said, pointing to the smoldering ruins of the explosives building.

Ben, J. L., and the other engineers stepped out into the parking lot of the work building. From their vantage point, everything was in chaos.

Dommer and his crew raced down the Bauxite Highway from their headquarters at the mines with their sirens going full blast. Outside on the work site, there was chaos. The old fire truck that served as the Bauxite Fire Department came close on the heels of the security sedans.

Ben turned to one of the other young engineers.

"Go down to the plant and make sure that everything else is in good shape. If you can, get everything else up and running. J. L. and I are going down to the shed to check out the damage."

Ben and J. L., with Sandy close behind, walked down the hill, across the parking lot in front of the plant, and up the hill to where the shed had been. The fire department was administering first aid to two men sitting on the ground. J. L. recognized them as members of Leroy's crew.

"What happened?" J. L. asked.

"Don't know. Snooky and me," he said pointing at his friend, "was running a little late. We was walking up the hill when all hell broke loose."

"Where's Leroy?" Ben asked.

"I guess he was in the shed," the man said. "He always got here a little early."

Ben turned to J. L.

"Didn't you write Leroy up last week for smoking in the shed?"

"Actually, he never smoked in the shed," J. L. said. "The guy smoked three packs of Camels a day, and the only time he didn't have a lit cigarette in his mouth was when he was in the shed. Most of the time, he'd just lay the cigarette on the top of a barrel just outside the door," J. L. said. "And I told him, if he didn't quit doing that, we were going to have to let him go. It's all in his file.

Ben turned back to the injured man.

"Is there anybody else who might have been in the building?"

"Nobody but Leroy, me, and Snooky ever come up here. It's kinda a no-man's-land. Most folks are scared of this stuff."

"What do you think happened?"

"Can't say. Could have been lightning, but there weren't any clouds. Leroy was telling us one day about this shed that blew up 'cause of static electricity."

As the man was finishing, Dommer came walking up.

"The site is now secure," he said. "Looks like sabotage to me; got all of the classic hallmarks. This site won't be available to you for a couple of days, Mr. Sebastian, and this time, you won't be overruling me."

Ben didn't argue. Most of the explosives work had been completed, and the minor work that needed to be done could be delayed until Dommer's investigation was complete. This would keep the War Production Board busy for several weeks.

"Would you like the file on Mr. Larson?" Ben asked.

"And who might that be?" Dommer asked.

"He was the lead man and was probably killed in the accident," J. L. said.

Ben turned to Sandy, who was standing about twenty paces away.

"Sandman, would you go back to the office and have Louise pull the file on Larson for the major?"

Junior nodded and walked back down the hill. It had worked just as he intended. His mind was going on to his next project.

Chapter 40

There was an urgent message waiting for Junior when he got home from work. The note read: "Meet me at the Red Gate, Thursday night, eight o'clock. It's very important. Bill."

It was six o'clock and almost seven miles to the Red Gate. Most days, that would be a snap, but it had been a hard day and a hard week. Junior was tired.

He could have gone to the work site and used one of the trucks he drove during the day. If anyone asked, he could say he was running an errand for Sebastian and Stein, but it would have raised eyebrows if the truck were seen at the Red Gate. There were strict rules about company vehicles and bars. Instead, Junior walked over to Mr. Mac's house on Silk Stocking Row and knocked on the back door. Mr. Mac, who had just sat down for supper, got up from the table and came to the door. "

Well, Sandman, you have perfect timing. We were just sitting down to eat. You want to join us?"

"No, sir, but thanks for the offer. I do need to ask a favor. I got a message from my father, and he needs for me to meet him in Little Rock. It's some kind of emergency. Coach, can I borrow your car for a few hours. I'll be real careful."

"Sure, you can. Just be careful," Mr. Mac said.

"Sorry, I haven't been to the gym much lately but working for those guys doesn't give me much time off."

"Man, I understand. We've all been busy." Mr. Mac disappeared back into the kitchen, came out with a set of keys and handed them to Junior.

"I shouldn't be more than an hour or two," Junior said.

"Don't worry about it. I'm not going anywhere this evening. Take your time and I hope it's not anything serious," he said patting the young fighter on the shoulder.

Junior had spent most of his life wanting to please his father and now he had added Mr. Mac to that list. Mr. Mac's door was open to all of the fighters; he treated them like they were his sons.

Like with company trucks, Mr. Mac would have frowned on his car being parked outside of the Red Gate, so Junior parked the truck a quarter of a mile away on County Line Road and walked to the tavern. There were only a couple of cars, none of which he recognized, in the parking lot. He had hoped that Fitts wouldn't be there, because that would mean that Stein was there.

Bill and Junior had a routine for most of their meetings. The first one there found a table in the back beyond the pool tables, where the lights were dim, and ordered a couple of sandwiches and beers. This was the one time they allowed themselves these luxuries. Both men looked forward to their meetings.

Junior walked in through the side door and looked toward the corner where they normally sat. His father was taking a bite out of a large cheeseburger. Junior made his way to the table, pulled out a chair, and sat down.

"Evening, Dad," he said.

Bill looked up and smiled at his son.

"Hey, boy, I got some real interesting news for you. You remember the last time I was over here you told me you were working for that guy, Stein?" Bill asked.

Junior nodded.

Bill continued, "I thought I recognized that name. I did some asking around, and it turns out he's the Jew nephew of one of the bigwigs in the Bund. It also turns out he is working for the same people we are. The comment I got from the folks in New York was that they don't know how reliable he is. You may have to take him out at some point. He hasn't been real good about sending data in the last month or two."

"I can tell you why that's true," Junior said.

"Why?"

"'Cause he's working twenty-four hours a day, seven days a week, as far as I can tell."

Bill put his sandwich down and continued, "Anyway, the boys want you to find a way to put the fear of God in him without him knowing who you are. Do you think you can do that?" Bill asked.

Junior nodded and smiled.

"Now I don't want you to endanger your position," Bill said.

"Don't worry; I know how to handle this clown," Junior said. "I'll have him pissing in his boots."

Terror was as easy for Junior as it was for his father; in fact, it was second nature. It required a cold, still nerve; it required the willingness to act when called for; and it required patience—all of those things, Junior had in abundance.

Stalking his prey was Junior's second favorite thing to do. Killing was now his favorite.

Chapter 41

"I really need a break," J. L. said to Ben. "All work and no play makes John Lewis Stein a very sad boy. You think you could do without me for a day or so?"

"Of course I can. Where are you planning on taking Miss Elrod?"

"And what makes you think I'm not going off by myself?"

"Are you kidding? I've known you long enough to know that you aren't that stupid," Ben said, smiling. "You did know that the men have started a betting pool about how long it is before you announce that you two are going to get married."

"Are you kidding?"

"No, I'm not kidding. You've been walking around here like a love struck fool for several months."

"I didn't know it was that obvious."

"Well, it is. When was it you were wanting off?" Ben asked.

"How about the weekend of the fourteenth of next month?" J. L. asked.

"So I was right. Valentine's Day?"

J. L. just grinned.

In was raining when they drove back into Benton that night.

"You mind if I use the company car to pick up Marty at the train station this evening?"

"I don't think anyone is going to notice personal use of the car just this once," Ben said.

J. L. enjoyed sitting in the waiting room of the station in Benton. It reminded him of home as a child when they took trips to see his grandparents, when the family went to the country. The long wooden benches, the sound of the telegraph key, the mechanical ticking of the large clock on the wall, the smell of freshly brewed coffee—he could sit for hours immersed in the smells and sounds. Marty's train would arrive at six thirty, and it was almost always on time.

At 6:29, he heard the whistle of the train as it crossed Edison Street and rounded the last corner just east of town.

The heavy rain had let up, but it was still falling. He walked out to the platform and opened his umbrella as the train came to a stop.

Marty appeared at the top of the stairs that descended from the train, shifted her books into her left hand, and walked down the three steps.

"Why, Mr. Stein, isn't it nice that you would meet me with an umbrella?"

J. L. started to laugh and then cry. "I love you with all my heart and soul. Will you marry me?" He had not intended to say it that way; it had just come out of his mouth. He had planned on taking her to the Arlington Hotel in Hot Springs, and after they had had a wonderful meal and danced for several hours, he would drop to his knee on the dance floor and propose. But since talking to Ben earlier in the day, proposing had been all he could think about.

"Yes, of course I will marry you."

Marty dropped her books and put her arms around his neck and kissed him.

The conductor, who was standing to her left, picked up the books and smiled at the other passengers waiting to get off of the train.

"Kids," he said. "I am very happy for you, but we have other people who want to get off of the train."

J. L. and Marty looked behind them, and there was a line of people waiting to disembark from the train.

"Sorry," J. L. said. He reached out and took the books from the conductor, and the couple walked arm in arm to the car.

When they were finally sitting in the car, J. L. explained his original plan to invite her for a night at the Arlington and propose there.

"I would like to take you to the Arlington in a couple of weeks. Valentine's Day, I mean. You remember I promised to take you to the lake, and with the war and all, we just never got around to it."

"That sounds wonderful," she said.

CHAPTER 42

Yesterday, an Italian Jew, known for his beautiful voice, was heard to be singing to himself during roll call. Gossip has it that he sang professionally before the war. When we arrived at the quarry, Niedermayer, one of the SS guards, pulled him aside and informed him that they wanted him to stand at the top of the quarry wall and sing the song "Ave Maria." Despite the fact that he was Jewish, he did know the song and was pleased that he had been asked to sing. Unbeknownst to the singer, the charges had already been set for the day's rock blasting. He was silhouetted against the morning sun as he began his song.

Ave Maria
Gratia plena
Dominus tecum

While the word tecum vibrated in the air and the singer took a short breathe, the SS officer pushed down on the plunger, detonating the charges and engulfing the singer and the sun in a cloud of horrendous sound and smoke.

It was just one more act of cruelty—neither better nor worse than the normal daily fare. The difference was this one involved the sun. For an instant, prisoners and guards alike were taken aback by the darkness that invaded our little space. The sound faded away, and there was a long, uncomfortable silence.

Poet of Mauthausen

CHAPTER 43

J. L. pulled into the driveway of his apartment.

The Roberts family was sitting at the kitchen table eating supper. Mr. Roberts looked up, smiled, and waved at J. L. as he passed the window. The canopy of trees that sheltered the house and garage was just beginning to put out buds, and the forsythia and quince were in full bloom.

For days, J. L. had been daydreaming about the future. His relationship with Marty and, the Friday night before, Larry had fueled the daydreaming with a proposal. They were at the Red Gate, having a beer, when out of the blue, Larry said, "I been thinking about something."

"What's that?" J. L. asked.

"Now, I haven't thought it through completely, but what would you think about—in a year or so, after this silly war is over—you and me going into business together. Now, I'm not making any money, mind you, but there are a lot of possibilities out there. And this isn't just beer talking. I came up with this idea yesterday while I was throwing a pot. With your business connections and all the stuff you know about chemical processes, we could do okay, I bet."

J. L. was speechless. Until recently, he had seldom allowed himself to think about the future, because most of the possible futures he could envision weren't good. Any good future required the Germans forgetting who and where he was, and that didn't seem reasonable. If the conflict ended tomorrow and his part in the war was left buried in some file cabinet somewhere, it was possible but, again, not probable. If Larry found out that he was using his pottery to advance the treachery, that would be the end of that. What would Marty say when she found out? What about his mother? What should he do? Was there any way that he could help her, beside what he was doing?

"Well, what do you think? Aren't you going to say something?" Larry asked.

J. L. took a drink from his beer. "I really don't know what to say," he said.

"Well, it's either yes or no,"

"It's not quite that simple," J. L. said.

"I'm not going to sit here and beg you," Larry said. There was an edge in his voice.

J. L. realized that his friend was in the process of getting his feelings hurt.

"No, stupid, it's not like that. I can't think of anything I'd rather do than quit my job and join forces with you, but my life is a little complicated right now. If I quit, they will deport me, quick as a flash, and more importantly, I've got some family obligations that I have to take care of."

"Wait a minute. You don't have to quit anything," Larry said. "This isn't like you have to sign a contract in blood or something. In fact, until we start making money, it would be good if you didn't. Think about it, you could give up the apartment, move into the back of the shop with Marty and me. The way you two have been getting on, we might not even have to build another room. When times are lean in the pottery business, we could eat off of part of your salary."

"Don't misunderstand," J. L. said. "What you're saying sounds great, but right now, it would be more than a little complicated."

"Well, you just think about it. The offer's on the table," Larry said. "Now let's get down to some serious business. Did you see that woman who just walked in the door?"

Nothing else was said, but for days J. L. had been dreaming.

J. L. stopped the car, turned off the lights, reached around into the backseat, and grabbed his briefcase. He had several things that needed to be photographed that night.

He walked to the top of the stairs, reached into his pocket, and fumbled around for his house key. When he had moved in, Mr. Roberts hadn't offered him an apartment key, and when J. L. had asked, Roberts had said he wasn't sure if there was one. The door was an old door that had been on a utility room he had torn down. J. L. had persisted, and Roberts had rummaged around through several drawers in his shop before he came up with a series of skeleton key look-alikes. What they had discovered was that several of the keys opened the lock to his door. Roberts had given him a whole handful of keys with the comment that he would have a spare if he lost one.

J. L. opened the door and went into the apartment and laid his briefcase down on the table by the radio. He went into the kitchen, opened a can of clam chowder, and put in on the stove to heat up. He opened a small icebox and took out a beer. He went into his bedroom, sat down on the bed, and took off his shoes. It was the second day for the pair of socks he was wearing, and they had a bit of an odor.

The small room in the southwest corner of the apartment, which could have served as a second bedroom, had a padlock on the door. The second day he had lived in the apartment, he had gone to Gingles Hardware and purchased the padlock and a dead bolt from Mr. Gingles; it was J. L.'s extra layer of protection. Unlike the big, ancient, unwieldy door keys Roberts had given him, this was new, modern, shiny, and small.

Before he opened the second door, J. L. always made sure that the dead bolt lock on the outer door to the apartment was secure. It wasn't burglars he was worried about; it was Larry and Marty. If either of them came barging in through the front door, then J. L. would have to find a way to explain why he had all of this complicated photographic equipment. Any reason J. L. could come up with sounded lame, so he simply made sure it didn't happen. Unlike Mr. Alred at the guesthouse, it was clear that the Roberts family respected his privacy.

J. L. went back into the kitchen, turned the gas burner off on the stove, and poured the hot clam chowder into a bowl. He opened a package of saltines and crumbled half of them into the soup.

He carried the soup back into the bedroom, placed it on the dresser that sat beside the locked door to the back room, pulled the padlock key from his pocket, opened the lock and door, picked up his soup, and went into the room. He turned the overhead light on and was immediately struck by the fact that something was different.

As an engineer, J. L. had a thing about order. At the end of work each day, his desk was clean; the chores for the next day were scheduled and notated. As a spy, the same principles applied.

On the top of his Zapp's cabinet was a single piece of paper. It read:

I KNOW WHO YOU ARE JEW STEIN.

DON'T DO ANYTHING STUPID.

I'LL CUT YOUR NUTS OFF, AND FEED THEM TO YOU.

The note was printed and rough; most of the letters were broad and smudged.

J. L. read the note a second time. Reading the note, it occurred to him that the person who had written the note could still be there, and instinctively, he ducked.

There had been few times in his life when J. L. had been really scared. Once as a child, when he, Franz, and Anna were staying with their grandparents in Linz, a summer storm had blown through the river valley and knocked over a tree in the side yard. The limb had come crashing down through the roof of the living room of their house. If he had been standing three feet to the left, he would have been crushed. The day that John Michael Krause had told him how his brother had died had created much the same feeling.

There was someone just out of his field of vision who could bring his life to an end, and he had no control. He sat down in the chair behind the desk where the camera was and looked around for anything else that had changed. There was no sign of any sort; whoever it was knew how to cover his tracks.

J. L. walked out of the back room and looked around his bedroom, then the living room and the kitchen. He opened another beer from the refrigerator and walked out onto the landing of his apartment. He sat down in the metal glider that the Roberts had provided and studied the note.

Hidden from view, behind the next-door neighbor's backyard shop, Junior Parkus watched J. L. while he studied the note. Junior enjoyed watching his prey in a state of fear.

CHAPTER 44

Yesterday, a large contingent of Russian prisoners of war was brought into the camp. Most were boys, sixteen and seventeen years old; they were dirty, hungry, and lice-ridden. The guards of the camp forced them to stand in the roll-call yard and sprayed them with first cold water and then hot water. One of their officers walked among them and encouraged them to live or die on their feet. By talking to his men, he attracted the attention of the hose man and, with that, extra sprays of water. In thirty minutes, the officer was frozen solid, leaning against the granite wall. By the next morning, all of the soldiers were dead.

Poet of Mauthausen

CHAPTER 45

Now that America has decided to challenge us, we will make them pay. As I speak, boatloads of saboteurs are landing on the shores of the United States. A call has gone out to all of the moles we have hidden in their society. We will strike terror in their souls. Their children will go to bed at night and dream of explosions; every time they get on a bus or a train, they will worry that someone has planted a bomb; they will be suspicious of anyone and everyone who looks or sounds different. We will paralyze them with fear.

Wilhelm Canaris, the German spy master, speaking to high command.

On Thursday night, Ben and J. L. worked late. It was almost midnight when J. L. parked in front of the apartment.

As he switched off the ignition and prepared to turn off the lights, he noticed that there was a letter in his mailbox. He didn't get mail, so he knew before he handled the letter who it was from. The letter was postmarked Hot Springs and read, "We have a letter from your mother. You need to pick it up this weekend."

On Friday morning, J. L. picked Ben up at the Sims's house. "Look, Ben, you haven't had a day off in months. I know you won't take off a whole weekend, but at least take off one day Why don't you take off Saturday and let me take off on Sunday? Both of us don't need to be there all weekend."

"You know that is a pretty good idea," Ben said. "You go on and take off; in fact, take both days. I'd just be sitting on my thumbs."

"I'm going to take off on Saturday, but I will be back on Sunday and I don't expect to see you here."

On Saturday morning, J. L. caught the train to Hot Springs and then a taxi out to Lorio's. Tommy was working on the roof of the dock when J. L. got out of the cab.

"Hey, friend, what do you know?" Tommy asked.

"Not much. You?"

"Since the war began, I've had more work to do than I can say grace over," Tommy said.

"Where's Jake?" J. L. asked.

"When the war broke out, he disappeared overnight, and I haven't heard from him since. That may be the one thing I don't mind. I never felt comfortable with him being around the kids. Speaking of somebody who has been scarce over the last couple of months, where you been?"

"We been working seven days a week on the new plant," J. L. said.

"Are you going to want a cabin for the night?" Tommy asked.

"No, I need to get back tonight."

"You hungry?" Tommy asked.

J. L. shook his head. "I had a sandwich on the train," he said.

"Well, get you a pole out of the bait room, and let's go fishing for a while. I got something for you. Get some minnows out of the box. There's a minnow bucket under the counter."

In a few minutes, Tommy came back with large manila envelope and a sack with three sandwiches.

When they were well out of the dock and heading for the main body of the lake, Tommy handed the envelope to J. L.

"I thought we would go down south of Rabbit Island. There's a cove down there where the water drops off real quick. Lot of bass and crappie back up in the brush this time of year."

J. L. barely heard his explanation as he opened the manila folder. First, he opened the letter postmarked Vienna. It read:

> Dear Son,
>   We are not getting a lot to eat, but what we do get is sufficient. Since the United States declared war on the Germans, it has gotten increasingly hard on us. We have to work more hours in the day than we did before. This war seems so unnecessary. I hope that, one day, we will have

the chance to see each other again. I'm told that you have helped the Germans to protect me. A mother could not ask for anything more. Eat well and keep yourself safe.

Your mother,
Helena

For the first time, J. L. knew for sure: that letter had not been written by his mother. How or why he knew, he couldn't say, but he knew for certain that his mother had not written that letter. Whether she was dead or alive, he did not know, but she had not written the letter, and he was mad. He had done everything that these people had asked him to do, and they were sending him fake letters from his mother. They had some clown at the plant threatening him, and they expected him to do their bidding.

He turned to Tommy.

"Shut it down, Tommy," J. L. said.

Tommy throttled the motor back and shut it off. They were floating out in the middle of the lake.

"What is this crap, Tommy?" J. L. demanded.

"What do you mean?"

"I mean this isn't a letter from my mother. This is a fake."

"Look, J. L., I don't know anything about that. I do know that's the letter they gave me to give you."

"These sons-of-bitches have been lying to me," J. L. said.

"This is the only place I can talk," Tommy said. "Out here, there are no listening ears. One thing you can take to the bank: these people have no honor, and you're not the only one they lie to. They wouldn't know the truth if it bit them in the ass. Jake threatened to kill my uncle. I know my uncle is a prick, but he's harmless. He and Jake had an argument down on the dock, and Jake pushed the old man off into the water. The old man can't swim, and if one of the kids hadn't seen it, he would have drowned. That asshole, Jake, was stealing me blind. You just don't hurt your family, and you don't steal from your own people. They tried to take over my bookie joint, and when that didn't work, they tried to muscle in on the resort. If I thought I could get away with it, I would pack up my whole family and move to Mena."

"What's in Mena?" J. L. asked.

"Nothing. That's why I would go there. I'm just thinking about a quiet place to raise my kids. What are you going to do about the deal with your mother?"

"I don't know. I don't have any idea at all. They say they will kill her if I don't continue to give them information," J. L. said.

"I'll tell you what, let's you and me fish for a few hours. We'll feed you some supper, and then I will drive you to Benton."

"I appreciate that, but I need to get back. I got a lot of work to do, and you don't need to spend the rest of the day and evening driving back and forth." What he didn't say was that the two-hour train ride was comforting to him.

When they got back to the dock, he asked Tommy to take him back to town. Riding past the racetrack, Tommy turned to J. L.

"Look, I have a feeling you won't be coming back over here, and I'll understand if you don't. If you get in trouble with these people, they won't hesitate to kill you in a second." He stopped for a second and then started again, "Look, J. L., I am about to break all of the rules. If you don't already know, there is another fellow at that plant who works for these people. At least, he was there about three years ago. I only met him once, and we didn't hit it off. I got the feeling he was mean and stupid. Watch your back. If you find that you need a place to hide, I can make you disappear for as long as you need."

"Thanks, I may take you up on that. As it is, I can't trust anybody else," J. L. said. "By the way, this guy at the plant … what do you remember about him?"

"Nothing, really. We talked on the back stairs of the shop, and I never did see his face. I do remember that he had on dirty, greasy gloves and wouldn't shake hands with me."

The train was almost empty for the four o'clock run. When they were heading out of town, J. L. reopened the envelope. This time, he opened the second packet. In it was a letter and a set of instructions. The letter read:

> Stein,
>
> The Americans must be made to pay for their arrogance. They think that, since we are separated by a large ocean, they are insulated from this war. This summer, we will show them that they are no safer than the fools in Hawaii. Our understanding is that the new plant will be dedicated with a ceremony at the community hall next month. We want you to bomb that building during the ceremony and, one hour later, bomb the small hospital where the patients are taken.
>
> They must understand that, even in the very middle of the country in rural America, they will feel the bite of our mighty forces.
>
> Included in this package are the instructions for constructing the two bombs.

He thumbed through the instructions. They seemed to be self-explanatory—a simple clock as a timer, wiring, fuses, blasting caps, and dynamite. All of this was to be encased in a canvas bag filled with fertilizer. It was all so cut-and-dried.

As the train traveled up the western slope of Ten Mile Mountain, a thunderstorm swept in from the northwest. One minute, the beautiful green countryside was still and serene, and the next, it was engulfed in winds that seemed to come from every direction at once. Cobwebs of lightning formed and disappeared in an instant. The thunderous voice of God rained down from the dark clouds and shook the windows of the train. Wind-whipped rain beat against the windows of the coach.

If the letter wasn't from his mother, was she dead or alive? He loved her more than life itself and would do anything to keep her out of harm's way. What about Marty? His friends—Larry, Ben, and Jim—wouldn't understand if he told them who he was and what he did. The people from Bauxite were like a second family, and the idea of bombing them—creating death and havoc—was beyond the pale. How to deal with the stalker was his greatest fear. If he didn't build the bombs, the stalker would know. If he failed to provide information, the Germans would know.

When the train reached the top of the grade at Lonsdale, the storm cleared, and the sky turned blue, but the storm that raged in Jean Louis Edit-Stein was nowhere near resolved.

The sun was beginning to set when the train pulled into the station at Benton. J. L. walked up the hill and stopped at the Lone Star. The place was almost empty, except for two old men arguing about the Cardinals and a hardware salesman. J. L. was finishing his second cup of coffee when he focused on a sign that the owner had placed above the front door. It was a picture of Hitler. A large, black *X* was drawn across his face. Below the picture were the words "Everyone welcome but Hitler."

His mother's words came back to him. *This man will bring us nothing but bad things. He appeals to our worst instincts of hate and anger and prejudice. Your self-interest will be pitted against the interests of those who are different, and he will dictate who is different. Your obligation is to truth and justice. If you can find the moral high ground, grab it and hold on, it's a hill that can't be taken by force.*

When J. L. walked out of that café on that warm night, he knew what he had to do; the question was how to do it and when?

CHAPTER 46

In my world, luck is more indispensable than God. It seems such a waste to plead with or curse God. For me, it's difficult to accept or find necessary some explanation of life that includes anything but what I see. In my simple world, the meaning of life is life itself, and the essence of life is living. There is no solace in looking back in regret or longing for some unpromised future. There is little that I can do but go about each moment, each hour, each day as if it were my last. If there is judgment about good and evil, that act must stand on its own. Each morning, I search for a quiet place within, a solitary port in the storm where I can view the struggle. My bread is the one part of life that I comprehend; it has taste and substance. The rest is in that cloud of unknowing.

Luck is with me, because I have not died today.

Poet of Mauthausen

J. L.'s plan was complicated, had some holes, and required a lot of luck.

Using the instructions he had received, J. L. spent a week assembling the components for three homemade bombs. He made an extra just to test the design. The dynamite and caps, he smuggled out of the newly rebuilt explosives shed and carried home in his tin lunchbox, each on different days. The wiring he got from the machine shop, and the three alarm clocks and the fertilizer he bought from Gingles Hardware.

His plan involved building the first bomb as a test. He would take it out into the country west of town somewhere along the river and detonate it. Most of that part of the county was cattle and goat farms with very few homes.

When he was comfortable that the bomb would perform as specified in the instructions, he loaded it into a canvas bag that he had fashioned into a backpack. He grabbed his fishing rod and several wooden lures as he was going out the door.

J. L. took off, walking west on Sevier Street. One block beyond his apartment, the street became a narrow wagon trail called Brent's Ford Road, which followed McNeil Creek down to the fish trap on the river. In the twenties, the city had built a low-water dam on the Saline River at the end of Brent's Ford Road. The low-water dam had formed a pool from which the city got its water. North of the fish trap, the river bottoms spread out with large pastures on either side of the river. Instead of crossing the river, he turned upstream and walked about a half mile north into the river bottoms until he came to the place where Salt Creek emptied into the river. On the opposite shore of the river was a high, sandy bank. The river was no more than twenty yards wide at that point and reasonably shallow.

J. L. waded across the river, almost falling twice. He dug a hole in the bank under a large cottonwood tree and carefully planted the bomb in the web of roots, sand, and gravel at the base of the tree. He set the timer for ten minutes and then went back across the river to wait. To protect himself against flying rocks and gravel, he stood behind a wide-based red oak just at the top of the opposite bank.

J. L. had worked around explosives, especially since being at the mines. He knew about the force that was generated. The one thing he wasn't prepared for was the sound. Most explosions were controlled and heard from a distance. The particular configuration of the bank and the river bottoms created a bowl that amplified the sound. The ground heaved, and then the sound wave came around the sides of the tree. It was like having someone clap you on both sides of the head at the same time. It was the most pain he had ever felt. For an instant, he passed out from the pain, and when he came to, the only thing he could hear was an intense ringing in both ears.

When he struggled to his feet and stepped out from behind the base of the tree, the next surprise came crashing down. The cottonwood tree had been undermined, and without its support, it came falling down across the river. Since J. L. couldn't hear, the first he knew of the falling tree was when he looked up as the first large branches came whipping down on top of him. One limb of note—about two inches in diameter—struck across his right shoulder, tearing his shirt and knocking him to the ground.

When the dust settled and J. L. was sure that there were no more surprises coming from the bomb site, he walked out into the river to survey the damage. He was awed by the damage created by the one small bomb. The force of the explosion plus the falling of the tree had changed the course of the river.

On the opposite bank of the river, just beyond the base of the tree, a cow and her calf had been grazing. The cow lay dying from the explosion, with half of its hindquarters missing. The calf was staggering about as if it had no equilibrium. When J. L. saw the mother and child wounded on the bank of the river, it again came home to him what he had been asked to do. For minute, he stood in the middle of the river and cried.

The bleating of the dying cow brought him back to the present. He had to find some way to put the poor animal out of its misery. Just as he crawled onto the opposite bank, the big animal gave out one last groan and died, saving him the job of killing her. The calf stood and watched him as he walked toward her. J. L. looked across the field and spied a field of cows with their calves. He picked the calf up and carried it toward the herd of curious animals. He laid the calf under a willow tree that stood out in the middle of the field. Somebody would find the calf and the remains of the mother.

As J. L. walked back to town, his shoulder began to hurt. When he removed his shirt, he realized that his shoulder looked funny. He went back to his apartment, got all of the river mud off, and changed clothes. By then, the shoulder was really hurting, so he walked down to Dr. Gann's. The elder doctor was gone for a vacation, but his son was there. He came to the door dressed in pajamas and smelling strongly of alcohol and urine.

Gann Jr. looked J. L. up and down for an awkward moment.

"If you needed pain medicine or some kind of surgery, you will have to go to Dr. Jones or Dr. Ashby, because I don't have a key to the clinic, but I can help you with that collarbone."

To this point, J. L. had not said a word. "How did you know that it was my shoulder?"

"Purely inductive reasoning. And it isn't your shoulder; it's your collarbone.

"Okay, my collarbone," J. L. said.

"To begin with, it is Sunday night, and you have presented to the doctor's office obviously in pain. You hurt yourself playing ball or falling down the stairs. Your right shoulder is dropped, making your shirt fit funny, but you are using your arm. If your shoulder was dislocated or the humerus was broken, you would be holding it still. And lastly, that funny looking bump is the distal fragment of your clavicle."

"I don't care what it is. It's hurting like hell. Can you help me?" J. L. said.

"Sure, won't take a minute. Come on in." Gann Jr. rolled a piano stool out into the middle of the front atrium. "Sit down here. I'll be back in a minute." The younger Gann disappeared into one of the back rooms, leaving J. L. sitting in the middle of the cavernous entryway to the beautiful, old home. It had an ornate circular staircase that extended to the second floor, large, solid-core, pocket doors, and a great, crystal chandelier. Though he had never lived in a home like that, it reminded him of the homes that had surrounded the Oldenberg house.

Soon the doctor returned with a roll of wide gauze and three strips of wide, cotton padding.

"This will hurt at first."

He fitted one of the cotton pads in front of each shoulder, and then standing behind J. L., he formed a figure eight, encircling each shoulder repeatedly. As he began to tighten the loop, the pain in J. L.'s shoulder surged, but as soon as the collarbone stabilized, the pain began to subside. By the time he finished, Gann Jr. had his knee in the middle of J. L.'s back to cinch up the harness. When the yoke was complete, he stuffed the third cotton pad between the shoulder blades.

"There, that should feel better," the doctor said. He walked around in front of J. L., admiring his handiwork. "Are you more comfortable?"

"Yes, sir, I am."

"Good. I left a special cinch knot in the last length of gauze. Every few days, it will need to be tightened. It's easy to figure out. You're going to have to leave this thing on there for about six weeks. Come back once a week so we can readjust the sling. I'm working on one with snaps and buckles that you can take on and off, sort of like a woman's corset. It's not quite ready. Now that I can't practice medicine, I have a lot of time on my hands.

"By the way, that is an odd accent you have. During my training, I spent a lot of time on the continent. Is that German or Austrian?"

"Boy, you have good ears. It's Austrian. My father was from Linz, and my mother from Vienna. They moved to Pittsburgh before I was born, but when I was a child, they always spoke in the native language."

"I thought so," Gann Jr. said.

"Thanks for your help. How much do I owe you?"

"You don't owe me anything."

"Well, thank you, Dr. Gann. It was a pleasure meeting you," J. L. said.

"Likewise, Herr Stein," Gann said.

"You probably shouldn't call me that, with the war and all."

"I guess you're right. But it wouldn't make any difference. All of these people think I am a fool. On second thought, there is one thing you could do for me."

"What's that?" J. L. asked.

"When you come in to let my father check your shoulder, if you don't mind, tell him that I did a good job on your shoulder," Gann said.

"Yeah, sure. I'll make a point of it."

"Thanks."

When J. L. climbed the stairs back into his apartment, he was ready to go to sleep. On his pillow was a brief note from the stalker. It read:

I KILLED THE CALF.

AND I'LL KILL YOUR GIRL

DON'T SCREW UP

The finishing touches were being put on the new plant.

Ben laughed at J. L. when he told him the story he had made up to cover his broken shoulder. In this bit of fiction, J. L. had borrowed an old bicycle from the Roberts family and, while he was racing down Conway Street, lost control of the bike. He couldn't stop and ended up in the creek at the end of the street.

"You mean to tell me that you broke your shoulder falling off of a bicycle?" Ben asked.

"No, you didn't listen to me. I was still on the bike when it hit the ground, so technically I didn't fall off of the bike."

"Okay, so how long is it going to take for this shoulder to heal?"

"Why?" J. L. asked.

"Because I have a proposal for you."

"And what might that be? You and I quit this outfit and go to work digging ditches?" J. L. asked.

"Well, it's not quite that drastic but close. The folks in Pittsburgh like the work that you and I have done on this plant. They want me to go to Surinam and build another just like it. After that, I'm going back to the East Coast. They told me that I can have whatever job I choose. I can take whoever I want with me. What do you say? You want to go south of the border? You might even meet some pretty little senorita down there."

"Ben, that sounds great. I have never enjoyed working with anyone as much as I have you." J. L. said.

"I know. We make a great team. You are super at taking care of the people problems, and I don't do that worth a damn. By the way, you do have another option."

"What?"

"I happen to know that if you don't go with me, they want you to stay on as the plant engineer for this plant," Ben said.

"Me? Man, there are a lot of people around with more seniority than me."

"That may be true, but you know this plant like the back of your hand. We could lose the blueprints today, and you could reconstruct them from memory. There is no one who could keep this place running better than you. I told them that. At the time, I didn't know that you couldn't keep a bicycle upright."

"I wasn't expecting this. That's a hard choice. I don't know what to say," J. L. said.

"Well, you got about a week to make up your mind. I'll be leaving for Surinam next Monday," Ben said.

"Have you talked to Gail at all?"

"She says that when I come back from the 'jungle,' as she calls it, we will see if we can pull our marriage back together. I think this is probably it. You know, old buddy, she's just too pretty for me. She's got more ambition than I do. There's a lot of things in life that she wants. I've known it since we met. I'm just an average Joe who wants a house with two or three rug rats underfoot all the time. I want to come home at night, have supper, kick off my shoes, and listen to radio. She's never going to be happy with that."

"I'm sure sorry to hear about this," J. L. said.

"Yeah, we did look good together, didn't we? Anyway, you are going to have to make a decision yourself, in the next week, as to what you want to do."

That evening, after J. L. dropped Ben off at the house, he circled back by Larry's. Larry had a series of pots set out for J. L. to choose from. As they went through, picking out the ones he wanted to send to Valencia in Mexico, J. L. told Larry about his shoulder, and Larry shared the latest Saline county rumor—this one was about the German bombing of Saline County.

"Old man Chastain, who owns a pasture on the river off Peeler Bend Road, heard an explosion down by the river last night. He grabbed his binoculars and raced out into the front yard. The old man swears that he looked up and saw a low flying bomber with large swastikas painted on both wings. When the airplane disappeared and he was sure there weren't any fighters tailing the big plane, he made off for the river, looking for the evidence of the bomb. When he got to the river, he found his prize-winning cow, the best of the herd, destroyed by a bomb dropped from the plane. The old man is convinced that the bomber got lost and was probably running out of fuel. He told the sheriff that a friend of his cousin told him there was an airfield over near Mena that the Germans were flying in and out of at night.

"Anyway, the sheriff went out and checked the bomb site. He says it looks like some fisherman was trying to dynamite fish and got carried away. The cow was dead all right, and the really odd thing was that the cow's calf was found about a hundred yards away. Didn't have any marks on it, but it was dead as a doornail. Must have had a concussion or something.

"Anyway, the old man went down to the paper, and the editor sent Marty out there to look around. They sent a cameraman out to get a photo. Apparently, Jim Sims called the FBI. They made an appearance this afternoon and took statements from everyone, had a good laugh, and then disappeared. Ain't that the wildest thing you ever heard?"

As Larry was talking, J. L. was admiring one of the pots. He slid the last letter to the Germans into the vase.

"I definitely want this one," he said.

"Good choice," Larry said. "Put in over on the workbench."

"Now, back to what you were saying about Germans and bombs. Why do you think that is so farfetched?"

"Oh, please, German bombers over Saline County, Germans landing in Mena? Give me a break. The Krauts and the Japs have got a whole lot more important things on their plate than scaring some poor farmer in the Saline River bottoms."

"Hold it just a minute. Let's say that there were German spies in this country. They get hold of some old planes, paint swastikas on the wings, drop a little dynamite in different parts of the country where the people think they are safe. The Germans are putting screaming noisemakers on their fighters to scare people in Europe. If these people can make people scared, they are already one step up."

J. L. had already decided that, at some point, he would tell Larry who he was, but it wasn't the time just yet. He had to get this shipment of pots out before he said anything. And then, he wasn't sure. Larry was a bit of a hothead, and it was hard to know how he would react.

"When do you think this shipment will go out?" J. L. asked.

"I'll pack everything up in the morning and get it on the five o'clock train tomorrow afternoon," Larry said.

"That's great."

"Man, you seem awfully edgy," Larry said.

"I am just a little. We've had a few last-minute setbacks at the plant in the last week. Nothing major, just stupid stuff. We are pushing hard to get everything on line before the bigwigs get here next week. On top of that, Ben is leaving next Monday, and I've had a couple of job offers. I got a whole lot on my plate right now." He told his friend about the conversation with Ben earlier in the day.

"Boy, I'd say that sounds like a pretty good dilemma. I got to tell you, I hope you end up taking the job here. I think you and I would make a good team. You learn real quick. You understand what I do, and you're interested in it. With your connections and business sense, I think, eventually, we could make some money. More than that, it would just be fun."

"That's one of the things that's hard for me," J. L. began. "A person doesn't make many real close friends in his life. You're like a brother to me. The people at that plant are like family. It would be real hard for me to ever do anything to disrupt that. As far as working with you here in the pottery and furniture business, I can't think of anything that I would like better. The aluminum business chews people up and spits them out. Ben has this thing about wanting to get back to the East Coast, but I think he knows that, after Surinam, there will be someplace else. I could tell by the way he talked this morning—he's already given up on getting Gail back."

"Okay, let's complicate your life even more," Larry said. "Here, today, right now, I want you to accept my offer of partnership in the business."

"But, I don't have anything to bring to the table. You got this building, land, your truck, all of the pots and furniture ..." J. L. said.

"This building and land aren't anything. Anyway, they were given to me. Somebody could just as easily come along and take it away. Look at what has happened to Bullet Hyten over the years. One year, he's on top of the world, selling more than he can produce, making all kinds of money, buying big cars, going on fancy trips. The next year, he's selling door-to-door for Camark. He's not the only one; that's the nature of this business. I'm just about as bad about managing the business part of my work as Bullet is. Now you, on the other hand, have a good job at the plant, and you get a regular paycheck. You can make money while we are getting this place up and running. You bring everything you have, and I'll bring everything I have. That seems like a fair partnership to me."

"It's a deal," J. L. said.

The two young men shook hands. Larry went to the back and took two cold beers out of the icebox.

Larry opened the beers, held his up and, said, "To a long-lived partnership."

"Here, here."

J. L. thought to himself, *This might the shortest partnership deal in history.*

"Can I assume that you are going to take the job at the plant?"

"Yeah, I guess so. If they offer it," J. L. said.

"Well, just as soon as things get settled down around here, I will start working on a room in the back of the building for you to live in so you won't have to be wasting money on rent for that apartment on Sevier Street. How does that sound?" Larry asked.

"Sounds great."

Chapter 47

In this time, there are things that I cannot comprehend.
The unknown is an event horizon that will be whatever
it will be. I go out and live my day and don't waste time
pondering the unknown. I force myself to open my eyes
and look, really look. I can't be a voyeur of life. I stick
my head well below the surface and look around. I must
think about what I see. If I am thinking, then there are
others in other places with other lives that are thinking
the same thoughts. It may sound crazy, but in the end,
the thoughts think the thinker. Down below the surface
is the answer to this mess.

Poet of Mauthausen

J. L. firmly believed that the success or failure of his plan was predicated on
figuring out who the stalker was. The only real clue he had were the notes
left in his apartment. The block letters and the awkward use of words were
oddly familiar.

By Tuesday, most of the finishing touches were beginning to fall in place
at the plant, so J. L. took off a little early and went to the funeral home.

"Mr. Sims, I'm trying to close up some files at the plant," J. L. said. "Can
you tell me whatever happened with the Hampton case?"

"Nothing's happened, and nothing will," Sims said. "I think I told you
that when we were working on the case."

"Yes, sir, you did. Would you happen to still have that sign that was found
on the body?"

"Sure don't. Sheriff keeps all of the evidence. I do have photos that Mr. Merrill developed for me."

"That would be just as good. All I need is a copy for the file."

"I always have him make three copies," Sims said.

He led J. L. into his office. Jim Sims was an organized man. All of his files were precise and ordered. The fingerprint file was kept separate and in a locked case.

"Here it is, John L. Hampton Jr.," he said. Sims pulled out an eight by ten photograph of the sign that had hung around the boy's neck. "You know, the odd thing about this case is that there weren't any fingerprints, none. There was a little smudge of oil on the top corner of the wooden sign, but no fingerprints anywhere. Most people don't even know about fingerprinting. The guy who did this must be pretty smart."

"Either that, or he wears gloves," J. L. said.

"Hadn't thought about that. That's another possibility."

"How much do I owe you for the picture?"

"Nothing, it's part of the job. Are you folks going to be through with the plant for the big celebration next week?" Sims asked.

"We will actually be in operation by this weekend. That way there won't be any surprises come the big day."

"Good luck."

"Thanks."

The last thing on J. L.'s mind was whether the new plant would work. They had tested each section of the plant already. It was just a matter of putting it all together. His concern was how to keep the whole place intact and not blow everyone up in the meantime.

When he got back to the apartment, J. L. took out the photo and compared it to the notes he had gotten. There was no question—it was the same guy, a nameless, faceless man who hated blacks and wore greasy gloves. There wasn't a lot to go on. The question was how to flush him out into the open.

The next evening when J. L. came home, he parked the car, went up the stairs, and turned on the lights and the radio. He waited about thirty minutes and then let himself down through an old attic ladder into the garage. He slipped out a small window on the west side of the garage and found a place in the shadows of the neighbor's toolshed. He hadn't been in place for more than twenty minutes when he felt the barrel of a gun come up beside his head.

"Don't move a hair," the voice said. "If you do, I'll kill you right here. What in the hell do you think you are doing, sneaking around out here in the dark? Hell, you can't even explode a bomb without damn near killing yourself. What a klutz. You do make a good bomb. Your bombs worked a lot better than mine. In fact, I'm gonna take one of yours, and you make another. As far as this crap of trying to figure out who I am … if I didn't need you, I'd kill your ass right now. Now when you wake up, go back in the house and act like a good little boy and maybe those bad old Germans will let your mommy live. Adios shithead."

With that, Junior came down hard on the side of J. L.'s head with the butt of the gun. For the second time in a week, J. L. had lost consciousness.

When he came to, his head was hurting. He had almost been killed, and he knew little more than he had when the evening had begun. The only new piece of information was that the stalker was going to bomb something as well.

The next morning, J. L. went by Larry's on his way to work.

"I need to use the phone. It's a long distance call. When you get the bill, let me know, and I'll pay you," he said.

"Hey, boss, it's partly your phone now and your phone bill." Larry said as he stood, watching him.

"It's private."

"Well, pardon the hell out of me."

He dialed zero on the phone.

"Minnie, this is J. L. Stein. I need a Hot Springs number, it is Wakefield four five seven seven, the Spa City Cigar Store, and I need to talk to Tommy Lorio.

In a minute, Tommy was on the line.

"Tommy, this is J. L. Stein. I need to talk to you."

"Who did you say this was?"

"Stein, J. L. Stein," J. L. repeated.

"Sorry, I don't know anyone by the name of Stein," Tommy said. "I sell tobacco and run a resort on the lake."

J. L. was taken aback for a minute, and then he realized that, in his anxiety, he had broken one of the rules.

"You probably don't remember me, but I stayed at the resort last summer, and I was just wondering if you had a room for the night."

"When?"

"Tonight," J. L. said.

"That's a bit of a short notice, but I think we can accommodate you. Would you like a room for one or a cabin?" Tommy asked.

"A room would be just fine."

"And when could we be expecting you?" Tommy asked.

"I should be there by eight o'clock."

"Fine. We'll be expecting you."

J. L. hung up the phone and walked up to where Larry was packing the pots they had selected the night before.

"Thanks for the phone. Now, I have one other, big favor. After you deliver the boxes down to the train station at five, can I use your truck for the evening? I can't tell you where I am going, but in a few days, I'll make everything clear."

"First, I was kidding about the phone. You can use anything I have, anytime you want, and you don't ever have to explain. I asked you to be my partner not my wife."

"Thanks a bunch," J. L. said. "I'll be back at about six."

"I'll have it gassed and ready. Should I put rubber bumpers on it, just in case you forget and think you're on a bicycle?"

"I don't think that will be necessary, but thanks anyway," J. L. said, smiling.

It was nearing dark when Tommy and J. L. began motoring out into the lake to talk about J. L.'s problem.

"Sorry about the telephone this morning. I just forgot," J. L. said.

"It's no big deal. What have you got on your mind?"

"First of all, you were right about there being someone else at the plant. He's been stalking me, and on several occasions, he threatened to kill me," J. L. said. "I didn't tell you, but the Germans want me to set two bombs—one to go off in the community hall during the dedication services. The second bomb is to be timed to go off one hour later in the small hospital where they will take the injured. The other fellow has taken one of my bombs, and I believe that he will probably try to blow up the plant.

"I am convinced that my mother is probably dead. I know that she didn't write the letters I've received in the last year. I didn't want to let myself believe it, but the last one was the kicker. There is no way my mother would write a letter like that. Anyway, my last letter back to the Germans was shipped this afternoon. In it, I told them that I wouldn't help them anymore. That was one of the hardest letters I ever wrote.

"I could have done almost anything, but when they asked me to kill innocent women and children to save my mother I knew I couldn't do it.

"I am going to turn myself in to the FBI. Jim Sims, the coroner, has connections with those people, but I don't want the stalker to know about it.

"Can you remember anything else at all about the first guy at the plant? Anything that might help me to identify who he is?"

"Other than the gloves and the fact that he hadn't had a bath in a month," Tommy said.

"If you think of anything else, call me through Fitts Pottery and Furniture," J. L. said. "I think you have Larry's number. I go by there at least once a day. That's where I called you from this morning.

"There are two other things I need you help me with. I need a meeting place so I can meet with the FBI and not let the stalker know."

"You mean you want to bring the FBI to my place? I don't think so," he said, smiling broadly. "I do have another idea though. There is a small campground just east of Carpenter Dam. It isn't used very much, because it is so hard to get to. You could come here. I could take you down to the Dam. They could meet you at the park. It isn't more than a half mile from our side down to the park. After you guys meet, if you are still a free man, I could be waiting up at the dam to bring you back. They would never have to know that I was there. It would be better for me if we could do this on Sunday."

"That sounds great," J. L. said.

"You said there were two things. What is the other thing?" Tommy asked.

"You remember you said you could hide a person and keep them safe, like in Mena?"

"Yeah, I can handle that."

"If I can talk her into it, I may have someone who needs your safe hands."

"Just let me know."

CHAPTER 48

There is a peculiar moment,
an instant really,
when breathing ceases.

In a little while,
there is a quiet as stillness
descends on this last act of life.

We look and wait
for the next breath,
the cycle of to and fro,

but it is the silence,
the quiet
that we hear.

To whom do these words provide hope? It's simple; it's
the writer. No one may read what I write, but I live with
the sure knowledge that I am not alone. Last evening,
the woman in the bunk with me died. She took the
second half of that breath that starts and stops life.

She has no name. I will not recognize anyone, any
person, any being, in that corpse that lies there. To put a
name to that cold flesh hastens my own demise. The only

thing that separates me from her is hope and luck. Mostly luck.

Poet of Mauthausen

"Sit down Larry, I've got something to tell you," J. L. said to his friend.

"Oh, so now I get to hear the big secret," Larry said, smiling

"Yes, I am afraid that you do, and you aren't going to like it. My name is not John Lewis Stein, it is Jean Louis Edit-Stein. It is pronounced 'Jon Louie.' I was born and raised in Vienna, Austria. My father was an engineer who fought for the Germans in World War I and died from the flu. I told you about my brother. He was a Nazi and a drunk. He was killed by a bunch of American Nazis. I think my little sister, Anna, was killed early in the war, fighting the Nazis. The last I heard, my grandfather who lived in Linz is still alive. I've had no contact with them since the beginning of the war.

"My mother, Helena, is a newspaper writer and editor and the most wonderful, smartest person I have ever known. She convinced me to come to the US under the ruse of looking for my brother when she saw what was happening in Europe. When the Nazis took over Austria, she hid and continued writing but was eventually caught. They've held her in a place called Mauthausen since the beginning of the war—that is, if she is still alive. They began contacting me when I lived in East St. Louis and told me that, if I did not cooperate with them, they would kill her.

"For the last several years, I have been spying for the Germans. Since moving to Bauxite, I've used you and your pottery to ship the information about bauxite production to Mexico City. The guy in Mexico City is a front for a spy operation.

"Now, they've demanded that I blow up the community hall and the hospital in Bauxite a week from Saturday in the middle of the dedication ceremony. I'm convinced that they also plan on blowing up the new plant or at least part of it. The explosion down at the river the other night was my clumsy attempt at trying one of the bombs. That's how I broke my shoulder.

"That's not all. There is another spy at the plant, and he's crazy. I know that he's mean as hell. He is the guy who killed your friend Hampton at the plant last year. He knows who I am, but I don't know who he is. For the last two months, he has been stalking me, and I'm convinced that he's the one who is going to blow up the plant."

There was a silence.

"Is that all?" Larry asked.

"Yeah, that's about it.

"So why are you telling me all this? Are you going to kill me now?" Larry asked.

"No, stupid. I'm turning myself in to you. I'm confessing. I'm giving myself up to you."

"Why me? Why don't you just go down to the sheriff, the FBI, or the WPB?"

"First of all, I don't want to do anything that will raise the suspicion of the stalker. I am convinced that he watches me all of the time, and if I do something that is out of the normal, he will either kill me or run. We need to catch this clown," J. L. said. "Larry, I am asking a lot of you, but I want you to help me catch him before he blows up the plant."

"What do you want me to do?" Larry asked.

"In the morning, I want you to go down and tell Jim Sims all of the things that I've told you. I want to set up a meeting with you, him, the FBI, and me at the little park just below the Carpenter Dam on Lake Catherine. I'd really like to do it the day after tomorrow at about seven thirty in the evening. To keep the guy from being suspicious, I'll meet all of you there. I get my information in Hot Springs, and he won't suspect anything by my going there."

"What if the FBI doesn't want to meet?" Larry asked.

"Trust me, they will want to meet. They have everything to gain and nothing to lose by meeting with me."

"They may come and arrest you tomorrow, you know," Larry said.

"Yeah, I've thought about that. That's what would happen if the WPB got wind of this, but then, we still have this other fellow out there, and I promise you he's a lot more dangerous than I am.

"One of my problems is that I don't want the Germans to know for sure that I double-crossed them. If they find out that I've been arrested, I can't be held responsible for that. I am willing to accept the consequences of them thinking that I took a moral stand based on the lives of the people in Bauxite, because I know that is what she would do."

"Why don't we try stalking him?" Larry asked. "What's good for the goose is good for the gander."

"I've already tried that and almost got myself killed in the process. He got the jump on me and then knocked me out. We really have to be careful. This guy seems to really like killing things.

"And, by the way, don't tell a word of this to Marty. I am going to try to get her to go to Hot Springs with me when I go."

The next morning, J. L. went to work, fully prepared to be arrested during the day. The work day came and went, and no one showed up. After he dropped Ben off at the house, he headed for Larry's.

"I did what you asked. After Jim picked his chin up off of the floor, he got on the phone to the Little Rock office, and they immediately agreed to the meeting. I'll bet you have more than one stalker tonight. Until this is over, you aren't going to be able to pick your nose without somebody knowing about it. You know, J. L., I really do admire you. You could have just picked up your stuff and disappeared, and no one would ever have known the difference."

"My friend over in Hot Springs said that he could hide me in west Arkansas, and no one would ever find me if I didn't want them to. But I just couldn't do that."

"Well, the next week should be interesting, if nothing else," Larry said.

CHAPTER 49

Yesterday,
a storm blew across our mountain.
Ahead of the rain, the quiet sky
turned yellow-green in color.
Then it came—
rain fell in sheets;
wind blew from every direction;
thunder and lightning shouted.

With no place to hide,
we stood in the mud
in the grime
and watched.

Some prayed to the storm,
"Take me, please take me."
Some drank the rain.
Some cried.

After the great fury passed,
the stale smell of smoke
and human waste
was gone.

Poet of Mauthausen

"Marty, I need for you to do me a favor and not ask any questions," J. L.
said.

"Of course, whatever you want," she said.

"I need for you to pack a small bag with enough clothes for a few days. I'll pick you up early in the morning."

"Can you tell me where we're going?"

"We are going to Hot Springs on the train but don't tell anyone."

"What time do you want me ready?"

"I'll come by and pick you up at about 7:00 AM."

Early the next morning after they had boarded the train for Hot Springs and were nearing Ten Mile Hill, J. L. bared his soul to Marty.

"I am so sorry that I couldn't tell you any of this before but I really didn't know what I was going to do. Tommy Lorio has offered to make one or more of us disappear until this is over. If anything happens and we don't catch the stalker, you are really in danger, because he has already made it clear that he knows who you are, where you live, and what you mean to me."

"I'll do whatever you ask, J. L., but if you are convinced that your mother is no longer alive, why don't we both leave?"

"I can't. This man is planning the death of many of my friends, and he has got to be stopped. I am the only one who can draw him out. In fact, I fully expect him to come looking for me.

"Larry told Jim Sims, and he is setting up a meeting with the FBI at a park east of Tommy's this evening. I will feel much better if I know you are in Tommy's hands, because I am certain that I can trust him, and I really don't know about them."

When J. L. and Marty arrived at Lorio's, they found that Tommy had set aside a cabin for them to have some privacy.

When they were alone, Marty said, "Jean Louis, I am really proud of you, and I am very scared that I may never see you again." Then she began to cry. "Please make love to me."

Slowly, gently, they undressed each other and made love.

Afterward, she turned to him. "I hope that one time makes me pregnant. Because even if you don't return, I will always have part of you with me."

At six forty-five, Tommy knocked on the door of the cabin. "Okay, lovebirds, we better get moving if we are going to make our appointment.

Tommy and J. L. loaded into a small boat and headed out across the lake. They motored to the boat launch just above the Carpenter Dam on Lake Hamilton.

"I'm going do some brim fishing while I wait for you," Tommy said. "Now, remember what I told you. You get in trouble, just take off running toward the bridge east of the Dam. There is a little creek just on the other side of the bridge. Run up the creek. I got some people up there that will take care of you. We got a few across the river on the bluff with rifles and scopes. Don't let them give you any grief."

"Thanks, Tommy. I won't ever forget this," J. L. said.

"Damn right, you won't, you owe me big for this." He smiled as he pushed the boat away from the shore. "This is my day off."

J. L. walked down the gravel road that led down behind the dam. The corp of engineers had been releasing water in the last hour, so the temperature had dropped a good fifteen degrees as he descended into the canyon created by the bluffs on either side of the river and the concrete dam to the west. A gentle mist rose off of the water and covered the campground.

At the far end of the campground were two black sedans, unmarked but obviously not fishermen. When J. L. approached the first of the two cars, several men in black suits got out and motioned for J. L. to put his hands on the car and spread his legs. After they thoroughly searched him, the doors to the other car opened. Two older FBI agents, plus a stenographer, got out of one side of the car. Jim Sims and Larry got out of the other side of the car. While everyone was being introduced, the men who had done the searching set up two collapsible tables and a series of chairs that they retrieved from the trunk of the first car.

In a short time, J. L. Stein was telling these men his life story. If they had any interest in Jean Louis Stein, they never let on. It was when he began to talk about the stalker that they seemed to take notice.

"Are you sure that this man is not just a racist who doesn't like Jews and coloreds?" the older officer said.

"Why do you ask that?" J. L. asked.

"Because we've never heard of this other fellow. We aren't convinced he exists."

"What do you mean you don't believe that he exists? I exist. If I exist, what makes it so unbelievable that he could exist?" J. L. said.

"It isn't really important that you know all of the details, but I can tell you this. We have known about you ever since you set foot in this country. We've known about Rudy, Franz, and especially your uncle Karl. We weren't too sure about Larry over here. We finally figured out you were just using him."

"I wasn't using him, I was using his pottery," J. L. said, looking at Larry. "He knew nothing about all of this."

"Well, that is to yet to be seen."

"And why do you say especially my uncle Karl?" J. L. asked.

"Look, Stein, doesn't it seem odd that the Germans, three thousand miles away, have known about your every move? Your uncle Karl is Rudy. He knows about your mother, he knows about you. He has been using you to curry favor with the Germans."

"What about all of the information that I have sent to the Germans?" J. L. asked.

"Most of the stuff you've sent, they could have gotten from a hundred different sources. We've been surprised that you haven't sent them anything in the last year. Just those wordy letters."

"What do you mean wordy letters?" J. L. asked.

"I mean, hell, man, you write letters that go on for six or seven pages and never say a thing. And your punctuation is horrible."

J. L. smiled. "You guys don't have a clue, do you?"

"What do you mean by that?" the older man said.

"I mean, I have been using microdot technology for the last year, and you guys had no idea what it was. What a bunch of idiots."

"You've been using what?" the agent asked.

One of the younger agents leaned over and whispered into his ear.

"Oh, yeah, we knew about that. Where do you get a lab to process the film?"

J. L. spent the next ten minutes explaining the Zapp's cabinet to the officer.

"And where is this magic box?" the agent asked.

"It's sitting in my bedroom on Sevier Street," J. L. said. "Look, officer, I don't want to get in a sparring match with you about all of this, but you didn't know about the photography. Now that suggests that there are a few things about me that you don't know. I have nothing to gain by telling you all of this stuff. I fully expected that you might just put me in jail, here, tonight. That would be okay for me, but there is another man at that plant, and he intends on blowing up the new facility and killing as many people as he can in the process.

"You have nothing to lose from letting me see if I can find him. If I am arrested, he will be spooked, but knowing this guy, he will still go after the plant and the people. If I am arrested, he will do the bombing of the community hall himself."

"What do you propose to do?" the agent asked.

"Like you said, this guy hates Jews. He knows that I am a Jew. I think he will try to kill me when he blows the plant up, but only after I have set my bombs."

"How do you know that he has a bomb?" the agent asked.

"Because he took one of the ones I made," J. L. said.

"How did he get it?"

"He broke into my apartment and took it," J. L. said.

"Again, I ask you how do you propose to find him?"

"I won't have to. He'll find me."

"We will inspect your bombs to make absolutely sure that they are duds."

"You can play with them all you want, but just don't change their appearance. This guy is sharp," J. L. said.

"If you figure out who he is, you will immediately come to one of our people."

"You bet. I have no desire to be a dead hero," J. L. said.

"If you come out of this, what is it you want for all of this information?"

"One thing. Make sure that the Germans and my uncle Karl think that I am dead."

"Agreed. Now, I can't promise you won't go to jail for espionage," the agent said.

"I understand that."

"If anyone is killed, you will get the death sentence," the agent said.

"I understand."

"How do we know you won't run?" the man asked.

"You don't, but you have my word, the word of a most unwilling spy," J. L. said.

Larry, who was sitting on the hood of one of the cars, added, "Yeah, that, and a nickel will get you a cup of coffee. You people about through? I'm getting hungry."

The older officer got up from his chair. This seemed like a good place to end the meeting.

"You deactivate the bombs, and my men will check them when you have gone to work."

J. L. reached into his pocket and handed the man the key to his apartment. "When your men go into the apartment, tell them to dress in work clothes and drive an old truck. If anybody asks, I sent them to the apartment to pick up some papers. That way it won't arouse any suspicion. Now I won't mess with them until Friday, just in case the stalker gets particularly nosy."

All of the men got into the cars, except for J. L. and Larry.

"Aren't you going with them?" J. L. asked.

"No, it smells better out here. Anyway, partners got to stick together." They stood and watched as the two cars drove off. "That was one hell of a performance. Did you ever consider a career on the stage?" Larry asked.

"Did you hear what that stupid clown said? He doesn't care if the guy kills people, because they are different as long as he's not a Nazi. At one point, I thought he was going to say it wasn't part of his job description."

"You really surprised him when you started talking about the photography. That poor kid behind him is probably going to get an earful when they get back to the station. You know, of course, they aren't going to be any help at all when it comes to catching the stalker."

"Yeah, I know. You got a cigarette?" J. L. asked.

"Yeah. Here," he said, handing him a smoke.

After the cigarette was lit, Larry said, "I've never seen you smoke before."

"I haven't. I mean, I don't. But it sure does taste good now. You know, I never felt comfortable around my uncle, but I thought it was me. He was always nice to me, but he always seemed distant. He wasn't anything like my dad."

"By the way, where are we going?" Larry asked.

"I got a friend picking us up in a boat in a little while."

"You've gotten pretty good at this."

"Well, after a while, you learn not to trust some people."

CHAPTER 50

The work in the quarry was hard. Each day, Helena felt herself getting weaker. The injury was simple. She was lifting a piece of flagstone, and it slipped from her hands, striking her left shin and tearing a small triangular flap of skin away from the bony surface. She ripped a small strip of material from the bottom of her blouse to staunch the bleeding. By late evening as she walked the steps back up to the compound from the quarry, the first red streak of cellulitis extended its way up her inner thigh.

Lying in her bunk that evening, she felt the first chill. Early the next morning, Helena Edit-Stein was a nameless corpse, one more life that luck had abandoned.

CHAPTER 51

Driving back to Benton in Larry's truck, J. L. turned to Larry. "I had no intention of you becoming involved in this business. This is my mess, and I have to clean it up."

Larry smiled. "Look, from the sound of those guys back there, they believe very little that you say, and I'm second on their list. So, my friend, it looks like we are in this together."

"I appreciate your offer, but you don't know the stalker like I do."

"What are you going to do, anyway?" Larry asked.

"I haven't the foggiest idea. I know that, on Friday night, I'm going to set the bombs in place, and then Saturday sometime after ten in the morning, I'll go back and set the timers. I'll set the one at the community hall to go off at eight PM and the one at the hospital to go off at nine PM," J. L. explained.

"And what will you do after that?" Larry asked.

"Wait, I guess."

"I could use a beer when we get back to town. How about you?"

"Absolutely. I could also use another of those cigarettes."

"Better watch out. These things are addicting," Larry said.

"Yeah, right."

On Monday, Ben left for Surinam. J. L. took him to the train station.

"Good luck, my friend. Be careful down there in the jungle."

"Good luck to you," Ben said. "I put in a word for you on that job. I think it's a done deal."

"Thanks for the help. Next time you talk to Gail, tell her I said hello."

"Yeah. We'll see," Ben said.

With that, J. L.'s mentor got on the train and left for Surinam.

When J. L. got back to the plant, there was a note that the superintendent wanted to see him. When he arrived at the office, Maxine seemed rather cold.

"The Superintendent wanted to talk to me," he said.

"He's busy right now. Have a seat," she said.

After about thirty minutes, the door opened, and he was motioned into the room. In the room were the superintendent and the two officers from the night before.

"I don't think I have to tell you what this is all about. The officers have filled me in on what you have done and what is going on. I must say that I am most disappointed in you. I honestly don't see why they don't take you out and shoot you. There was talk of giving you the job as plant engineer, but at this point, I think that is completely out of the question. As of now, you are to be designated a staff engineer. Until this is all cleared up, you will have access to none of the production data or the design information for the new plant, and you most certainly will not go near the new plant unless you are accompanied by the new plant engineer, Harold Johnson. Do you understand me?"

"Yes, sir, I do," J. L. said.

"The agents said we had to make things look as normal as possible," the superintendent continued. "We will put it into the rumor mill that you were caught embezzling funds and that is why you have been demoted."

"I understand, sir."

"As for the car, leave the keys with Maxine on your way out," the superintendent said.

Every action we take in life has unintended consequences, and J. L. hadn't factored this in to his equation.

For the next week, the FBI came and went from his apartment at least twice a day, always in the guise of workmen. Unlike the stalker, these guys left their tracks everywhere. One of them even stole a quart of beer. Each evening, J. L. rearranged his stuff in the way he would have had it so as not to arouse the suspicion of the stalker.

Each night, the stalker left a new note.

DO YOUR JOB AND YOU MIGHT LIVE.

DON'T GET COLD FEET, JEW BOY

WHAT'S THIS ABOUT STEALING?

The twenty-first came, and everything was in place. He packed the bombs, minus the explosives, in two new briefcases.

The first bomb was to be placed in the false ceiling above the men's bathroom, just to the right of the entryway going into the main area of the community hall. The bomb he had exploded on the riverbank had had enough power to kill most of the people sitting in the back of the hall. The secondary effect would have been to cause the roof to collapse, multiplying the dead.

The second bomb was to be placed under the operating room at the hospital. It was an outside wall and was fronted with large shrubs. There was a vent grate that he used to get under the building. It was perfect. The plan was to kill the doctor and his nursing staff as he worked on the injured patients.

On Friday evening, he borrowed Larry's truck, drove to Bauxite, and parked up the hill in the high school parking lot. It was a summer evening, and no one noticed him as he walked across the lawn, briefcase in hand, to the community hall. Inside the men's bathroom, he locked the doors, stood on one of the commodes, put the case up in the false ceiling, and walked out as if it was the normal thing to do. The hospital was easier. It was dark and quiet. Since it was midsummer, there were few patients. With everything in place, he returned to his apartment and tried to sleep. That night, there was no message from the stalker.

The next morning, J. L. caught the morning bus to Bauxite with the rest of the men. No one sat near him. The rumor mill had worked to perfection. People who stole from the plant during the war were as bad as spies. This was a person who would take candy from a baby.

The day began as a beautiful summer day in Bauxite. The roar of the Ukes and trains continued as they did on any other day. These great mechanical beasts raised a haze of dust not unlike a west Texas sandstorm. Small knots of men stood around, waiting for orders to go somewhere and do something. For the last year, nothing had stopped at the mines, and today was no exception. For those who were not working, a Fats-and-Thins baseball tournament was planned for the afternoon. A large picnic was set out on the grounds of the community hall to welcome all of the big shots.

When J. L. got to the plant, it didn't take him long to complete his work. For completeness' sake, he went through every motion as if it were real. He never knew when his nemesis was spying on him.

It had never occurred to Jean Louis Stein what would happen if he exposed himself for what he was. By branding him as a thief, it was as if they had broadcast that he was a traitor. The people he had managed just days before turned away when he walked up. The empty feeling inside built as the day went on.

With time on his hands and nothing to do, he decided to walk over to the new plant one more time. Standing on the hill south and west of the plant, J. L. had a great deal of pride in what he, Ben, and the other men had accomplished in the last year. It was a magnificent structure—shiny and clean. It dwarfed the old production facilities and would bring the operations in Bauxite into the twentieth century.

The cleanup crews were readying the grounds for the final inspection.

J. L. descended from the hill with the idea of making one last inspection, himself.

Walking toward the front gate, he noticed a bar ditch on the south side of the road leading to the plant. A week earlier, he had instructed one of the crews to drain the hole, dig out the mud, and then fill it in with sand and gravel. When it rained, the shoulder of the road washed into the ditch, making the shoulder weak. On top of that, it was an eyesore at the new plant.

A new guard gate had been constructed, even though the perimeter had not been fenced. J. L. recognized the guard at the front gate as Homer Peeler.

"Morning, Homer," J. L. said.

"Morning, Mr. Stein."

"Got you a new job I see," J. L. said.

"Yeah and a uniform, too," Homer said. "No more mine work for me."

"Looks good. Thought I would take one last look around, while it's still clean."

"I'm sorry, Mr. Stein. The folks upstairs were real clear that you weren't to go into the plant. I'm real sorry. Tell me something. Is it true what they are saying?"

"What do you mean?"

"That you was caught stealing part of the payroll," he asked.

"Is that what they are saying?"

"Yes, sir, it is."

"No, Homer, I didn't steal anything from the plant," J. L. said.

"Well, that's the story. That you and Mr. Sebastian was caught stealing from the plant and that he ratted on you. Said it was all your idea."

"Homer, I didn't steal anything, and neither did Ben. All of this is a misunderstanding. Someday, we'll get it cleared up," J. L. said.

"I sure do hope so. We was all hoping that either you or Mr. Sebastian would be the new plant engineer. None of us like this Johnson fellow."

"Oh, he'll work out. Just give him a little time."

"Maybe you can get this thing cleared up, and then you can come back down here to the plant," Homer said.

"I would like that Homer. I would really like that."

J. L. turned and walked away from the plant. He knew he could never get his old world back. It was gone, never to be recaptured. J. L.'s biggest worry was whether the plant would be there in the morning.

"How did it go at work?" Larry asked.

"It went okay. Everything is in place. Do you know what they are telling everybody?"

"No. What?"

"They're saying that Ben and I were embezzling funds," J. L. said.

"What funds?"

"Well, I think the phrase was 'part of a payroll.' I don't know which would be worse: just disappearing off of the end of the earth or letting them think that I'm a thief. What's worse—now they think Ben was in on it."

"Well, you can't do anything about it now," Larry said. "I know you've got a lot on your mind, but there's a lot of work to do here at the store. It might help if you just keep your hands busy. How about putting a finishing coat on that chair for me? It has got to go out by Monday. It's a wedding gift for one of the Baxley women, and they want it at the house when the couple gets back from their honeymoon in Eureka Springs. The varnish is out by the chair."

"Sure, that's a good idea. But before I do that, I need to go down and talk to Jim Sims."

"That would be real good. Jim is a good fellow. He's just real serious. He ain't like those other clowns."

It was a busy Saturday afternoon at Sims Furniture and Undertaking. When J. L. caught his eye, Sims motioned him into the back.

"You want a cup of coffee?" Sims said. "Have a seat."

"No, sir. Thanks. I'm just fine."

"Do you have any word about the stalker?"

"No, nothing yet," J. L. said.

"I want you to know that I believe you about the other guy. It all fits."

"Do you have any idea what the FBI is up to?" J. L. asked.

"No, I don't. I know that they don't believe you, but I am out of the loop in this process."

"Mr. Sims, the main reason I came by is to apologize for breaking into your home."

"Don't worry about it J. L. I understand," Sims said.

"I didn't get a chance to tell Ben before he left. If you talk to him, would you tell him my side of the story?"

"Sure. What do you think is going to happen?"

"Nothing, maybe. But we will know in a few hours."

"Well, I got to go back to work. You be careful," Sims said.

He got up and offered his hand to J. L.

"I don't know what I would have done if it had been my mother."

"Thanks."

Most of the afternoon was spent doing odds and ends around the shop. "When do you think this guy might try to contact you?" Larry asked.

"I don't expect to hear anything till after dark."

"Where do you think he will be?"

"I think he will leave a note at the apartment, but it could be anywhere," J. L. said.

As the afternoon passed, the sky began to cloud up. One small thunderstorm came through with a small shower. It cooled things down for a while, and then the steam and humidity added to the heat.

At six, the temperature was lingering around ninety degrees, and it was sticky. J. L. was hesitant to go back to his apartment; he had no idea what he would find.

At six thirty, he forced himself to leave the shop and head home. Climbing the stairs into the darkened apartment was one of the hardest chores of the day. He fully expected the stalker to meet him at the door, gun in hand.

To his surprise there was nothing amiss. The FBI had not even done its usual job of ransacking his apartment.

When he went to check on his photo equipment, the note was sitting on the camera.

MEET ME AT LOST LAKE 8:00.

YOU HAVE A JOB TO DO.

ANYTHING GOES WRONG, YOU ARE DEAD.

For weeks, he had known this note would come. He had known that the stalker wasn't doing this for the fun of it. There was no doubt in his mind that, if he didn't do as he was told, he would be killed; it might not be today or tomorrow, but it would happen. If anyone else showed up at the lake, the stalker would disappear and strike somewhere else at another time. In the meantime, he would kill J. L.

When J. L. left the apartment, his heart was beating hard, to the point of distraction. He had no real plan, because the unknown factor was the stalker. The man was crazy and mean, but he wasn't stupid.

As he walked the streets of downtown Benton, there were children playing on the courthouse lawn. Old men sat under the pecan trees whittling as they did every day. There were people coming and going from Gingles department stores, laughing at private jokes. None of them realized that the world had changed, that the war across the sea had been brought to their doorstep.

He opened the door to Larry's shop, and a small bell attached to the door announced his arrival. Larry looked up from his work table. "Hey, bud, any word?" Larry asked.

"Yeah, sort of. There was a note in my apartment when I got home. I need to borrow your truck."

"Where you going?"

"It's probably better that you didn't know."

"Well, you can't have my truck if you don't tell me," Larry insisted.

"Damn, don't make this hard. You don't have any business being involved in this."

"Look, J. L., we are partners. What happens to you happens to me."

"All right, All right," J. L. said, giving in. "Come on. We're going to Lost Lake, but you keep out of sight."

"I'll be as quiet as a church mouse," Larry said.

"I'll believe that when I see it."

The two men jumped into the delivery truck and headed for Bauxite. The sun was setting behind them as they rounded the hill heading down into Swamp Poodle. It was 7:50 when they drove by the community hall and headed out to the lake; like at church on Sunday morning, many of the old men lingered around on the steps of the hall. There was something about being cooped up inside the hall.

As they neared the lake, J. L. stopped the truck. "Get out Larry. This is stupid, and I can't let you go with me."

"Look, if there are two of us he will be less likely to try something stupid. So I'm going, and I don't care what you say. Anyway, I'm the one with the gun." Larry reached into the glove compartment and pulled out a snub-nosed pistol and a half-dozen shells.

"What are you doing with that gun?"

"I carry it for shooting snakes at the river. As I see it, this ain't much different."

"Keep that thing out of sight," J. L. said. "You're liable to hurt somebody with that thing."

Larry tried to stick the gun into his pants the way they did in the movies, but he couldn't find a way that was comfortable, so he just laid it on the seat. About the time his hand left the gun, the truck hit a bump, and the gun when sailing off the seat onto the floor.

"Would you pick that thing up and put it back in the glove compartment?"

"Okay, okay, but I am going to take it with us when we get to the lake," Larry said.

Just beyond the Pine Haven Apartments, a narrow lane turned off of the wide-based road and headed down to the lake. It wasn't really a lake but more of a bauxite pit abandoned back in the thirties. The kids went there at night to drink beer and get away from their parents. A quarter of a mile before they got to the lake, J. L. pulled the truck off into a little cul-de-sac.

"We'll leave the truck here. Let's go and see if he's really here."

Larry reached into the glove compartment and retrieved the gun.

"Keep that gun out of sight," J. L. said.

"What are you planning on doing? You've already said that this guy is mean. You just going to walk up and say, 'Okay, Mister Bad-Guy, come with us. We are the good guys, and we are taking you in.'"

"I don't know how I'm going to handle it, but I hadn't planned on walking up and shooting him in the back. The first thing I was going to do was cut through the woods and find the trail that goes around the lake. I figure he will be over at the put-in where the diving platform is. That way we can get an idea of who this guy is. To do this we are going to have to be really quiet."

"Okay, okay, you've made that point," Larry said.

As they walked through the woods, the wind began to blow, and a small shower began again. Off in the west, lightning lit up the sky. The trail was covered with pine straw, which made it easy for them to silently move around the edge of the lake. Just before they came to the boat ramp, a small brush covered point jutted out. The two young men walked out onto the point making a point to stay in the trees.

Sitting on the bank by a small campfire was a lone figure who had covered himself with a piece of tarp to protect himself from the rain.

"What now, Sherlock?" Larry asked.

"Do you really know how to use that gun?"

"If you mean have I ever shot a human, the answer is no. If the question is, can I shoot straight, I can hit a turtle at fifty yards," Larry said.

"The real question was: can you handle it without shooting one of us?"

"I think that I can do that," Larry said defensively. "If you are so worried about me and the gun, you take it."

"I have never had gun in my hand in my whole life, and I don't want to start now. I am not particularly wild about killing this guy, but at the same time, I don't want him to get away. If he gets away, then I am dead—sooner or later"

"Well, just let me handle the gun. If I have to shoot him, I'll just wing him."

J. L. and Larry eased themselves back onto the trail and walked quietly toward the launch site. Ten yards from the fire, the trail emerged on to an open site that served as a gravel and sand beach. The rain was falling in a steady stream by then.

"Are you ready?" J. L. whispered to Larry. Larry nodded his head. The two men stepped from the shadows and J. L. said in a loud voice, "Stand up and turn around. We have a gun, don't try anything stupid."

The figure by the fire didn't move. The two men walked closer to the fire.

J. L. said again, "Didn't you hear me? I said for you to stand up and turn around. We have a gun."

Behind them, Sandy Scroggins emerged from the trail.

"So do I," he said.

J. L. and Larry turned around and looked into the shadows off to the edge of the trail.

"Sandy, is that you?" J. L. asked.

"Shut up, you stupid shit," Sandy said.

"The Sandman. I never would have guessed that," Larry said.

"You two shut up before I shoot you," Sandy said.

J. L. tried to reason with him. "Look, Sandy, there are two of us, and we've got a gun just like you have."

Junior looked at Larry with his gun and smiled. "He wouldn't shoot me. Here," he lowered his gun to his side, "take your best shot."

For an extended moment they all stood with their attention focused on Larry.

"I didn't think so," Junior said. "He ain't got the nerve to use that gun."

"But there are still two of us and only one of you."

Sandy aimed his gun and fired two shots in quick succession at Larry's chest. Unlike in the movies, the wounded man didn't fall over or cry out in pain. Instead, he stood dumbfounded, looking at Sandy. The gun dropped from his hand as he turned toward J. L. He coughed, clearing his throat, and then spit out a mouthful of blood. Larry opened his mouth as if to speak, but before he could utter a word, he fell to the ground, unconscious.

"Now there are just the two of us," Sandy said.

"You son-of-a-bitch," J. L. exclaimed.

"It ain't my fault," Sandy said. "He didn't have to come out here in a rainstorm and pull a gun on me. I gave him a fair chance. That's enough talking, Jew boy. Come on."

"But what about Larry?"

"Are you kidding, that stupid shit is dead. Now move, you've got a job to do," Sandy said.

With Sandy behind him, J. L. walked away from his friend, who lying motionless on the bank of the lake.

"What do you mean I have a job to do?"

"I mean you're about to bomb the new plant. That bomb you built is loaded into the back of a deuce-and-a-half and wrapped in a hundred pounds of fertilizer. It will go off in about twenty minutes as you drive the truck through the front gate of the plant. The sad thing is that you will be killed in the explosion. There won't be much left of you, but there are enough hints left around for them to figure out that it was you. If you try anything stupid, I'll kill you on the spot. If you don't believe me think about Hampton and the Gimp. That ought to convince you."

"Why?" J. L. asked.

"Why what?"

"Why are you doing this? Why did you kill the colored man? He hadn't done anything to you."

"It ain't none of your business," Sandy spit out.

"It's not going to hurt anything. Like you said, I'm going to be dead in twenty minutes anyway."

"Being a Jew, you wouldn't understand. Somewhere along the way in this country, we got lost. This land belongs to white people. We're God's chosen people. Those stupid clowns in Washington decided that they were going to start letting anybody and everybody into this country, and look what happened. We get the bottom of the barrel from everywhere. The only reason we had a Depression was because of all of the lowlifes that we let into this country. Hitler is our wakeup call. He's not our enemy; he's our savior. The communists are the enemy. You are the enemy. The coloreds are the enemy. The unions are the enemy.

"The French are a bunch of bloodsucking crybabies who won't stand up to anybody. They needed a strong leader, and now they got one in Hitler. The English used to be strong, but they lost their way. That Jew president in Washington, if he has his way, will hand this country over to the socialists. For once in our history, we white people have got to stand up and defend ourselves."

How do you respond to something like that? J. L. wondered as he walked, listening to the diatribe that his question had triggered.

"Turn up this little road," Sandy said.

Just across from the place where Larry and J. L. had parked the delivery truck, Junior had hidden and camouflaged his truck full of explosives.

"Now get in on the passenger side and slide across. You're gonna drive."

It would have been hard for J. L. to claim that he didn't know how to drive the truck, because he had made it his goal to know the basics of how to operate all of the equipment on the plant site. That was one of the things that the men liked about J. L.; he never asked them to do something he wasn't willing to do. Sandy knew that.

"I'm a little surprised that you didn't freak out and go to the FBI when this bomb stuff started. I bet my father ten bucks you would," Sandy said.

"You were right. I did go to the FBI. They didn't believe me," J. L. said.

"I'll be damned. I knew I was right about you. You're such a weak sister. I knew you couldn't kill the men who were working for you. I bet you did something to keep the other bombs from going off. For that, I'll make sure you're still alive when this bomb goes off."

Sandy's plan had been well thought out. The hill that led to the plant entrance was a long downhill grade. He had removed the governor from the truck, so they could get the speed up to at least fifty miles an hour. When they were seventy-five yards from the plant entrance, he would shoot J. L., throw the truck into neutral, and roll out the passenger side of the truck onto the soft shoulder. He had thought it through hundreds of times as he had rehearsed the bombing.

"Put the pedal to the medal, Mr. Stein. We got a plant to bomb," Sandy said.

J. L. worked up through the gears and was reaching peak speed as he rounded the top of the hill. The steering of the truck wasn't designed to handle the speeds they were moving at, but by struggling, he kept it in the middle of the road. His right shoulder was just about to fall off. It was then that he remembered the bar ditch and soft shoulder he had noticed earlier that morning. There was one chance that he could derail this speeding freight train and still not die.

"Are you ready to die, Amigo?" Sandy asked, pointing the gun at his head.

"Not quite yet," J. L. said, jerking the truck into the soft shoulder. Had Sandy's gun been more accurate or the momentum of the truck less, J. L. would have been dead in that instant. The right front wheel dropped off the road into the soft dirt. One shot fired from the pistol, grazed the top of J. L.'s head, struck the top of the cab, and ricocheted into his left shoulder. At the same time, he succeeded in throwing the door open and was attempting to jump out when the wheel hit hard clay, quickly flipping the truck on its side. The open door acted as the arm of a catapult and thrust J. L. high into the air in a grand arch over the water-filled pit. The impact of the bullet and the wrenching motion of the truck door dazed J. L. as he did a face-first dive into the blue-green water of the bauxite pit.

Sinking into it, he remembered a nice spring day in the Prater of Vienna. The sun had been warm, lovers had come and gone, and his father had surprised him with cotton candy. He had been sitting under a tree, slowly going off to sleep. It had seemed to be very natural thing.

While J. L. sank into the pit, Junior was trapped in the front of the truck. He had done an excellent job of securing the bomb in the back, and as the last five seconds of his life ticked off, he felt a fear that he'd never known.

What next? he thought. That was the last thought to go through his mind as the bomb and fertilizer exploded.

The bomb destroyed the truck. The metal sides of the bed, before they disintegrated, acted as a cannon, aiming the force of the explosion across the top of the watery pit. The force sucked most of the water from the ditch and left J. L. laying in one piece on the bank of a dry hole.

The thunderstorm that had started earlier added its voice to the choir. A cobweb of lightning filled the sky, followed by a loud, long, low, rumbling thunder that seemed to go on for minutes.

The taste of confectioner's sugar faded from J. L.'s brain.

CHAPTER 52

There was no funeral or memorial to mark the passage of Helena Edit-Stein. Her clothes were divided up among those who could still use them. Eventually, death came to the new owners and then the next. Several generations down the line, when the person of Helena was long forgotten, Myra Goldener, a young girl from Salzburg whose crime had been picking the wrong parents, came to possess her ragged coat.

The second day the jacket was in her possession, it fell apart. Inside the threadbare cloth garment was toilet paper that had been used for insulation. Written on the coarse paper, were the thoughts and poems of Helena. To Myra, this was a sign from God that she would survive. She did not survive, but the poems did.

Luck works in mysterious ways.

It was quiet, except for the ringing in J. L.'s ears. The sheets were cool, and the windows were open. A breeze was blowing through the windows, causing the thin, white curtains to flutter. A faint smell of ether was the only odd note. *That's strange*, J. L. thought to himself. *What is this and where am I?*

He moved his head slightly to his right, and there in the chair by him was Marty. She was thumbing through a copy of *Look* magazine. Out of the side of his eye, she caught the movement of J. L.'s head. Without saying a word, she smiled, reached out, and touched J. L.'s arm. She started crying. "We were scared you wouldn't wake up," she said as she kissed him on the forehead. "I'll get the nurse."

Shortly, a silent young nurse came in and took his blood pressure and pulse. She recorded those on the metal clipboard she was carrying and then inserted a thermometer under his tongue. As she was finishing, a distinguished looking older man in a white coat came in, took the chart, and leafed through the pages.

"Good morning, Mr. Stein, we have been waiting for you to wake up. The truth is we have been hoping you would wake up."

"Where am I?" J. L. asked.

"You are in St. Vincent Infirmary in Little Rock."

"What happened?" he asked.

"You were knocked out by an explosion. You had a fracture of your skull, and a bleed into your head. We had to put a burr hole in the right side of your skull. I don't think you will recover any of the hearing in your right ear. Other than that, it doesn't look like you had much brain damage, but we won't know about that for a while.

"You are here in a private ward, and these people will be at your beck and call. From what these men tell us," he said, pointing to suited men in the back of the room, "we all owe you a lot. You are a hero."

When the medical people left, two men in dark suits came forward. The older of the two did the talking.

"Mr. Stein, we owe you an apology." It was then that it dawned on J. L. who these men were—they were FBI agents.

"You mean because you didn't believe me?" J. L. asked.

"No, we believed you all along. We knew there was someone else, but we couldn't let you know. We didn't know who he was, and we didn't know who was directing his actions. No, our apology is for one of our men going to sleep at the switch. He was supposed to let us know when you guys started to move, and he literally went to sleep in his car down the street from your apartment. By the time he woke up and realized it was dark, we had no idea where you had gone."

"Did you find Larry?" J. L. asked.

"Well, it was more like he found us," the man said.

"What do you mean?"

"I mean right after the explosion he came driving up in his delivery truck. He had blood everywhere."

"You mean he's still alive? Where is he?"

From the other side of the curtain divider came the familiar voice of his friend.

"I'm right over here, you dumb shit."

The second agent pulled back the curtain, and there in the bed next to his was his grinning friend. Larry had a series of tubes leading from his chest to two bottles on the floor. One of the bottles was full of blood.

"I thought you were dead," J. L. said.

"No joke. So did I," Larry said. "I asked the doc if there were enough body parts between the two of us to make one good human. He didn't think it was very funny. We've been waiting for you to wake up for the last three days. Good to see you, old buddy."

"Good to see you, too," J. L. said as he turned his attention back to the agent. "Did Sandy get out of the truck?"

"Are you kidding? Not only did he not get out of the truck, there was hardly enough left to get an ID."

"So what's going to happen to me?"

"When you get well, you can go back to the plant if you want. The superintendent can get the rumor mill revved up again and let it be known that you and Ben were framed. After looking into the matter, it was determined that you were completely innocent. According to what the doctor tells us, it will take about a year to get you back into shape. Both shoulders are screwed up, you've got a hole in your head, and you can't hear out of your right ear. Where would you like to do your recuperating?"

"There is a fishing resort on Lake Hamilton," J. L. said.

"You mean Lorio's?"

"Yeah."

"He's done work for us in the past. He's a good fellow," the younger agent said.

J. L. turned to Larry.

"Want to join me and Marty? Close the shop up for a few months, eat some good spaghetti, drink Chianti, and fish?"

"Works for me," Larry said.

EPILOGUE

Spring 1999

When J. L. and Larry finished telling the story to Maggie, J. L. went into the back of the store and began rummaging around. Soon, he came back with a dusty, old accordion file and a clean piece of tying paper.

J. L. put the paper down on the worktable.

"Did you notice that the letter you found has no punctuation?" he asked.

She shook her head.

Larry and Maggie looked closely at the letter, and sure enough, there was no punctuation.

"Look," J. L. said. He took the yellow envelope and turned it upside down onto the piece of typing paper. Several dozen little, black dots fell onto the white paper. "The glue we used was only designed to hold for a week or so. That way, it was supposed to be easier for them to get it off the paper and reverse the process. Those little dots you see are the production numbers for the bauxite mines for the second quarter of forty-two."

"Why didn't you ever tell anybody about all of this?" Maggie asked.

"The boys from the FBI told us that what happened was top secret, and if it ever became public, I would end up in jail. I've always thought that they were just covering their butts, because the truth was they didn't know what was going on, and they damn near screwed it up."

"Sounds like you guys were banged up pretty bad," she said.

"Yeah, but we bounced back pretty quick. Larry was up and moving in a week or so. It took me a while longer. While we recuperated, the three of us went over to Tommy's place on the lake. Marty and I got married. The FBI set us up with cabins and paid our expenses. Larry only lasted about three months, and then, he started getting itchy feet. He came back to Benton and took up where he left off.

"I had a little harder time of it. The head injury and the surgery had taken their toll on me, but I had really good nurse. I had trouble remembering things like numbers and people's names. I set up my own rehab program. Tommy had a small casino set up at the lake for his regular customers. I spent hours at the craps table, memorizing numbers. If I wasn't shooting craps or playing cards, I was fishing.

"Met a bunch of people with money and made some good connections. We worked a deal with Tommy where we put a lot of our furniture and pottery at the resort and let it be known that all of it was for sale. While the men were gambling, playing the horses, and fishing, the women were buying furniture and pots.

"When the FBI got wind of what we were doing, they cut me off. Can't say as I blame them. I do have to say, though, they were true to their word. After a year or so, they got me a job back at the plant, despite the misgivings of the superintendent. The explosion had been reported in the local paper as lightning striking the fuel tank of the truck. Soon afterward, a rumor was circulated that Ben and I had been set up by the real payroll thieves. I went back to the plant as a staff engineer near the end of the war. Probably would have stayed a lot longer, because we needed the money.

"It was somewhere around early forty-seven; I got another one of those calls to come to the superintendent's office. This time, it was about my sister. When the government was going through the records at Mauthausen, they found a folder indicating that, not only had she been a prisoner at the camp, she was a communist. It was explained to me that, because of my connection to my sister, I could no longer work in an intelligence-sensitive industry."

"What about your mother?" Maggie asked.

"They knew nothing about my mother, or at least, they said they didn't."

"Were you ever able to find anything out about her?"

"Yes and no," he said. "The boys at the FBI weren't too keen on me traveling overseas after the war. They kept me on a pretty tight leash until the mid-fifties. About that time, they seemed to lose interest. By the time I made it back to Austria, there weren't any traces left of my family. Grandpa Stein was killed in the bombing during the war. Mr. Gruber died of a heart attack. I was able to get access to some of the old records at Mauthausen but couldn't find any mention of my mother or her friends. The Nazi's kept accurate records about most things, but when it didn't serve their purpose, a person or group of people just disappeared.

"As I talked to people who had been in the camp, I kept hearing reference to someone known only as the Poet of Mauthausen. No one seemed to know who this person was. One lady from Munich told me she thought the poet was a group of people who circulated poems and sayings on toilet paper. After the war, some survivors gathered up the poems they could remember and published them in a small book. When I read the collection, I knew without a doubt the identity of author of those poems."

J. L. reached into the accordion file and pulled out a small, black book.

"Listen," he said as he opened the small volume to a well-worn spot with the corner of a page turned back.

Hawks Are Like That

I have a friend—
we talk every day—
a red-tailed hawk
who rises above
this grey, granite prison.

He sits on the wind
and drifts
from side to side.
He uses the air currents;
together they climb
the mountain, then
dip over the quarry walls.

We speak of things
great and small.

I've told him
of my childhood in Aigen,
my wonderful father,
the teacher,
and his love.

We've gone on for hours
about sweet Willie,
his soft shoulders,
his warm smile,
his ease with life.

I've cried my regrets
for Anna and Judith,
great warriors
for Truth and Justice,
my daughter and my sister.

I've stewed over
the fate of my sons;
the oldest, lost in a storm
he didn't create.
His brother,
banished
to a faraway land.
I dream of the man
he has become.
I see my father.
I see his father.

My friend, the hawk,
promises to bring me news
of the world beyond these walls,
word of my son.
Every day, he promises,
but he gets busy;
he forgets.
Hawks are like that.

J. L. put the book down, held up the letter, smiled, and said, "For the first time in fifty-seven years, I know for certain that I was not the cause of my mother's death."

AUTHOR'S NOTES

This novel is strictly a work of fiction; however, there are individuals and events in this story that have their basis in history. Every attempt was made to portray these events and people in their real contexts. Some of the dialogue is verbatim from recorded speeches.

Helena Edit-Stein and the women of Oldenberg are composite characters, but they represent a feminist movement that flourished in Vienna between World Wars I and II.

Naomi Mitchison was a member of the British parliament, who spent time in Vienna during the worker uprisings of 1934 and in the Mississippi delta during the share cropper strikes of 1935 and 1936.

H. L. Mitchell and Norman Thomas, socialist and presidential candidate, were very active in the share cropper strikes of the mid-thirties.

Bill Parkus and Adolph Krause are both fictional, but much of what they say in this story was taken from recorded speeches given by the KKK and the German-American Bund during the thirties.

Mr. Jim Sims, Constable Jeff Davis, Mr. Bullet Hyten, and the Doctors Gann were prominent figures in Saline County, Arkansas, during the twenties, thirties, and forties.

About The Author

Sam Taggart is a family practice doctor who has lived in Benton and Hot Springs, Arkansas, for the last thirty years. An avid outdoorsman and marathon runner, he is the author of the novel *We All Hear Voices* and is currently writing two other novels about the Delta.